Once You Know

Madeleine Van Hecke

Once You Know

Trigger warning:
The story in *Once You Know* is set against the backdrop
of the *Me Too* movement and includes references to
sexual assault that may be disturbing to sensitive readers.

For Kalyn

Chapter 1

The moist spring air smelled of newly-mown grass, and Colleen inhaled it greedily, as if the past dry months living in Arizona had left her parched. Just ahead, Izzy grabbed her father's hand and jumped a puddle. Her black patent shoes didn't quite clear the water, and gray droplets splattered her white tights. Colleen swallowed a reprimand.

Her restraint felt like a bargaining chip. She would be her best self this visit. In return, Izzy would behave as well as could be expected of any eight-year-old. Rachel, already at the end of her first year in college, would be happy and *easy* after her performance this evening. And the sense of romance in the springtime air would linger through the night.

Oh, Colleen had so many hopes for this weekend!

They waited outside the auditorium for Colleen's brother Shawn and his family. Derek was listening patiently to Izzy describe her favorite parts of the Children's Museum when the soothing hum of their conversation suddenly broke. "I thought I was staying at the hotel with you and Mommy," Izzy cried.

"No, hon," Derek said.

Colleen interjected. "I told you, Izzy. You're going home with Aunt Bea after the concert for a sleepover with Amber."

Izzy glanced from one parent to the other, her mouth trembling. "I want to stay with you."

Colleen pursed her lips.

Izzy spun toward her father. "Daddy!"

Colleen gave Derek a warning glance. But he wasn't looking at her; he stared down at Izzy's tear-streaked face. "It's not a good idea, honey. Mommy's right. You stay with Aunt Bea tonight."

"But Daddy!" Izzy slammed herself against her father and clamped her thin arms around his waist. Derek had developed a small paunch this past year, and her cheek rested on the swell as if it was a pillow. His face went rigid. He unwound Izzy's hands from his waist, bent down, and pressed her arms close to her sides. He held her in place and stepped back, almost at arm's length. "No 'but Daddy!' We're going to do what Mommy wants."

Relief vibrated through Colleen. But it was a relief mixed with a jittery feeling. How uncharacteristically stern Derek had sounded! And hadn't he—if she admitted it to herself, if she let herself recall details she'd rather ignore— hadn't he seemed tense once or twice earlier this trip, and not his usual, easygoing self? He'd been irritated at the long coffee line in the airport, at the delay taking off.

Derek seemed himself again. He straightened up, tousled Izzy's wild dark curls, and gave her nose a friendly tweak. "You don't want to listen to Daddy snoring all night in a hotel room." He emitted a loud honk.

Izzy laughed and covered her ears. "Oh! There's Amber!" and she raced to meet her cousin.

They entered the auditorium, where the discordant sounds of the young musicians tuning their instruments blended with the chatter of audience members. Settling next to Derek, Colleen watched Amber skitter around her parents to sit by Izzy. *My family*, Colleen thought, looking down the row. Unexpectedly, she got that prickly feeling at the edges of her eyes and blinked back the tears before they formed. Izzy wrapped her little finger around her father's, and he clasped her small hand. Izzy was a Moretti through and through, the skin of her hand nearly as dark as Derek's. In contrast, the Irish came through in Rachel, who was seated onstage. The hints of russet in her upswept hair gleamed, and her pale skin stood out against her lacy black shell.

The conductor strode out to a burst of applause, and then a hush fell. Colleen focused on Rachel who sat ramrod straight, concentrating on the maestro. The moment she moved her bow across the cello strings, Rachel's face took on an ethereal quality. *When the music starts, everything goes away.* That's what Rachel had confided to Colleen, years earlier. Hadn't that been unusual, in so young a child? Didn't that say something about her daughter's talent?

After the performance, they searched for Rachel in the milling crowd. Colleen spotted her in the distance, talking animatedly with a heavy-set young woman whose long blond braid trailed down her back. In a sheer dark tunic that flowed over her navy dress and nearly touched the crossed straps of her cork sandals, Rachel's friend carried her weight like a goddess. In contrast, pretty Rachel, trim and petite like Colleen herself, failed to reach elegance, despite her long black skirt and the rhinestone comb that held her hair in a sophisticated sweep.

"This is my friend Mandy," Rachel said when they approached. Izzy offered her sister a bouquet of roses, Bea commented on the program, and Derek exclaimed, "You look beautiful, Rach; so grown up!" But an awkward silence followed that flurry. Colleen waited for Derek to fill it the way he always did.

"So, are you and Rachel in a class together?" he asked Mandy.

Mandy answered, "Yes, but we actually met back in September. We were in the same small group during orientation."

"Yeah," Rachel said. She ducked her head a little and

added, "Mandy was the only one in the group willing to answer my question."

"What question?" Derek smiled.

"It was a stupid question," Rachel said. Colleen's heart tightened at her daughter's words, at the downward bob of her head that accompanied them.

"It wasn't a stupid question," Mandy objected, in the same tone Colleen herself might have used to defend her daughter. "Rachel asked where we'd want to live if we could live anywhere in the world for a year. It was an interesting question."

"But it didn't really go with what we'd been talking about," Rachel stammered. She cast an accusing glance at her mother. "It came out of that book."

Colleen imagined the scene: The other students misinterpreting Rachel's shyness as aloofness. Rachel recalling the book Colleen had given her, *Questions to Start Any Conversation, Anywhere,* then blurting out a total non sequitur that interrupted the ongoing discussion. Apparently, Mandy had rescued Rachel from the embarrassing moment. A wave of gratitude swept over Colleen, and she directed a warm smile toward her daughter's friend.

But in the next moment, Mandy said, "Yeah, so we're in a sociology class now, and also kickboxing. And we hope to find an apartment to share." Rachel startled at these words, a reaction that Mandy blithely ignored.

"We're looking for an apartment for this summer and next year."

"Rachel's staying with her aunt over the summer," Colleen said. She shot a look at Rachel and stumbled a little on her next words. "Unless you want to come to Arizona?"

"I don't want to come to Arizona, Mom. I told you that when you decided to move there."

"Well," Derek declared, all cheery and smiling, "let's not worry about summer and next year. Let's just enjoy this wonderful night. This weekend together."

Easy for him to say, Colleen thought, recalling the conversation later. She wouldn't bring that up. Not now, when Derek was holding the door of their hotel room open and pressing his hand to the small of her back to guide her over to a desk where a vase of pink roses stood. "Oh, hon. They're lovely." She brought her freckled nose close to a bloom and sniffed. When she looked up, Derek was waiting, expectant. But for what?

"Remember the bed and breakfast where we stayed on our honeymoon?" he asked.

Colleen racked her brain. "We stayed at a lot of places."

"Come on, honey. You must remember." He nodded toward the bathroom and said meaningfully, "You wait in there. Give me ten minutes."

Colleen blinked. "No! Not that again. I was stuck in

that bathroom for an hour."

"Only ten minutes," he laughed. "Okay, maybe twenty." He lifted a rose from the vase and carried it to the bed. A smile tugged at the corner of Colleen's mouth. He plucked petals and lay them in a heap by the pillow. Painstakingly, he lined up five to form the letter "I," then began creating an "L."

"When you finally let me open the bathroom door, the draft blew the petals every which way," Colleen recalled.

"So this could be a do-over."

"Derek."

His knee pressed down on the mattress, fracturing the "I," and he had to realign it.

"Derek," Colleen repeated. "We don't need rose petals." With a sassy smile, she dangled her lacy black negligee in the air with one hand and pressed the music icon on her phone with the other. Sultry jazz swelled. She unzipped her dress and slid one sleeve down, baring her shoulder and the black strap of her bra. A slow grin crossed Derek's face. He tossed the handful of rose petals into the air in a victory salute and settled against the pillows to watch.

The next morning, Colleen scooted up the mattress so that Derek could set the breakfast tray across her legs. Naked from the waist up and shaggy as a bear, he looked comical posing as a waiter. The white cloth of the napkin he'd folded over his arm glowed against his olive skin. He lifted a silver dome with a flourish, revealing scrambled eggs, toast, bacon, and a little pot of strawberry jam. "Madam," he bowed, his salesperson's smile gleaming. When he settled himself in the bed, the mattress dipped, and he reached out a hand to steady the tray. "So," he exclaimed in a hearty voice. Too hearty, Colleen thought, suddenly wary. He went on. "What would you like first? The good news or the bad news?"

Colleen's hand stopped midair, a strip of bacon hovering an inch from her lips. "What bad news?"

"The good news," Derek said, not meeting her gaze, "is that we'll be back home this summer. No more Arizona. No more 110 degrees at midnight, no more desert."

Colleen set the bacon strip down. "What's happened?"

The smile left his face, and he gave her an apologetic shrug. "The Arizona office isn't going to make it, hon. Tony's decided to cut our losses while he can."

Her brow furrowed. "You mean they're closing the whole thing down?"

"Lock, stock, and barrel."

Colleen scrutinized her husband, but his ingrained optimism made it hard to know whether she should trust the unworried look on his face. "Do you still have a job?"

His eyes widened. "Sure I do. You don't have to worry about that, Col. Tony's letting all the Arizona hires go, but me and Cynthia are coming back to Chicago. There's no question of me losing my job. If he had to, Tony would find a place for me in one of the other offices. Michigan or Indiana. Or, God forbid, Iowa." His fingers did a quick tap dance on the tray. "But it would be good if we could get the Arizona house on the market right away. Eliminate that mortgage payment. That would give us a cushion."

A coldness crept over Colleen, and she hugged her bare arms. "What aren't you telling me?"

He rested a warm palm on her shoulder in a tender gesture. "I might have to take a cut in my base pay. But maybe not. We'll see." He gulped down more coffee. "It'll be fine," he assured her. "And you're a whiz at organizing stuff. You'll have us back home before we know it."

A jumble of images from last August crowded Colleen's mind: hours spent searching realtor.com, arranging for movers, packing, signing agreements with the agency to rent their house in the Chicago suburb of Wilmington. And the work she'd need to do now to get the Arizona house ready to sell. In their haste last fall, they'd ignored features that they'd need to fix now to have a quick sale. Izzy's bedroom needed to be painted for sure, there were cracks in the stucco wall surrounding the yard, and they should probably have the patio doors replaced. And after all that work, she'd be back home in Wilmington, unpacking the same boxes she had packed less than a year ago. Dismay and fear about the future churned inside her, a dangerous brew. "This time you have to help."

Derek kept his gaze straight ahead, but his profile revealed the thin, tight line of his pursed lips.

"This time," Colleen insisted, "I'm not doing everything myself. Even if all you do is take Izzy off my hands so I can get stuff done."

"I'll do what I can, Col. This week. But after that, Tony wants me back in Chicago. Jim said I can stay at his condo until our renters move out."

Colleen slammed her cup on its saucer with a satisfying bang. "So, I'll be alone in Arizona? Moving will all fall on me, just like last summer?" She turned narrowed eyes toward her husband. "I don't think you have any idea how hard that was. And for what? For nothing, apparently."

Derek stopped drumming on the tray. "I begged you to stay here. I told you, 'Let me rent an apartment in Phoenix and see how things go.' You were the one who insisted on moving. And not even just moving, but buying a house."

Colleen raised a stubborn chin to her husband. "I was trying to keep our family together." She flushed. Even at the time, she'd known it was crazy to insist that they buy a home. But how could she explain the dread she'd felt when Derek had talked about living in Arizona without her? With Rachel at college and Derek two thousand miles away, her family would unravel. She had needed to be with her husband, in a home that bound her and Izzy and Derek together with a permanence that renting couldn't provide.

"You've never really understood," Colleen accused him now, "how terrible last summer was for me. You traveled more than you had since Izzy was a baby. Only she wasn't a baby anymore, was she? She turned eight; she was old enough to *notice*." Her face grew warm. "You know Izzy. It was the end of the world every time you cancelled a trip to the beach, every time you missed her gymnastics or couldn't find the time to take her to a Sunday movie." Another thought seized her, and her voice shook with anger. "It was your last chance to spend time with Rachel before she left us, our last chance to be a *family*, and where were you?" Her rage grew with every word. "Not home! And then, out of the blue, you tell me about this Arizona deal? You want to go to Arizona—*alone*." Her heart pounded with a fury that spoiled for release. "See us once or twice a *month*?" With a jerk, Colleen upended the breakfast tray. The eggs and toast spilled off, and the strawberry jam dribbled onto the sheet. Derek tried to right it, but Colleen knocked it over again when she swung her legs to the side of the bed and hurtled off. She stuck her arms through the sleeves of her robe, pulling it tight around her, and paced, barefoot, at the foot of the bed. She felt out of control, not caring what she said or did. It felt great. She approached the vase of pink roses, her hands itching to pitch it.

"Colleen," Derek pleaded. "Please. Calm down."

But Colleen was not the sort of woman who stuffed her

anger down into some dark place. Get it out! That was her philosophy. She lifted the vase and slammed it on the carpet. After a single bounce on the rug, it landed sideways, spilling roses and water. A stream ran toward Derek's pants, which he'd let fall to the floor the night before. Colleen kicked his clothes out of the way. "That's not a family, Derek. We wouldn't have been a family. I *had* to move us to Arizona. I had to. And after all that, we got there, and you disappeared. We would have seen more of you if I *had* stayed here and let you fly home twice a month." Her face was on fire; even the tips of her ears burned. "You know, every time you went looking for new clients, Izzy and I baked your favorite double-chocolate brownies for when you got back. Put the oven on, in that Arizona heat. And you wondered why our air conditioning bill was sky-high! But the brownies dried out before you got home, because you kept adding days to your trips." She lifted her chin, daring him to deny that. Derek stayed silent. Colleen stormed on. "Even when you were home, you weren't. You were like a cardboard figure sitting at the kitchen table." She mimicked Derek's perfunctory responses to her every remark or question. "'Mm hm.' 'Oh, yeah?' 'Sure, hon.' You were a million miles away. So, don't you dare blame me, Derek. This is not on me."

Having made the circuit of the room once again, Colleen now faced the mirror that hung on the back of the bathroom door. She stood there, following Derek's movements in the mirror. He ran his fingers through his hair. Then he assessed the damage on the bed. He righted an overturned cup, sopped up coffee with a napkin, straightened the breakfast tray and smoothed the crumpled sheet.

Her flow of adrenaline slowing, Colleen watched the changes in her own face in the mirror. First, her flaming skin toned down to pink, then faded to a blush, and finally neutralized into her normal pale coloring with a sprinkling of freckles across her nose. In the mirror, Derek moved the tray half-way down the bed to make room at his side. Watching him prop her pillows up and fold the bedding back like an invitation, Colleen exhaled deeply. The pot had boiled over, the volcano had erupted, and Derek remained steadfast as ever. He patted the empty spot next to him. "Col. Come here."

She picked up Derek's socks from the floor and rolled each of them into a ball.

Derek smiled.

She aimed for his head.

He caught the socks easily, gave her a considered look, and then tossed them back at her. One of them bounced off the top of her head. The skirmish only lasted a minute. Colleen hurled the socks, and Derek batted them back, that boyish grin on his face. Then she drifted back to the bed, slipped out of her robe, and climbed in. Derek put his arm around her. "Feel better?"

A chuckle escaped her. "You know I do."

"Yeah." He embraced her so closely that the hairs on his chest tickled her cheek. "I'm sorry you've had so much to deal with. I've been under a lot of pressure in Arizona. Things will be better when we're back here. And I will help you with the move. As much as I can. I promise." He kissed the top of her head. "And Rachel can forget this nonsense about getting an apartment. She'll be home with us for the summer."

"Yeah." Colleen took a deep breath. "And we won't be in that Arizona heat. We'll be near my brother and Bea and Amber. Izzy can go with them on vacation again, and back to Mrs. Anderson for violin." Her forehead scrunched. "I'll have to contact the realtor as soon as we get back." She opened the notepad feature on her phone and tapped the keys. "And call a plumber about that leaky faucet."

"I can fix that, Col." At her skeptical look, Derek nodded firmly. "I promise."

But would he? A spark of anger at everything he hadn't done this past year ignited. Colleen squelched it, and instead looked into her husband's dark eyes. "I wanted this weekend to be a new beginning for us." Her voice hitched.

Derek put his tanned arm across her pale shoulder and drew her to him. "I know you did. And it could be. It still could be, couldn't it?"

She nodded and snuggled into his warm embrace.

Chapter 2

The second Rachel took a chair next to Mandy in class, Mandy said, "So how did it go with your parents?" Rachel grimaced and quoted her father's comment on Sunday afternoon: "'You can get your own apartment when you can pay for it.'"

Disappointment pulled the corners of Mandy's mouth down. "I shouldn't have said anything after your concert. I should have let you bring it up."

"You were afraid I'd chicken out."

Mandy conceded that with a nod.

"It's going to be tough," Rachel said, "because they're moving back here. And I know how it'll be if I'm home with them." She did a parody of her mother. "'What time are you going to be home? Who are you going to be with? Who's driving? Text me when you leave so I know you're on your way.'"

In response, Mandy assumed a similar hectoring tone: "'*That's* what you're wearing? How much did those tickets cost? There aren't going to be any drugs, are there?'"

Rachel sighed, "Oh, God." A moment later she added, "I can't do it, Mandy. Live back home with my hovercraft mom. I'm not going to do it." More firmly, she added, "I'm going to find a part-time job."

At the lectern, Professor Malley lectured on Freud, telling the class how the man had initially listened sympathetically to his female patients' stories of sexual abuse. Only later had he deferred to his colleagues' protests that the women's memories must be false. "And why?" the professor demanded. "Because they couldn't believe that so many well-respected, upper-class men could have sexually abused their own daughters."

The class broke into their small groups at the end of the lecture. Tall, lanky Gregorio crossed the room, with Aaron in tow, and folded himself into a student desk across from Rachel. "Look at Ms. Sophisticate," he winked, taking in Rachel's auburn hair, still swept back in the French roll she'd worn for her concert. "Oh, it's all coming down now," Rachel demurred, self-conscious, though she knew she looked good today. That morning, the sight of her fancy hairdo in the mirror had made her reject her usual jeans and t-shirt and instead choose black leggings and an off-the-shoulder dress printed with tiny violet flowers. She ducked her head and tucked stray hairs behind her ear. At that moment, Kaitlin came up behind her. Instead of sitting down immediately, she loosened the comb at the back of Rachel's head. Rachel felt the pull when Kaitlin tightened the French roll and pressed the comb more firmly in place. Then Rachel glanced around their little group. Kaitlin, dragging a chair into the circle. Aaron's compact body next to gangly Gregorio, his Cubs cap pulled over his curly brown hair. And Mandy, who had urged Rachel to sign up for the class. Initially, she'd resisted. A course in *gender and violence*? The very name had disconcerted her. But here, to her surprise, she'd found her first real friends on campus. It struck Rachel that after a lonely fall term, this little group had filled the void created by her family's exodus to Arizona.

Gregorio told the group, "Be careful what you say." He inclined his head toward Aaron. "We have a Freudian in our midst."

"No, that's not what I…" Aaron began.

Gregorio stretched his long legs out. "No one insisted more than Freud that being gay was an illness. So, pardon me for being skeptical about your hero."

Aaron twisted one of the curls that periodically dangled on his forehead. Rachel momentarily felt a little sorry for him, but then he protested in that pedantic tone he sometimes fell into. "I'm not saying Freud was right about everything. But give him a break. He was a man of his times, right? And a man way ahead of his time in many ways, with his theories about unconscious motivation and dreams—"

Normally, Rachel was patient when Aaron started holding forth, but not today. "Aaron, those women trusted him. They remembered something really awful, and at first, he believed them, so probably they trusted him even more, and then—boom! He told them they were making it all up?" To her astonishment, Rachel choked up on the last words. Her classmates' heads swiveled toward her. "What?" she demanded.

Gregorio and Mandy exchanged glances. Then Gregorio said, "We've just never heard you so emotional before."

Aaron nodded sagely and rested his chin in his hand. "You want to say more?"

"Oh my God, Dr. Freud, where's the couch?" Rachel folded her arms across her chest. "Not being believed would upset anyone!"

After a silence, Kaitlin gently said, "Sure it would. It's just that you seem really bummed out."

Rachel waved her hand dismissively. "It just reminded me of something that happened when I was a kid. That's all." But at those words, her friends drew in even closer, looked even more concerned. Rachel threw her hands up in the air. "It's not a big deal. Look," she went on, "one time I caught my cousin, my boy cousin, peeking at me. That's it." She settled back in her chair. But her explanation failed to dispel their troubled looks. Shaking her head, she added, "We were only, I don't know, five or six? We were at a picnic at this park where there were bathrooms. He must have followed me into the washroom, because when I finished and I stood to pull my shorts back up, I could see him lying on the tile floor, staring straight up at me. It scared the crap out of me. I actually screamed. He banged his head trying to get away fast. My mom thought I was making a big deal out of nothing. She didn't really believe me, and she didn't want me to say anything in front of his parents." Rachel scanned the circle. Her friends' solicitous looks had faded. "I told you it was nothing."

Mandy launched into a furious attack on Freud then, freeing Rachel to lapse into her usual quiet for the remainder of their discussion, but she felt unsettled. Because earlier in the term, she had listened while Kaitlin confided about the mail room boss who had stuck his hand up her skirt. Her heart had broken when Gregorio had described being beaten at thirteen when he'd had an erection in the boy's locker room. And though she didn't know for sure, she suspected that something terrible and sad lay behind Mandy's periodic outbursts. But until today, it hadn't occurred to her that this class could become personal for her as well.

Rachel stepped lightly through the shower of pink apple blossoms on the path. They reminded her of all the bouquets she'd been given over the years after recitals and concerts. In middle school, a boy had offered her some violets that had been growing at the edge of the grass in front of her house. She'd backed away from his outstretched hand and stumbled inside without speaking. Why had she done that? And more to the point, why had she turned Aaron down after class today when he'd suggested she walk with him to the lakefront path where he ran? It was, as he'd mentioned, almost on the way to her dorm. She liked Aaron. Why did she dodge every hint that the two of them might spend some time together, without the group?

In today's world, you were supposed to believe that everything was normal, just "different." Different gender identities, different sexual preferences, different orientations. So how did people figure out whether they were queer or straight? Gay, lesbian, bisexual, cisgender, transgender, pansexual, asexual? Had she missed anything, she wondered? Another category, maybe one yet to be acknowledged?

And then there was the whole question of sex. Sometimes she felt like the only virgin in the world. Everyone she knew had done it—*everyone*. Rachel had had the opportunity at more than one drunken party in high school, and again this fall, but the very idea made her shrink back. Could she be asexual? Was that it? Supposedly that was as normal as being highly sexual. But she didn't want to be asexual. A memory came to her, of watching girls in the mall sauntering past with their boyfriends, hands in one another's back pockets. Envy rose up from a place buried so deep inside her that she hadn't known it existed.

A breeze blew, and Rachel felt some of the strands that Kaitlin had secured in the comb loosen again and blow against her cheek. She thought of how she had wandered around almost her whole sophomore year in high school with *The Tibetan Book of the Dead* in her backpack. It took her all those months of trying to read the tome, starting and stopping and not really understanding much, before she admitted to herself that the Eastern spirituality book was nothing but a prop. Part of her high school persona as an intellectual, offbeat kind of student, a Buddhist in a Catholic high school. *So*, she thought, using her ID card to release the turnstile in the lobby of her dorm, *maybe you find out what you really are by trying out different experiences*. Maybe the next time Aaron asked if she wanted to walk on the lake path, she should just say yes.

Ralph, the security guard in the lobby, smiled at her, and she gave him a friendly wave. Upstairs, she unlocked the door to her room and set her backpack by the small desk. She still had more than an hour before her practice room became available. She should take the shower that she hadn't had time for this morning. Instead, she found herself wishing she had joined Aaron at the lake, and that restless sensation stirred above her thighs. Surely she couldn't be asexual if she felt that. If she couldn't resist *that*.

It had been a long time. She tried the door handle to make sure it was locked. Her roommate Serena rarely showed up at this time of day. Rachel breathed in the musty air of the dim room, with its curtains still closed. Passing her desk, she picked up her notebook. She sat on the edge of the bed and took off her shoes. After propping her pillow against the headboard, she slipped under the handmade quilt and put another pillow by her side, creating a little wall between herself and the door. Rachel opened the notebook and leaned it against the pillow. If Serena returned unexpectedly, all she'd see would be Rachel, deep in study. Under the quilt, Rachel unzipped her jeans and wriggled halfway out of them. Finally, she slid her fingers inside her panties and closed her eyes.

It took three rounds of compulsive stroking before she felt completely spent. Her eyes shut, Rachel took short breaths until her pounding heart slowed. Then she lay very still. She'd learned not to fight what came next. It was better to stay quiet, her hands limp at her sides, and let it happen.

The sense of revulsion crept over her as if it were a physical substance, slime that inched across her face, making her squeeze her eyes tight and hold her breath. It trickled down her throat, slithered over her breasts, her abdomen, her thighs. She stayed taut on the bed until it had snaked all the way down her calves and seeped between her toes.

In the bathroom, she waited until the water grew nearly too hot to bear before she stepped into the shower.

Chapter 3

"It would be so much easier if Izzy was with you." Colleen talked to Derek over her shoulder while scrounging through the junk drawer to find a box cutter. "There are twenty things the realtor said we should do if we want a quick sale." She settled for a pair of scissors and turned to face her husband. "I can't paint the back bedroom with Izzy here, not with her allergies. And she'd love having time with you. You could use some of your vacation time."

Derek set his plate of toast on the counter and squared his shoulders. "Taking vacation time when Tony is downsizing is not a smart idea. And I don't even know for sure what my territory will be when I'm back in Chicago. I might have to travel downstate."

Colleen gave Derek a long look. "Okay. How about this? I'll come home after Izzy gets back from vacation with Bea and Shawn. So, we're only talking about a week without me there. Rachel can help, and Bea can take Izzy overnight if you absolutely have to travel." Derek frowned, dumping his half-eaten toast into the garbage and emptying the cold coffee into the sink. Colleen put her hands on her hips. "You promised you'd help."

"I know, Col. It's just…"

The helpless gesture he made with his hands infuriated her, and she turned away sharply. "I have to take Izzy to gymnastics."

In the car, she continued to hear Derek's forlorn tone in her head. He acted like he was powerless. But he always managed to get time off for his fishing trips, didn't he? She glimpsed Izzy's sad face in the rearview mirror and snapped, "What's the matter with *you*?"

"I thought Daddy was coming. I wanted to show him my ring flip."

Colleen's hands tightened on the wheel, but she forced a cheerful tone. "He's taking you to the water park tomorrow. With Ritu and her dad. That'll be fun."

"Yeah." Izzy's voice brightened, and Colleen relaxed a bit. But then Izzy let out a heavy sigh. "I'm going to miss Ritu so much!"

"But you'll have Aaliyah again, right next door. You can ride your bikes on the prairie path."

In the rearview mirror, Izzy's brow creased. "I wish Ritu could move to Wilmington, too. I wish Aaliyah lived on one side of me and Ritu on the other side."

"But we can't always have what we want, Iz. Can we?

You're almost nine years old—old enough to understand that. We have to be grateful for the good things we do have." Her daughter's mouth turned downward. "I have no patience for sulking today, Izzy." Colleen entered the gym parking lot. "Look on the bright side. You'll have Mrs. Anderson again for violin, you can go with Aunt Bea and Amber to the cabin in Michigan, and you'll see your sister all summer."

"No, I won't," Izzy said. She burst into tears. "Rachel's going to get a job and live in an apartment."

Colleen turned down the nearest aisle, looking for her friend Geeta's car. "Izzy." She fought to keep her voice calm. "Rachel's not getting an apartment." She slowed as she approached a silver SUV, but it wasn't Geeta's.

"She is too! She told me. She's getting an apartment and she's going to be a waitress. I thought it would be fun, talking to all the people, but Rachel said you get really tired, standing all the time."

Colleen hit the brakes, shifted to park, and twisted around to face her daughter. "When did Rachel tell you that?"

"When she called yesterday. You were taking a bath."

A black SUV loomed behind her. Colleen ignored it. "That's not happening. That's what Rachel wants, but like I said, you can't always get what you want." The SUV beeped, a long, impatient blast. Colleen glared at the driver, then shot forward and scanned the cars in the next aisle for silver SUVs, for the emblem of the Arizona Diamondbacks on the rear window. There! Geeta's car. She nosed her van into a spot a few cars down.

All the way to the building, with Izzy plodding next to her, Colleen throbbed with anger. Inside, Izzy gave her a wary look and then sped toward the girls' locker room. Colleen moved to a deserted corner of the hallway and stabbed the keyboard on her cell phone. *You want to get a job? You think you're getting an apartment? What's the matter with you?* Breathing hard, she hit send and jammed the phone back in her pocket, where her hand brushed against her mother's old rosary. She leaned against the wall and fingered the beads. Sometimes just rubbing the beads with her thumb soothed her, but not today. *Hail Mary, full of grace.* She repeated the prayer until her heartbeat returned to normal.

In the gym, Colleen spotted Geeta in her usual place in the bleachers. Geeta turned her five-year-old son Ajay in Colleen's direction and pointed. His soft black curls exploded in a halo around his dimpled cheeks. How dear that little round face! Colleen's heart ached. *I miss Izzy at that age.*

She sank down to the bench to tell Geeta about Derek's transfer back to Chicago. While she talked, the older girls sauntered out of the locker room, and the younger ones skipped. "Derek acts like it will kill him to take care of Izzy on his own for a week," Colleen complained. "And now,

Izzy tells me that Rachel still plans to get a job and move into an apartment."

Geeta listened quietly. That was one of the things that Colleen would miss. Geeta didn't jump in with questions, with advice. She just waited, like an open hand, for whatever Colleen offered. "Rachel used to be happy," Colleen went on. "In high school, she loved her cello, she had nice friends, she studied hard. All these other parents complained about their teenagers, kids yelling—you know—'blank' you! right to their parents' faces. And I thought, well, obviously these parents are doing something wrong. Not teaching their children the most basic respect. But now—" Colleen blinked back the prickle of tears. "Now, when she knows we're moving home, and we could be a family again, she's trying to get an apartment behind our backs?"

In a careful voice, Geeta said, "Srini and I have talked about going back to India. And not just because my father's health is poor. But for the sake of the children. American culture has so many good things about it, but it doesn't require the respect expected from Indian children. Oh, there's Izzy!" Geeta pointed, and Colleen dutifully watched Izzy mount the balance beam. Even at this distance, she saw Izzy's legs tremble when she got to the point where she had to make a turn. But though she hesitated a bit before that maneuver, Izzy made it through, and landed with only the slightest stumble. Colleen stood and gave her a thumbs-up sign, but Izzy ignored her.

"Mostly I'm afraid that when we're all back in Wilmington, it's going to be a repeat of last summer," Colleen said, "when I hardly saw Derek at all."

Geeta looked thoughtful.

"What?"

"I don't know, Colleen. I hope it is different."

Colleen protested, "We had a great weekend in Chicago."

"Well. That's good. But maybe you need to talk to Derek. About why you hardly see him."

"Derek's the head of his team," Colleen said. "The whole burden of getting enough clients to make a go of it in Arizona fell on him. I get that, I really do. It was a huge challenge. And one he failed at. Obviously." She took a sip from her water bottle. "Of course. That's why he's been so distant. Derek's not used to failure," she told Geeta. "Not in sales."

"Amma, juice please." Ajay inserted himself between Geeta and Colleen, and Geeta stuck a straw through a juice box and handed it to him. "If that's what's bothering Derek," she said, "it might bring you closer to talk to him about it."

Colleen squinted. "Maybe. But sometimes the only thing talking accomplishes is to make mountains out of molehills. I'm more of a 'let well enough alone' kind of person." She chuckled.

"Hmm," Geeta murmured. She scrounged through the woven bag next to her and handed Ajay a cookie.

That 'Hmm" inched into Colleen's mind and nagged at her. "C'mon, Geeta. What are you thinking?"

Geeta gave a tiny shrug. "Just that this didn't just start. You've complained about Derek's business trips the whole time you've been in Arizona. And now you tell me he was distant even before you moved here, and you're afraid it will be the same when you go back." Geeta bit her lip. "Me? I'd want to talk to Srini. I'd want to know."

"Know what, exactly?"

"Nothing," Geeta said quickly. Too quickly. The two friends stared out over the gym floor at their daughters, even though Izzy and Ritu stood idly in line waiting for their turns at the rings.

Colleen said quietly, "You think Derek's having an affair."

"I didn't say that."

"But that's what you think, isn't it?"

Geeta dabbed Ajay's plaid shirt where some orange juice had dripped on it. "I don't know, Colleen. How could I know? But if it was me, I'd ask Srini what was going on. I'd want to know."

Colleen thought again of how Derek had left her alone with Izzy while he ping-ponged across Arizona seeking new clients. She shook her head briskly. "Derek wouldn't," she told Geeta. She leaned toward her friend, searching for the right words. "I know he wouldn't. He would never hurt me like that." A wave of relief flooded through her with that conviction, and she let out a breath. "Never," she repeated.

But the next day, after Derek and Izzy had left for the water park, Colleen's mind circled back to that conversation. Why *had* Derek been so reluctant for her to join him here last year? She told herself that he'd been afraid, even then, that the business might fail. In the living room, she passed his laptop and crouched by the shelves, dusting off the plastic cases of old DVDs before packing them. But the presence of Derek's laptop on the coffee table behind her drew her like a magnet. She told herself only a wife with no faith in her husband would be tempted to search his computer. *Let well enough alone*, she admonished herself. Then again, she knew that if she did search his files, she'd find nothing. Right? And then she'd stop worrying.

Derek had had the same password since he'd opened his email account more than two decades earlier. What a lot of emails he had! Did he never delete any? Colleen filed her own messages in folders with labels like *bills* and *family* and *medical*. She never had more than a dozen active emails in her inbox. Feeling sneaky, she scanned one innocuous email after another. She sighed. The email she'd been reading was months old, and she hadn't found one hint of indiscretion. *Because there's nothing to find*, she reminded herself. All the packing she still had to do, and she was wasting time on this? She was about to close the laptop when she noticed the file folder in the corner of the home screen. *Documents.*

She found folders labeled *Contracts, Prospects, Follow-up,* and... *Personal.* Tucked into the *Personal* folder were two sub-folders, marked *Fantasy* and *Temp.* Images of girlie magazine covers flashed through her mind, and she opened *Fantasy* with a sense of foreboding. It turned out to be information about playing fantasy football. She almost didn't bother with the folder labeled *Temp.* That probably held contact information about the temporary help the company sometimes hired during its busy season. But then she hesitated. Why would that be filed under *Personal?* Better to be thorough, she thought, and put her fears to rest once and for all. She clicked on the icon.

A list of document names appeared on the screen, and Colleen's heart stopped.

Chapter 4

The red-and-white canopy over the small snack bar in the social science building felt like a welcome to Rachel. For once, she had time to select a scone from the display and sit with her coffee at one of the small tables before she went to class. Absorbed in an article she'd printed out, she missed seeing Mandy come in, and only looked up when a shadow fell over her paper. "You look terrible," Mandy said, setting down her coffee and a cherry-filled Danish.

Rachel took in Mandy's loose-fitting khaki jacket and pants. Mandy was having another Brown Day. Rachel sighed. No sense in trying to cheer Mandy up, but she gave it a shot anyway. In a joshing tone, she said, "I thought I looked good. This top matches my eyes."

"If anyone could see your eyes," Mandy said. She plopped down. "They're half-closed."

Rachel yawned. "I slept right through the alarm this morning and missed math. Last week, I was late for my cello lesson because I fell asleep in the library."

Mandy sat up a bit. "What's going on?"

"This research for my paper." Rachel glanced toward the article on the table. "I'm doing it on child sexual abuse."

Mandy pulled her thick braid forward and twisted the end of it around her finger. "Awfully hard to read about." She tilted her head. "Where do you get your statistics from?" Professor Malley was big on documenting claims with statistics.

"I found some crime stats. But that's only the people who get caught. I did find one study they did in California a million years ago. They interviewed almost 1,000 women in San Francisco, just random people on the street. One in six said that their stepfathers had abused them. It wasn't as bad with biological fathers, but even then—one in forty. Isn't that unbelievable?"

Mandy's face blanched, and the hand twirling her braid into a corkscrew stilled. After a moment, she said, "I thought I might do my paper on sex trafficking. But I'm afraid if I read too much more of that stuff, I'll shoot somebody." She jerked her shoulders as if sluffing off the impulse. "Thank God for Valium."

Rachel blinked. "You take Valium?"

"When I need it."

Rachel swallowed a bite of her scone. "So, it helps you sleep?"

"Better than any of those sleeping pills. Why? You want some?"

"No, I just…"

Mandy sprang to life and fished around her bag. "I can give you some. We think my grandma stockpiled her pills. Probably just forgot to take them. She got kind of messed up the last few months."

Rachel stared at her friend's outstretched hand. "It's just that I'm so tired," she said. She pocketed the vial. "Thanks. Just until I get this paper finished." The two friends launched into a discussion about what Professor Malley expected in these papers and how she'd be grading them, until nothing was left on their plates except crumbs, and it was time to go to class.

There, they watched clips from old teenage sex comedies, supposedly funny scenes that involved humiliating or assaulting women. A strained silence settled on their small group when they gathered for discussion afterwards. Finally, Kaitlin broke it. "I tell myself that people laughed at those movies because they just didn't *see*. Not because they thought rape was funny."

Mandy bristled. "The fact that they didn't see makes it even worse. It means that toxic masculinity is so much a part of our culture that it seems normal, even funny."

"Well," Aaron began, "the *Animal House* scene with Belushi's devil and angel arguing was kind of funny."

The three women stared at him, and Rachel noticed that they were all sitting together on one side of the circle.

Aaron opened his hands. "What?"

Kaitlin said, "A girl is lying there unconscious."

"Right," Aaron said. "But Belushi never took advantage of her. I mean, in the end, his angel won out."

"So," Mandy said, "you see a guy staring at an unconscious girl, wondering whether he should rape her, and as long as he makes the right decision, that's funny to you?" She made a disgusted sound. "You think you're so enlightened, but you're just as big a part of the problem as any other guy."

Gregorio blurted, "Did I ever tell you guys about the time I had to give this book report in front of my class? This was really funny."

"Do you have to joke every time a discussion gets serious?" Kaitlin interrupted.

Gregorio's flush darkened. "A feminist discussion," he muttered to Aaron. "No humor allowed."

"Because that's the way you guys make light of our concerns!" Mandy flared. "That's the way you try to make us feel like there's something wrong with us if we're upset or angry. Gaslighting. Well, I'm angry and that doesn't make me crazy!"

"Mandy," Gregorio pleaded, "the story I was going to tell makes fun of *me*!" No one said anything for a minute. Mandy's face stayed florid. She avoided their glances and shook her head, looking toward the whiteboard at the front of the room. "You just don't get it."

"Great!" Aaron erupted. "We don't get it. So, there's no

point in talking to us. Give up, Gregorio. Nobody with a dick has a chance once they get to that point."

Rachel and Mandy and Kaitlin all reacted at once, saying, "Wait a minute!" and "Hey!" and "*They?*"

"Rachel," Aaron said, his voice quieter. "Do you really think guys like me and Gregorio are the enemy here?"

"Nobody's saying that," she said.

Aaron pulled his baseball cap lower so that it shadowed his face. "You know, it's not easy being a cis male in this class."

"Poor you," Mandy said.

Aaron whipped around. "Really, Mandy? You? You're the one who keeps saying how emotional this stuff is. How do you think it makes me feel to think about what other guys have done?"

"Oh, my God!" Mandy exclaimed. "So we should feel sorry for you? We should worry about you? Because, oh, dear, this is so hard on *you*, to face something you've ignored all your life. Your own toxic masculinity." She shot a withering glance at Aaron. "Right now is not a good time to ask for my sympathy."

"Well, fuck!" Aaron exploded. "When is a good time? What do you want from me? I'm here, aren't I? Learning what women go through, learning to appreciate what you have to deal with. You think I'm part of the macho culture? Do I look macho to you? I'm a 140-pound Jewish nerd! I whizzed through high school calculus, but I couldn't figure out what it meant if a girl smiled at me. Then I get in a class like this. There are a lot of cool women in this class. Smart. Funny. I *like* a lot of the women in this class. But you got to admit, your faces can morph from smiling to pissed off in a nanosecond. And half the time I don't even understand what some guy said to make that happen. I mean…I thought this would be different from high school. And it is, I mean, it has been," Aaron stammered. "I made friends here. I thought you were one of them, Mandy. And now you look at me like that?" His voice faltered, and a tiny muscle at the corner of his eye twitched.

Rachel stretched a hand toward him. "Aaron."

He kept his gaze locked on Mandy. "You should see your face right now. Full of disgust. I'm not perfect, but I'm not the enemy here either."

Mandy stiffened. "'It takes a village to rape a woman,'" she quoted from one of their course books. "It takes that mindset—'it's just a joke, it's kind of funny, you're overreacting.' That's what lays the groundwork. You think you understand, Aaron, but you don't. You have no idea what it's like to be female. You're not afraid to walk across campus at night, you don't ask your friend to guard your drink at a party when you go to the bathroom, you don't worry that someone's going to stick their hand down your pants on a crowded subway. You don't know what it's like to be afraid, not because of anything we have any control over, but just because of who we are."

"Thanks for explaining that," Aaron said, his voice gritty. "Because to me as a Jew, oppression seems like something that only happens to other people."

Big pink blotches erupted on Mandy's face. "Fine. Play that card."

"Oh, now…" Gregorio said, but before he could finish, Aaron shoved his chair back so hard that Gregorio had to grab it to keep it from falling over.

Seeing Aaron disappear out the door, Rachel longed to race after him. But inches from her elbow, Mandy hunkered down in her chair looking miserable, tugging the edges of her beige jacket together as if willing the loose-fitting clothing to swallow her up. Rachel couldn't leave her. Yet she couldn't think of what to say to her friend either. Kaitlin touched Mandy's arm and murmured supportive comments. But Rachel could only sit silent and confused, wondering how it had all gotten out of hand so quickly.

When Kaitlin went off with Mandy after class, Rachel hurried to the circular path where Aaron ran. The path curved along Lake Michigan, and she crossed over to the jumble of boulder-sized rocks that descended to the water. Sitting on one of the flatter boulders, high above the churning lake, she angled herself so that she could see both the path and the water spewing through crevices below her. She took comfort in the repetitive crashing of the waves against the rocks. *This lake will be here, its surf pounding whatever lies in its way, long after we're all gone.* The thought soothed her. She focused on a slate-gray rock just far enough above the water to be splashed only intermittently. The hot sun began drying it the moment the wave receded. That was how quickly Aaron and Mandy's argument would evaporate, Rachel thought, if you took the long view of it. Just then, she looked toward the graveled track. Aaron came pounding around the bend, his head down. But he must have spotted her, because he stopped abruptly while he was still some distance away, and paused a long moment before coming nearer.

"Hey," she said.

Aaron slumped on the rock next to her and stared at his running shoes. "I'm not some macho asshole."

"I know." After a moment, Rachel added, "Mandy knows that, too."

"That was a cheap shot," Aaron said. "About playing the Holocaust card."

"Yeah," Rachel conceded. She listened again to the crashing surf and took a breath. "You both got upset."

"When I said I thought part of that scene was funny, I was just being honest. I thought our group was a place where we could all be honest. I thought, 'Gregorio, Mandy, Kaitlin, you—these are my friends. And suddenly there's Mandy looking at me like I'm *vomit*, and I just couldn't deal, you know?" Aaron's chest heaved. For a second, Rachel thought he might cry. She didn't know what she would do if he cried.

Aaron said, "I don't think this was all my fault."

"Forget about who's at fault," she responded quickly. "Don't get into a big discussion about what happened. Just wait a few days, then tell Mandy how bad you feel about all of it. Tell her you want to figure out how to make things right. Then see what she says. She feels bad, too."

Aaron looked skeptical.

"What's the alternative?" Rachel demanded. "The two of you avoiding each other for the rest of the term?"

Fiddling with the loose lace on his running shoe, Aaron muttered, "And after." He snuck a look at her. "I mean, we're not going to stop seeing each other when the term's over, are we? And you're going to be living with Mandy."

Disconcerted, Rachel said, "Oh, I always pictured our group staying together after this term ended. Going to movies, sharing pizzas…" Her voice trailed off.

"Our group," Aaron repeated. He sat up straighter and gazed at the squawking seagulls careening over the lake. "If a girl is going to like me," he said, "it's not going to be because of anything she can take in within minutes of meeting me. She's going to have to get to know me. And we did that, didn't we? In our class discussions? And then our group started doing things together, so I hoped." He took a shaky breath and looked directly at her. "I wasn't sure how you felt."

Rachel flushed. "I like you, Aaron."

His mouth curved into a crooked smile. Then he shifted on the rock, close enough that she felt his leg pressing against her thigh. When he leaned in, it was like a movie scene, the way they looked into one another's eyes, the way she felt his warm breath on her cheek. Rachel lifted her face to his. But at the last second, she twitched away, and his kiss landed off-center, on the corner of her mouth.

Rachel sprang up, flustered. "I have to get to cello practice."

Aaron stuttered. "Oh. Well. Um. Listen…are you doing anything Friday? We could do something Friday night." He glanced at the lake, then back at her. "I mean, just the two of us?"

Rachel swallowed. "Friday is good."

They both let out a breath. Then they stood there, grinning and awkward and happy, in the warm May sun.

Chapter 5

Two days after discovering Derek's *Temp* file, Colleen sat cross-legged on the couch and flipped again through the documents that she'd printed out.

"Change Your Brain: Ten Ways to Resist Temptation."

"How to Resist Temptation: A Christian's Guide."

"*And lead us not into temptation*—the Power of Prayer."

"God is Faithful."

She set the article about changing your brain aside. With its heavy focus on resisting chocolate as an example, that hadn't been worth printing out. She picked up the "God is Faithful" article and reread the opening.

"No temptation has overtaken you that is not common to man. God is faithful, and he will not let you be tempted beyond your ability, but with the temptation he will also provide the way of escape, that you may be able to endure it (1 Cor. 10:13)."

Derek had highlighted the words "he will also provide the way of escape." One treatise gave explicit advice about handling sexual temptations. "Stay away from the people that tempt you," the author counseled. "Avoid situations that enable you to be alone with a member of the opposite sex."

He wouldn't, Colleen told herself for the umpteenth time. Derek would never hurt her like that. Aggravate her, yes. That he could do. But not truly hurt her. But what if there had been someone, someone who laughed at his tired old stories? Someone who never tried his patience? Someone younger who looked up to him, all dewy-eyed? One of the new hires in Arizona had been fresh out of college. The thought made her heart thud.

This, Colleen thought, was exactly why she should have left Derek's laptop shut tight. She drew her mother's rosary from her pocket and clasped the pale blue beads. Shawn had wanted to leave the rosary in their mother's casket, wound around her cold, dead fingers. But Colleen had retrieved them, sure that her mother would have wanted her to have the comfort of those beads. She kissed the cross the way she'd seen her mother do so many times and began the Apostles' Creed.

Temptation probably assailed most married men from time to time, she thought, moving from the Creed to the first decade of the rosary. "Hail Mary, full of grace." Not that that justified Derek cheating. *If* he had cheated, she reminded herself. *If.* "Blessed art thou among women." She had the horrible notion that believing Derek *might* have betrayed her could somehow increase the odds that he had done so. "Blessed is the fruit of thy womb, Jesus." *It's not true*, her mind insisted. "Holy Mary, Mother of God." *If it is true, make it be not true.* She ignored the illogic of that wish and pressed on. "Pray for us sinners, now and at the hour of our death." *Please. Make this go away. Just make it go away.* "Amen."

With each prayer, she ping-ponged back and forth between her hopes and her fears, until sheer repetition blunted that emotional turmoil. *Amen.*

Amen.

Amen.

Just when she reached the last bead, light from the window fell on the rosary entwined in her fingers. Some quirk of the light created a prism effect, so that tiny patches of amber and green glinted across the shimmering beads. She raised her eyes to the window. The beam of light fell across Izzy's photograph on the mantel, and Colleen abruptly recalled the moment her mother had pressed this very rosary into her hands like a talisman. Initially, Colleen had accepted it out of politeness. Such an old-fashioned approach to religion, she'd thought. But as time went by, and one miscarriage followed another, Colleen had taken the rosary from its wedge of cotton in the small, white box and prayed it out of desperation. Within a year, she was holding Izzy in her arms.

Colleen stared at the sunlit beads nestled in her palm.

The power of prayer. Derek had been tempted, but he had sought God's help to resist temptation, and God had helped him. Gratitude swept through her. Derek had not betrayed her. She sunk deeper into the couch and let out a deep sigh of relief.

Amen.

Chapter 6

On Friday night, Rachel craned her neck backwards to inspect her image in the mirror. Did her short navy skirt cover enough of her butt that she could wear black leggings instead of jeans? Yes, she decided, tugging the hem down a bit. She'd just finished arranging her black-and-white checkered scarf into a loose scoop around her neck when Aaron texted to say he'd arrived at her dorm. Slipping into her fawn-colored boots, she headed downstairs.

Aaron waited just on the other side of the turnstile, clutching a cardboard holder with drinks in one hand and a pizza box in the other. "Hey," he smiled. She swiped her card to let him in and relieved him of the drinks. When the two of them passed Ralph, Rachel gave the security guard her usual friendly smile. But instead of returning it as he typically did, Ralph's eyes darted from her to Aaron, and he smirked knowingly. Rachel reddened and turned her face toward Aaron, who was saying, "So, Mandy and I had a long talk last night." A moment later, they entered the elevator, and Aaron gave Rachel a rueful look. "It wasn't easy. Well, I didn't expect it to be easy." The elevator doors opened at Rachel's floor, and Aaron traipsed behind her down the hall. "At the end, when I asked her what I could do to make things better, she said I could help the two of you move when you find an apartment."

Rachel grinned. "Good." She led Aaron into the lounge at the end of the hall and set their drinks on a scarred end table. Aaron put the pizza box on the center cushion of the old leather couch and pulled a fistful of napkins from his jacket pocket.

"My mom is totally against me getting an apartment," Rachel told him. "She reminded me that I was a nervous kid. I used to hide behind the couch when people rang our doorbell. She thinks I'll be terrified without a security guard." Ralph's smirk flashed through her mind. The creep. What business was it of his if Rachel brought a boy upstairs?

Aaron handed her a slice of pepperoni pizza on a napkin. "What else scared you when you were little?"

Rachel gave him a look. "Don't go all junior shrink on me."

"No, I just think it's interesting, don't you? The things that kids are scared of." He chose a piece from the onion and green pepper half. "The boogeyman. The monster. The witch."

"The man under the bed," Rachel added.

"The man under the bed?"

Rachel futzed with the plastic top on her cup, which had come loose. "Oh, you know. I used to be afraid that there was a bad man lurking under my bed who would try to grab my feet." She nearly told him how she'd sometimes raced across the dark room and taken a frantic, running jump that landed her on her mattress with a thump and then laid there, pressing her pillow against her beating heart. But the look that crossed Aaron's face, a mixture of curiosity and cool assessment, kept her from saying more. Instead she asked, "What about you?"

Aaron freed the melted mozzarella stuck to the cardboard and extracted another slice. "I pretended to be a superhero. I could fly and fight the villains, but mostly I outsmarted them."

"Of course you did," Rachel teased, and then felt protective when Aaron blushed a little.

Aaron went back to his conversation with Mandy. "We basically ended with a truce," he said. "It might be a little awkward for a while, but I think it's okay." They talked a while about parents and families. Rachel described her mixed feelings about her family moving back to the area. Of course she wanted to see them. But to live with them again? After the freedom of this first year away from home? Rachel found herself talking faster, laughing more often, as triangles of pizza disappeared one by one. Finally, Aaron indicated the last piece. "You want that?" He finished it off when she shook her head, then gathered their napkins and the pizza box and carried the trash to a receptacle in the corner of the room. Watching him, Rachel moved to the far end of the couch and perched at the edge of the cushion.

"You always sit so straight," Aaron said, crossing back toward her. He sat right next to her on the middle cushion, where the pizza box had been.

"Oh, that's cello training," Rachel explained, straightening even more. "My teacher drummed that into me since I was three."

"It makes you look tense." Aaron leaned in and put his fingers lightly on her shoulders. "Are you tense?" He barely touched her, but her breath caught. She tried to relax. "No. I'm good." Aaron kneaded her shoulders. "Your muscles are really tight." She found herself unable to take a deep breath, so instead she focused on taking short ones in a steady rhythm. When Aaron's fingers pressed little circles into the base of her skull, she exclaimed, "Oh my God, that feels good!"

"That's it," Aaron said. "Just breathe into it." A funny feeling swept through her at his words. That was what she did when she played cello. Breathed into the music. She tried that now, breathing into the pressure of his fingers and feeling her muscles relax. *Breathe into it.* A melting sensation ran from her abdomen down her legs. It was, and it wasn't, like what she felt when she touched herself. This was more diffuse. More like a soft glow that ran through her whole body rather than a throbbing demand from that triangle between her legs. She shut her eyes and let the warm waves stream over her. Aaron's hands finally came to rest on her shoulders. Turning her toward him, he brought his hands to her face, lifted her mouth to his and kissed her.

She'd never realized how *sensitive* lips could be. Aaron ran his tongue, just barely, over the underside of her lip. It sent a jolt through her, and her body rose to him. But then her face grew warm, the way it did just before that red-hot shame came, and she propelled herself back into the corner of the couch.

Confusion flooded Aaron's face. "What's the matter?"

"It's not you, Aaron."

"What is it, then?"

Rachel looked at the golden flecks in his eyes. She rearranged her scarf and tucked herself more deeply into the corner of the couch. "I've never had a boyfriend."

Aaron opened his mouth, then shut it again. He brushed a few crumbs off the couch into his hand, then stared at his palm as if uncertain what to do with them. After a moment, he whisked them onto the floor. "I've never had a girlfriend."

"Oh. Right. Okay. Good." Rachel wrapped her arms around her chest. "I mean, not good, but..." She took a breath and faced Aaron squarely. "I don't really know how to do this."

Aaron broke out in a wide smile. "That makes two of us."

She didn't smile. How could she explain to this Jewish boy how problematic this whole sex thing was for a good Catholic girl? She hugged herself, rubbing her upper arms and hating that tension had returned to her neck and shoulders.

Aaron gave her a long, considering look. "Rachel, I'm just saying, it's not like I'm experienced either. You and I are pretty similar that way."

But they weren't similar. Aaron hadn't grown up in a religion that said the feelings she'd just had—those warm, incredible feelings that had swept through her when he'd massaged her shoulders—were wrong. Outside of marriage, just *having* those feelings was sinful. And here she was, experiencing those same feelings now, when Aaron wasn't even touching her. Her whole body tingled just because he looked at her steadily. Aaron shifted close to her again. He kissed her mouth, her neck, her throat, and a moan escaped her. The next thing she knew, Aaron slid her hand over his jeans where a mound had formed. Curious and a little excited, she ran her index finger along the crease. The bulge hardened.

Rachel jerked her hand back and pushed Aaron away. "I can't do this."

"I'm sorry."

"It's just that—"

Deep furrows ran across Aaron's brow. "I get it." He looked away.

Rachel couldn't think what to say. Why had she pulled her hand away as if he were some kind of freak?

Aaron turned toward her. "It's okay," he said softly. "We could…I don't know. We could go to a movie. See if Gregorio or Mandy are around. Walk the lake path. Whatever. We can take things slow."

Rachel's shoulders relaxed just as they had after Aaron massaged them. She glanced at him. The curl dangling on his forehead charmed her; his anxious look melted her. With a shy smile, she held her hand out to him. He stood and tugged her to a standing position. Then he slung his arm over her shoulder, and that tingly feeling enveloped her and floated her down the hall, weightless as a breeze.

Chapter 7

Colleen held out her parcel, wrapped in white tissue and tied with a silver ribbon. Suddenly unsure, she said, "Geeta, I hope you're not offended, but you wanted something to remember me by." With some trepidation, she watched Geeta untie the ribbon.

"Oh!" Geeta lifted a small statue of the Virgin Mary holding baby Jesus. "It's lovely, Colleen."

"I'm not trying to convert you or anything. It's just…I do pray for you. I pray especially these days, because I know you're worried about your father. But if this is the wrong thing to offer—"

Geeta smiled. "It's fine. It's better than fine."

"Good," Colleen sighed. But her brow still wrinkled.

"Come. I want to show you something," Geeta said. In her home, Geeta wore simple, short-sleeved tops with flowing, traditional print skirts that nearly reached her bare feet. Colleen followed the colorful peacock pattern on Geeta's skirt up the stairs. "Hinduism is a very accepting religion," Geeta said, leading Colleen into the master bedroom. "We have many gods. See?" Atop an ornate table with gold inlay, there were dozens of small statues in brass and marble and silver, set on a mat woven with threads of red and gold. "This is Lord Vishnu," Geeta said, pointing to the large bronze statue in the center, "a very important god for us. Dancing here is Shiva, and this is Krishna playing the flute. I have two statues of my favorite, Saraswati, the goddess of wisdom and learning. In this figure, she's playing a musical instrument, but I really like this one, where she's holding a book."

A very fat, smiling Buddha squatted at the edge of the group. Geeta moved the Buddha over a bit and set the Virgin Mary and baby Jesus in the space she had made. "See? Your god is welcome here," she smiled, "just like the Buddha is." Geeta bit her lip. "And your prayers for my father, they're so welcome, too."

"The only one I recognize is the Buddha," Colleen admitted. "I don't know the Hindu gods."

Geeta hesitated a moment, then lifted the Buddha. "Would you like this one? To remember me?"

"Oh, Geeta, I'll never forget you!" Colleen exclaimed. "But of course I'll accept your Buddha. Thank you." She blinked back tears. To seal them in, she hurried on. "We'll stay in touch. We can talk and Skype, and I'll come back to Arizona sometime to visit."

Geeta dabbed at her own wet eyes with a tissue. "This

isn't like me. You know this isn't like me. All this with my father—it doesn't take anything, and I turn into a puddle."

"Me, too," Colleen said, wiping at tears. "This isn't like me, either. And I have no excuse for being weepy."

Geeta's eyes widened. "But of course, you're worried about Derek."

"Oh, I…" Colleen stammered. "I'm not. Really. I have no doubts about Derek." Geeta's eyebrows rose, and Colleen rushed on. "See, I found these articles on Derek's laptop about resisting temptation. Whatever he might have been tempted to do, I know he didn't give in."

Geeta frowned. "Maybe," she said. "But couldn't it mean the opposite?"

"No, it couldn't." The words came out brusquely. Colleen softened her tone. "I can see how you might think that's what it means. But it doesn't." How to make Geeta understand?

Geeta led Colleen to the queen-size bed with its silky duvet, and the two women sat. "You don't really know Derek," Colleen said. "You've only seen his funny, light-hearted side. But he can be…" She swallowed. "I had a really hard time when my mom got sick. I took her to the doctor; she'd had an x-ray because her back hurt, and we were going to find out what the x-ray showed. My mother complained the whole time in the waiting room about how the x-ray probably wouldn't show anything, and what was the use? The doctor probably couldn't do anything anyway, but…" She choked up.

"It did show something."

Colleen nodded, her throat too constricted to talk. After a long moment, she said, "Lung cancer. Already spread to her spine." She stared at Geeta's altar, at the Virgin Mary, who looked incongruous among these Hindu gods. "Derek was such a comfort to me at that time. The way he took care of me." She gave a little shrug. "I just know that he wouldn't hurt me."

Back home, after Izzy had yawned her way to bed, Colleen paced the bare kitchen. She'd packed many nonessentials: the knickknacks, the decorative ceramic tiles with brightly painted fruits and vegetables, the canisters, the dreamcatcher. Only her mother's needlepoint of the Irish Kitchen Prayer still hung on the wall. Her mother had stitched little green shamrocks to border the words: "May the kitchen be a gathering place blessed with family and friends where love is always the key ingredient." Colleen lifted the needlepoint off the wall and considered it. Aloud, she said, "Geeta thinks that Derek is having an affair, but she's wrong. My husband is not having an affair." In Colleen's mind, her mother responded. *It wouldn't be that surprising, though, would it? The way you nag. And you're still throwing stuff around? Almost forty years old and you're still having tantrums?* Colleen's hands gripped the frame, and she argued back, "Better mad than sad! Better than keeping everything inside and sitting in a dark room for the rest of your life." She slammed the needlepoint on the counter and continued, "Derek is back in Chicago, a hundred miles away from whoever tempted him."

What about Cynthia? It was as if the needlepoint had whispered the insinuation.

Cynthia. Cynthia had gone to Arizona at the same time as Derek and, like him, had now returned to Chicago. But pushy, know-it-all Cynthia? Who had once gone behind Derek's back to complain to his boss about his expense vouchers? "Derek doesn't even like Cynthia," Colleen declared.

The perfect cover, her mother's voice rejoined.

The only light in the dim kitchen came from the bulb above the stove. Colleen caught an image of herself reflected in the dark patio doors. Her vaguely-defined silhouette almost blended with the shadowy shapes of the cabinets behind her, and she had the disturbing feeling that she could fade into the gloom. Be sucked into an endless gray void, untethered from hearth and home. She stumbled against the wall in the corner of the kitchen and sank to the floor.

Where she remembered her six-year-old self.

Her six-year-old self, huddling in the corner of her bedroom because Daddy was yelling. Then the door slammed, and the house became quiet. Still, she waited, her back pressed against the wall, until it had been silent for so long that she feared she might be alone. She stumbled down the hall to the mound of covers on her mother's bed. "Mommy?" The covers stirred. "Mommy?" She snuck her hand under the bedspread, felt her mother's shoulder and shook her. "Mommy!"

Her mother thrust her away with a push as rough as a slap. "Can't you let me have five minutes of peace? Can't you leave me alone for five minutes?" Colleen shrank back and tiptoed to her bedroom, where she latched onto Paddington Bear and rocked back and forth in the corner with the bear in her arms. Quiet. Not crying.

Later, her mother sat in the dim living room and stared at the muted television. Colleen carried her book and a plate with two ginger cookies into the room. She lifted the plate toward her mother. When her mother didn't look in her direction, she extended the dish further. It hovered over her mother's lap until her thin arm ached. Her mother kept her eyes focused on the silent TV screen. The muscles of her skinny arm burning, Colleen slumped to the floor and set the plate down. She leaned her cheek against the knobby fabric of her mother's chair while she turned the pages of her book and whispered the story to herself in the dark.

How strange, Colleen thought, *that such an old memory is still so vivid.* She lifted the edge of her t-shirt and dried her tears with it. Feeling for her mother's rosary in her pocket, she ran her thumb over the small cross. *I am not a child*, she reminded herself.

She extracted herself from the corner and strode toward the stove, stopping to snap the wall switch on. The kitchen flooded with light. *I am not my mother.* Briskly, she filled the teapot with water and told herself that she needed to think over her situation like an adult. Waiting for the water to boil, she mulled things over. She was a good wife. A good wife should trust her husband. But if a wife can't trust her husband one hundred percent, if he may be in danger, then what? Then a good wife should *do* something. She should help her husband resist temptation.

The teapot whistled. If Colleen sent Izzy to Derek, the way she had originally planned, Izzy's presence would remind him of his family, of his obligations. Colleen turned the burner off and inhaled the scent of a chamomile teabag before dropping it in her cup. Her hand wavered over her cell phone, sitting on the counter. She picked it up to call Derek, then set it back down. Why give him a chance to argue?

She poured hot water over her teabag and settled herself in front of her laptop to search for a flight for Izzy. *I am not my mother*, she thought. *I know how to take action.*

Chapter 8

On Saturday, Rachel rang Aunt Bea's doorbell and shifted from one foot to the other while she waited on the stoop. The May winds in the suburbs were much warmer than the lake breezes by her dorm, and she unzipped her jean jacket.

Bea's plump arms enfolded Rachel the moment she crossed the threshold. "This is so nice!" Bea exclaimed, stepping back and considering her niece with a wide, welcoming grin. "We barely had a chance to talk the night of your concert." She led the way to the kitchen, her ample hips swaying under her brightly-patterned skirt. "You want a scone?" Bea asked over her shoulder. "After you called, I took some of those scones you like out of the freezer."

"Oh, you didn't need to do that." In the bright light of the kitchen, Rachel noticed Bea's hair. "You had your hair streaked."

Bea's hand flew to her short brown waves, now splashed with the color of caramel. "What do you think?" She extracted a cookie sheet from the oven and laid it on the stovetop. The smell of cinnamon filled the kitchen.

"It looks really nice," Rachel said, though in reality she preferred her aunt's familiar, mousy-brown color. She glanced around the empty kitchen, taking in the quiet of the house. "Is Amber home?"

Bea pulled a spatula out of a drawer. "She's at Saturday soccer practice. After you called, I asked her dad to take her."

"I didn't mean for you…"

Bea set four scones on an old-fashioned plate with roses on it. "He was glad to get out of putting more paving stones down in the garden."

The cups and saucers on the table had the same roses and gold edges as the plate. "Aren't these your good dishes?" Rachel wondered.

"Uh-huh. I decided that it's silly to only use them two or three times a year. And I kind of feel like it brings my mom into the room, you know?" While they sipped tea, Bea talked about the Christmas feasts her mother had prepared when Bea was a child, and Amber's soccer coach, and the motorcycle Uncle Shawn wanted to buy.

Finally, Rachel brushed some crumbs off her olive t-shirt and interrupted her aunt. "There's something I wanted to ask you." She wished her voice didn't tremble so. She took a breath and explained about not wanting to move back home for the summer. "I missed my family so much when they left last fall," she stammered at the end, "but I need space from Mom. I don't know if you can understand that."

"Oh honey," Bea laughed, "I know what your mother can be like."

Rachel blinked. For the first time, it occurred to her that friendly, garrulous, nonjudgmental Aunt Bea was not only aware of how her mother behaved, but had some opinions of her own about that. "Of course, things were hard for her," Bea went on. "She might as well have been a single mom half the time, with your dad traveling so much. But I don't think you can blame everything on the infamous Irish temper." Bea rolled her eyes. "As if your mother has no control over that." She added quickly, "Of course, she's much better now."

Rachel grew thoughtful. "We joke about her Irish temper, but we never talk about it. Not really."

Bea gave a noncommittal shrug. "Maybe you need to, honey. You're older now. Tell her why you want to be on your own. It's not easy walking on eggshells in your own home. Have a heart-to-heart with her." Bea gave Rachel a long look. "She might really like that. In the end."

"I know she'd like to be closer to me," Rachel admitted. "But when I try to talk to her, she gets so snippy, and then she says stuff, and I get mad." Rachel glanced at her aunt. "I'm afraid of what I'll say if we're living together. Mom looks tough—"

"But how quickly that tough cookie crumbles," Bea said.

"Exactly! That's why I can't talk to her. 'Heart-to-heart'? It would kill her if she knew how I felt about her sometimes." Rachel leaned forward. "I can't live with her all summer. That's why I want to rent an apartment with my friend Mandy."

Bea's brow creased. "Your mother will be devastated."

Rachel lifted her chin, getting what she knew her mother would call "that stubborn look," but she didn't say anything.

"Izzy's been looking forward to being with you this summer, too," Bea added.

"I thought about that. I could visit; I could take the train to Wilmington and then take Izzy downtown to spend the day. She'd love that, just me and her. That would be way better than me living at home. It would be more special." Bea looked skeptical. "The thing is, Aunt Bea, I applied for a job at this restaurant, and I'm almost sure I'll get it. So, I could pay you back, but I need money for a deposit. And you know Mom is never going to give it to me."

"Oh, Rachel."

"My half is $1,000, but I have some saved. If you could just lend me $800…or even $750, I could manage it. I would pay you back, I promise."

"It's not the money. It's…" Bea gave a nervous laugh.

"Your mother would never speak to me again."

"We wouldn't have to tell her. I'll tell her I earned it at my new job."

Bea raised her eyebrow. "The one you're *almost sure* you have?"

Rachel pleaded, "Mom doesn't have to know that."

Her aunt sighed. "See, that's what happens. One lie leads to another, and in the end the truth comes out, and then where are you? And she wouldn't just be mad at me, would she?" Bea took their cups to the stove and poured boiling water over their teabags. "Can you imagine the fireworks? Well, you know your mother." She gazed at the yard beyond the window and shook her head. "When I first married into this family, I couldn't believe her. Throwing your toys and books onto the lawn!"

"Onto the lawn?"

"Oh," Bea said, handing Rachel a refilled cup, "you were little; you probably don't remember. Anyway, I think it's better if you're honest with your parents. Maybe talk to your dad alone first? Don't tell him your mom will drive you crazy. Talk about the value of working, of developing more independence."

But the shocking image of her mother throwing *books* on the lawn distracted Rachel. "Why did mom throw books on the lawn?"

Bea frowned. "I don't remember. The stress of the holiday, I guess." She squinted, trying to recall. "Something went wrong with the lamb roast one Easter, I think." After a moment, she threw her palms open. "It doesn't matter. So, tell me, how is school going this term?"

"What I remember," Rachel said, "is the time Mom got so mad because Dad was late for a brunch, and when he got home, she scraped his meal into the garbage right in front of him." Rachel chuckled, then became somber. "It wasn't funny then. But when I think back…my hundred-pound spitfire of a mother."

A troubled expression pulled down the corners of Bea's mouth. "Sometimes it was funny. But I hated when you got yelled at. It broke my heart. It really did. You tried so hard. I've always believed parents should present a united front. But when your dad made fun of your mother, I was secretly glad."

"Dad made fun of Mom?" It seemed inconceivable.

"Not in front of her," Bea added hastily. "Or other people, I don't think. I only knew because I eavesdropped." She plucked self-consciously at her sleeve. "I overheard him once. I was walking your colicky sister up and down the nursery. Lord, how that child could scream! And you came bawling down the hall to your bedroom. After a while, your dad went in there and pretty soon you stopped crying. I was curious." Bea's face colored a little. "I listened at the door. And there was your dad telling you, 'Mom doesn't mean it, you're a good girl.' Stuff like that. And I thought, 'Good!' But then I heard him *mimicking* her! Talking in exactly that tone of hers, but in a squeaky voice. 'Oh, no, someone left a sock on the couch! Easter is ruined!' And you laughing." Bea gave Rachel a fierce look. "I don't think parents should undermine one another, but I could have clapped for your father."

Rachel's throat went dry. Gravel crunched in the driveway outside the window, and Bea stood up. "Here's Amber and your uncle now." A car door slammed.

"I have to go to the bathroom," Rachel croaked, and rushed down the hall. She locked the bathroom door, shut the lid on the toilet seat, and buried her face in her hands. A weird sensation, unlike anything she'd ever experienced before, came over her. It was as if there were two parallel worlds going on at the same time. In one, she sat on the closed lid of the toilet in her aunt's blue-tiled bathroom, the light so bright that she had to shield her eyes. In the other, she sat with her father on the edge of her childhood bed, the room dim, with just a sliver of light coming through a gap in the curtains. His arm around her, he murmured, "It's okay, Mommy's just tired. The baby was up all night. She didn't mean it." Then her father made her laugh through her tears, with his silly faces, mimicking her mother.

But then.

He kicked off his loafers. Slipped off her shoes, cupped her stockinged foot in his warm hand. Pulled the bedspread back, patted her Little Princess sheet, patted the empty space he'd created next to him. She could see his hand, his big hand with the black hairs on the backs of his fingers, patting that sheet.

The blue tiles of the bathroom swam around Rachel, and her breaths came more and more rapidly. She lowered her head and waited for the dizziness to pass. She didn't know how much time had gone by when a knock came on the door.

"You okay, honey?"

Rachel barely got the words out. "I'm fine. I'm good. Just be a minute." She stood and splashed water on her face. Her skin looked very pale in the mirror. She cupped her hand and captured tap water from the faucet, forcing some down her dry throat.

In the kitchen, she talked quickly. "I just realized how late it is." She didn't look at her aunt, her uncle, her cousin; she focused on the stitching on her jean jacket, on the geometric pattern on her bag. "If I run, I can catch the next train."

Bea said, "Uncle Shawn will drive you to the station."

"No, no; it's beautiful outside. I need the exercise. I can make it." She waved, barely glancing at them, and pulled the back door shut behind her. Then she sped away, faster and faster, as if the house could suck her back in. Could suck her all the way back to her childhood bedroom.

At the station, Rachel scrounged through her bag for the vial of Valium Mandy had given her and downed a pill, dry, just as the train pulled in. She moved to an empty seat near the back of the car and shut her eyes. The rhythmic sound of train wheels had always seemed to chant words to Rachel, and today the wheels repeated *Did that happen did that happen did that happen…* Three stops down the line, when a small girl in a princess dress put her thumb in her mouth and stared at Rachel, she realized that her face must be streaked with tears, her lavender eyeshadow smudged. She twisted her body and rested her forehead against the cool train window. At the next stop, a large crowd got on: families going downtown to spend the day at Millennium Park or Navy Pier. An old woman plopped down next to Rachel. The train moved deeper into run-down neighborhoods, and Rachel stared out the window at junkyards, huge heaps of tires, abandoned buildings. The train wheels repeated, *Did that happen did that happen…*

Her eyes shut tight, Rachel listened to the sounds in the train car. Thin whining from some unhappy child far behind her. A squabble among children two seats ahead of her, followed by a mother's sharp, "Leave her alone!" From somewhere else, a sudden belly laugh and a child's surprised voice, "Look, Mommy!" Then in Rachel's mind, another child's voice—her own voice, amazed. *It popped up! Daddy, it popped up!*

Chapter 9

Rachel awakened late Sunday morning, her eyelids stuck shut. After she rubbed them half-open, she peered at the papers and books stacked on her desk. They blurred in the distance, and even her backpack, flung onto the floor close to her bed, appeared vaguely unreal. Then she remembered, and her eyes went wide.

Maybe that never happened.

Just last week, she'd read an article about false memories, about the suggestibility of children. What did she really recall? Her father's hand, patting a sheet? A light stroke across her abdomen? Did she truly remember these things, or had her mind been invaded by images from the research she'd done, the case studies she'd read?

But.

It popped up.

She heard her child's voice saying those words as clearly as if she had spoken them aloud now. Her hand drifted down to her backpack, and she fumbled inside the pouch until she touched her pills. She swallowed another Valium and slept.

The clock showed almost noon when she staggered, woozy, toward the bathroom. Uncharacteristically, Serena's bed was tidily made. Perhaps it had never been slept in Saturday night. Serena herself was nowhere to be seen, thank God. Rachel soaped her naked body under the hot shower, steam filling the room. Yesterday's events seemed to dissolve in the cloudy mist. Rachel raised her face to the cascade of water as if it could wash away her confusion. What was real? If only she could know for sure. If only there was someone who could tell her. But there was no one.

That's not true, she realized, turning so that the water pounded her tight shoulders. Her father knew. One way or another, her father knew the truth. Images of him played across her mind. He had a barely perceptible shadow outlining his body, so thin that she could ignore it and focus instead on the smiling face, the dad who cracked jokes and made up funny games and sometimes came to her defense against her mother. Rachel shivered despite the heat in the bathroom. Maybe it was better not to know for sure. She could turn a blind eye to that shadow then. She could go on with her life.

In the lobby, Ralph gave her the same sleazy smile he'd been bestowing ever since the night she brought Aaron to the dorm. *Fuck you,* she thought, turning crimson at his glance. She headed for the doors, her music in hand. Ralph muttered something as she raced past him. Bursting through the doors, she slipped her dark glasses on and ran. She ran all the way to the music building, ran with the fierce energy of someone desperate for sanctuary: a suppliant to her church, a lover to her beloved, a child to her mother's arms.

The music building enveloped her with the sweet familiarity of its marble floors and cathedral-like ceiling, the light that poured through the glass wall, the muted sounds of piano, violin and saxophone that escaped the closed doors along the hallway. Rachel retrieved her cello from her storage unit and headed to Practice Room 8. There, she lifted her beautiful, burnished instrument out of its case and rosined her bow. She planted the cello firmly on its spike and drew her bow across the C string. Tightened the peg. Cocked her head and listened again. A stillness settled in her while she carried out the ritual tuning. Then, her back hardwood straight, her concentration on the music in front of her, she arranged her calloused fingertips on the strings and raised her bow. A deep sigh escaped her. The notes lifted her above it all: her father's violation, her mother's impending devastation, her own anger. With the chords rising pure and clear, she breathed into the music and lost herself in it.

Chapter 10

The following afternoon, Rachel tried to sustain the peace she'd felt during her practice. But moments after she began taking notes in the library for her term paper, she had to set her pen down. She glanced at the words she'd scrawled in handwriting so shaky that she hardly recognized it as her own. "Victims experience anxiety, self-blame, shame."

She turned back to the research notes she'd made a week earlier, before her visit to her aunt. Here, her clear writing reflected a steady hand. "Not all pedophiles are predators," she'd written. "Majority of P's not exclusive (they have relationships with adult women); P's who abuse family members have lowest rate of recidivism. P's often abuse same-age children. Brain scans reveal P's attraction to children."

She forced herself to take notes on a very long article that discussed a complicated classification system, defining a dozen different types of pedophiles. Next, she disciplined herself to read all about the Sex Offender Registry and the constraints imposed on where sex offenders were allowed to work, to live. She read a series of journal articles on the effectiveness of different types of therapies for victims of child sex abuse. In this way, article by article, she got through the hours until evening descended and a wave of dizziness came over her. She had barely eaten. Suddenly, she yearned for mac and cheese, chocolate milk. Leaving the library, she put on her sunglasses, though it was already dark outside, and pulled the hood of her sweatshirt forward. With leaden feet, she made her way to the huge cafeteria in Rothchild Center.

She ate her mac and cheese outside on the near-deserted, shadowy patio, watching the lights of the Chicago skyline shimmer in the distance. By the time she swallowed the last spoonful of pasta and downed the last drop of chocolate milk, she felt a bit better. She thought again about false memories and truth, what was real and what was imagined. She took out her cell phone, but the thought of phoning her father made her short of breath. Instead, she scrolled to her mother's number.

Colleen picked up on the second ring. "Rachel, hi!" Rachel's voice stuck in her throat. Her mother asked, "Is everything all right?"

Rachel stood so abruptly that she banged her knee on the plastic chair. "Everything's good. I just wanted to…I was visiting Aunt Bea, and we got to talking about when Izzy was a baby, and…Did you really throw my toys onto the lawn?"

A snort came over the line. "This family never forgets a

thing, do they? Bea had it easy. Amber slept through the night at three months. Your aunt has no idea what it's like to be up half the night for months on end." She coughed. "You were an easy baby, too. But Izzy? Which reminds me. I'm glad you called. Here's the thing, Rachel. I really need your help with Izzy."

Rachel blinked. "What do you mean?"

"Well, our renters are moving out June first. I'd like to send Izzy back home soon after that. Dad will be working a lot, so I thought you could be home to help out, and I could stay in Arizona for as long as it takes to get the house ready to put on the market." Her mother's voice tightened. "That's another reason you moving to some apartment isn't a good idea."

"God, Mom! You always—"

"No, Rachel, I'm not. I promise, I'm not being a hovercraft. This isn't about stopping you from being on your own. This is about me needing your help."

Rachel's shoulder muscles knotted up painfully. "But you'd get me home all the same."

"Okay. True. But look. If I think we can swing it financially, I'll help you set up in an apartment next summer. I promise. But for now, it makes so much more sense for you to live at home. Dad can't totally take care of Izzy on his own. Not while he's working."

In a wooden voice, Rachel said, "Izzy would be home alone with Dad?"

"Exactly. That's why I need your help." Her mother's voice broke a little. "Things are really hard for me right now, okay? Your dad's job, the move…other stuff…"

In Bea's story, Izzy had been a baby. That meant that Rachel would have been eight, the same age as Izzy was now. Rachel's head swam. "Don't send Izzy home without you."

Her mother's angry voice slammed across the line. "You can be so selfish, Rachel. Do you have any idea how much Izzy's missed you this year? It would mean the world to her to have some time with her big sister. Is that so much to ask? If you won't do it for me, do it for your sister."

"But Mom—" Rachel said, clutching her phone tight. She stopped herself. What could she say, when her memories were as vague and shadowy as the dim patio? *Did that happen? Did that really happen?*

Colleen snapped, "'But Mom' what?"

Rachel's heart beat like a drum. "I'll think about it. I have to go." She ended the call, sank down on the plastic chair and stared at her contact list. Her father's name gleamed at her. Would he tell her the truth? And if he denied it, could she believe him? Her finger spasmed so badly that it took her three tries before she could press the icon by his name.

On the fifth ring, he picked up. "Rachel! This is a nice surprise. How you doing, hon?"

Rachel heard the background noise of a sports bar,

cheers and boos and yelling at an umpire. "I'm okay. Listen…"

"Hang on a second, sweetheart. I can hardly hear you. Let me move somewhere." Slowly, the raucous cheers and noisy conversation faded to a distant murmur. "So, how are you? Everything okay?"

Rachel's breath came out in spurts. "I need to talk to you…" She let out a squeaky gasp. "I remembered… I think I remembered something. I think when I was…like eight…you used to touch me."

Silence.

"Touch my private parts."

She heard a bang, as if her father had knocked into something. A bark of a laugh. "Sweetheart. What are you talking about?"

"And I think," Rachel forced herself to say, "maybe you made me touch you."

It took a second, but then her father's voice thundered across the line. "Good God, Rachel! What a thing to say!" When she stayed silent, he said, "Pumpkin. You know that's crazy, right?'

And in the next moment, she did know that it was crazy. Of course it was crazy. Of course her father had never abused her. The truth of that thought burst in her like a firework and exploded, sending shimmering sparks of relief through every cell of her body.

He rushed on. "You're the world to me, Rach. You

know that, don't you? My gosh, I remember the day you were born. I held you in my arms, you with this little white cap on your head. Your little scrunched up face. Such a darling. *That's my girl!* I thought. I'd kill anyone who hurt you, Rachel. You know that, right?"

She did know that. Her eyes welled up, and for a moment she couldn't speak.

"You know," her father went on, "your mother said something to me after our visit, about that class. How it's affecting you."

She let out a sound that was half-sob, half-laugh. "Yeah," she sniffled. "I think it's been doing a number on me."

"You and Izzy are the light of my life," he told her.

If he had stopped there. Perhaps, if he'd stopped there. But he didn't. Her father's words tumbled on, recounting a time long before Izzy was born, when he and Rachel had gone sledding. "We hit this patch of ice," he said, "and then we were shooting straight for this tree," and he went on and on about how devastated he'd been at the thought that something might have happened to her, and then he repeated that she meant the world to him, she was his treasure, and she thought *it's too much he's protesting too much* but maybe not, maybe this was the normal reaction of a father who couldn't believe his beloved daughter would levy such an accusation at him. But in the next moment, he said, "I knew your mom would be so upset if she learned how close we'd come to an accident."

"We never did tell Mom," Rachel said, the memory coming back to her. She ran her fingers over her mouth in a "my lips are sealed" gesture, and automatically added that twist that meant she'd turned the key.

Her father chuckled. "Of course we didn't tell her. Why upset her when nothing happened?"

But Rachel's hand remained frozen in the corner of her mouth. Because she saw her father, clear as day, swiping his own lips in that gesture, and then winking while he waited for her to do the same. And after she'd done that, after she'd given that imaginary key a final twist, he lowered his face and grazed her lips lightly with his own, as if sealing them a second time.

Rachel asked, "Did you used to come into my bedroom and make fun of Mommy?"

"What?" Then, "I don't know, honey. I don't remember that."

"You don't remember that?"

"No."

"You don't remember how you'd try to calm me down after Mom had one of her fits?"

Her father stammered, "Well, I always tried to keep the peace." A phony chuckle came across the line.

Rachel answered dully, "You're lying."

"What?"

"If you remember that, then you remember everything."

After a long silence, her father said, "I have no idea what you're talking about."

The cicadas clamored in the trees, and Rachel's heart drummed as if in concert, the two sounds pounding in her ears. "If you're not lying," she cried, "then I'm going crazy." Mac and cheese clumped at the top of her throat, and her breaths came in gasps.

"Honey, listen."

"Dad," she wheezed, "I can't breathe."

Her father's tone became urgent. "Are you sitting down, Rach? Sit, okay? Okay, hon, you're going to be okay. Do you have a paper bag, something you can breathe into? It's okay if you don't; just put your head down, and slow now, breathe slow, exhale, then hold it, like this…" Her father demonstrated, all the while murmuring reassurance. Rachel lowered her forehead onto her hand, cell phone on the table by her ear, listening to his voice and mimicking his breathing, the way she had as a child when inexplicable panic overcame her and made her heart stampede. It had been years since this had happened.

After a while, her father said, "Are you doing better now? Less dizzy?"

She sobbed. "Dad. I need you to tell me the truth. Please. Just tell me the truth."

A long minute passed. Finally, he answered, "I prayed that you would never remember. Sweetheart. I'm so sorry."

The roar in Rachel's head was as deafening as the cicadas.

"Hon?"

She pressed her head against her palm. "How could you do that?" She heard her father's labored breathing.

"I don't know. I never meant to hurt you. I kind of left home, you know, for a while. I took on more travel."

"But why?" she cried out. "Why would you do that to me?"

Her father's swallow was so loud that she heard it. "I was so sure you had forgotten all that. It was such a long time ago, and you never said anything. I thought you were okay. And look at you now. You looked so grown-up at your concert, so beautiful. I mean, you are okay. Aren't you?"

A group of students emerged from the building carrying trays. "*Okay?*" Rachel said. The students veered in her direction, and she stumbled away from their chatter.

"Sweetheart," her father began.

"Stop calling me sweetheart," she whispered between clenched teeth. Two students set their trays down on a distant table, but then a girl detached herself from their group and walked straight toward Rachel. "These are cleaner," she called out to her friends. With her father's murmurs in her ear, Rachel backed away from the girl's approaching figure. Turning, she fled the patio and ran down the dark path away from the Center.

"I'm going to make this up to you," her father said.

Coming to a halt, Rachel pulled her hood forward, as far past her face as it would reach. "I talked to Mom."

"Oh!"

"She wanted me to know that she's sending Izzy to you. Before she comes home herself. She wanted to make sure I'd be home to help out with Iz."

"Rachel." Cold fear echoed in his voice. "You can't say anything to Mom. You know that, right? This would kill your mother."

She licked her dry lips. She found herself scratching at her arms, scraping them with her bitten fingernails.

"Rach. What did you tell your mother?"

"Nothing. I didn't tell her anything. But Izzy can't be alone with you."

"That wasn't even the plan. That was your mother's old plan. I told her no weeks ago. God, she can be so stubborn! I knew nothing about this. Nothing."

"You can't be alone with Izzy," Rachel repeated.

A beat passed. "You don't have to worry about Izzy. I give you my word."

A disgusted sound burst from Rachel's lips.

"No, listen, Rach! Here's the thing. You can't imagine how much I regret, how I wish I could go back in time."

Suddenly, Rachel couldn't bear the sound of her father's voice. "I don't care about your wishes or regrets! All I care about right now is Izzy."

His words flew into her ear. "But that's how you can know that Izzy is totally safe with me. How terrible I feel. That would keep anything from…Hang on a second." A group must have been moving toward him, because a murmured conversation grew louder, and then he said, "How's it going?" Another man's voice boomed. "They're up by three!" She knew her father would be nodding now, perhaps even smiling, waiting for the patrons to pass. That morning, when she'd showered, she had pictured him outlined with a thin shadow. She imagined him standing in the bar now, that shadow darkening, thickening, so that the joking fans would see it and edge away.

"All I'm trying to say, Rach, is that Izzy is safe. And if Izzy is safe, and you tell your mother, you will have destroyed her for nothing. Think this through, Rachel, please." After a long silence, he added, "I'm so sorry you remembered. If only you could know how sorry I am. I wish I were with you now. I wish I could give you a big hug."

Rachel pulled the phone from her ear as if her father could reach through it and embrace her against her will. Her voice trembled. "I think of Izzy," she said. "So open. And laughing. Isn't that how you picture Izzy? I mean, if she just pops into your mind? Laughing. And I think, maybe I used to be like Izzy." She blinked back tears.

"Nothing's going to happen to Izzy," her father pleaded.

Suddenly exhaustion overcame her, and Rachel's shoulders slumped. "Mom has to be told."

Her father's patient, even-tempered tone, the one he used to calm her mother when Colleen was overexcited, came across the line. "Look, Rach. If you tell your mother, don't you see, it's just spreading the pain. Why cause even more suffering?"

Rachel shut her eyes. For a fleeting moment, she wondered, *Could I? Keep this secret? Go home for the summer. Be the good sister who watches over Izzy. The good daughter who protects her mother.* But what about when summer ended? And what might happen even while she was home, on alert? Her mother had been home…

"Rachel," her father begged. "Please. Promise you won't tell Mom."

Rachel steeled herself. "I'm not going to tell Mom." Her voice was ice. "You are, Dad. You are."

Chapter 11

Rachel stared at her image in the mirror. The forecast had warned of temperatures near 90, unseasonably hot for May, so she'd slipped on her favorite sundress, a creamy print dotted with pale pink roses. But it left her shoulders and arms bare, and in some obscure way, it just didn't feel *right*. She stripped and grabbed the same black jeans and long-sleeved gray top she'd worn the day before.

Professor Malley had already begun her lecture when Rachel slipped into the room. Mandy craned backwards and motioned her into the empty seat next to her. "Where have you been?" Mandy whispered. "I tried to reach you when you didn't show up for our kickboxing workout. Didn't you get my texts? We have to give them a deposit today to get that apartment."

Rachel nodded vaguely in response. Mandy's agitation felt totally removed from her. Throughout the lecture, she ignored Mandy's pointed looks while her own glance darted around the room, from one woman to another.

How many? she wondered. *Her? Her?*

"Earth to Rachel," Aaron said when she joined their discussion group later. "Friday or Saturday? Does it matter to you which day we go?"

Her lips parted to ask, "Go where?" But it didn't really matter where. "I don't care," she answered, and sat quietly while their words flowed around her.

When class ended, Mandy followed close behind her. "Rach, I could call now," she said. "This place is perfect. It's kind of old, but it's got two bedrooms and it's partially furnished. The mattresses on the beds looked brand new, and there was a couch and a kitchen table. An ugly couch, but still. My mom will co-sign, but I have to give them a deposit today."

"Today?"

"Haven't you been listening? Didn't you see my texts? I texted you all weekend, and yesterday too. Is your phone even on?"

Rachel came to a stop. She drew her cell phone out of her backpack. The battery was low, but not dead. Why hadn't she heard from her mother? Hadn't her father told her yet? Was he chickening out?

Mandy shadowed Rachel down the path. "Don't you *want* to get this apartment with me?"

Heat rose from the pavement. Beneath Rachel's long-sleeved jersey, sweat dribbled between her breasts, and her black jeans burned in the sun. Another concern leapt to her mind. Where exactly was her father? Still in Chicago? Or back in Arizona? "Of course I want to get the apartment," she told Mandy. "But I don't have the money for a deposit."

Mandy's face fell. "No help from your aunt?"

"No," Rachel said. "My aunt was no help at all."

"What about your dad?" Mandy pressed. "He seemed more open to it. Did you try asking your dad?"

"My dad?" A caustic laugh burst from Rachel. "Yeah. Maybe I could get money from my father. I could blackmail him for it." She laughed again, slightly hysterical, sounding more and more crazed. She clutched at her stomach, leaned against an oak tree near the path.

Mandy approached her. "Rachel—"

"I should have thought of blackmail sooner," Rachel croaked. "It's probably too late now."

"What are you talking about?"

Between guffaws, Rachel gasped for breath and pressed her palm against the tree. "He's probably already told my mother."

Mandy stared at Rachel. "What happened?"

Peering at the narrow slits of Mandy's eyes, Rachel suddenly had the idea that Mandy would be able to answer the questions that had woken her in the middle of the night. "Why didn't I stop him?" she cried out. She scraped the heel of her hand against the rough bark of the oak tree. "Why didn't I tell my mom?"

Mandy's face paled. "Oh, Rachel." She lifted Rachel's chafed hand from the tree and held it between her own. Her face, so white a moment earlier, now flamed. "Maybe you thought she wouldn't believe you."

Tears sprang to Rachel's eyes. "Don't, Mandy. I'm so mad at my father. I can't be mad at my mom, too." She twisted her hand from her friend's grasp. "I have to go." She moved down the sidewalk, Mandy silent by her side. In less than an hour, she would be able to shut the door of the practice room behind her, shut the world out. To calm herself now, she replayed her last practice session in her mind.

"Goddamn motherfuckers!" Mandy's shout startled Rachel so much that she stumbled. Not noticing, Mandy forged ahead, spewing out a rant against men, against fathers, uncles, brothers. "Goddamn perverts!" she thundered to the skies just as they arrived at Rachel's dorm. Mandy's chest heaved, stretching the material around the buttons of her bright yellow top, and she took a shaky breath. "I'm sorry, Rachel. I don't mean to upset you even more."

"You're not upsetting me."

Mandy gave her a look.

"Really, Mandy, it's fine. The more upset you got, the calmer I got. So. That's good."

Mandy frowned. "I'm not sure that's good."

"No, it is. It's like I can be more reasonable now."

Rachel took her sunglasses off, eliminating the dark wall between herself and her friend. "You're like my outrage, so I can calm down."

Mandy turned Rachel's hand over. Little dots of red had appeared where she'd scraped it raw against that tree. "I'm texting you my therapist's number," Mandy said. "Monica could help you get through this. She's really good. If you ever want to talk to someone."

"Thanks, but I don't need to talk to anyone."

Mandy latched onto Rachel's hand again. "Don't bury your anger, Rach. That anger can help you."

Rachel pulled away and pursed her lips, reluctant to argue. Then a slow smile spread across her face. "You're right," she told Mandy. "My anger did just help me. It told me how I can get the deposit for our apartment." She scrounged through her backpack. "My father transfers money from his account into mine when I need some." Unzipping one of the pouches, she drew out her phone. "He uses the same password for everything." In the next moment, she stepped into the shade of the dorm building so that she could see her screen more clearly, and triumphantly entered her father's password.

Mandy grinned conspiratorially. "Get more than the deposit if you can. You might need it."

"Yeah. Fuck it." She beamed back at Mandy. "I never knew anger could feel so good." But a moment after, she frowned. "It says I'm logging in from an unknown device.

It wants me to answer a security question." She scanned the screen. "The only pet I remember him mentioning was King. But he had lots of pets growing up." She hesitated.

"Just try it," Mandy urged.

Rachel typed, then shook her head. "Nope." Energy drained out of her.

"Will it send him a message saying someone's been trying to access his account?"

Rachel's eyes widened. "I don't know." A frisson of fear rippled through her, and hard on its heels, guilt. She pondered that, then burst out, "Why should I feel guilty?" Lifting her chin, she hit her father's name on her contact list and put the call on speaker. The ringtone sounded loudly in the shadow of the building, where she and Mandy waited. When her father picked up, Rachel spoke before he had a chance to say a word. "I'm calling because I need money for a deposit on that apartment. I tried to transfer money from your account, but they wanted the name of your favorite pet." Silence. "Will you tell me that?"

A long moment passed before he answered. "Are you saying that if I give you the money, you won't say anything to Mom?"

"No! God, no. You still have to tell Mom. I figured you'd already talked to her. Haven't you?"

A soft sigh. "I will soon."

"When?" He didn't answer. "I'll give you 'til Sunday,"

Rachel said. "Then I'm calling her."

"Give me a week," he begged. "Until Tuesday."

Rachel did a rough calculation. That would leave enough time for her mother to cancel Izzy's trip. "Okay," she said. "But will you give me the money?"

After a long silence, he said, "How much do you need?"

Mandy held up two fingers.

"Two thousand," Rachel answered, her heart pounding with an unfamiliar mixture of fear and power.

In a dull voice, her father answered, "I'll transfer the money to your account."

"Can you do it now?" She heard a sharp intake of breath.

He said, "I'll do it as soon as I hang up."

"Okay," Rachel answered curtly.

"But, pum—

She cut off the old endearment midstream, pressing hard on the red phone icon. *Pumpkin.* Her father's utterance drifted in the air. *Pum.* Repeating itself, it became meaningless, a nonsense syllable. *Pum pum pum.* Then it took on the cadence of the little drummer boy song—*pum pum pum pum pum*—and reverberated faster and faster. Rachel jumped up—*pum pum pum pum pum!*—and spun her leg out in her favorite kickboxing move, shouting at the top of her voice, "I did it!" Her foot whirled out two more times before it came to rest on the tender grass. Rachel's face flushed with excitement, and she grinned at her friend. "This morning I was in the pits, but now I'm flying!"

Mandy regarded her thoughtfully. "Yeah," she said. "It's a rollercoaster."

Chapter 12

Colleen used a thick green magic marker to print "Kitchen" in block letters on the cardboard box, followed by "Dishes" on the line below. She loved how these packing boxes had preprinted lines that made it easy to identify exactly where the boxes should go and what was in them. She surveyed the growing row of cartons with immense satisfaction. Humming, she stuck a bright red "Handle with Care" sticker on the glassware box and admitted to herself that Derek was right. She was terrific at organizing things, and the challenge of preparing for the move had absorbed her attention and lifted her spirits.

She rested a moment at the kitchen table, checking her to-do list. *Call Derek*. June loomed, and Colleen still hadn't gotten a response to the email she'd sent her husband. She regretted now that she hadn't told him she'd actually bought a ticket for Izzy, already arranged for movers, instead of describing it as a possible plan. He so often accused her of being impulsive that she'd wanted to ease him into it. Disclose her plan in steps, win him over in stages, so that in the end, the decision would seem like it had been mutual. But she couldn't do that now; she couldn't wait any longer. In a little over a week, Izzy's plane would touch down at O'Hare.

Colleen braced herself and made the call. Derek's phone rang and rang, then went to voicemail. She didn't leave a message. Derek would call her back; he always did when he saw that she'd phoned. Just then, she heard the clank of their mailbox. Grabbing the stack of mail, she peered down the street, but no school bus was in sight. She left the door unlatched for Izzy and sorted the mail at the recycle bin: a free hearing test, grocery coupons, an advertisement for cable service. And tucked into a sheaf of newspaper ads, a letter from Derek. A soft smile curved Colleen's lips. She turned the envelope over. In the early years of their marriage, Derek had often sent letters while he traveled, adding a whimsical drawing on the envelope flap—a dragonfly, a unicorn, a heart with a sad face to show that he missed her. This flap was blank. Still, the fact that he'd written touched off a warm nostalgia for those old, pre-email days. She tucked the letter in her pocket and let a happy flutter of anticipation grow while she made herself a glass of iced tea. Finally, she carried her drink outside to the walled-in concrete patio.

Soon, she thought, plopping down on the worn cushion of a wrought-iron chair, she'd be gardening in a real back yard again, with grass and flower beds and the purple blossoms of lilac bushes filling the air with their scent. Smiling, she slid her finger under the envelope flap and drew out Derek's letter. She smoothed the blue-lined pages on the glass-topped table.

"Dear Colleen," Derek began. "Writing this letter is the hardest thing I have ever had to do. Something happened…"

Colleen's head jerked up, and she stared at the top of the stucco wall. *Something happened.* With a sidelong glance at the blue lines, she caught the words, "hoped you would never have to know." She flipped the pages over quickly, before she could see anymore.

A lizard scrambled on the rocks around a potted cactus. Colleen's freckled skin burned in the Arizona sun, but she shivered. How odd, to be shivering when her skin felt scalded. She glanced back at the letter. It stood in accordion-like folds, upside down on the table. Only the final two lines at the bottom of the last page were visible. But she didn't need to read the rest of the letter to understand. Derek had written, "I'm hoping against hope that you can forgive me. Or tell me that it might be possible to forgive me someday. I love you." Those last words were underlined three times, the ballpoint pen pressed so hard that Colleen felt a ridge when she ran her finger over them.

She tried to take a sip of her iced tea, but the glass, moist with condensation, slipped and slammed against the tabletop. The patio door banged open, and Izzy stuck her head out and grinned. "Hey, Mom! When is a number not a number?" Colleen's voice remained trapped in her throat. Izzy declared, "When it's a *negative* number!" She laughed. "I made that up. Can I have a Pop Tart? The bananas are old and there's no more yogurt." Colleen nodded mechanically. The moment Izzy whipped back into the house, Colleen shoved Derek's letter between the pages of an old *House Beautiful* magazine.

She remained inert in the heat of the patio. *Geeta was right.* The words repeated themselves flatly, as if the desert air had sucked the emotion out of them. *Geeta was right.* After a long while, Colleen roused herself. Clutching the magazine, she stumbled through the kitchen, past the crumbs by the toaster where Izzy had made her Pop Tart, past her red plastic cup in the sink, with milk in the bottom.

The sounds of Izzy practicing violin filtered down the hallway while Colleen made her way to the master bedroom. She shut the door behind her and paced around her bed, pressing her pillow tight against her chest. She passed the window where the sun had discolored the sill, approached the bedside table where her romance novel lay face down, its pages splayed, then turned back to make the circuit again. When she became aware that her legs ached, she flopped down on the foot of the bed. In the mirror, her freckles stood out more than usual against her pale skin. Her eyes were red-rimmed, though she hadn't cried. She stared a long time at the wedding photo atop the dresser. Derek looked fondly down at her, his bride. "You fool," she burst out, unsure if she was yelling at Derek or herself.

Colleen turned the frame face down on the dresser and sat again. The notes of Izzy's piece broke through her daze. *I have to get a grip.* Her hand slipped into her pocket and drew out her rosary. She prayed through numb lips. "Hail Mary, full of grace." But instead of calming her, her whispered words harshened with each repetition, until she was spitting them into the air. She stopped, staring at the little heap of white and blue pearly beads in her palm, and then she hurled them against her dresser mirror with all her might.

Chapter 13

Waiting for the rally to start, Rachel pulled her hoodie forward and peered at the crowd milling around the quad. Behind a table, Mandy handed out magic markers to students bent over poster board. A few feet away, Gregorio stood on his stork-like legs, talking with Aaron. Rachel focused on her friends. *I can do this*, she thought. She watched Kaitlin and Prija spread out a long red banner, revealing the first three words. *This part of…*Rachel lifted her face to the cool lake breeze while her friends continued to unfurl the banner. *This part of my past affects…*Her heart thudded. *This part of my past affects every man in my life.*

The unfairness of it! Rachel stomped over to the table and grabbed a sheet of poster board. Next to her, a woman wrote "Me Too" in thick black magic marker. How were so many women able to shout to the world what they'd kept secret for so long? Rachel wondered. A tall woman whose jet-black hair made her pale skin appear even whiter taped a photograph of her face onto the poster board and wrote SHAMELESS in large letters across the top. Catching Rachel's startled look, she said, "Shame-*less*—the ones without shame. That's us. The ones who didn't do anything wrong." When the woman turned to go, Rachel saw that the right side of her head was studded with short, shaved hairs.

Rachel had just scrawled "Believe Women" on her sign when Aaron came forward carrying his placard. *I am an Ally*. A red marker rolled across the flagstone, and Aaron stooped to pick it up. The woman who had dropped it approached him. Rachel watched Aaron extend the marker toward her, smiling. Then he took in the woman's sign: *Me Too*. He averted his eyes. He still looked flustered when he reached Rachel. Through gritted teeth, she said, "You want to be an ally, but you can't even look at a woman who's holding a 'Me Too' sign?"

"What?"

"Nothing," Rachel muttered. "Forget it." She turned aside.

Aaron grabbed her elbow, clamping his fingers down. "What are you upset about?"

Rachel jerked from his grasp, snarling, "You don't know what I'm upset about? Read these fucking signs."

"Jeez, Rachel," Aaron exclaimed. "Take it easy. I'm an ally, remember?"

"You can take it easy," Rachel shot back. "Me? I'm angry, okay?"

Aaron's face clouded with confusion. "I'm angry too, you know."

She shook her head. "Not angry enough."

Aaron opened his mouth, but before he could speak, two guys on their way to class catcalled the group. One of them, tall and ginger-haired, homed in on Tiana, who stood out in a striking red choker sweater that left one brown shoulder bare. Her sign said, "Flirting is Not Consent."

"Your flirting might not be consent, but mine is, sweetheart," Ginger Hair told her. He edged up to Tiana, a sneer on his face. "So," he said. He stepped closer, towering over her. "What's this all about?" Glancing at his friend and smirking, he added, "Babe."

Two things happened so quickly then that Rachel could hardly take them in. First, Tiana ducked out from under the jerk's arching figure, clearing a space in front of him. Next, Mandy reared up from the crowd like a mountain and body-slammed him, yelling, "I'll tell you what it's all about, '*babe*.' It's about getting assholes like you to stop harassing us."

Ginger Hair's face suffused with rage. He regained his balance, and for one suspended moment, Rachel thought he might strike Mandy. Then his friend grabbed his arm. "C'mon, Kurt, we're going to be late." Kurt shrugged off his friend's grasp and read Mandy's sign, loudly. *Whatever we wear, wherever we go, yes means yes and no means no.*"

He looked her up and down. "Don't worry—whatever *you* wear, wherever *you* go, we'll always say no."

His friend guffawed and punched Kurt in the arm. "Come on."

Kurt kept his eyes on Mandy and added, "Which is too bad for you, because you'd probably loosen up a lot if you could just get laid."

A chorus of disgust rose from the women. Mandy's face flushed purple, but instead of backing down, she stepped toward Kurt. In the next moment, Aaron dropped his sign and insinuated himself between them. Laying his smallish hand flat on Kurt's broad chest, he said, "Back. Off." Aaron looked like a cartoon character in a modern-day David and Goliath tale, and a hysterical giggle surged in Rachel's throat. She had to bite the inside of her mouth to keep it from escaping. But this David had no stone to catapult into his enemy's face. Kurt's steamroller of a hand shot forward and propelled Aaron backwards into the throng of women. The closest ones grabbed him in mid-stumble. Even as he teetered, Aaron shouted at Kurt, "How would you like it if someone talked to your sister that way?"

"Nobody would talk to my sister that way, because my sister isn't a tub of lard."

Kurt's friend pulled at his arm. "Come *on*." The two of them backed away, yelling a barrage of insults at Aaron. "Wuss! Pussy! Wimp!"

Watching them move further away, Rachel's heartbeat slowed almost to normal. Then Aaron shouted, "*Hey!*" His hands clenched at his side, he marched toward the bullies. They stared at him, open-mouthed. A hush came over the crowd. Aaron glanced straight at Rachel and raised a stubborn chin as if to say, "Am I angry enough for you now?" Then he threw his shoulders back and marched ahead. Kurt and his friend exchanged smug smiles.

Someone has to stop him, Rachel thought, searching the crowd. There! Gregorio stood a few feet away, next to a boy whose name Rachel couldn't recall. But the two of them merely gawked at Aaron, then cast uncertain glances at one another. In the next moment, Aaron hurled himself forward and landed a punch in Kurt's gut. Not much of a punch, because Kurt grabbed Aaron's wrist mid-movement and then bashed him right in the face. Aaron staggered backwards, blood streaming from his nose. Kurt stood, palms open, grin on his face, his whole stance saying, *That all you got?*

A jet of anger shot through Rachel. She despised Kurt's hotshot grin, his height, his wide hands that beckoned to Aaron in a *come on, wimp* gesture. Her gaze dropped down the sheer bulk of his body to the place where he was most vulnerable. She stared at that mound, while Kurt remained intent on Aaron, who pressed the edge of his t-shirt against his nose to staunch the flow of blood. Rachel's body balanced itself in kickboxing mode, and the next thing she knew, she had leapt forward, a ninja warrior. Her leg whipped up and her pointed shoe smashed into that unprotected target.

Kurt roared. White-faced, he clutched himself, staring wild-eyed at Rachel. She stepped out of his reach. He raised his fists. The tableau froze: Rachel in her stance, Kurt simmering with rage, Aaron dumbfounded, the crowd momentarily stunned. The lull probably only lasted a few seconds, but to Rachel, the frozen piece of time seemed to go on forever. It ended when Tiana's strong voice rang out, "Rise up for the women of the world." A handful of women joined in the response: "For the women of the world, rise up." They moved forward, forming a knot of bodies that tightened around Rachel and Aaron. The group repeated the call and response, more forcefully each time, while advancing toward the bullies. Kurt and his friend muttered insults, but at the same time, they backed up until they stood on the grass that edged the quad. The chant grew stronger and louder, filling the quad. Making one final obscene gesture, Kurt and his friend lurched toward the science building and disappeared through a side door.

After a few more repetitions, the chant shifted from a battle cry to a celebratory anthem. "For the women of the world, rise up!" Rachel chanted. She let her hood fall back on her shoulders and raised her face to the sun.

Shortly after the rally ended, Aaron helped Mandy and Rachel move. They filled his car with their belongings and drove to their apartment. Gregorio and Kaitlin waited for them in front of the Chinese restaurant that occupied the street-level floor of their building. Then the five of them, energized by the excitement of the rally, clambered up the stairs to the third-floor walkup with armfuls of clothing, pillows and bedding, boxes of toiletries and kitchenware. When they finished, they sprawled in the living room on its horrible fuchsia couch and lumpy armchair, eating carry-out from the Chinese restaurant below and rehashing the rally.

"I couldn't believe you," Mandy exclaimed, fist-bumping Rachel. "Let's hear it for kickboxing!"

"A guy from the journalism school took a photo of Tiana giving her talk and a group shot with all our signs," Kaitlin said.

"I wish he'd been there when we stood up to those jerks," Mandy said. "That would have been a great shot."

Rachel dipped an egg roll into sweet sauce. "Someone probably got it on their phone. Somebody's probably posted the whole thing by now."

Aaron groaned. "I hope not."

Mandy laughed. "Why?" She gave Aaron a friendly punch in the arm. "You started it, you idiot!"

"Me?" Aaron captured a water chestnut with his chop sticks. "Who body-slammed that asshole?"

"Yeah, but then you—"

They all began talking at once, replaying the fight. When their recap of the rally petered out, they reminisced about the ending of the term and the class that had brought them so close. "I'm going to miss you guys this summer," Kaitlin said mournfully. A flurry of reassurances about seeing one another in the fall and possible summer visits from Kaitlin and Gregorio followed. "Lucky," Kaitlin told Rachel and Mandy, "to be staying here all summer."

Rachel had an image of enjoying summer a stone's throw from Lake Michigan. Plunging into the chilly waters, the sun hot on her skin. Long summer evenings and campfires on the moonlit beach. She gave Aaron a sidelong glance and he smiled back, then squeezed her hand.

"Well, the term's not over yet," Mandy said, rising from the armchair. "I have to meet with my study group today." She picked up a half-empty rice carton and a paper plate with two egg rolls. "We done with this?" At their nods, she carried the leftovers to the kitchen. When Mandy returned, Gregorio and Kaitlin were shrugging into their jackets, ready to walk back to campus with her.

After the door shut behind them, Rachel found herself alone with Aaron for the first time since their date. Less than two weeks had passed, but it seemed like a million years. Aaron gestured toward the beanbag chair on the floor. "You wanted that in your room?" At Rachel's nod, he carried the lumpy velvet bag down the hall, while she followed with a small lamp. The full-size bed, with its bare mattress and pile of sheets and blankets, dominated her cramped bedroom. It would have felt claustrophobic but for the huge window, through which they could see white clouds billowing in the blue sky. Rachel set the lamp on the tiny bedside table and plugged it in before moving aside so that Aaron could drop the beanbag in the corner. The moment it hit the floor, he stretched out on it, his hands behind his head.

Rachel was acutely aware that they were in her bedroom in an empty apartment. From his spot on the floor, Aaron pointed a finger toward the miniature bedside table. "The table I made in woodworking would have fit there. It was supposed to be an end table for our family room, but it got smaller and smaller."

"What happened?" She wasn't that interested, but she'd learned in recent days that the easiest way to get through conversations, the easiest way to *be* with other people, was to keep the focus on them.

"Well, I used this router. You know what that is? It makes a fancy edge. But I kept shaving off too much, then I'd have to do the other edges to make it square. The tabletop just got tinier and tinier. Another disappointment to my mother." He grinned at her. "Basically, I'm doomed to disappoint my mother."

"But you're going to be a doctor!"

He made a face. "She's pleased about that, but it's a long way off. I have to finish undergrad. I have to get into med school. And of course, she's thinking neurologist. Or surgeon. Better still, neurosurgeon." He paused. "She's not thinking psychiatrist."

"Oh." Rachel felt increasingly awkward standing above Aaron's sprawled body. But she didn't want to sit on the bed, the only other possibility. Instead, she sifted through a box that held a jumble of hangers and candles and notebooks. She extracted a coiled poster and taped the top of it to her wall. While she unrolled it, Aaron read the opening line. "'Dance like nobody's watching.' That's cool."

Rachel turned away from the next line, "Love like you've never been hurt," and wiped her sweaty palms on her black jeans. "My mother doesn't get 'disappointed,'" she told Aaron, removing the quilt and pile of linens from the bed and setting them on the floor. "She throws tantrums and screams." Rachel shook out the fitted sheet and reached across the bed to tuck it in the far corner. Aaron leapt up and pulled the other end over the mattress edge near him.

"Sometimes I wish my mother *would* just yell," he said. "When she says, 'I'm not angry, I'm just disappointed,' I think, oh, please, just hit me, would you? Get it over with. A tantrum—that's like a thunderstorm, you know? A big burst, but then it's over. Disappointment is like a dreary rainfall that can go on for days."

"That's what my mother thinks," Rachel said. They snapped the last pockets of the bottom sheet into place. "She thinks blowing up clears the air."

Aaron reached over to help her unfold the top sheet. "You don't?" He straightened the sheet at the head of the bed while Rachel knelt at the foot and tucked it in.

She shrugged. "I never used to. But I'm starting to see how good it can feel to just let loose." She thought about the surge of power she'd felt when she'd kickboxed that jerk.

"Maybe you're more like your mom than you realized," Aaron grinned.

Rachel stood. She needed to stop talking about her mother. Her father must have talked to her mother by now. But if so, why hadn't Mom called her? Rachel shook her head as if she could shake the question away. "I'm going to get my cello."

"I'll get it." Aaron disappeared into the hallway. Quickly, Rachel unfolded the quilt and smoothed it across the bed. Her mother had stitched this quilt from patches of clothing Rachel had outgrown. It hit her, suddenly, that this quilt had been on her bed when *all that* happened. Aaron strolled into the room with her cello and leaned the case in the only available corner. "Would you play something for me?"

She stuffed one of her pillows into a case and shook her head. "I don't play in front of people."

"What are you talking about? You play in concerts, recitals."

Rachel plumped the second pillow at the head of the bed. "I play in public. I don't play in intimate settings." Facing him across the bed, she blushed at the word. *Intimate.* "I don't like to play when people sit two feet away. I need the distance of the stage. For me, playing is…" She trailed off. "It's hard to explain."

Flustered, she failed to notice Aaron stepping toward her, and startled to find his hands on her face. He kissed her—a soft kiss. Then another, this one on her ear. Her nose. *It's all right. It's Aaron.* But she felt the edge of the mattress pressing against the back of her calves, and feared she might tumble backwards onto that childhood quilt. She pushed away from the bed. Aaron took the opportunity to tug at the neckline of her gray sweatshirt and kiss the back of her neck. "I still need to unpack the dishes that my aunt gave me," Rachel murmured.

"Mm," Aaron answered. He drew her down to the velvety beanbag and took her in his arms. Her whole body hummed. Aaron nibbled on her ear. He kissed the base of her throat. When his hand drifted to her breast, she shot up to a sitting position. It was an automatic reaction, as instinctive as a blink when dust blows in your eye.

Aaron propped himself up on his elbow. "What's the matter?"

"I don't know." She shook her head. "Sex is mixed up for me."

"Didn't you like what we were doing?"

"The problem isn't that I didn't like it. The problem is that I liked it a lot."

"So…"

"But I've grown up learning that it's wrong. Until you're married. It's wrong." She reddened. "Shameful."

Aaron lifted her foot and peeled off her sock. She jerked her foot away. "Don't."

But he held on and peered at her toes, one by one, as if studying the little space between each of them.

"What are you doing?" she demanded. She tried to wriggle out of his hand.

"Looking for shame." He scrutinized the space next to her little toe. "Nope, not a bit of shame here." He scooted up and traced the ridge of her ear. "Definitely nothing shameful there," he declared, kissing it. The next thing she knew, Aaron had lifted her arm straight up and palpitated her armpit through her sweatshirt.

She laughed and pulled away. "That tickles."

"No shame there either," Aaron said.

His finger circled the swell of her breast, and Rachel's breath caught. "No shame here." He smiled at her, then his hand moved, feather-light, up to her throat, and he kissed her mouth. *No shame,* Rachel thought. She remembered the woman at the rally who'd posted her photo under the proclamation *Shameless*. Rachel shut her eyes and let herself float in the waves of warmth that rippled from every spot where Aaron touched her. She lost all sense of time.

Until her phone dinged. At first, she ignored it. Then a series of dings distracted them, and at the end of one last, long kiss, she extracted herself from Aaron's arms. But it wasn't her mother texting. All the alerts were related to a video from the rally.

"I hope my bloody nose isn't on there," Aaron said while they peered at Rachel's screen.

"So what if it is?" Rachel answered. "You were brave, standing up for Mandy."

Aaron's mouth drooped. "I don't really know how to fight." He gave an embarrassed chuckle. "I guess that was obvious. And I'm not brave. The truth is, I was scared shitless."

"But you went after those jerks anyway."

"Yeah," he said, his voice slowing. "I don't know why I did that." He glanced at Rachel. "Usually I run down a rabbit hole at the first raised voice."

What would it be like to be Aaron? To live in a society where being a man meant being fearless and strong, showing little emotion except anger. He wasn't like that at all. "It was my fault," Rachel said. "I made you think you had to prove something."

Aaron shook his head. "That's not why I wanted to

fight those guys." Was he blinking back tears?

"See," he said, "one time I saw something. And I didn't do anything to stop it."

Chapter 14

"Watch it, Izzy!" Colleen pulled her daughter away from the doorway and back into the kitchen. Two muscled men, soaked in sweat, lugged Izzy's mattress down the hallway. "Where am I going to sleep?" Izzy cried.

"You're sleeping over at Ritu's. You knew that."

"Yeah," Izzy pouted, "but I didn't know it was because they were going to take my bed." She leaned out of the kitchen doorway to follow the movers' progress, her lower lip trembling.

Colleen made an exasperated sound. "I *told* you the movers were coming today. You knew that, right?" When Izzy stayed silent, Colleen grabbed her by the shoulders, hard. "Answer me! I told you that, right?"

Izzy nodded, but her eyes filled with tears. "I didn't know how it would *feel*." A man passed the kitchen doorway, carrying Izzy's bedside table in one hand and her unicorn lamp in the other. Tears coursed down her daughter's cheeks. Colleen sighed. She'd been on a short fuse ever since she'd gotten Derek's letter. She still hadn't read it. She hadn't even touched it until last night, when she'd transferred it from the dresser drawer to her carry-on suitcase, averting her eyes. Despite her pitiful attempts to keep it out of her consciousness, Derek's affair hovered constantly on the edge of her mind. No wonder she was irritable. "Come on, Izzy. We'll wait on the patio until they're done. We can put our feet in the wading pool." Izzy rocked back and forth on her heels. "Come on," Colleen urged. "When they're done, it will be time to go to gymnastics."

But it took the movers longer than anticipated, and Izzy scowled all the way to the gym. When Colleen stepped out of the car, the heat rising from the asphalt was suffocating. Izzy slammed the car door and stomped toward her mother, hands on hips. "We're late," she exclaimed. "It's my last time, and we're late because you keep changing things."

Colleen's waistband slipped down her hips a bit. Impatiently, she pulled her shorts higher. "Izzy, I'm warning you, I don't have the patience for this."

"First, I'm going to see Daddy by myself, then I'm not, and now I am again, so now this will be my last gymnastics, and I'll miss Ritu's party next week."

"Things change," Colleen sputtered.

Izzy dragged her feet. "Why?" she whined. "What changed?" Colleen marched forward, ignoring her. But at the last minute, Izzy barreled ahead of her mother. At the heavy door, she turned sideways to squeeze through the narrow opening she'd made. Colleen grabbed her daughter's arm. "Don't you dare!" She spat the words. "Don't you dare shut that door in my face."

Izzy tried to wrestle out of her mother's grasp, and they stumbled into the hallway together. Colleen's fist clenched Izzy's skinny arm so hard that Izzy let out a howl of real pain. She wrenched herself away and fled down the hallway. At the door to the locker room, Izzy turned and screamed, "I hate you!"

A tide of fury blocked Colleen's throat. A good thing, too, because she wanted to scream, *I hate you too* right back. Izzy disappeared behind the locker room door, and Colleen backed against the wall, trembling. She searched her pocket for her rosary, but of course it wasn't there. She no longer carried it with her. She stood bereft on the scuffed brown tiles of this dismal hall, twisting the lining of her empty pocket. Suddenly she was overwhelmed with the need to see Geeta, to sit by a friend. She pushed her way through the gym doors, barely noticing the girls who stretched and tumbled just a foot or two from her side.

In the bleachers, Geeta was showing Ajay a game on her phone in which black ants scrabbled across blue floor tiles, disappeared into cracks, and then emerged again. Ajay smashed an ant, only to have two more surface. "That looks horrible," Colleen said.

Geeta laughed. "I know. It's creepy, isn't it? Lately Ajay's developed this *thing* about ants. He never lifts his head anymore when we're walking. He searches the sidewalks for ants. When he sees one, he stomps on it like his life depends on it. Like he's truly afraid. I'm hoping the game might help."

"Geeta," Colleen interrupted. "You were right. Derek's having an affair. I mean, he had an affair."

Geeta opened her mouth, shut it again. "Oh, Colleen!" The two women regarded one another. "With someone here?" Geeta asked. "Or in Chicago?"

"I don't know. I think it was here. But maybe not."

"But you don't know?" Geeta pressed. "I mean do you know for sure he had an affair, or do you just suspect?"

"I know for sure." At Geeta's cocked head, Colleen added, "He told me."

"Oh." Geeta pondered that a bit. "But you don't know who it was?"

Colleen wondered if Derek had told her that, if he'd disclosed the name of the woman in that unread letter. "It could be Cynthia," she said. "She came here from the Chicago office, like Derek. But maybe not." She started to explain about the letter. But Geeta jumped up, the better to wave back to her daughter Ritu, who was approaching the balance beam. After she plopped back down on the bench, Geeta gave her son a sideways glance, and then whispered, "Is Slut Cynthia back in Chicago?"

Slut Cynthia. Colleen liked the taste of that in her mouth. She nodded. "So is Derek."

"Oh." Geeta watched Ritu do flips on the rings. "But it's good that he told you, isn't it? That means it's over, right? He told you because it's over, and he wants to work things out?"

Colleen recalled the plea for forgiveness she'd glimpsed at the end of Derek's letter. "Yes," she agreed. "He wants to work things out."

Geeta gave her daughter a thumbs up sign, but Ritu didn't notice. "Do you think they were traveling together here on all those trips that Derek took?" Geeta's eyes were bright with interest.

Suddenly, Colleen did not want to say another word about Derek. It felt to her as though Geeta's curiosity had a voyeuristic edge now: a tinge of the ambulance-chaser, of a bystander drawn to a street brawl. "I don't know, Geeta. I don't even know for sure if it was Cynthia. I don't really want to know."

"If it were Srini," Geeta declared, "I would want to know. I would demand to know who it was. How long it had been going on. Where they met. How often."

"But Geeta," Colleen protested, "you can't unknow a thing! Once you know it, you can't unknow it." She glanced around. "If there were an envelope here on the bench with, I don't know, a report, photos from some sleazy private detective, I wouldn't want to open it."

"Oh, I would," Geeta said. "I would have to."

Colleen covered her wet eyes with her hands. "I can't believe I'm crying. I never cry. And I'm not sad." She scowled at Geeta. "I'm not! I'm angry, is what I am. This morning I yelled at Izzy. And for what? Because she'd gotten toothpaste all over the bathroom sink. Before that—because she didn't put a DVD back in its case. And then we got here, and she was whining about moving." Colleen was on the verge of telling Geeta how roughly she had grabbed Izzy, but she stopped herself. She picked at a thread on her navy shorts. "She just screamed at me downstairs." Suddenly she wanted to tell Geeta. Seeing Geeta's eyes soften with compassion would make Colleen feel less like a terrible mother. "She yelled, '*I hate you.*'" Colleen searched Geeta's face for the sympathy she so needed.

But Geeta's forehead was furrowed in concentration. "Does she know about Derek?"

"What? No, of course not."

"I meant maybe she knows you're fighting. You know how kids pick up on things." Colleen scanned the gymnasium floor. Izzy ended her flip on the rings and raced toward Ritu, grinning. "Izzy only notices things that affect her," Colleen said. Her voice broke. "I can't deal with her right now."

"Then it's good she's sleeping at my house for the weekend," Geeta said. She gave Colleen a long look. "You know, the girls will be together in Ritu's room. Ajay can sleep with us, and you could use our guest bedroom. A lot more comfortable than a sleeping bag on your bedroom floor."

Colleen shook her head. "Thanks. But I need a break from Izzy." She hesitated. "Would you mind if I left now? I could pick Izzy up tomorrow morning for church."

"Of course," Geeta answered. "You go ahead."

Colleen heaved a sigh of relief. "I just have to get through a couple more days with Izzy. Then she'll be Derek's responsibility."

"And he's okay with that?"

Colleen leveled a look at her friend. "What can he say? Right now, he can't complain about anything, can he?"

On Sunday morning, Colleen tapped her foot impatiently in the hallway of Geeta's house. Izzy emerged from the kitchen warily. Then her eyes opened wide. "You're wearing shorts!"

"Yep."

Izzy turned to Ritu, who stood at her elbow. "My mom's wearing shorts to church!"

"We're not going to church," Colleen said. "We're going somewhere else. It's a surprise. You'll like it." She gave Izzy a reassuring smile, but Izzy looked away and followed her mother through the front door in silence.

A half hour later they approached a long, curved

building made of adobe-colored sandstone. The building looked as if it had grown naturally out of the sandy desert. "Where are we?" Izzy wondered aloud. They passed a wall that sported three huge silver letters. "What's MIM?"

"Musical Instrument Museum," Colleen answered. She pulled into a space and twisted around. "You're going to like this." They crossed a courtyard dotted with cacti and rock formations. Izzy went silent again, but inside, she let her mother take her hand, and they wove their way through the crowd. "Let's go to the Experience Gallery first," Colleen suggested. Long before they entered the spacious room, they could hear thrumming. Stools circled a huge drum in the center of the room. All the stools were occupied, children and adults alike drumming the skins. Izzy skipped past the drummers and made her way toward a dark-haired woman who wore a pale green top and a long skirt, richly patterned in red and yellow zigzagged stripes. The woman played an unfamiliar stringed instrument that rested on her lap. It was shaped like a huge letter C tipped on its side, with one end of the C curving high into the air. Izzy read the sign. "It's called a Burmese harp," she told her mother. She watched the harpist's hands pluck and strum the strings.

"This is a very old, very famous Burmese song called 'Full Moon Night,'" the harpist said. Izzy's head tilted slightly, her gaze on the thin, graceful fingers that flitted effortlessly over the strings. The woman shifted to make space on the bench. "You try," she said, offering the harp to Izzy, who responded with a dazzling smile. First, the harpist arranged the instrument on Izzy's lap. Then she took hold of Izzy's bare arm and positioned it above the strings. She did this with gentle care, as if Izzy were as much a treasure as the harp. Just above the crook of Izzy's elbow, inches from the harpist's guiding hand, Colleen saw greenish-yellow bruises where she had grabbed her daughter's arm the day before.

She flushed. *Did I do that?*

Izzy plucked tentatively at the strings, occasionally lifting her head to monitor the harpist's reaction. Colleen moved to a spot where she couldn't see those marks on Izzy's arm. Moment by moment, her shame turned into frustration. *Why does Izzy have to provoke me so? She knows better.* Then a different thought hit Colleen. Whose fault was it that she was so edgy these days? Not Izzy's. But not hers, either. It was Derek's. Why, oh why, had Derek had to tell her about his affair?

The moment Izzy slid off the bench and thanked the woman, Colleen hurried to her side, shielding her daughter's bruised arm from the harpist's view. "Come on, Iz. There's a free stool at the big drum now." *I'm a good mother*, Colleen told herself, rushing to procure the spot. *I'm giving my daughter a really fun day.* For two hours, the two of them banged on gongs; beat on small, colorful African drums; and stared at original instruments once played by Elvis Presley, Johnny Cash, John Lennon, and Carlos Santana while the music of these artists streamed through their earphones. Eventually, they ended up in a room where children could construct guitars out of cigar boxes. Busy decorating hers with stick-on musical notes, Izzy burst out, "This is so fun, Mom!" Colleen's heart lifted. But a moment later, Izzy frowned. "I wish we'd come here when we first moved to Arizona. I wish I could have taken one of the classes here."

"Can't you ever see the glass half full, Iz?"

Izzy's face fell. Colleen twisted away from her daughter before Izzy's gloom triggered her anger. She studied the instructions for the next step in making the guitar. *Fold the cardboard to create a teepee.* In a tone that struck Colleen as bragging, Izzy said, "I'm glad I'm going to be with Daddy." She gave her mother what seemed a sly look, appraising Colleen's reaction to her words.

"Yes," Colleen answered evenly. Her voice became slightly vindictive. "I'm glad you're going to be with your dad, too."

A boy about Izzy's age approached their table and called out. "Here, Mom! There's space here."

"Daddy and me are going to have a lot of fun," Izzy sing-songed. "Maybe we'll go to the zoo."

"Maybe you will," Colleen agreed, her tone flat. She focused on the sheet of instructions in front of her. *Place the paint stick in the center of the cigar box with the bridge resting on top.* She mustered a friendly nod for the boy's mother, who settled herself at the opposite end of the table.

Izzy pressed on. "Maybe we'll go to the Children's Museum, too. And ride our bikes on the prairie path, and make popcorn, and watch movies, and play Pass the Pigs."

"I'm sure you'll have a lot fun," Colleen answered woodenly. She handed Izzy a small hammer and read, "Carefully nail the bridge to the paint stick."

Izzy complained, "Don't you *want* me to have fun with Daddy?" She dropped the nail, and it rolled toward the edge of the table. Colleen caught it before it fell, aware of the other mother's stare. "Of course I want you to have fun."

"Your voice doesn't sound like you mean it," Izzy said.

Suddenly Colleen didn't care what the other mother thought, didn't care what any other mother might think of her. "Well, your voice didn't sound like you meant anything you were saying, either." She mimicked Izzy. "'Daddy and I are going to go to the zoo. Daddy and I are going to have a lot of fun.' It was like you were *pretending* to be excited about those things."

Confusion filled Izzy's face. "Why would I pretend?"

To gloat about being with your dad, Colleen thought. *And because you're still mad at me.* Aloud, she said, "You tell me. Why would you?" The other mother turned her back to Colleen, but the boy stared at her.

"I was trying to see the glass half full," Izzy cried. "Like you said." Her lip trembled. "That's what you always say. 'Stop feeling sorry for yourself.' 'It's not the end of the world.' 'Look on the bright side.' You got mad when I said I wish we didn't have to move. I was looking on the bright side."

"Oh, Izzy!" Izzy's voice had been such a precise pantomime of her own! Colleen hunched down and drew her daughter close. When she rubbed Izzy's back, Izzy sobbed, "I miss Daddy." Colleen went rigid. She forced her shoulders, her arms, to relax. "I know," she said. "You're going to see Daddy soon."

"But you're going to stay here for maybe a long, long time, and then I'll be missing you."

Oh! Colleen held Izzy for what seemed forever, even though her back ached, and Izzy's chin dug sharply into her shoulder.

That evening, when Colleen found a flight reminder in her email, it hit her: she'd never forwarded Izzy's itinerary to Derek. How was that possible? Super-organized, list-making, always-on-time Colleen! But she'd been in a fog. She had emailed him that she wanted to send Izzy on Tuesday; she was sure she'd done that. But she'd never sent him the details. And had she let him know that the movers were already on their way? Would be there *tomorrow*? She forwarded Izzy's itinerary to Derek, then called him. She hadn't talked to her husband since she'd gotten that terrible letter. Her heart pounded. The ringing stopped, but no one spoke. "Derek?" Colleen said. "Are you there?" She moved toward the patio doors, where the reception sometimes improved. "Can you hear me? Are you there?"

"I'm here," Derek croaked, his voice hoarse.

"Listen, I just sent you an email. Izzy's coming Tuesday. And the movers will be at the house tomorrow. You knew that, right? I forgot to forward Izzy's details to you, so I just did that now. Check your email and make sure you got everything. There's a form you have to have so you can go through security and pick her up at the gate."

"You're still sending her?"

"Of course I'm still sending her!" Colleen snapped. "Are you checking your email now? See the one I just forwarded? There's an attachment with instructions. Do you see that?"

"I got it," Derek said.

"So, listen," Colleen went on, "The movers are coming tomorrow afternoon. You have to be home to meet them, okay?"

Derek said, "When are you coming?"

"When I can get there! When I'm done with everything here."

A pause. "Did you… did you get my letter?"

Colleen swallowed. "I can't talk about that now."

A second passed. "Right. Sure."

She paced around the wobbly card table. "I need time to figure things out."

"Of course you do. I wish there was something I could say. I—"

"Not now," Colleen cut in. "Except…have you gone to confession? Did you ever go to confession?" She waited.

In the long silence that followed, she stabbed the red phone icon and ended the call.

Chapter 15

Three days after the Me Too rally, Rachel sat cross-legged on her bed, rubbing her feet. They ached from another long shift at the Mexican Grill. She still hadn't heard from her mother. Should she phone? But what if her father hadn't talked to Mom yet? She could call him and find out, but she didn't want to talk to him.

There was a knock on her bedroom door, followed immediately by Aaron springing into the room, juggling a backrest pillow in his arms. "My mother doesn't use this anymore," he said, setting it at the foot of her bed. "It gives you back support. See?" He slipped his shoes off and reclined against the pillow to demonstrate. His weight made the mattress sag so that Rachel slid a bit toward him, and she pushed herself back up to the headboard.

"I didn't hear the bell," she told him.

"Mandy let me in. I ran into her on her way out." Aaron held out a white paper bag.

Rachel frowned. "What's this?"

"A present." He upended the bag, and socks in a rainbow of colors tumbled out. Aaron picked up a pair that had lemon-colored stripes edged in green. He glanced at her black cut-offs, her charcoal top, her gray socks. "Try these. You can wear them while I give you a foot massage."

Rachel went back to rubbing her foot, but he kept dangling the socks toward her. With an impatient sigh, she snatched them. Pulling off her drab socks, she remembered how Aaron had inspected her toes the last time they'd been together, proclaiming "No shame here!" He lifted her foot, now encased in yellow and green, and pressed his thumb in exactly the sorest spot and massaged it.

"Oh, wow." She sighed. At first, she stayed upright and watched him work his way around her foot, but after a few minutes, she relaxed against her pillows. He had the perfect touch, not light enough to tickle, but not hard enough to hurt. She let herself sink into the relief of the massage and tried to banish her worries about her mom. Shutting her eyes, she practiced deep breathing and felt the tension in her body melt away. "That felt good," Rachel told Aaron when he'd finished.

Aaron scooted higher up the bed. "This knee has the cutest dimple." He kissed her bare knee with an exaggerated smack, and Rachel swatted him playfully. Aaron slipped all the way to the top of the bed and stretched out next to her. "Your elbow has freckles on it."

He rubbed a freckle, then his hand slipped down her forearm and his thumb landed on the inside of her wrist. He stroked the soft skin there, and her breath caught.

They lay there a moment. Rachel glanced down the length of Aaron's jeans, and a wave of desire rippled through her. When he leaned over to kiss her, her body lifted of its own accord. She pressed up against him, her face growing warm. He kissed her. When he pressed the palm of his hand against the curve of her breast, her face flamed with an intensity so like the heat of shame that she jerked away. "My face is on fire."

Aaron tilted his head. "So?"

"It's like the shame is coming back."

"You feel ashamed?"

Rachel gave that a little thought, then glanced up, puzzled. "No. No, I don't."

He touched the palm of his hand to the heat of her flushed cheek. "Maybe," he said, "this is passion."

Passion.

Rachel grinned. *Passion.*

Aaron took his shirt off and laid back on the pillow, bare-chested. She touched him, liking the feel of her palm on his smooth skin, the tickle of the trail of hair that ran down the center of his chest. She laid her ear against the spot where his heart drummed. Aaron slipped his hand, tentatively, under her charcoal top. Rachel pulled it over her head and undid her bra. A moment later, she slid down on the bed and pressed her bare chest against his. "Nothing below the waist," she whispered.

Time took on a different quality. She felt like she could lay beside him forever, nuzzling and touching and kissing. Or perhaps it wasn't time that changed. Maybe it was that her body's needs dissolved. She had no need to eat or sleep, work or study, think of anything but what she was feeling, right now. No need to worry about anything or anyone else…

Her mother's face floated through her mind, spoiling the moment. Why hadn't her mother called? Was she too upset to talk to Rachel?

Did she *blame* Rachel?

The next thing she knew, Rachel was sitting up on the bed and reaching for her bra. "I need to call my mom."

"Right now?"

"Yeah, I'm sorry. I just…I didn't even know you were coming over today." She put her bra back on, pulled her top over her head. "I just remembered something that I need to talk to my mom about." She flung her legs over the side of the bed and stood up.

"I knew I shouldn't have told you," Aaron said.

Rachel blinked. "What?"

"As soon as I told you that I'd seen something and didn't do anything to stop it, everything changed. The last three days, you've only answered my texts once."

Rachel barely remembered the last three days, filled as

they had been with trepidation about her mother, about what she should do if her father failed to speak to her. Irritated, Rachel answered, "Not everything is about you, Aaron."

"Isn't it? One second you're all friendly, and the next…I wish I'd never told you."

Rachel forced herself to be patient. "You didn't really tell me anything, Aaron. You made this vague statement about seeing something, and then Mandy came back, and you never told me what actually happened."

Aaron looked flustered. "Okay, but if that's not what's bothering you, what just happened? Why did you pull away again?"

"I told you. I just remembered I have to call my mother."

Aaron got that thoughtful look on his face. "What's worrying you?"

Rachel turned away. "I don't want to talk about it."

After a moment, Aaron said, "You're always shutting me out."

Abruptly, everything that had happened that morning—Aaron's unexpected barging into her room, his invasion of her bed, his insistence on giving her a foot massage, his pressuring her to talk now—seemed intrusive. "Why don't *you* talk?" Rachel challenged. "Finish your story. Tell me about what you saw. You're the one who left things hanging."

Aaron slipped his knit shirt back on, then stared at her for a long time. Finally, he said, "Fair enough." He got off the bed and stood facing her window so that she was looking at his profile. He squared his shoulders. "This happened last fall. I had gone to the lake path to run. It was dusk. It was one of those really hot September days where it still feels like summer, you know? I love running there, the Chicago skyline in the distance, the little pools of light from the street lamps along the path, the lake lapping at the rocks. On my first go-round, I saw two people sitting by the fire pit. The next time I came around, the pit was deserted, and I passed them on the path a little further along. A guy and girl. She was leaning against him, kind of staggering, and I thought, *Somebody's been drinking.* On my next circuit, they were gone. I figured they'd left the path. It surprised me a little that I hadn't passed them again. Because they'd been moving so slow, I didn't think they'd make it off before I came around again. But I honestly didn't think any more about it; I just kept running. And then…You know where those weeping willow trees are, near the duck pond? There's a light there on the path, but it's all shadowy under those trees. They're quite a way off, and the willow branches, they make this veil—"

"Aaron," Rachel interrupted. "Spit it out."

He swallowed. "The girl was on her back, half-hidden by those ferny branches. The guy was on top of her. I didn't know for sure, but I figured they were fucking. It embarrassed me. It was still light enough to see them. I just wanted to get away, so I kept running. But I looked. I turned and looked one more time, then I ran and ran until I crossed the bridge, got off the circle path, and I kept running until I was way past Kegan Hall. I didn't stop until I got to the quad. And…the thing is, the look I saw on that girl's face was…" Aaron's voice fell. "Imploring."

For several seconds, Rachel heard nothing but his harsh breathing.

"You know," Aaron said, "how you can hear something, or see something, but not have it register? That's how it was. Not until I sat on that bench in the quad did I really *register* that look. I thought: That girl was *imploring* me. But then I second-guessed myself. Was she? Was that what I'd seen? I mean, it was all so quick, and it was almost dark, and I was twenty feet away, and those green leaves were fluttering around her face. I kept going over it in my mind, trying to decide." That little muscle in the corner of Aaron's eye twitched, and he pressed the heel of his hand against it. "I knew I should go back. I knew I should find out, try to help her, if …Instead, I thought and thought until so much time had passed that I told myself there was no point. Whatever had been happening, it would be over by then."

Rachel shoved past him, nearly knocking him over, and strode down the hallway to the living room, where she paced in front of the couch. The first time they had talked in class about men being allies, Aaron had insisted that there ought to be some kind of course in high school that would teach guys what to do. Some of the women had scoffed. Men needed *training* to figure out what to do? When a woman is harassed? When they see a guy feeding drinks to a tipsy girl, or leading her out of a party when she can barely stand up? From out of the corner of her eye, Rachel watched Aaron slink into the living room and come to a standstill behind the armchair.

"That girl," Rachel choked. "That girl will live with what happened to her for the rest of her life."

"I know."

"And you could have stopped it."

Aaron slumped. "I know."

The fury that had been gathering in Rachel exploded, and she found herself shrieking like her mother, screaming and out of control and not caring if the patrons in the Chinese restaurant below heard every word. "What is the matter with you? With all of you? How do you keep letting these things happen? Don't you give a fuck about us? What are we to you? Pieces of meat? Something to stick your dicks in?"

"Rachel!"

But she couldn't stop. She grabbed the arm of the couch, her hand a claw. She scraped her bitten fingernails along the plush material over and over, shouting. "Are we just body parts? Boobs and mouths and…*cunts*? That's what you call us, isn't it?" She looked down at her bent fingers, at the ruts she had grated into the velvety material. That's when the memory hit her. It wasn't so much that *she* remembered. It was more like her fingers themselves remembered and spoke to her in their raking across that couch arm. She no longer saw the fuchsia velvet; she saw her bitten nails scratching the faces of Snow White and Cinderella and Tinkerbell on her child's bedsheets. *This is what we did,* her fingers told her. *This is what we did when your father…*

"You should have stopped it!" Rachel shouted. "You could have kept it from happening! You could have protected that girl!"

Aaron threw his hands up in a helpless gesture. "I know I should have done something. I'll regret that for the rest of my life."

How tired of men's regrets Rachel was! Of their apologies and their appeals for her understanding. She folded her arms across her chest, and the air between them thickened. Aaron shifted from one foot to the other, but finally, he stilled. After a moment, he drew himself up. "Rachel, you're acting like *I'm* the rapist. Like I'm the one who raped that woman. And that wasn't me. That would never be me." His mouth trembled and tears welled in his eyes.

Rachel stood stone still. Because it was true. Somehow,

Aaron had gone from being the worthless bystander to being the perpetrator. How had the two transgressions blended? "I don't think you're a rapist," Rachel said. "But you were there."

Aaron's hands clenched. "I've been holding that story in for almost a year. I thought I'd never tell anyone. But I trusted you. And the way you're looking at me now—it's worse than Mandy. It's way worse."

Contradictory impulses ricocheted in Rachel's head. She wanted to attack Aaron. To pummel his chest, shove him out the door, push him down the stairs. And she wanted to take his solid, compact body into her arms. Lift that damp curl from his forehead. Stroke his back.

Aaron unclenched his fists and held his palms outward in supplication. "God, Rachel. Haven't you ever done anything that you were ashamed of?"

A little cry escaped her, and her hand flew to her mouth.

Aaron went on, his voice more forceful. "You know," he said, "I have a sister. I've *never* said that word. The c-word."

She pressed her hand hard against her teeth. *Ever done anything you were ashamed of?* Her teeth plunged into her finger and held on tight, quashing the scream that rose in her throat.

"I don't know what you want me to do," Aaron said. "I took our class. I'm doing what I can."

Rachel willed the image of the black-haired woman who

had shaved one side of her head to come to her mind. She focused on the stubble of hairs down the side of that woman's scalp. *Shame-less*, she insisted to herself. *We are shame-less.*

Aaron talked on. "I can't go back in time. God knows I would if I could."

So like her father's words.

The red banner from the rally flashed in Rachel's mind. *This part of my past affects every man in my life.* Aaron looked off to the side, toward his jacket hanging on the hook. His cheek glistened in the light from the tears running down his face. He stepped toward the entryway.

*Affects every man in my life…*Rachel sat on the couch and laid her hand on the spot next to her. "Come and sit." After a moment, Aaron came over. Without looking at her, he lowered himself down on the couch, his fingers tightening around the edge of the cushion. Tentatively, Rachel rested her hand on the back of his knit shirt, feeling the dampness there. "I know you're not like that, Aaron. I know you're a good person. A good man." Under Rachel's palm, a shudder rippled down Aaron's back.

Long moments passed. "You think we can get through this?" Aaron said. His back grew rigid.

"I don't know."

Aaron's back rose and fell against her palm. He asked, his voice hoarse, "Do you *want* to get through it?"

Rachel felt like her bones had crumbled into sawdust. "I don't know," she repeated.

Chapter 16

After Izzy left, the emptiness of the house hit Colleen hard. She hadn't expected that. The creaking floors echoed more loudly in the unfurnished rooms, and the bare walls greeted her with blank looks. This morning, she had dipped her rye toast into the yolk of a fried egg and taken a bite, wishing that Izzy was sitting hunched over a bowl of cereal across from her. How lonely the house felt!

Lonely. The word *divorce* had flashed in the air like a neon sign, and a cold finger of dread laid itself across Colleen's heart. She had stared at her plate, nauseated, then gotten up and scraped the remains in the garbage. No wonder the skirt she'd put on that morning for her visit to the rectory hung on her frame.

"I know I'm supposed to forgive, but I don't know how," she confided to Father Lopez now. She sat across from his desk in the rectory parlor, uncomfortably warm despite the air conditioning. "When I saw those articles? I was sure, I was positive that Derek had never given in. And then to get this letter? I felt like a fool!" She wiped her damp palms against her skirt. "The signs were all there. His long trips. His moods. The distance I felt when he was home. I wasn't such an idiot that I didn't notice. But don't make mountains out of molehills, right? Most things kind of take care of themselves over time, don't you think?" She gave the priest a challenging look. "Trust in the Lord. And don't they say that most of the things we worry about never happen? So why make yourself sick with worry? That's what I told myself."

She forced herself to take a deeper breath. "Look where that's gotten me. And now I'm supposed to forgive and forget? How does anyone do that?"

Father Lopez rubbed a finger across his small, neat moustache and leaned back in his office chair. "Is that what you think forgiveness means, Colleen?"

"Well, doesn't it? I'm supposed to say 'It's okay that he had an affair,' instead of wanting to kill him." She laughed nervously.

There was an earthen bowl filled with pale stones on the desk. The priest moved it nearer to Colleen. "Forgiveness doesn't mean pretending that what Derek did is no big deal. In fact, my belief is that you can't really forgive him until you acknowledge how badly he's hurt you."

Colleen's head shot up. "That's what I'm saying. He hasn't really acknowledged that. Not to my face. Not even on the phone." She made a *pfft!* sound and shook her head. "He wrote a letter."

"I'm not talking about Derek acknowledging how much he's hurt you," the priest said, "though he needs to do that, too. I'm saying that *you* have to acknowledge how much Derek has hurt you before you can begin to forgive him."

"I just told you," Colleen objected. "I'm mad as hell."

Father Lopez tipped the bowl of stones forward a bit, offering her one. She refused it with a brusque wave of her hand. He picked up a white stone and rolled it between his thumb and forefinger while he kept his eyes on her. "Not acknowledge how mad you are. Acknowledge how *hurt* you are."

A moment passed. "I don't know, Father," Colleen joked, "my motto's always been 'Get mad, not sad.'"

But the priest didn't smile. Instead, he gave her a searching look. "Colleen? Can you let yourself feel the hurt?"

Her heart clenched. She licked her dry lips and shifted in the chair. As casually as she could, she said, "Well, we've been married a long time. More than twenty years. We talked about renewing our vows for our silver wedding anniversary. I mean, formally, in the church."

Father Lopez rested his chin on steepled fingers. She wanted to shout, *Say something! Stop staring at me and say something.* When the silence became unbearable, she surprised herself by blurting, "You read these advice columns, you know. All these people. But you never think it could be you."

The priest nudged a box of tissues toward her. Colleen regarded it with distaste. "I get it. You probably talk to a lot of people whose marriages are in trouble. You're used to women weeping in your office. That's just not me." She forced a smile. "Oh, if you only knew the stories my family tells about my temper!" Thinking of the perfect story to tell him, she chuckled. "Why, last summer, when Derek said he wanted to come out to Arizona without me…"

Her throat closed. She started again. "Without me—" but then she breathed in sharply, cutting herself off.

Without me.

The priest moved the tissue box to the edge of the desk, inches from Colleen. She wanted to shove it right back at him, but in this musty, formal, old-fashioned parlor, she managed to stop herself. *Without me.* Her hands itched to hurl that stupid dish of stones to the floor. She twisted them together instead. *Without me.* Her nails dug into her palms so hard that her eyes stung with tears. "It hurts," she cried.

It was as if the cry released a deluge of pain that she'd held inside since the day she'd gotten Derek's letter. She dropped her face into her hands and wept. The sobs were like shards stabbing her poor, sore heart every time she took a breath. They went on and on, racking her. After a long while, Colleen became aware that her face was slick with tears and mucus. How disgusting she must look! She tore a wad of tissues from the box, then turned away from the priest, blew her nose, wiped her face, and waited until her breathing had slowed. Finally, she turned her swollen eyes toward Father Lopez again. "That," Colleen whispered, "was terrible."

"That took a lot of courage."

She slumped in her chair, smoothed her skirt, and took a shaky breath. "How is that supposed to help?"

He offered her the bowl of stones again. Putting two in her palm, a light blue one and a pink one, she said, "It's not as if I feel more like forgiving Derek now."

"But forgiving isn't about what you feel like doing," the priest said. "Forgiveness is a choice, not a feeling. The first choice involved in forgiveness is the choice to let yourself feel the hurt. And now you've done that."

"Okay, then," Colleen said. A weak smile wavered on her lips. "I'm glad that's over."

Father Lopez gave her a smile that was almost fond. "I think you know it's not all done. But you've made a big start." He paused, as if waiting for some sort of acknowledgement from her.

"That was the worst pain I have ever felt in my life," Colleen told him.

He nodded. "I understand how hard that was for you."

"Do you?" Her voice shook. "Do you know what it's

like to build your whole life around another person, and then have them betray you?" Sobs threatened to erupt again. She swallowed hard to hold them back.

"I don't, Colleen. I don't know what that's like. I do know how important your marriage is to you. That's why I believe you'll be willing to endure the pain that will come up more than once if you take the next steps."

She gave him a wary look.

"The next step is to make the choice to honor your commitment to Derek, to your marriage, by working through this crisis with him. Maybe seeing a counselor. I could meet with the two of you, or you could seek couples' counseling with someone else."

Colleen slipped the pink stone back into the bowl. "Derek's not even here now. That would have to wait until I move back to Chicago. And I don't know if he'd be willing to do it."

"What about you, Colleen? Are you willing?"

Her fist tightened around the blue stone. "Sit with some stranger while he dissects our marriage? I don't know. I'm not sure what good that would do."

Father Lopez looked at her steadily. "Do you want to forgive Derek?"

Colleen clutched the stone. "Of course I do. I want my marriage back. But…"

Father Lopez nodded encouragingly.

"I want it back the way it was before."

"Gift-wrapped," the priest said.

"What?"

"You want God to give you your marriage back like a gift. Without you having to make any effort."

Colleen stared at him a moment, then set the blue stone back in the bowl. "You've certainly given me a lot to think about, Father." She leaned to the side of her chair, picked up her bag, and headed for the door.

"I'll pray for you, Colleen," he responded, the words drifting behind her. She stumbled outside into the stifling heat and a yellow haze caused by a nearby building site. The air filled with particles despite the stream of water that shot over the construction area. A toxic environment. She glared at the relentless Arizona sun. *Don't ever,* she warned the God who supposedly loved her, *don't ever let me hurt like this again.*

Chapter 17

The room that the therapist led Rachel into had the same corded carpeting as the waiting room, the same cream-colored walls. But here, delicate watercolors that barely hinted at their subjects hung on the walls. A curved road lined with autumn trees in crimson and gold, the two figures walking the road hardly more than smudges in the distance. A hillside against a blue-green haze of sky, so deep in snow that you caught only a glimpse of the tiny roofs dotting it. And instead of the wall of water in the waiting area, there was an aquarium where small fish darted in and out of the ferns in flashes of indigo and amber.

Only after she'd sat on one of the chairs covered with worn, chocolate-colored corduroy did Rachel notice the box of tissues. It sat on a small table at her side. Apparently, people were expected to cry in here. Her heartbeat quickened. She scrutinized Monica as the therapist settled in her chair. Rachel liked the unkemptness of Monica's salt and pepper hair, strands escaping the combs that pulled most of her hair away from her face. She didn't care for the woman's full mouth or her eyebrows, which were so faded you could barely see them. But she liked her wide, gray eyes and the crow's feet around them.

Monica wasn't smiling. She wasn't exactly frowning, but she had a very intent look on her face while she scanned the sheets Rachel had filled out. "Before we start," she said, "you signed this sheet explaining the limits of confidentiality in here. Do you have any questions about that?"

The phrase *child endangerment* had stopped Rachel cold when she'd seen it on the form. She'd re-read the warning that therapists were mandated reporters and were required to contact the Illinois Department of Children and Family Services if they believed a child to be in danger. After seeing that, she'd asked the receptionist for a fresh form. There, she'd changed her answer to an earlier question that had asked her to list her family members. The second time, she'd left Izzy out.

She tried to sound nonchalant. "I don't have any questions. Basically, it's saying you don't have to keep stuff confidential if you think I might kill myself or someone else, or if you think a child is in danger. Right?"

"That's pretty much it," Monica smiled. She read from the form. "You wrote that you want help to sleep better and you want medication to help you feel less anxious." Rachel nodded. Monica set the papers down on the ceramic-tiled table next to her. "If I asked you tell me one other reason why you wanted to come here today, something you wish you could talk to someone about, what would you tell me?"

What would she tell this woman? Certainly not about *what happened*, not within the first minutes of meeting her. What else to talk about? To her surprise, Rachel blurted, "I'm afraid I'm turning into my mother." She told Monica how furious she'd become when Aaron had told her what happened that night on the lake path. "We're kind of okay now," she concluded. "I don't know. I'm still angry underneath. Like there's an underground crack that could turn into an earthquake with no warning. And that's not me. It's my mom who has a short fuse. I'm the one who stays calm. Now, it's like I can't let go of my anger."

"Okay," Monica said. "Let's take a look at what's happening right now. Are you aware of what you're doing with your hands?"

Rachel instantly stopped scratching the arm of the chair and brought her hands to her lap. "Sorry." Her face flushed.

Monica looked at her steadily. "What are you feeling right now?"

"Embarrassed. Like I just got into trouble."

"Like I was scolding you?"

"Yes. Exactly like that."

Monica asked, "And now what are you feeling?"

After a second, Rachel gave up. "I don't know." A long, uncomfortable silence grew. Rachel repeated, "I don't know!"

"I think it's hard for you to let yourself know," Monica said. She paused. "When I asked if you noticed that you were scratching the chair, it wasn't because I cared about the chair. I'm not your mother, Rachel." She leaned forward a bit. "I asked because you want to get control of your feelings, and the first step in doing that is to become aware of what those feelings are. So, when I see a sign that you're feeling something strong, I invite you to investigate that with me."

Rachel took a moment to digest that. Then she said, "I did feel scolded. And then you asked me how I felt, and I didn't feel anything. So that's what I said." She raised her chin and looked at the therapist. The next instant, her eyes widened. "Oh." Her fingers were scratching again, this time on her own arms, which she had folded across her chest. She stilled them.

"Instead of stopping yourself," Monica said, "would you be willing to let your body do whatever it's doing? And see what you notice?"

It felt odd to fold her arms and purposefully allow her fingers to graze the gray sleeves of her sweater. But after some moments, Rachel found her fingers digging in. "I'm angry. That's what I'm feeling." She blinked. "My heart is pounding." She let her fingers scrape up and down. Then abruptly, the movement stopped, and she was left clutching her arms. "I'm hanging on to myself," she said. "I don't understand what I'm doing." After a minute, it came to her. "I'm hanging on to myself because I don't want to pick stuff up and start throwing things." Her hands dropped to her side, and she followed the sweep of the angelfish in the tank while she took this in.

After a bit, Monica said, "So, you're angry, and at least some of your anxiety comes from the fear that you'll lose control of that anger and throw things?"

Rachel nodded.

"And where is all this anger coming from?"

The question hit Rachel like a fist. *I don't have to answer. Just because she asks me a question doesn't mean I have to answer.* "Can't you just help me stay calmer?" she asked. "Give me a prescription so I don't feel like I'm having a heart attack? Give me something to help me sleep at night?" The fatigue that had haunted Rachel since the day she saw her aunt overcame her. "I'm so tired," she cried. Hot tears burned her eyes. "I'm so tired."

"I'll talk to you about some over-the-counter medication that might help you sleep," Monica said. "But let's also help you learn how to relax. See, I don't think you've paid much attention to your body. It's been like a handy vehicle to carry your mind. You don't notice it unless it's giving you trouble."

She then took Rachel through a relaxation exercise. Would it help? That seemed doubtful. True, Rachel had never noticed the tightness of the skin on her face, or the grimace in which she held her mouth much of the time. The relief she felt when those muscles relaxed surprised her. She could see how this exercise of intentionally tightening and then relaxing her brow, her jaw and the muscles around her eyes might help her feel less tense. But cure her insomnia? Stop her nightmares? Curb her anger? Quiet her heart when it sped toward a panic attack?

"It's not an easy fix," Monica agreed when Rachel voiced her concerns. "It takes effort. Becoming aware of your tension and then consciously relaxing your body will be a challenge for you. But I know you can do it. All it takes is practice, and I know you have the discipline to practice."

Rachel raised a skeptical eyebrow that said *you just met me*.

"Rachel, you've been playing cello since you were three. The discipline that sustained practice requires—you've been developing that since you were practically a toddler."

Rachel had never thought of it that way. The idea encouraged her. She also liked the relaxed state that the exercise had induced in her, and she made a promise to herself to keep practicing. Then, with only a few more minutes left, Monica said they needed to talk about some practical issues. Like the fact that Rachel's insurance only covered twenty sessions a year. "That would take us close to Christmas," Monica said. "But the good news is that your insurance resets in January, so that would give you until almost the end of the school year if you needed that."

Astonished, Rachel said, "It's June now. I figured I'd come for the summer. Finish before school starts in the fall."

Monica rested her chin in her hand, a patient look on her face.

"What?" Rachel demanded. "How long do you think this will take?"

Monica gave a noncommittal shrug. "That depends. On how you're doing. On what you want. Right now, you think all you want is to sleep better and feel less anxious. But I think you want a whole lot more than that. From what you've said today, you want independence from your parents, a closer relationship with your boyfriend, a better relationship with your mother. It will take time to understand what keeps you from having those things. It'll take time for you to be ready to take whatever risks you need to in order to get what you want."

Under her sweatshirt, the hairs on Rachel's arm stood up. "I've never been a big risk-taker."

Monica tilted her head. "Don't you take risks as a musician?"

Rachel took a moment. "I guess every piece that stretches you is a risk."

"So, you're used to doing that, aren't you? Taking risks in small increments? That's how you can do it in here, too."

Rachel's brow furrowed.

"Rachel, who determines, in cello, how challenging the next piece will be?"

"Well, my instructor. But he bases that on what he thinks I'm capable of. He gives me exercises to get me to the point where I can handle the challenge, where I have the confidence. Once in a while, I tell him I'm not ready for that yet, and then we work out what I need to do to get ready."

"So you are ultimately in control of how much you risk?"

Rachel considered that for a moment. "Yes."

"Same in here," Monica said. "Same in here."

Perhaps the exercise *had* increased Rachel's awareness of her body, because she sensed immediately how her forehead smoothed and her face relaxed at those words.

Chapter 18

Colleen peeled a banana partway and bit the end off. Nibbling, she wandered through the rooms and gave them a last-minute check before the open house. The living areas had been staged, with a colonial kitchen set replacing the card table and blandly tasteful furniture carefully arranged in the living room. *Plants*, Colleen thought wearily. She should pick up a few plants. But she knew she wouldn't bother. There wasn't much that she had bothered with since her talk with Father Lopez. It seemed as though all her energy had seeped out of her along with those tears. No wonder she hated crying. Colleen had just swallowed the last bite of banana and thrown the peel in the garbage when her phone chimed. Rachel's name appeared on the screen, and Colleen brightened. "Hey!"

"Mom."

That brusque tone. Colleen pressed a hand to her forehead, but said nothing.

"I'm so upset, Mom. I can hardly talk."

She tried to sound sympathetic. "What's the matter, hon?"

"Dad said he'd tell you. He promised. And I believed him, God damn it! I believed him. What a liar, what a fucking liar he is!"

Colleen winced, but bad language was another thing she lacked the energy to deal with right now, so she ignored it and merely asked, "Tell me what?"

"Tell you how he couldn't keep his fucking dick in his pants!"

Colleen jerked the phone away from her ear. *How could Rachel know about the affair?* With the phone hanging by her side, Colleen couldn't make out what her daughter was saying, but the angry tone was clear enough. She brought the phone to her ear again and interrupted the stream of words. "How did you find out?"

A pause. "How did I find out? I was talking to Aunt Bea, and…What difference does it make, Mom? The thing that matters is that I was sure you'd keep Izzy with you in Arizona, or you'd come home with her. And then today Izzy texts me a photo of her and Dad at Navy Pier, and I text her back, 'Is Mom with you?' and she says no, you're still in Arizona. God damn it! Dad said he was going to tell you!"

"He did tell me."

"He did?"

"Well, he wrote. He wrote me a letter. But how… did Aunt Bea—"

"He *wrote* you. What a coward! And you still sent Izzy to him? Jesus Christ! How could you do that?" Rachel's sobs made her next words almost incoherent. "I can understand with me. I can understand that maybe you didn't know, but now you know."

The room telescoped. "Rachel, are you saying that your dad…" Almost simultaneously, she thought, *No.*

"I thought you said he told you. Didn't you just say he told you?"

Derek's words echoed in Colleen's mind. "*Writing this letter is the hardest thing I have ever had to do. Something happened…*" Her legs trembled. She landed on the floor with a thump and banged her back against the handle of the cabinet. The banana she'd just eaten rose in her throat so fast she couldn't get up in time to reach the sink. She leaned to the side and threw up clumps of slimy banana on the floor. Her eyes watered. She wiped them with the edge of her t-shirt and picked up the phone again. "Rachel, I'm so sorry. I didn't realize. I never read the whole letter that Dad sent."

A pause. "How could you not read the whole letter?"

Colleen swallowed hard. "Well, from the first lines, I thought he'd had an affair, and I didn't want to know the details—"

"Oh, my God," Rachel exclaimed. "You buried your head in the sand? Even about this?"

Colleen stumbled over her words. "I just couldn't

handle…and I never imagined…I'll read it, Rach. I'll read it the second we're done talking." She heard a squeaky hiccup that reminded her of how Rachel had cried as a child. That helpless sound. "You want to tell me about it now, Rach?"

Terrible words poured out of Rachel and seared themselves into Colleen's brain: *I was only eight* and *our special time* and *in my bed.* Every once in a while, unable to bear it, she pressed the phone to her thigh and muffled Rachel's voice. But then she would think, *Rachel is hurting, I have to listen.* Once again, the words would stun her, numbing her until they no longer made her jerk with shock. She became stupefied.

Finally, Rachel's voice petered out. Colleen whispered into the phone. "I'm so sorry, sweetheart. We'll talk more. But I have to go now. Okay? I'll call you tomorrow, okay?"

Rachel's voice was small and distant. "Okay."

"I love you, Rachel."

"I love you too, Mom."

Colleen stared at the now-silent phone in her hand, hating it. The vile words she'd heard seemed to have spewed from the phone itself rather than from Rachel. She shut the phone off completely and sat like a lump on the kitchen floor. The ticking clock had a rhythm in which every third *tick* sounded slightly louder than the previous two. She found herself waiting for it, breathing into that cadence.

The longer she remained, the more dreamlike the whole phone call became. She might almost have believed that it was a dream, except that something cold and wet touched her thigh—a disgusting gob of banana from the pool of vomit she'd produced. Colleen jerked her leg away and pulled herself up. At the sink, she wet a paper towel and washed her leg carefully, then used a wad of towels to clean the floor. An odd notion grew in her mind while she worked: if she got rid of the signs of the phone call, she could somehow make the call itself unhappen. By the time she disposed of the trash where she'd thrown the dirty paper towels, Rachel's revelation seemed like a vague, half-forgotten nightmare.

Then Colleen remembered the letter. The letter would make it all real again. Or would it? It might explain, or show that Rachel had misunderstood something. Children misunderstood things all the time. Colleen shuffled to the bedroom, empty now except for her sleeping bag and an open suitcase on the floor. When she sifted through her clothing, her rosary slid to the side, a little pool of blue and silver. She imagined praying the rosary, and it taking her, bead by bead, to some untroubled place where God loved her and Derek's letter didn't exist and Rachel's phone call had never happened. She picked the rosary up. It felt nearly weightless in her hand. Had it always been so light? She remembered it as more substantial.

The edge of Derek's letter stuck out from under her khaki

shorts. She lifted it by the corner, as though it was contaminated. There were matches in the bathroom, next to the aroma-therapy candle the realtor had suggested. She could burn the letter in the sink and rinse the ashes down the drain. It seemed possible. To burn the letter, then come back here and let the rosary beads slip through her fingers, let each repeated prayer slide her deeper into oblivion.

Making her way to the bathroom, Colleen pinched the letter between thumb and forefinger and held it away from her body. When she lowered the letter into the sink, the edge of the paper sucked up two fat droplets of water. She tried to strike a match, but it bent. The second match flared. But as she moved the flame toward the letter, she remembered Rachel's shriek. *My God, Mom. I could understand that maybe with me you didn't know, but now you do.*

Once you know something, you can't unknow it.

You can't unknow it.

The flame scorched her finger and she dropped the match. She snatched the letter from the sink, then ran cold water over her stinging finger. Dragging herself back to her sleeping bag, Colleen leaned against the wall and opened Derek's letter.

Dear Colleen,

Writing this letter is the hardest thing I have ever had to do. Something happened, years ago, that I need to tell you about. Please believe me when I say

I would give anything to go back in time and undo it. I hoped that you would never learn about this. Please, just for a moment, remember all the times that I've been a good father to our girls and a good husband to you. I'm so afraid that all that will mean nothing when I tell you what I have to tell you.

Rachel remembered something that happened when she was eight years old, after Izzy was born. I don't know if you remember how hard those months were. I know I left you on your own too much. I know you were hurt and angry and you thought I was selfish. You thought I wanted to travel to get away from Izzy's crying, to be able to sleep through the night in a hotel room. But the real reason I volunteered to travel more was because I started having these feelings for Rachel. Feelings of attraction. I know that reading that must be shocking to you. It was shocking to me! At first, I thought maybe it was just because we didn't have sex much those last couple months of your pregnancy, and then for a while after Izzy was born. None of that made it okay. I know that.

To my everlasting regret, I acted on those feelings, for a short time. I touched Rachel (just on the outside). A few times, I had her touch me. I would give anything to change that. I'd give my life. Literally. I'd give my life not to have to be writing this to you, not to cause you this pain. But Rachel told me that I had to tell you, or she would. Otherwise, believe me, Colleen, this secret would have gone to the grave with me. I would never, ever have hurt you the way that reading this must be hurting you now.

You'll think I'm a monster. You'll picture these sickos hanging around school yards. That's not me, Colleen, I swear. I'm not a monster. I'm not a predator. This was just something that happened in a moment of weakness.

I'm so, so sorry, Col. I love you. I do. I will always love you. I'm hoping against hope that you can forgive me. Or even just tell me that it might be possible to forgive me, someday. I love you.

Numbly, Colleen traced the thick line under those last words. Past moments jumped into her mind and took on new meaning. The articles on resisting temptation. Derek's silence when she'd asked, "Have you gone to confession?" Derek saying, "You're still sending Izzy?"

Izzy.

Izzy!

The dazed feeling that had filled her body left instantly, replaced by panic. Panic made her jump off the sleeping bag and stuff her clothes back into the suitcase. Panic raced her car so fast that the sallow sodium lights over the highway blurred. Panic made her cry out Izzy's name in the dark all the way to the Phoenix airport.

Chapter 19

In the moonless night, Colleen squinted through the rain-spattered windows of the taxi, straining to make out the street signs in their subdivision. If there hadn't been plexiglass between her and the driver, she would have grabbed his shoulder when she spotted the turn. Instead, she shouted, "Let me out here," though they weren't yet at her door.

Once out of the cab, she stood at the mouth of their cul-de-sac and stared at the four brick-and-stone Tudor-style houses that edged it. Light rain dripped down her face and obscured her view. She rolled her suitcase past the dark drive of the first house and came to her home. The bronze lamp hanging just beyond the curved arch of the entryway gave off a welcoming light. The three windows to the left of the entry were black, but a cheerful glow shone through the family room windows on the right. Probably Derek was in there, watching TV. Suddenly Colleen imagined Izzy cuddled next to her father. She raced forward, her suitcase rumbling behind her.

Not until she had mounted the two steps and escaped the drizzle under the covered entry did Colleen realize that she couldn't slip into the house unseen the way she'd planned. She only had the keys to their Arizona house on this ring. She peered through the beveled glass in the front door, but she couldn't see anything except the bench in the empty hall. A feeling of dread came over her, and she stabbed at the bell. At the same time, she pounded the front door with her fist and cried out, "Izzy! Izzy!"

The door swung open. Derek stood there, looking confused. "Colleen?" He wore a yellow knit shirt and his bare feet stuck out at the bottom of his blue jeans. Nothing seemed awry. Derek wasn't furtively tucking his shirt back into his pants. He just looked normal. "Colleen?" he repeated, opening the door wider. "What's happened? What are you doing here?"

"Where's Izzy?" Colleen dropped her carry-on and lunged past her husband. "Izzy?" She darted toward the family room, where a commercial blared, then wove her way around the couch and the recliner, still calling Izzy's name. She passed stacks of boxes lining the walls, then bumped against an end table, causing a bottle of Stella to wobble. Hurrying past the grandfather clock, she peered idiotically into the fireplace, as if Izzy could be hiding behind the mesh screen. Abruptly, she rushed out of the room and crossed the hallway to the formal living room.

But the brilliant light she turned on revealed nothing but a circle of empty couches and armchairs, their silken pillows askew.

Colleen sped down the hall toward her chrome-and-quartz kitchen, which was at the back of the house. There, she saw signs of Izzy—a box of Pop Tarts on the counter, a book of Sudoku puzzles on the breakfast table. Colleen entered the formal dining room on the other side of the kitchen. She rounded its gleaming table, scanned the curio cabinet and buffet, and ended up back in the kitchen, at the glass doors that led to the deck. Staring into the night, she realized why Izzy wasn't to be found anywhere downstairs. Her daughter would have gone to bed long ago.

More slowly, Colleen retraced her steps to the front of the house and mounted the stairs to the bedrooms. There she called her daughter's name, still urgently, but more quietly. "Izzy?" But Izzy's bed was vacant. All four upstairs bedrooms were dark and empty.

When she came back down, Derek stood as still as a statue by the fireplace at the far end of the family room. The TV still flickered, but he had muted the sound. "Izzy's not here, Colleen. She's at the cabin with Bea and Shawn. Remember? They left yesterday for vacation. Izzy won't be back until Saturday." He took a step toward her.

She held up a hand. "Don't."

Derek stumbled back, hitting the edge of the mantel. Neither spoke for a moment.

"If you touched Izzy…"

"Colleen, I would *never*—"

"Shut up!" she howled. "Just shut up! Why would I believe *you*?"

Derek steadied himself against the brick of the fireplace with the palm of one hand. "But you sent Izzy to me. I thought…"

They stared at one another.

Colleen took a step toward her husband. "You thought I sent Izzy to you because I trusted you?" The horrible phrases Rachel had spit out during that phone call came back to Colleen now, like prompters in a play, feeding her lines that she spewed out as if possessed. The hoarse voice that rose hysterically from her mouth seemed to belong to someone else. "Trust you to keep your goddamn dick in your pants? Trust you?" She paced back and forth across the room. "Who told his little girl that she could have special time with Daddy? Who put his fucking hands on her?" Her own hands itched to throw something. She passed the end table, picked up a container that held three remotes and a bunch of pens and pencils, and slammed it to the floor. The contents scattered. "And I…" Colleen laughed, a crazed sound. "I was upset because I thought you'd had an affair." She pressed her palms against her flaming cheeks and shrieked. "An affair! I thought that was the worst thing you could do to me. You fucking bastard!" All this time, Colleen had paced to and fro, getting closer to Derek and then backing up again. She let out a roar. Lowering her head like a bull, she careened into him, smashing her skull into Derek's gut so hard that he gagged. While he fought for breath, she sprang back and stood panting a few feet away. "Oh, God. How could this happen? Oh, Jesus…" She circled the room again, her hands clenched into fists that spasmed periodically. She—who had never in her life said the f-word, never said "Jesus" or "God" except with reverence—yelled, "Jesus fucking Christ!" Not once, but over and over again while she pinballed from one side of the room to the other. "Jesus fucking Christ!"

Derek cradled his stomach in his hand and slumped by the fireplace, silent and haggard. He looked like he *wanted* her to go on and on. When she came to a stop by the recliner, he said, "You can hit me, if you want," then glanced down. She followed his gaze to the heavy metal poker leaning against the fireplace. "I wouldn't try to stop you. I wouldn't fight you."

His feeble tone incensed her. Colleen screamed her way across the room. "Don't act like you're the victim! You're not the victim!" She grabbed the poker. "You're the fuck who couldn't keep his filthy hands off our daughter!"

Derek took a tiny step back. "Col…"

She couldn't stand to look at him. She shifted her gaze, and it landed on an unfamiliar photo in a cheap metal frame on the mantel. In it, Izzy stood with her father in front of the huge Ferris wheel at Navy Pier, her face tilted up in that sappy, adoring look. Colleen raised the poker high above her head. Derek looked truly frightened, but he didn't back away; he clung to the edge of the mantel. A martyr struggling to be brave. Disgust shot through Colleen, and she swung with all her might.

The photo crashed to the floor. At the same time, the poker cut deeply into the wood of the mantel and wedged there. Colleen struggled to free it.

Derek made a futile gesture, as if to help her extract it.

"Get away from me!" she shrieked, wild-eyed. "Get out!" In the next moment, the poker came free, and Colleen swung it hard. Derek leapt out of the way, his eyes horrified. Colleen swerved the poker in a wide arc. Derek moved just fast enough that it missed him and clanged against the brick of the fireplace instead. He raced toward the front door. "That's right," Colleen shouted. "Run! You better run." She pursued him, slicing the poker through the air. "You won't fight me, but you'll run, won't you? You'll run! You'll run for your life, for your fucking miserable life!"

Chapter 20

The next morning, groggy from her poor sleep, Colleen held tight to the banister and lowered her body down the stairs step by step. The night before seemed unreal. When her bare feet hit the cold tiles at the bottom of the staircase, she heard the percolator and smelled coffee. She almost returned to Izzy's bed, where she'd crushed Pooh Bear against her chest all night.

At the sink, Derek popped a handful of antacid pills into his mouth and chewed. He hadn't shaved. His face was puffy, and a line creased his cheek, as if he'd fallen asleep pressed against the edge of something—a magazine, a twisted sheet. But otherwise, he looked the same. How could he look so much the same? He tightened the top of the pill container and cast a wary glance at Colleen from under heavy lids. "You want some coffee?"

"What are you doing here?"

Derek's hand shook. The two empty mugs he held struck one another with a clang. He lowered them to the quartz countertop. "We need to talk, don't we?" The coffee stopped percolating, and the blue light came on. "Don't you think we need to talk?" He nudged a pastry box toward her. "I got donuts."

Colleen blinked. Did Derek think donuts and coffee could somehow restore them?

They didn't speak again until they were sitting across from one another with their steaming mugs, the donut box wide open on the honey-oak table. Pink frosting dripped down the side of one of the pastries. The sight of it made Colleen's throat close up. She added extra milk to her coffee, but she still didn't think she could manage a single swallow.

Derek's laptop yawned open near his elbow. He shut the lid and turned his full attention on Colleen. "The first thing I want to say again is how sorry I am. I don't have the words to tell you how terrible I feel."

She searched his face the way she might examine some exotic specimen, but found no outward sign of the man she now knew him to be. "I never would have believed it if you hadn't told me yourself."

You'd think her words had revealed common ground, the way Derek pounced on them. "I can hardly believe it myself, Col. Our girls are the light of my life. I'd kill anyone who hurt Rachel or Izzy. You know that."

Colleen's mouth dropped open. "But you did hurt Rachel."

Derek mumbled, "I know." He slumped in his chair,

speaking so quietly that Colleen had to lean in to hear him. "I'm not trying to excuse what I did. But what happened was just, you know, touching."

"'Just,'" Colleen repeated. The early morning chatter of the birds came through the open patio door, and her eyes drifted to the feeder on the deck. "She was eight years old, Derek. Eight years old."

"I know. I know."

His face took on the same hangdog expression it had worn the night before, and disgust, acrid as bile, rose in her throat.

"I just mean," he said, "there's degrees. What I remember—"

Colleen slammed her palms against her ears. "I don't want to hear about what you remember!"

Derek pleaded like a defendant throwing himself on the mercy of the court. "What I did was terrible, Col. I know that. But please, give me a chance. I will do anything to fix this, I promise you. Anything. Just tell me what you want. I'll do whatever you want."

"What I want? I want you out of this house. Today."

"Col—"

"And I want you to never see Izzy again."

He reared back. "Hang on a second!"

Colleen folded her arms across her chest. "I want you out of this house," she repeated. "I want you out of our lives."

"Colleen." His voice rose in supplication. "Think about this. What's that going to do to Izzy? Isn't it bad enough that you're hurt now, too? You want to spread that to Iz? And what are you going to tell her? What are you going to say when she gets back from Michigan and says 'Where's Daddy?'"

Colleen gazed through the patio doors at her lovely green yard, where all the Midwestern flowers she had missed in Arizona bloomed—orange tiger lilies and top-heavy lavender balls of hydrangea and a ton of lilac bushes at the back of the yard, so tall that they hid the prairie path from view. Finally, she said, "We'll tell Izzy you're traveling. She's used to that. She's used to not having you around. Which I, fool that I am, regretted."

Derek pursed his lips and drummed the table. "And on Izzy's birthday? Her Fourth of July birthday party in a couple of weeks? You going to tell Izzy that I'm too busy traveling to be here? What about Thanksgiving? And *Christmas*? Are you going to be the one to tell her that she's never going to see me again? You going to explain why?"

She had no answer. After a long while, Derek opened his laptop and fiddled with some keys, then angled the screen toward Colleen. Izzy appeared there, squealing, "Daddy's home!" In the film clip, Izzy was perhaps three years old; Rachel, eleven. "Daddy's home!" The two girls hurried to the front door. The camera jerked while it followed Rachel as she reversed course back to the kitchen, where she picked a cake up from the table, then raced toward her sister. In the next shot, Derek had already come in and lifted a giggling Izzy to his shoulders. Rachel shouted, "Look, Daddy! I made it myself!" and she slanted the cake so that her father could read the icing: *Happy Birthday Daddy!* But she tipped it too much, and the cake slid. Derek and Rachel saw it at the same time, slipping off the plate. Derek still had Izzy on his shoulders, and was holding her ankles with one hand. He grabbed the falling cake with the other, and ended up crushing it against his suit coat. In the next moment, he was wiping cake from his lapel and licking his fingers. "Mm, this is the best!" He tried to feed some cake to the girls off his suit, but they cried out, "Ick! No, Dad!" They were all laughing, even Colleen, unseen behind the camera. Abruptly, the clip ended.

The shards of pain that had pierced Colleen in Father Lopez's office tore through her again. This time, she recognized the pain. She could name it. *Grief.* She pressed her fist to her heart.

Derek turned moist eyes toward her. "I've been watching old clips all night."

Tears coursed down Colleen's cheeks, and Derek reached out a solicitous hand.

Colleen shrank from it. "You know the craziest part of all this? All night, I kept thinking I could handle this, I could do this, I could get through it." She swallowed. "If only I had you to help me. You." She shook her head, bewildered. "As if you could be the one to help me."

Derek leaned across the table. "But I could be. I want to be. We could figure out how to get through this. We could figure that out together." He turned his broad hands over, his open palms an invitation. Without her consent—nearly without her awareness—Colleen's own hands reached for his, and were swallowed in the warmth of his grasp. She stared at her small, pale hands clasped in his olive ones. Dark hairs rose on the back of his thick thumbs. In the next moment, she pictured those thumbs insinuating themselves under the thin white elastic of a child's panties. She yanked her hands off the table and onto her lap.

After a long moment, Derek slumped in his chair. The two sat silently, listening to seconds pass. Tick-tock. Finally, Colleen gathered herself together and said, "You'll come to Izzy's party. We'll have the same kind of cookout we always have, with Bea and Shawn and Amber, and Izzy's friends." She hesitated. "And Rachel." She forced a swallow of tepid coffee down her dry throat. "You find somewhere else to stay. But leave a few clothes here. We'll pretend you have to travel, even more than before. You can come home once in a while and see Izzy. But I have to be here. You can never be alone with Izzy. Never."

Derek let out a heavy sigh. "I promise you, Colleen, you can trust me." She stiffened. Hastily, he added, "Okay.

Whatever you want." He drummed on the table, then caught himself and instead closed his hands around his mug. "I know you don't want my help right now. But I can do things. Like I can arrange to get your car back from Arizona. I can deal with the realtor if you want to give her my number." At her skeptical look, he became more insistent. "If you need something, you can call on me." He went on in that vein for a while. He could go to Mass with her and Izzy on Sundays. Come early on July 4 and put up decorations for the party. He described all the things he could do to help make her plan work. As if it were *their* plan, not hers. He had become the involved partner she'd always longed for.

Derek leaned forward. "I'm just saying that I'm here for you." He turned his hands, palms up, on the table again— half supplication, half invitation—and raised his dark eyes, shining with tears, to hers.

Colleen's hands twitched on her lap, and she slid them under her, so that the weight of her thighs would hold them fast to her chair.

Chapter 21

Striding across the park near campus, Rachel spotted her mother slumped on a hard bench near the swings, where Izzy propelled herself high in the air. Up close, her mother looked as exhausted as Rachel herself felt. The skin under Colleen's eyes sagged, forming little dark pools that aged her. Her cheekbones stood out sharply, too. Rachel felt a pang of guilt. It had been her phone call, hadn't it, that had wrought these changes?

"Hey, Mom." She watched her mother pull herself upright and lift a hand in greeting.

"Rachel!" Izzy shouted from her swing, beckoning, and Rachel escaped the sight of her mother by joining her sister.

"I bet I can go higher than you," Izzy challenged. She soared. While Rachel swung, her mother wandered over. Each time Rachel swept past, she caught the dark blur of her mother's navy top from the corner of her eye.

After a while, Izzy slowed, and they swayed lazily side

by side while Izzy babbled about the fun she'd had with Amber in Michigan. Rachel gave her sister a sidelong glance. "How was your time with Dad?" Her mother leaned in a bit.

"Fun! We went to Buckingham Palace." Izzy giggled. "I mean Buckingham Fountain. Dad kept calling it Buckingham Palace!" She laughed. "And we went to the zoo and the Children's Museum. He took me and Aaliyah to Buckingham Fountain and the zoo. Aaliyah couldn't go to the Museum." Izzy scraped the heels of her gym shoes on the ground and brought her swing to a full stop.

"Iz… did Dad… did Dad ever act strange while you were with him?"

"Strange?" Izzy frowned. "You mean goofy?" She grinned. "Dad always acts goofy." With that, she sped to the jungle gym and scrambled on all fours toward the top of the dome.

Her mother moved directly in front of Rachel, blocking the sun. "I think Izzy was fine with your dad," Colleen said. "I'm almost positive."

"Oh, God, I hope so," Rachel cried. She looked away. "I should never have left it up to him. The minute he admitted it, I should have called you. If I'd done that, we wouldn't be watching her today, wondering."

A strange look crossed her mother's face. "I watch her all the time," Colleen said. "I wonder all the time. Not so much about last week, but about this whole past year. I tell myself he was hardly ever home. I tell myself that I was there." She bit her lip. "But I was there with you as well."

Rachel opened her arms. "Oh, Mom." Her mother returned her hug, but stiffly. Perhaps, Rachel thought, because it was the first time they'd been together since that terrible phone call. Rachel rested her head lightly on her mother's shoulder.

"It's all right," Colleen murmured, "everything's going to be all right." But when Rachel tried to sink into her mother's arms, Colleen pulled away. "Here comes Izzy."

Colleen put on that phony smile. At her side, Rachel repeated flatly, "Here comes Izzy." She looked at her mother. "Izzy always comes first."

Colleen turned sharply. "That's not true."

Just then, Izzy bounced up to them. "What's not true?"

Colleen stammered. "That you… that we give you better birthday parties than we gave your sister. Just because, you know, you always get fireworks."

Izzy gave Rachel a look. "Well, duh! If your birthday was on the Fourth of July, you'd get fireworks too." She rubbed the side of her red tennis shoe against the gravel. Little bits of mud came loose. "You were lucky—you got to go to different places with your friends. I always have the same old barbecue at home. I asked Dad if he would do something different this year, roast a pig like Aaliyah's father does. But he said he doesn't know how to do that. So it will be hot dogs and hamburgers like always."

"Dad is grilling?" Rachel said.

Izzy tugged at her mother's arm. "Take a picture of me upside down on the bars, okay? I want to send it to Ritu." She raced away, calling over her shoulder, "Wait 'til I tell you."

Rachel folded her arms across her chest. "Dad is grilling?" Her mother drew her cell phone out of her bag and kept her gaze steady on Izzy, who sped toward the climbing equipment. "Mom. You said in your phone message, 'Dad is gone.' So what exactly does 'Dad is gone' mean?"

Her mother's face closed up. "It means he's not staying at the house. He's not living with us. But Izzy doesn't have to know that. She thinks that he's traveling a lot; that's why he's not home."

"That's your plan? You're pretending that you and Dad are still together?"

Colleen shifted from one foot to the other. "For a while."

Rachel was stunned. "I was sure you'd divorce him. I was sure that the minute you knew, you'd leave him."

"I *have* left him. I threw him out. But then I asked myself, what is this going to do to your sister? Why not keep our family together, for Izzy's sake, just for a while? Until I can figure out what I'm doing." Her mother's face reddened. "Is that so terrible?"

Rachel tried to imagine Izzy's upcoming party. Her

father grilling and sharing beers with Uncle Shawn, Aunt Bea asking Rachel how her new job was going, her mother smiling like a grotesque caricature of herself through the whole ordeal. "I'm not coming," Rachel said. "If Dad's going to be there, I'm not coming."

Izzy hung upside down from the bars, her bright yellow t-shirt a smudge in the distance. She waved frantically. Colleen trained the camera lens on her. Click, click, click. Then she faced Rachel. "Please, Rach. Come to the party. For Izzy's sake."

Rachel answer came out slowly. "After I told Dad that he had to tell you, I waited for you to call me. I didn't want to call you because I didn't know for sure when he was going to talk to you. But I was sure you'd call me as soon as you knew. I couldn't understand why you didn't call to see how I was." She looked directly at her mother. "You're the hovercraft."

Colleen laid her hand on Rachel's shoulder. "I didn't know. I misunderstood the letter. I didn't know until you phoned me."

Rachel covered her mother's hand with her own, holding her at her side. "I understand that, Mom. But even after…" She shook her head. "Like right now. You don't think about how hard it would be for me to show up at Izzy's party, make small talk with Dad in front of Aunt Bea and Uncle Shawn." She looked off to the side again. "All your concern is for Izzy." A jet of anger, hot as the

June sun, shot up in Rachel. "If you'd been half as vigilant with me, would any of this even have happened?"

Her mother's mouth contorted. "I will never forgive myself for that." Then it was as if she made a valiant effort to rearrange her face, to hold the planes of it together. It gave her a stony look. It struck Rachel that her mother's rigid mask was like an eggshell. It felt hard to the touch, but it was pitifully thin and fragile.

"But you're all right," Colleen went on. Her voice grew fervent. "You've always been mature, level-headed. You keep things in proportion. You're strong! I know that you're going to be all right, Rachel. I have faith in you, you hear me? You're going to be all right." She beamed her eager, pathetic smile until Rachel squeezed her hand and forced a smile in return.

Chapter 22

"Mommy, there's no more cereal."

Colleen forced her bleary eyes open, then narrowed them again against the bright morning sun. Izzy leaned over the bed, so close that Colleen picked up the scent of her unwashed hair, a mixture of sweat and summer sun. "There's no more cereal," Izzy repeated. "There's no Pop Tarts either. And I don't have any clean tops." Colleen propped herself up. How could Izzy be out of tops? Colleen had only been home a week. Then she remembered that Izzy had left Arizona nearly two works earlier than that, plus she'd brought home a bagful of dirty clothes from her vacation with Bea.

"I'll wash clothes this morning," Colleen said. "After I take a shower." She scratched her scalp. "And then I'll go grocery shopping." Suddenly, these small, domestic tasks felt overwhelming, and Colleen lay back on her pillow and half-shut her eyes.

"Are you sick, Mommy?"

"No, I'm just tired."

Izzy rocked back and forth on her heels. "Can we make the invitations for my party today? I found some balloon pictures on the computer."

"Listen, Izzy," Colleen said, sitting up straight again, "don't be too disappointed if your sister can't come to your party. She might have to work."

"I know," Izzy said, breezily. "If she can't come, she's going to do something special with me, just the two of us. Maybe the Field Museum. Whatever I want, she said." Izzy's eyes shone.

Colleen forced enthusiasm. "That's great! That'll be so much fun!"

Izzy nodded, but then the smile left her face. "What's the matter, Mom?"

"Nothing," Colleen said. "Nothing's the matter." She searched the floor, found one worn slipper and slid her foot into it.

Izzy retrieved the other slipper and handed it to her. "Then why are you crying?"

Colleen swiped at her eyes and stared at the wetness on her palm. "I'm not crying. I'm just a little tired."

In the bathroom, she set the shower nozzle to "mist." A soft touch, that's what she needed, to help her meet another day. By the time she padded down the staircase, she felt—not energized, but at least shielded. Then the smell of something burnt hit her.

"I'm sorry, Mom." Izzy bent over the garbage pail in the kitchen, scraping charred pancakes off a blackened frying pan.

"Be careful, Iz. Isn't that pan still hot?" Colleen took the pan from her daughter and set it in the sink.

"I wanted to surprise you," Izzy said in a small voice.

The sound of coffee percolating came to Colleen's ears. "Are you making coffee?"

"Uh huh."

Colleen peered at the suspiciously pale brown liquid dripping into the glass pot. "Did you put new grounds in?"

"New grounds?" Izzy's thin shoulders slumped. "I thought you just had to put in water. There was already coffee in the basket."

Colleen sighed. "Those were old grounds from yesterday." She unplugged the pot and managed a weak smile. "It doesn't matter."

Izzy's chin trembled. "I wanted to cheer you up. I was going to make smiley faces on the pancakes with chocolate chips like Daddy does."

"Oh, Iz." Colleen opened her arms to her daughter. But somehow, midstream, the hug meant to comfort Izzy changed, and instead of hugging Izzy, Colleen clung to her. Izzy stiffened, and when Colleen pulled away, her daughter's dark caterpillar eyebrows drew so close together that they almost touched. Colleen announced, brightly, "I'll make new pancakes. You set the table, okay? And get the orange juice out."

Izzy didn't move.

"Izzy," Colleen said. "I'm fine, okay?" She hummed the opening bars of "My Favorite Things" and began to sing. "Cream-colored ponies and crisp apple strudel…" Izzy joined in on the chorus while Colleen produced a fresh pot of coffee and a dozen small pancakes with big, smiling chocolate-chip faces, and the two of them sang on about vanquishing fear and sadness just by remembering their favorite things.

That night, minutes into a documentary on the earth's oceans, Colleen dozed off in the recliner, only to be jarred awake by a ringtone. By the time she recognized that the insistent sound came from a Skype call, it had stopped. The digital numbers on the cable box said 10:05. The only light in the family room came from the television, the volume so low Colleen could barely hear the narrator. It disturbed her to find herself in this tomb of a room, so like the TV room at her parents' house on one of her mother's gray days.

She leaned over the side of the recliner and peered at the laptop sitting on the table. Geeta had called. A weary guilt invaded her. But what would she say if she talked to Geeta? In her mind, she heard her friend's solicitous voice. "How are you? How are things going with Derek?" How could she answer that question? And what if she lost control of herself and blurted out the truth? Her face flamed at the thought. Just then, the ringing started again. Colleen sat very still, as if Geeta would somehow detect her presence if she moved.

The ringing stopped, and Colleen let out a breath of relief. But then, she heard *Ping!* and a text message appeared. "Colleen, are you there? I need to talk. Are you there?" Another *ping!* "Colleen, please call me."

She slumped in the recliner and stared at the TV, where an enormous number of sharks converged on a dead whale in an orgy of eating. In the next moment, unbelievably, the Skype program rang with another call from Geeta. It hit Colleen that her friend could tell she was online. There was a way to make yourself invisible on Skype, but she didn't remember how to do that. *I could be upstairs,* Colleen told herself. *Or in the bathroom.* The ringing went on and on. *All Geeta knows is that the computer is connected to the internet. She can't know I'm sitting right here.* Still, the ringing continued. Colleen slammed the lid of the laptop down and silence filled the room.

Only then did she realize what she'd done. Wouldn't Geeta now know that her call had been cut off? Know that Colleen had heard the ringing, seen her pleading notes, and deliberately shut her out?

Colleen gazed at the gloom around her—the shadowy edges of the couch, the end tables, the grandfather clock. It was so like the darkness in the room where her mother would draw the drapes tight, then nap on and off all day in the dim light of the flickering screen, while Colleen and her brother tiptoed around the house.

Colleen pulled herself upright. She was not her mother. She, Colleen Agnes Riordan Moretti, was a woman of action. She snapped the television off. In the kitchen, she filled the dishwasher and wiped the stove and countertops. She vacuumed the floor tiles and got on her hands and knees to scrub every sticky spot, every scuff mark. Tomorrow, she would finish unpacking all those boxes, wash clothes and shop for groceries. Setting the alarm on her phone, she vowed to get up early and walk on the prairie path the way she'd dreamed of doing all those long months in Arizona.

The next morning, dew dampened Colleen's running shoes when she crossed the yard and slipped through the gap in the bushes to the prairie path. She'd forgotten how heavy the morning dew could be, forgotten how the gravel on this path crunched beneath her shoes, and she relished the sweet familiarity of these sensations. She felt like she could walk forever in the dappled sunlight, so much gentler than Arizona's blazing heat. When she eventually spotted the railroad tracks in the distance, a reminder that she needed to head back, her spirits fell a little.

On her return trip, the path grew more crowded. Runners pounded past her, while cyclists called out warnings of "On your left," before they whooshed past.

Dog walkers reined in their pets. Two women strode by, their heads bent together as they talked. Seeing them, Colleen felt a pang of longing for Geeta and a deep unease about ignoring her friend's messages the night before. But how could she talk honestly to Geeta? In fact, how could she ever talk honestly to any friend again? The thought brought a terrible sense of isolation, and Colleen broke into a run, as if she might outrace it.

Nearing her yard, Colleen heard a group of laughing women coming from the opposite direction. It wasn't just that they were loud. They were doubled over, holding their stomachs, gurgling with the kind of laughter that makes other people chuckle even when they have no idea what's so funny. Approaching her, Aaliyah's mother, Jackie, called out from the center of the group. "Hey, Colleen!" A tall, raven-haired woman next to Jackie made some comment that Colleen didn't catch, but which made them all laugh again. In the middle of this, Jackie tried to introduce her. "Hey, this is my neighbor, Colleen. Her daughter Izzy and Aaliyah play together." The women attempted polite responses, muttering hellos and trying to explain what was so funny. But mostly they hiccupped and said things like, "Oh, stop, I have to stop laughing; my stomach hurts." Jackie glanced at Colleen's running shoes. "You should walk with us, Colleen. We meet by my house about eight o'clock every morning." The tall woman interjected. "Not *about* eight o'clock. No later than eight. If you're going to walk with us, be on time. I don't like to wait."

Colleen blinked. Jackie said, "Pay no attention to Rose; she used to be a team captain in high school."

"I'll be there," Colleen told Rose. "I'll be *early*." She was earnest, but the others acted like she had made a joke, and they burst out laughing again, then laughed even harder when she protested, "No, it's true. I'm always early for things."

"Good," Rose declared. The youngest-looking woman told Rose, "You're not the boss of us," a remark apparently connected with their earlier hilarity, because it set them all off again. The fourth member of their group, a gray-haired woman with pale, thin eyebrows, snorted then, triggering another flood of laughter.

After Colleen ducked into her yard, she reviewed their names. She knew Aaliyah's mom, Jackie, of course. She stood out as the only black woman in the group. Then there was tall, bossy, you-better-be-on-time Rose. Letitia, whose tattooed ankle sprouted a vine with delicate pink flowers, was clearly the youngest. And Pat, much older but plump enough that her face remained unlined. When the group drifted further away, their easy chatter faded, and the loneliness that Colleen had tried to outrace returned. She gripped one of the lilac bush branches. She had lost Geeta. She would never be close with these new friends like she and Geeta had been. But she would walk with them. And maybe, one day, she would at least laugh again.

Chapter 23

On Izzy's birthday, Rachel cut over to the prairie path so that she could avoid the deck where her father would be grilling. She dragged her feet over the graveled path, then peered through the leafy branches. On the deck, her father swigged a beer, leaning against the railing in that expansive way he had, arms extended while he talked with Uncle Shawn. Her mother elbowed her way through the patio doors, a crush of paper plates and cups and napkins in her arms. Her father sprang over to help, and her mother, all smiles, worked with him to arrange the items on the serving table. Rachel wrinkled her nose in disgust, and her back seized up. She tried to relax her muscles the way Monica had taught her, but her back continued to send out spokes of pain. She retreated down the path a little. She could be back at the train station in ten minutes. Get a coffee at the shop across the street while she waited for a return train. But then Rachel glimpsed Izzy barefoot on the lawn, playing croquet with her friends. *Do it for your sister.*

She washed a Valium down with a long draw from her water bottle and pulled her visor low, then headed toward the croquet game, raising a hand vaguely toward the adults on the deck. Her mother waved back enthusiastically. Izzy skipped over and wrapped her arms around her sister.

"Happy birthday, Iz."

Her eyes bright, Izzy shook the small gift box that Rachel handed her. "Is it a game?"

"It's a used gift," Rachel said. "But you'll like it. Go ahead and open it."

"Now?"

Rachel nodded. "Why not?"

A moment later, Izzy shouted, "OMG!" She lifted Rachel's old cell phone from a nest of yellow tissue paper and waved it in the air. "OMG!"

Her mother called from the deck. "I don't want to hear that, Izzy. That's still swearing."

"But look, Mom!" Izzy swirled the phone in the air, then threw herself into Rachel's arms. "You are the best sister!"

Rachel watched her mother hurry across the grass toward them.

Izzy studied the cell phone, squinting. "Can I get a different picture on the screen?" Turning her back on her mother's advancing figure, Rachel said, "I'll help you set everything up later. We should probably charge it now."

"Izzy's a little young for that, don't you think?" her mother said, huffing.

"I'm nine today," Izzy protested.

Rachel gave her mother a stony look. "I think it's a good idea for safety," she said.

"Yeah, Mom. Did you hear about that girl? The man put her in the trunk of his car, but they found her because she had a cell phone."

"Yep," Rachel agreed. "And you don't have to be kidnapped to call for help, Iz. If you find yourself in any kind of trouble, if you're upset by anything, you can always call me." She paused. "Or Mom."

Izzy nodded. excited. "Or Dad."

Colleen did an about-face and headed back to the deck. Rachel joined the last few minutes of the croquet game with Izzy's young friends. By the time Derek called out, "Come and get it!" the Valium had kicked in, and Rachel felt calm and controlled. Still, she hung back while Izzy and her friends raced to the deck, and watched her mother and father work in tandem there. Her mother opened buns on the girls' plates, and her father slid burgers or speared hotdogs onto them. The girls added chips, potato salad or fruit salad and carried their plates down to a picnic table several yards from the deck. Keeping her back to her father, Rachel helped herself to the salads on the serving table.

She paused by the cooler that held beer and cans of hard lemonade. Mandy had told her, "If you have a drink with one of these pills, you won't feel anything but happy, even with your father there." Rachel grabbed a can of hard lemonade and turned to join Izzy at the picnic table. But Bea called out, "Here, Rachel. Sit by me. I haven't seen you in ages," and Rachel thought, *Why not? Why not sit at the same table as my parents?* Where she sat no longer seemed important. In fact, nothing seemed important, nothing worth worrying about. Her father said, "Hamburger or hot dog, Rach?" and she answered, "Hamburger," held out the flimsy paper plate, and even returned his brief glance.

When she plopped down next to Bea, her aunt remarked, "Your dad said you got an apartment."

"Best thing for a young person, really," her father called out from the grill. Rachel blinked and took a long draught of her hard lemonade. "Maybe not for every young person," her mother chimed in. "But Rachel's always been very independent. It's actually not much more expensive than the dorm, and she's paying the difference with her part-time job." Her parents went on in that vein for a bit, smiling and nodding as if they were proud of her. When Uncle Shawn turned the conversation to sports, Bea leaned toward Rachel and lowered her voice. "I'm so glad that worked out for you. It turned out better this way, didn't it, with everything above- board?" Some of Rachel's drink sputtered out of her mouth. She dabbed her top with a napkin and murmured "Excuse me" before leaving the table.

In the kitchen, her mother scraped most of her hamburger and half of her potato salad into the garbage. "Lost my appetite," Colleen muttered. In a dull voice far different from her cheerful patter at the table, she said, "I suppose you bought yourself a new phone. I guess it wouldn't occur to you to check with me before giving Izzy a phone."

In the past, her mother wouldn't have been speaking in this lifeless voice. She'd have thrown her arms in the air and ranted and raved while her face darkened from pink to purple. But today her tone remained flat. Even her sparkling green eyes seemed dull. *My mother has lost her fire*, Rachel thought.

On the deck, her father was gesturing, telling Bea and Shawn a story and grinning as if he didn't have a care in the world. Rachel and her mother watched him pantomime rowing a boat. "You'd think he'd get tired of telling that old story," Colleen said. After a long moment, she added, "Sometimes I look at him, and he seems the same, you know? Like now, all I see is your same old dad telling that same old story." Her mother shook her head. "Other times, all I see is… the man who did that to you."

Rachel studied her father, who now laughed heartily with Shawn and Bea. "Like those reversible figures," she told her mother. "You know, the one that can look like a very old woman or a very young one. You've seen that? It shifts from one to the other."

Tears pooled in her mother's eyes. "I wish you were here at home this summer."

The idea appalled Rachel. To watch her mother fade a bit more each day? To see tears in the eyes of the woman who never cried? To witness her carrying on this charade each time *he* visited?

Rachel squeezed her mother's shoulder. "I'll visit, Mom. I'll see you and Izzy a lot." She escaped back to the table, where she gulped down her hard lemonade. Her father explained to Uncle Shawn that the new stain he'd just used on the deck had taken forever to apply, but would last longer. Bea launched into a detailed complaint about Amber's soccer coach. Each time Rachel took another swallow, her father's comments about the stain became less boring, and Bea's criticisms of the coach less annoying. She poured more hard lemonade over a tall glass of ice and thought about how cheerful the red, white, and blue birthday balloons looked, bobbing in the breeze. Each sip lightened the day. Uncle Shawn's teasing became friendlier, her father's jokes funnier. The bits of conversation she overheard from Izzy's table struck her as amusing. When one of them reminded her of something funny that had happened at the Mexican Grill, she started telling her family about that. But she found herself stalling and restarting because she kept getting confused about what had happened next. That struck her as hilarious, and she laughed so uncontrollably that she snorted. Her father cast an amused glance down the table. "Someone's getting tipsy." He smiled. "I'm glad you're having a good time, kiddo. I'm glad you're doing okay."

Suddenly, all humor drained from Rachel. She stared at her father, speechless. A moment later, she was overcome by nausea. When she stood to make a beeline for the bathroom, the world spun. Bea grabbed one arm and her mother the other, but before they could get her into the house, she puked right onto the newly-stained redwood deck.

It was Bea who helped her upstairs and into her old bed. But her mother came with a glass of water and aspirin. "Sorry, Mom," Rachel muttered.

"I think you need help," her mother said.

"Not now, Mom," Rachel moaned.

She revived nearly two hours later, just as dusk settled. In the kitchen, Izzy's opened presents lay on the table in a crush of wrapping paper and ribbons, her nearby cake almost obliterated. Rachel heard Izzy's friends calling goodbye outside. The next thing she knew, Izzy had grabbed her hand, and the whole family was walking the five blocks to the fireworks.

When they reached the football field at the high school, Izzy left Rachel and went to join Amber. The family meandered through the bleachers, looking for a space big enough for the seven of them. Her uncle gestured and made his way into a near-empty row, pressing past a young couple with a toddler. When they filed in, Rachel realized that her father would end up next to Izzy, and her heart pounded. Just then, Colleen called to Izzy and straightened the ribbon in her hair, then deftly inserted herself between Izzy and Derek.

The hovercraft was back. A confused mixture of relief and resentment swelled in Rachel.

Chapter 24

Colleen didn't think she could keep her eyes open during Mass without a shot of caffeine. So, despite the heavy mugginess of the early morning July air, she sipped coffee on the deck and wished she could nap later to make up for her poor night's sleep. That would mean leaving Derek alone downstairs with Izzy while Colleen slept. Not going to happen.

In contrast, Derek was full of pep. He buzzed around the yard in his tank top, watering the flowers, his shoulders looking pale and faded compared with the dark tan of his arms. He dragged the hose over to the bed of irises. "You have to really soak them," Colleen called out. Derek flashed her a thumbs-up sign. It was such a familiar gesture, one that Colleen had seen countless times. Time snapped like a rubber band, bringing into focus the Derek that Colleen had lived with and loved for almost twenty years. For the briefest of moments, she imagined that these past weeks had been a bad dream. She tried to extend that sensation, to live a little longer in the ordinariness of a Sunday morning where her biggest irritation was that Derek had moved too quickly from the irises to the hydrangea bushes.

Of course, she failed, just as she'd failed each time these sorts of experiences had occurred over the past few weeks. What was so disconcerting about Derek brewing coffee in the kitchen on Sunday mornings, or folding clothes while the three of them watched television in the evening, was how ordinary it seemed. Two weeks ago, she'd pointed out some yard-tool organizers on the internet, and now their rakes and shovels and clippers hung neatly along one wall of the garage, next to a new set of shelves. Sometimes Colleen could almost believe the story they'd told Izzy. Sometimes, just for a minute or two, it seemed they were a real family. She knew that wasn't true. Nevertheless, when a tabloid at the checkout counter announced a celebrity divorce, and the word jumped off the page and froze her heart, she could tell herself she was still married. Still a stay-at-home mother. She still cooked, cleaned the house and worked in the garden. Not everything had changed.

Not yet.

She pulled herself up from the table to dress for church.

Entering the low-slung modern building of St. John of the Cross, Colleen moved into the sunlit nave, with its pale oak pews and light streaming through stained-glass windows. It used to feel like she was walking into a warm embrace. Now the space felt sterile. Even the light seemed cold and thin, mimicking Colleen's own feelings. Because God wasn't there anymore. As far as Colleen could tell, God wasn't anywhere anymore. Bitterly, she thought that perhaps He never had been. She marveled that her signature volcanic rage had not erupted against God. Would it be a relief when that happened? Or would it shatter something irrevocably?

Ahead of her, Derek flipped his elbow out in a jaunty gesture. Izzy spun so that her rainbow-colored skirt twirled, and then slipped her skinny arm through her father's. Resentment welled up in Colleen. *Look at those two pals jostling down the aisle together!* She sped up and thrust herself between the two of them just as Derek entered a pew, separating father and daughter. Her gaze fell on the golden tabernacle that sat in the center of the altar and held the chalice and consecrated hosts. She raised her chin to it. *What? I'm protecting my daughter.* Though she knew, of course she knew, that nothing bad was going to happen to Izzy sitting right next to her in church. Izzy fiddled with a loose barrette, and Colleen swiveled around to help her, turning her back on the altar. It felt good to literally give God the cold shoulder. When the congregation rose to sing, "Enter, Rejoice, and Come In!" she didn't make a sound.

Later, Father Conklin mounted the stairs to the pulpit. "Forgive us our trespasses as we forgive those who have trespassed against us," he began. "But what does it mean to forgive? Does it mean that we pretend what the person said or did never happened?" *Good luck with that*, Colleen thought.

"Does it mean we downplay the hurt, deny the feelings of betrayal that we have?" A lump swelled in her throat. "Does it mean that the offender should suffer no consequences as a result of what they did?" Colleen felt Derek sneak a look at her. She kept her eyes straight ahead. The priest launched into a long story about two brothers who didn't reconcile until one lay on his deathbed. He closed the sermon by saying, "Forgiveness is an act of compassion, because it is very hard to be hurt by the people we love. But it is also very, very hard to be the person who needs to be forgiven."

Colleen was sure that Derek peeked at her again at that moment, and she was equally certain that his dark eyes were as sad as a dachshund's. She gave the altar another cold stare. *That's Your message? It's very hard to be the person who needs forgiveness?* The priest's final words were, "Remember what you do for the least of my brethren, you do for Me." Colleen recognized the quote; it came at the end of a familiar litany. "I was hungry and you fed me. I was thirsty and you gave me to drink." She frowned. It seemed to her that Father Conklin was implying that they should add another line to that litany: "I betrayed you and you forgave me."

She nearly didn't go to Communion. But when the time came, she followed Izzy out of the pew, muttering to God. *Fine. I'll go through the motions. But if You want me to feel anything, believe anything, You'll have to make that happen.*" On the way back, the wafer sticking to the roof of her mouth, she cast a bitter look toward the crucifix.

The car was an oven by the time church ended, the leather seat burning through the thin linen of Colleen's skirt. Derek made the short drive home with the windows down, but the breeze was hot, and sweat dripped between Colleen's breasts. The heat reminded her that it was nearly August. That brought back memories of her unhappiness last August, when Derek had announced his decision to go to Arizona. *And I thought I was miserable then.*

The moment they returned home, Izzy disappeared to change into shorts. Colleen sat on a stool by the island while Derek flipped pancakes that she knew would lodge in her throat after two bites. He talked fast, describing a training exercise he planned to use with his sales crew, but he kept his eyes averted. He hadn't looked directly at Colleen since the sermon.

After he set the platter on the table, Izzy bounced into the kitchen, her cheeks flushed with excitement. "Ritu's grandpa died!"

Colleen's head jerked up. "What?"

"Ritu's grandpa died. She Skyped me." Izzy grabbed the maple syrup.

"The grandpa who died," Colleen asked, "was that her mother's father, or her dad's father?"

Izzy looked blank. "I don't know."

Colleen sprang up. "I have to call Geeta."

Geeta answered on the fourth ring. Her face loomed at an odd angle on the screen. "Hello, Colleen."

"Geeta, I am so sorry. Izzy just talked to Ritu. She said…" Colleen gulped.

"My father died."

"I'm so sorry, Geeta. I feel so bad."

Geeta looked at her, somber. "You never called me back. You never answered my emails."

Colleen grew hot with shame. "I know. I could tell you I was depressed, which is true, but it's no excuse. I don't know what to say, Geeta. I feel terrible."

"You feel terrible," Geeta repeated in a dull voice. "I have spent the past month caring for my dying father."

Colleen said, "You went to India."

"Of course I went to India." A pause, then Geeta raised her eyes to Colleen. "Did you not even read my emails?" When Colleen failed to answer, Geeta shook her head sadly and leaned her face into the palm of her hand. "I took Ajay with me, and Srini stayed here and took care of Ritu. There weren't many times that I could call the States with the time difference, plus of course I often really couldn't get away, between caring for my dad, mum, and Ajay. But sometimes I needed to tell someone besides Srini how hard it was getting, like when my father was in pain—" She cut herself off.

"I'm so sorry, Geeta. I can't tell you how sorry I am."

Geeta didn't answer. Colleen felt utterly helpless. *It is very hard to be the person who needs forgiveness.* On the screen, Geeta stared into the distance, one fat tear running down her cheek. Colleen's own eyes brimmed. "Please, Geeta," she whispered.

"Remember the day I met you?" Geeta said. "You probably don't even remember this, but I got on that bus for parents for the regionals, and of course there were no other Indians on that bus, only white people. I always tell myself that it doesn't matter; these are just mothers like me. I'd spoken to them at practices, I'd seen their daughters in the gym, so I smiled and started down the aisle, but no one acknowledged me until you looked up and said, 'Want to sit here?' It was so kind of you, Colleen. So welcoming."

Colleen thought, *But I didn't know anyone either. I was afraid no one would sit with me.* She didn't say that. How could she admit that now? Her presumed kindness that day, her supposed generosity, now held their friendship together by the thinnest of threads.

"I know you are not a cruel person, Colleen. But it was cruel not to call me. Not to explain what was the matter, what I had done that you would move away and I would hear nothing from you. Nothing."

"Oh, Geeta, you didn't do anything. It was me; it was all me. My fault."

Geeta looked incredulous. Two little lines creased the space between her eyebrows. "I thought I must have offended you in some way. I went over that last afternoon we were together. I thought there must have been something that I said, or did…or failed to do? But I couldn't come up with anything. I kept thinking, what could I have done that offended you so badly that you would not even answer an email? Not even *read* an email."

Colleen's breath caught. How impotent she felt! How many times could she say that she was sorry before the word lost its meaning? "When I get depressed," she tried to explain, "I get really bad. I can't eat or sleep. I'm awake until the middle of the night, and then I can hardly get up in the morning. And this was a bad depression, Geeta, the worst I've ever had. I just had to hide away, from everyone." She raised desperate eyes to her friend.

A long minute passed before Geeta responded. "I need more time," she said.

Colleen opened her mouth to tell Geeta that she understood, she wasn't asking for anything more right now, but before she could speak, Geeta ended the call, and the screen went blank.

Usually Derek left right after Izzy went to bed, but that Sunday the thermometer barely dropped below 90 even after the sun set, and Colleen said, "I'm going to make myself a strawberry-banana smoothie. You want one before you go?"

They sat on opposite ends of the couch, Derek with his legs outstretched on the ottoman, but angled so that he faced her. Colleen tucked her feet under her and hazarded a glance in her husband's direction. "I've been thinking about this morning's sermon. I don't know what it means to forgive. I used to know. But I don't anymore." She looked away from Derek's steady gaze. "I don't know how to act with you. Or feel about you." She busied herself wiping some condensation from her glass. Her smoothie was so cold it almost hurt to swallow. She took a tiny sip.

Derek said, "I'd be grateful if you'd just look at me once in a while. Because most of the time, you don't. You turn away. Like you just did." His hands flapped open in a helpless gesture.

"I hate it when you do that!" Colleen cried, swiveling back to face him. "Make me the bad guy." She shook her head. "I can't help how I feel about you. How do you expect me to feel?"

Derek sighed. "I don't expect anything, Col. That's what I'm learning. Not to expect anything." He rubbed his hand across his forehead. "I get it," he went on. "I get that you don't see me when you look at me. You don't even see a person. You see a monster."

Colleen flinched. Remembering how she'd felt just that

morning, when Derek had given her that thumbs up, she said, "Sometimes I do see you. Sometimes I almost forget. And I see…how you used to be."

Derek's dark eyes brightened. He ran his fingers through his hair, the way he did when he was thinking hard. "Do you remember what you told me once about gay people?"

"Gay people?"

"A few years ago. Before they legalized gay marriage? And you were all, 'I don't know what to think.' Because the church said homosexuality was a sin, but then you heard some radio show where they interviewed some gay people. And you said that what they did seemed unnatural to you, but it was natural to them." He gave her a long look. "You said that you couldn't judge them for feeling something they didn't choose to feel."

Colleen stiffened. "I see where you're going with this. It's not the same."

"I'm not saying it's the same, Col. All I'm saying is that I'm just people, too. I'm a person. I'm a person who did a really terrible thing that I'll regret until the day I die. But I'm more than the worst thing I've ever done. I'm not garbage."

Not garbage. Colleen wondered: Could she see him, no longer split into the good Derek she remembered and the monster she'd learned about? Could she see a good person who was terribly, terribly flawed, and so had done terrible things? But still a person. Not garbage. "Did you ever go to confession?"

Derek drummed his fingers on the couch cushion. "I tried to."

"Oh, Derek!"

Now it was he who turned away from her, picked up his smoothie and sipped. After he'd returned the glass to the table, he slumped so much that his chin nearly touched his chest. "I was too ashamed."

She made a disgusted sound. "I suppose you never tried to get help from anyone else, either."

"I couldn't, Col. They might have reported me. And where would that have left you and the girls, if I'd gone to prison?"

He didn't say it aloud, but the fear in his eyes said *and where would that have left me? A convicted pedophile in prison.* He seemed to take her silence for understanding, or at least a sign that she wanted to understand, because he launched into a long description of websites he'd gone to, searching for help and advice from these anonymous sources.

"I didn't want to have those feelings," he said. "At first, I kind of discounted them. I thought, they couldn't, I don't know, they couldn't be *me*. It took me a long time to admit: this is who I am."

The phrase struck Colleen. She'd sometimes used similar words, "That's just who I am," to defend herself after losing her temper. Surely Derek wasn't using that as an excuse, was he?

Derek was going on about "virtuous pedophiles," men who had these urges but never, ever acted on them. The expression seemed a contradiction in terms to Colleen, and she said so.

"You wouldn't feel that way, Col," Derek answered, "if you read what some of the men on this site write, how they struggle, how committed they are to never hurting a child. I mean, think of it. A lot of them aren't attracted to adult women at all, so basically, they're committed to never having a relationship, never having a lover. And they've never crossed that line, not even once. You can't even join this site if you've ever touched a child."

"But you did." She gazed at him steadily. "That's the thing, Derek. Even if I could live with the idea that you have these…urges, how can I live with the fact that you acted on them?"

"I lost control, Col."

"That doesn't excuse it!"

"I'm not saying it excuses it. I'm just trying to explain. I mean, you of all people know what it's like to lose control." The moment the words were out of his mouth, he tried to take them back. "I don't mean it that way. I know you never hurt our girls."

"Don't you dare make this about me!"

"I'm not. I'm sorry; I didn't mean to. You get upset,

you throw things, but I know you've never hurt the kids and you never would."

The image of bruises on Izzy's arm flashed through Colleen's mind. She told herself it wasn't the same and shifted her attention back to Derek. "If you're not trying to excuse yourself, what are you trying to do? You don't want to face any consequences. Just like at first you wouldn't admit it when Rachel told you what she remembered." She could tell from his taken-aback look that he didn't know Rachel had told her all about that phone call.

"Colleen," he said. "Hear me out for a minute, would you? I probably *was* trying to protect myself. It was instinctive, you know? A reaction to the shock of hearing something I never thought I'd hear. But I swear to God, the main thing in my head was how to protect you." His fingers stopped their nervous tapping, and his voice grew gentle. "What has ever mattered more to you than creating the happy family that you never had growing up? I thought, what good would all this truth-telling do, compared to the harm? Harm to you and to Izzy. And, yeah, to me, too. I didn't want to add the guilt of hurting you to the guilt I already had."

Colleen's head swam. "You haven't lived like you were crushed by guilt. You've lived your life like it never happened."

"That's true. In a way, that's true," he admitted. "More

and more time went by, and I didn't see anything terrible coming from it. Rachel seemed fine, didn't even remember. I told myself no major harm had been done; I'd stopped it so soon. So, yeah, I didn't dwell on it, but that doesn't mean that I ever stopped wishing I had acted differently. I just didn't let myself think about it, most of the time." He searched her face. "I don't know if you can understand that."

But of course she could understand that. That was the easiest part of this whole sad story to understand. "How clever of you," she answered, "to know just how to get to me."

Derek sighed. "The more I try to explain, the more you think I'm trying to manipulate you." A long silence followed. "Why do you think that? Have I ever been some kind of conniver, trying to change you?"

"You try to calm me down when I'm upset," she pointed out.

"Okay. True. But how do I do that? Not by trying to talk you out of your feelings. I accept them, let you have them. I just stay with you while you go through them, so you know you're not alone."

Not alone. It was true; she knew that what Derek was saying was true. A vivid memory came to her then, of crouching behind the couch in a darkened room, and Derek coming to her…

A storm had brewed that night, howling winds beating

against black windows. The murky shadows in the living room took on a sinister quality. She reached out a hand and turned the lamp off, wanting to darken the room because it seemed that only total blackness could hide her and keep her safe. When a particularly violent gust rattled the window nearest her, she dropped to the floor like a frightened animal. Crawling, she backed into the narrow space between the wall and the couch, and crouched there, pressed in so tightly that she could barely take a full breath. She waited desperately for the creak of the front door, Derek returning. Yet when she heard him come in, she didn't make a sound. His footsteps—going up the stairs and, a bit later, coming down again, moving to the kitchen, and then back to the front hallway—inexplicably frightened her. She listened with a thudding heart.

Derek called out softly, "Colleen?"

Her whimper alerted him.

"Colleen?" The lamp on the end table flickered, shedding light into the opening to her tunnel. A strangled cry escaped her throat. In the next moment, Derek dropped to his knees and peered in at her. "Col?" He shifted the couch.

"Don't make me come out!" she cried.

"I'll come to you. Okay?" He waited for her nod before he started toward her.

"My mother has lung cancer." He enfolded her in his arms. "Don't make me come out," she repeated.

He rocked her. "We can sit here together as long as you need."

The memory receded, and Colleen blinked. She grew aware of Derek, waiting as patiently now as he had that night. "I know you're not a monster," she whispered. "I know you're better than the worst thing you ever did."

When he raised his eyes to her, she met his gaze. But she held onto her heart tightly, keeping some essential part of herself aloof. Because letting his humanity touch her too deeply felt perilous.

Chapter 25

Rachel settled back in the corduroy chair in her therapist's office. Watching the angelfish swim in and out of the pale green ferns, she tried to decide what to talk about. For the past several weeks, she'd discussed her anxiety, her frustration with her mother, the faltering steps she and Aaron were taking to regain the closeness they'd had before he told her about the possible rape he'd seen. An indigo guppy darted out of a rock formation, and it struck Rachel that the problems she'd discussed were like the greenery where the fish hid. They were real, they were issues she needed to find her way through like the guppy threading through the fronds now, but they were also camouflage for what Mandy called *the real problem.* "When," Mandy had demanded, "are you going to tell Monica what your father did?"

Rachel's favorite guppy, the one with the crimson-and-indigo tail that flared out like a swirling skirt, meandered around the tank. She wished Monica would say something, but the therapist appeared content to wait for whatever unfolded. *Maybe it would have been easier*, Rachel thought, *if I had just blurted it out the first time I came here.* She let out a breath. "There's something I need to tell you about."

Her guppy glided by. "I don't know why I didn't say anything about this before." Her face heated up, and she snuck a glance at Monica. Her therapist's expression revealed nothing but quiet interest. "In the spring, I remembered something." Perhaps the sun had come out from behind a cloud, because suddenly the brightness of the room hurt Rachel's eyes, and she unzipped her backpack and retrieved her sunglasses. When she slid them on, dimness surrounded her like a soft, velvet cloak.

"I know this happened," she began, "but sometimes, even now, I can't believe it. It feels so unreal, so distant. Sometimes I even think maybe it doesn't really matter. Maybe I'm making a big deal out of nothing." Her words tumbled out faster. "But then I think of the shame I've experienced, and how I feel so abnormal, and how I can't sleep. There's something the matter with me, how scared I've always been of boys. Then I think *fine,* who cares? Who needs it, sex and love…but I have that now with Aaron, to some extent, and I don't want to lose it, and I'm afraid that talking about this it will make it real, and I won't be able to—"

Rachel stopped talking and did some of the deep

breathing Monica had taught her. Finally, she forced herself to say the words out loud. "My father abused me when I was a child." She peered through her dark glasses, trying to make out the expression on Monica's face. Perhaps Monica had leaned forward; perhaps she looked a little more concerned. Rachel explained, "It's all so vague—just bits and pieces. Like, I can tell you what I remembered in my aunt's bathroom and then on the train, and then what I remembered when I talked to him, how we had this secret." She recounted those details, then asked, "Is it important? To remember more about what he did? Because I don't really remember the part about him touching me, except maybe, I don't know. The feeling of skin…"

A wave of nausea cut off her words. "I know that he never—he never penetrated me. I think mostly he had me touch him, under the covers. I do remember him moving my hand under the covers, and my surprise that I felt *hair* down there. And then my surprise that something popped up so I guess that's when he put my hand on him, but I'm not sure. I think he put his hand over mine, and I guess then he must have moved my hand, you know, up and down, but I don't really remember that. That's what I mean; it's like a film that someone spliced helter-skelter, and all I have are disconnected bits and pieces."

She stopped, because suddenly she could feel the small bones of her hand being crushed, even while her father's steel grip jerked her hand up and down. "He squeezed my hand too hard, and I told him that hurt, but he didn't stop." She looked through her dark glasses at Monica's shadowy form. "He squeezed my hand too hard." She began to cry. She didn't realize that she was cradling one hand in the other until Monica came over, sat on the footstool near her chair and enfolded Rachel's hands in her own.

Rachel's nose started dripping. She pulled her hand from Monica's and grabbed tissues from the box on the side table. She blew her nose and took her sunglasses off to wipe her eyes, and then she stared at Monica, whose kind gray eyes looked back at her.

"Why didn't I stop him? Why didn't I tell my mom?"

Monica took Rachel's hands into her own again. "You were eight years old. You had this 'special time,' this 'my lips are sealed' secret with your father."

"I was special to him," Rachel said. "I mean, not just special time, but special *me*." The feel of her father's tight grasp on her hand came back to her again, and her bottom lip trembled. "I hate these flashbacks."

"Of course you do," Monica said. "They're painful and upsetting. But they're helpful, too. Often trauma memories are stored in your body. Your body is telling us what happened to you."

Rachel recalled how she had clawed the couch, and how that had brought back the memory of mauling the sheets on her bed. "Yes," she answered. "I understand that. I do." She swallowed hard. "But what if I don't want to remember?"

Monica rested her chin in her hand. "Do you recall what I told you your first session? In here, you're the one who controls where we go and how fast we travel. We don't have to excavate your memories as fast as possible, as if there's a treasure chest at the bottom with a road map to your recovery. We don't necessarily have to excavate them at all. But when things come up spontaneously, it's good to bring them in here. They'll help us understand what you need to deal with, and they'll help us figure out how you can do that."

Monica sounded so reasonable. She meant to be reassuring; Rachel knew that. And Monica cared about her, genuinely wanted to help her. Rachel believed that, too. She should nod in agreement now. She should force a smile. Instead, she cried, "I really hate this! I hate it."

Monica leaned so far forward that Rachel could have touched her. "Rachel, what is the 'this' that you hate? What is the 'it' that you hate?"

A moment passed before the words pounding in Rachel's head burst from her lips. "I hate that it's real." She leveled a look at Monica. "You think that I hate my father. I don't hate my father. I love my father."

Rachel lowered her forehead almost to her knees. "But I don't want to love him."

Chapter 26

Heading back from their walk, Colleen and her friends came to a point where the prairie path narrowed, and tree limbs formed a dripping canopy over the pinched track. At the head of their line, Rose and Letitia had been talking quietly, but now Rose's voice grew loud. "I don't see how anyone can stay a Catholic these days."

The group came to a standstill as the two friends faced each other. "The Catholic Church isn't the only one that's had scandals," Letitia answered.

Rose made a sound of disgust. "But so many! Come on, Letitia. And the cover-ups." Rose ducked her head and went deeper into the leafy tunnel.

Colleen held back to trail behind the group, and barely heard Letitia's argument. Just ahead of her, she saw Pat, whose crown of gray hair glistened with drops from the drooping leaves. Colleen focused on the crunch of wet gravel under her feet, ignoring the faint murmur of conversation that continued at the front of the line. Then

Rose twisted her head and shouted, "I'd like to castrate every one of them. And every father, every uncle, every brother, too." Breathing hard, Colleen concentrated on the muddy ridges at the sides of the path and the slippery leaves underfoot. Letitia made a comment that she couldn't catch. But then Rose turned and her voice rang out again. "Of course the mothers know!" Colleen glimpsed Rose's face, framed by her dark hair, her mouth a red slash. "How could anyone not know?" she called out.

In front of Colleen, Pat turned away from Rose, and Colleen found herself staring right into the older woman's eyes.

Rose's voice, insistent and righteous, demanded, "You'd know, right? If someone was doing that to your child?"

Colleen flushed a deep red.

"It makes me sick," Rose exclaimed, then strode forward, and the group moved again. Colleen bent her head down and watched her feet plod along. The next thing she knew, she had slammed into Pat. Pat staggered against the branches of a tall bush, and Colleen held out a hand to steady her. For a moment, the two women regarded one another. Colleen flamed to the roots of her hair. "I have to get out of here," she choked.

Rose's voice filtered back toward them, faint but discernable: "Well, if they didn't know, they should have known."

"I have to go," Colleen repeated, twisting away.

Pat put a plump hand on Colleen's arm. "If you leave now, they'll wonder where you went. They'll wonder why."

"Tell them I felt sick." Colleen swiveled again, but Pat latched onto her elbow. "They'll turn back to stay with you. They'll want to make sure you're all right." Her brow furrowed. "Hang on." With that, Pat unclasped the gold chain around her neck and flung it back toward the area they had just passed. "Go look for it," she directed. "Go as far as you can down there." Then Pat spun around. "Hey, guys! Hang on! I lost my necklace."

No one paid any attention to Colleen's burning face as they focused, heads down, on the trail. Pat kept up a constant patter. "I've got to find it; the locket was my grandmother's and then my mom's." By the time Jackie yelled, "Here it is!" Colleen's face had cooled down.

When the path widened again, Colleen slipped next to Jackie. They talked about Aaliyah and Izzy, and whether or not they should involve them in more organized activities or let the rest of the summer stay unstructured. On and off, Pat hovered at Colleen's elbow and cast concerned glances her way. Colleen stayed glued to Jackie until the women approached their starting point, then abruptly called out, "See you," and headed toward her lilac bushes.

But Pat pursued her, tripping up to her and then

staying alongside, even when Colleen picked up her pace and almost ran through the opening in the bushes to her yard.

"Colleen?" the older woman called out. "Can I come in a minute?"

She wanted to say no. She wanted to turn her back on the dangerous mix of sympathy and eagerness to talk that she heard in Pat's voice. But then she thought of how Pat had tossed that chain to distract the others. *A kind person,* she told herself. *And she doesn't know anything, not for sure.* She could pour them each a glass of iced tea and say of course Rose's comments had upset her, she was a devout Catholic…

They reached the stairs. "Come on in," Colleen said.

Inside, Pat wandered to the kitchen table and inspected the quilting book there. "I used to quilt, a long time ago. Before my hands got too arthritic."

Colleen made a quick circuit to the refrigerator. "You want some iced tea?" From the corner of her eye, she saw Pat move to the African violets. Sunlight fell across the delicate pink and blue blooms.

"I never had much luck with these," Pat said. She began talking very quickly. "I did everything people said you should do; I even bought grow lights. The plants still died. My sister thought I put the lights on *too* much. But she was the one who told me to buy them in the first place. I do what she says, and she still finds a way to criticize."

Colleen set the pitcher of iced tea on the island. "People can be very judgmental."

After a long pause, Pat said, "Almost everyone thinks like Rose." She fiddled with her gold chain. "Everyone thinks the mother should have known. Must have known."

Colleen breathed harder and poured tea over ice cubes in two tall glasses. She carried their drinks to the table, color rising again in her cheeks. Pat rested her hands on the back of a kitchen chair and gave Colleen a nervous look. "Don't you find it hard, not to have anyone you can talk to? I mean anyone you know wouldn't judge you? I'd find that hard."

At least, that's what Colleen thought she had said. But then Pat added, "I find it hard, to be so alone with it." *I find it hard.* Not *I would find it hard.*

Colleen stared at the older woman for a long moment. "I do find it hard," she whispered.

Pat plopped onto the chair. Her mouth trembled, and the smile she attempted melted away. "There's never been anyone I could tell." Pat emitted a bark of a laugh. "I'm sorry," she said at Colleen's startle. "It's just such a shocking idea. To tell someone after all these years." She squeezed a lemon wedge into her tea and stirred. "I don't know where to start."

Colleen fidgeted with a napkin, moved the quilt book further down the table, and nudged a plate of oatmeal cookies closer to the center. "How did you find out?"

Pat gazed into the yard. "In those days," she began, "we lived in this tiny two-bedroom apartment. The boys in the bedroom down the hall, the girls just off the living room. That was the thing. When we opened the hide-a-bed for me and Joe in the living room, it almost touched the television next to the girls' bedroom door. How could I have imagined anything happening behind a door six feet in front of me?"

"You couldn't have," Colleen assured her. "No one would have."

Pat opened her mouth, then seemed to think better of whatever she'd been about to say and shut it again. She took a sip of tea. "Most nights we did watch TV. Joe sat there after dinner and watched sitcoms and game shows and drank a few beers. He never got drunk. He wasn't an alcoholic. It was just what he did, how he relaxed, in the evenings."

Pat twisted her gold chain around her finger. With a determined look on her face, she went on. "Joe always tucked the girls in. He'd go into the bedroom and read them a story. He started that when Ellen was four or five, and then he kept it up with Katie. Katie had a hard time sleeping, scared of monsters and boogeymen and who knew what else."

A flash came to Colleen of Rachel's nightmares, her terrified cries in the night. She pushed the memory away.

"I was grateful," Pat went on, "that Joe would sit with Katie until she fell asleep. I thought that's why he stayed in there such a long time. It was the same thing he'd done with Ellen when she was younger. I never thought a thing about it." Pat threw a challenging look in Colleen's direction. "I never thought a thing about it."

With an abruptness that startled Colleen, Pat scraped her chair back. "Where's your bathroom?" she asked. Her eyes had turned red-rimmed, though no tears spilled from them. Colleen half-stood and pointed, then watched Pat move stiffly down the hall. *Don't fall apart. If you fall apart, I will too.*

When she returned, Pat said, "I've wished there was someone I could talk to about this so many times." Her chest rose and fell under her floral top. "It's just hard to say the words."

"Of course it is," Colleen answered. Then she waited, the way Geeta used to wait for her. Like an open hand.

Pat swallowed. "The night this happened, Katie was nine. I could hear her crying and Joe hushing her from behind the bedroom door. But she didn't stop. It made me mad. Why did I have to do everything? Finally, I pushed the door open. Joe tried to wave me out of the room, like 'I've got it,' you know? But Katie sobbed and reached out to me, so I sat on her bed and asked, 'Sweetheart, what's the matter?' and she said, 'I don't like the way Daddy touches me.'"

"Oh, Pat!"

Pat went on as if she hadn't heard. "You could have knocked me over with a feather. I had talked to the girls about stranger danger, all that stuff. And not just strangers, either. I'd talked about uncles, cousins… told them, it doesn't matter who it is, you know? I was stunned. I couldn't take it in. I said, 'What do you mean, honey?' and Joe says, 'Nothing, she's just upset, I hugged her too hard or something.' And I might have believed him. I wanted to believe him. But Ellen had come to the doorway by then. She'd been in the kitchen, doing her homework. She was fourteen. She looks at me, and these are the exact words she says, I'll never forget them. She says, 'Dad is feeling her up. I know the difference between hugging and feeling someone up. I know what Dad's doing because he did it to me for years.'"

Colleen yearned to slam her hands against her ears.

Pat pressed a hand to her heaving bosom. "Joe tried to say something, but I yelled at him to get out of the room, so it was just me rocking Katie, who was still crying, while Ellen sat next to the two of us on Katie's bed. A minute later, Joe stuck his head inside the door, but before he could say anything, I yelled, 'I'm getting a divorce.' And all hell broke loose." Pat shook her head at the memory. "Katie was wailing, 'No, Mommy, I didn't mean it, Daddy didn't do anything.' Ellen shook so hard that the mattress jerked. I told them, 'Don't cry, don't worry, everything will be okay.' I sat on Katie's bed for what seemed like hours until she fell asleep, and I waited there until Ellen slept too. When I finally left the bedroom, the TV was off and the living room was empty. Joe had pulled out the hide-a-bed and put our pillows on it, turned the sheet and blanket down, like they do in a hotel. I heard sounds from the kitchen.

"The stink of beer hit me halfway down the hall. Joe stood at the kitchen sink, emptying one beer can after the other down the drain." Pat looked up and appealed to Colleen. "He stopped drinking that night. He blamed it all on the liquor, and promised he'd never touch another drop. He told me that none of this would have happened if he'd been sober." Pat grabbed Colleen's wrist, her blunt fingers digging into her flesh. "I wanted to believe him. Can you understand that?"

Colleen found the pressure of Pat's grip distasteful, but she forced herself to stay still because Pat held on as if Colleen's hand was a life-line.

"I was 17 when Joe stormed into my house and told my dad that he'd beat the crap out of him if he ever hit me again." As if coming back to herself, Pat loosened her hold. "Six months later, we were married. And here I am, after almost fifty years."

"Fifty years," Colleen murmured.

Pat jerked back.

"I'm not criticizing," Colleen rushed to say. "I'm just wondering how you did it."

Pat took a minute with that. She looked like she was considering various possibilities before she answered. "I decided that the Joe I loved didn't do that. Beer Joe did that. And Beer Joe didn't live there anymore. I lived with a man who looked and acted like the man I loved, treated me even better than he had before, never drank. That man was not Beer Joe, the… the pedophile." She hurried past the word. "That's what I told myself. After a while, it was as if… not as if what he did never happened, but as if that other person had done it."

"So," Colleen stammered. "Eventually the love came back?"

After a long moment, Pat sighed. "We all settle, Colleen. How many couples do you know who are truly happy after fifteen, twenty years of marriage? And most of them never have to deal with anything like what happened to us. Most just bump along, avoid the potholes that lead to big fights, enjoy the times when things go smoothly. What Joe and I had—it was never what we'd had before. But it was pretty much what I saw all around me. It was better than what some had."

"And your girls?"

A philosophical shrug from Pat. "Katie would be glad to never see her father again. But Joe walked Ellen down the aisle at her wedding."

Down the aisle. Colleen tried to imagine Rachel in a bridal gown, reconciled with her father.

They sipped their tea in silence, nibbling the cookies. At length, Pat asked, "What about you?"

Quid pro quo, Colleen thought. It was only fair that she too should tell her story. "The light of our lives," she told Pat. "That's who Derek was. When he came home with his teasing and his silliness, it could be pitch-black outside, but it felt like light flooded the house when he opened that door." She raised her gaze to Pat. "How could I have been so blind?" She posed the question as if the older woman might actually be able to answer it. But Pat just rested her chin in the palm of her hand and waited.

"Izzy still lights up when her dad walks in the door," Colleen went on. "Sometimes, when she tells me, 'Daddy this, Daddy that,' in that adoring voice, I want to shake her. I want to say, let me tell you about your precious father, and see if you still think the sun rises and sets with him." The bitterness in her voice took Colleen aback. "Forgiveness is a big deal in my religion," she added. "But I've been telling God He better show me how to do that, because I don't know how."

"You still pray?" Pat said. "I never set foot in a church again."

A worm of resentment turned in Colleen. Pat had no faith, and yet she had managed to sustain her marriage, her family.

"How did you find out?" Pat asked.

Colleen felt the sharp edge of the cookie piece she'd just

swallowed force its way down her throat. She gulped some iced tea before she began the story of Rachel recovering her memories. She'd just told Pat how Derek now pretended to still live at home when the deck doors slid open, and Izzy bounced into the kitchen.

"Yum! Oatmeal cookies. Do we have milk?" She trotted across the room and peered into the refrigerator.

Pat rose. "I should get going." She gave Colleen a quick hug and slipped out the patio doors.

Izzy poured milk into a plastic cup. "Can I go over to Aaliyah's?"

Colleen nodded. After Izzy left, she selected Brahms on her playlist, and the music filled the kitchen. She buried her face in her hands. Pat's marriage wasn't perfect, but she'd sustained it for fifty years. And one of her daughters had forgiven her father. Wasn't that a sign that forgiveness was possible? Yet Pat had no faith. *So, what's that about?*

Colleen directed the question to God, but God remained silent.

You better not be giving me false hope, she warned Him.

Chapter 27

Colleen watched Izzy show Derek how to manipulate the pulleys at one of the water tables. Her bare feet on the artificial turf, Izzy told her dad, "You pull this rope and I pull the other one, then the water makes a funnel down here." Derek patiently followed Izzy's lead to navigate a ship through locks and dams, but Izzy kept mistiming the release of the water.

"Oh, Izzy!" Colleen protested, seeing water spray and a damp blot spread across the front of Izzy's red t-shirt. Derek winked and splashed Izzy, soaking her even more. Then he pulled her, laughing, to the bank of hairdryers where children dried their clothes.

Izzy turned the hair dryer on her father. He pretended to be upset that she'd mussed his hair. Izzy giggled and flashed a smile at Colleen. When Derek chased Izzy around the water obstacle course, she twisted around to mist him with her squirt gun. Colleen thought of all the times she'd wondered how she could have been so blind to what Derek had been doing. The scene before her seemed like the answer to that question. When Izzy shot a spray of mist at her father, and then whooped at his pursuit, Colleen lifted her phone and captured the chase on film. Replaying it, she couldn't help smiling. In a burst of optimism, Colleen forwarded the clip to Rachel with the text, *Maybe we can get through this.*

Rachel's brief response came hours later, just before the family left Water World. "Good to know that *you* are doing okay." Colleen's brow furrowed. Was Rachel implying that she herself was not doing okay? If only she had seen her father and Izzy in real life instead of in a 40-second clip. But Rachel had refused Colleen's invitation to join them, saying she had to work.

It was a little after five o'clock now. "Hey," Colleen said when the family reached their car in the parking lot. "Why don't we eat at the Mexican Grill? It's not that far. And when Rachel's shift ends, we could go see her apartment."

Izzy leapt in the air. "Yes!"

Derek frowned. "I don't know, Col. Did you ask her?"

"I can text her, but she won't answer unless she's on break. Which isn't likely, since she's off in an hour. I think it'll be all right." She thought of Rachel's message. *Glad you are doing okay.* A friendly response. "She sent me a nice text a little while ago."

Izzy jumped up and down. "Please, Daddy, can we?"

"I think it will be all right," Colleen said. "I really do."

While Izzy continued to tug on her father's hand, Colleen allowed herself one brief, rosy fantasy: Rachel brightening when she spotted her family coming into the Mexican Grill, and leading them, with self-assured pride, to a table in her area.

But the restaurant turned out to be less upscale than Colleen had pictured, and overly chilly, the way so many restaurants were in August. A young man with a streak of green in his hair and an eyebrow ring took their order at a counter, then handed Colleen a numbered sign. She scanned the noisy room while they meandered between the packed tables, but Rachel was nowhere in sight. Noticing a group gathering up their belongings, Colleen shot over to claim their table. She wrinkled her nose at the bits of chips and salsa that littered the tabletop.

Just before he slid into his seat, Derek's phone vibrated. "The realtor," he told her. Wiping the table with a napkin from the dispenser, Colleen tilted her head to catch his conversation. Despite the din of the restaurant, she heard enough of Derek's call to realize that the most recent offer on their Arizona home had fallen through.

"Okay," Derek told the realtor. "Go ahead and shave five thousand off the asking price and relist it."

Colleen shook her head in dismay. "It's been on the market more than four months."

"It'll sell, Col." Derek gave her a smile meant to

reassure. "It's just a temporary setback." But his fingers tapped the black plastic tabletop nervously, and she wondered how long they could manage two mortgage payments.

Just then, Izzy squealed. "There's Rachel!" Izzy half-stood at her seat, craning her neck to see her sister lift a tray of platters from the countertop. Colleen gave a little wave and beamed at Rachel. In the next moment, Rachel recognized them. Her expression shifted from surprise to alarm to a moue of distaste.

When she got to their table, Rachel turned a stiff back to Colleen and set Izzy's tacos down. "Hey, Iz."

"Hey," Izzy responded, rocking a little on her chair. "We're going to see your apartment after we eat."

"Really," Rachel said. Her voice was flat, and her back shut Colleen out. "Whose idea was that?" Before Izzy could respond, Rachel swiveled and smacked Colleen's plate down roughly. Grains of rice scattered on the table. Then she shoved her father's tostados across to him.

Colleen said, "We were practically in your neighborhood—"

Rachel stalked away, threading through the tables back to the kitchen.

They ate in silence. Even the loud chatter around them couldn't drown out the heavy stillness that fell over their table. A dark cloud of depression weighed on Colleen, and she pushed her food aside. But during the next few minutes, the cloud churned into an angry storm. Couldn't Rachel at least be civil? Was that asking so much? Most mothers would have been invited to see their daughter's first apartment long before now. An apartment that she and Derek had partly paid for! Colleen shoved back so hard her chair banged another at the table behind them. She ignored the startled, "Watch it!" of the young woman sitting there, and strode toward her daughter, who was now serving customers in the far corner of the room. Colleen blazed her way through the crowd. Turning away from the table she had just served, Rachel almost rammed into her mother.

"I thought this would be a fun surprise," Colleen sputtered.

"Mom, I'm *working.*" Rachel glared, then glanced around the room.

"Can't you just be civil—"

"See that woman who's staring at us?" Rachel interrupted. A frizzy-haired woman leaning near the end of the ordering counter squinted in their direction. "That's my boss. I can't stand around talking to you."

"But you can throw food onto our table. You're not worried about what your boss thinks of that."

Rachel answered Colleen through clenched teeth. "I'll talk to you after my shift."

Back with her family, Colleen avoided Derek's questioning glances, and Izzy's "What happened? Are we still going to Rachel's?" Instead, she studied her phone and picked at her food.

The August heat outside came as a relief after the chill of the restaurant. Her heart pounding, Colleen watched the door for Rachel. Izzy, nut-brown from hours in the summer sun, twirled around a telephone pole, but the moment Rachel emerged, Izzy rushed to her sister's side. "Dad said he could drive us to your apartment."

Behind her dark glasses, Rachel dismissed the idea with a shake of her head. "There's never any parking near my place. I walk."

"We can walk with you!" Izzy said. "Can't we, Mom?"

Rachel stepped away from all of them. For a moment, Colleen feared she'd stalk off alone. But when Izzy reached her hand out, Rachel clasped Izzy's hand and led her down the street. Colleen and Derek trailed behind. Derek slumped, a resigned look on his face. "Go up there with them," Colleen told him.

"Col…"

"Just *try*. Please. You don't have to talk. Just walk with them."

He shook his head despondently, but he quickened his pace and caught up with his daughters. Rachel came to a halt the second Derek reached them. Colleen watched Rachel's body tauten. She kept her face averted from her father. Izzy took Derek's hand, placing herself between the two of them. Together, the three moved forward a few steps. But then Rachel dropped her sister's hand and waved them off, turning back to walk with Colleen.

The moment her daughter reached her, Colleen blurted, "You can't walk with your dad for ten minutes? Meet him halfway?"

"Oh, my God, Mom." Rachel pursed her lips, then said, "I meet him halfway every day I don't go to the police. Every day I don't tell Izzy."

Colleen jerked back. *Tell Izzy?* She had to get a grip before she could speak. "I'm not begging just for his sake. If you'd let yourself see your father, see how bad he feels, how he'd do anything for you, I think it would help you."

Rachel came to a standstill and gave her mother a long, searching look. A lake breeze ruffled the dark tunic that covered her black leggings. "I'm never going to forgive him for what he did."

"You don't know that," Colleen protested. She yearned to tell Rachel about Pat's daughter, but how could she betray Pat's confidence? Suddenly inspired, she said, "I read this advice column the other day. A letter from a daughter who experienced…the same kind of thing you did. It took a long time, but in the end, she forgave her father. He walked her down the aisle on her wedding day."

Rachel made a disgusted sound. "What a charade that would be."

They were passing a large park now, and Colleen noticed that Izzy and Derek had drifted onto the grass, playing a kind of hide and seek, ducking behind trees. "But maybe it's not a charade," she pleaded. "Maybe sometimes things really do get better. That's all I was hoping for. For things to get a little better, not even so much for your dad. But for you." She shook her head. "If you could understand how terrible he feels, how much he wishes he could fix this."

"Well, he can't," Rachel answered sharply. "He can't fix it. And you pushing him into my life—bringing him where I work, for God's sake—is not helping."

"You're so angry, Rach." Colleen took a breath to build up her courage. "Sometimes forgiveness can just mean letting go of your anger. Because your anger is killing you."

Rachel gave a bitter laugh. "I think my anger is killing *you*, because you can't get what you want. You pretend your concern is all about me, but it's not. It's about you. You just don't know how to center me. You've never been able to center me."

A wave of impatience ran through Colleen. "I don't even know what that means. *'Center'* you."

They were past the park now, back to where stores dotted the street, and the cars sat nose-to-trunk in the metered spaces. Rachel said, "You start by accepting what I feel. You try to understand what it's like to be me instead of trying to make me see what it's like to be you or dad. For me, some things are unforgiveable."

Colleen glanced back and spotted Derek and Izzy quite

a distance behind them, peering into a store window. In a careful voice, she said, "You remember it as something unforgiveable."

They'd arrived at the red door that led into Rachel's building. "What's that supposed to mean?"

Colleen sent up a wordless prayer before she spoke. "Maybe it wasn't as bad as you remember. Don't you think that class might have affected you?"

Rachel's mouth dropped open. "Dad himself *told* you…"

"I'm not doubting you. I'm just saying. Like you said, it's all hazy, bits and pieces, and if it wasn't as bad as you think, then maybe your feelings about your father could change."

Rachel's eyes widened in astonishment. "You're building a house of cards. One breath and it will all collapse."

Izzy ran down the street toward them, dragging her father by the hand and shouting, "Wait for us! Wait for us!" She skidded to a stop just as Rachel put the key in her lock.

"You can come up," Rachel told her sister. "But Mom and Dad are going to wait down here."

"Why?" Izzy asked.

Colleen froze. Rachel's earlier phrase rang in her ears. *I meet him halfway every day I don't tell Izzy.* "You go on up, Izzy," Colleen said. "I don't feel well. I think the stairs might be too much for me." She started to say something else, but Rachel cut her off.

"I don't want Dad in my apartment, Iz. That's why."

Derek's head jerked back as if she'd slapped him. "Rachel," he pleaded.

Rachel pushed her sleeves up to her elbows, baring her forearms, and began scratching at them. Colleen heard the scrape of Rachel's nails across her skin.

"I don't want your shoes on my stairs," Rachel told her father. "I don't want your jeans on my couch. I don't want your mouth on my water glass."

Droplets of blood oozed where Rachel dug into the same reddened line. "I don't want anything you've touched to touch me."

Colleen put her hands on Izzy's shoulders and drew her back.

Izzy cried, "What happened? Why is everyone mad?"

Colleen tightened her arms across Izzy's chest. At the same time, she longed to let go of Izzy and reach out to Rachel, stop Rachel from gouging herself. The three of them stood facing Rachel, Izzy's back pressed against Colleen, Derek still as a statue at her side. Izzy began to cry. "Why is everyone mad?"

Rachel quivered in front of Colleen, a dangerous amalgam of power and fury. "Good question," she said. "You guys want to tell her?"

It seemed to Colleen that, with one wrong word, Rachel

might erupt and spew the whole sordid story into Izzy's small, shell-like ears. She tightened her grip on Izzy's shoulders.

Rachel spat out, "I didn't think so."

Colleen watched her own arm, as if detached from her, stretch toward Rachel over Izzy's shoulder.

Rachel backed away and slammed the red door shut. It loomed in Colleen's face like an open, screaming mouth.

Chapter 28

Rachel had feared that talking in therapy about what her father had done might trigger more flashbacks. She was especially afraid that those might rear up when she was with Aaron and contaminate the feelings she experienced with him. But one day followed another that September, and none of her fears materialized. She and Aaron sped down bicycle trails and hiked in the Morton Arboretum. They raced hand in hand down the Indiana sand dunes until they tumbled, laughing, into a heap at the bottom. And in the bedroom, she had only to remind herself that the heat burning through her was passion, not shame, to give herself over to the astonishing pleasure of touching and being touched.

Today, at the zoo, Rachel breathed in the crisp autumn air and smiled at Aaron's efforts to win over her sister. "Look, Iz, baby hippos!" he called out.

Izzy rolled her eyes. "Those aren't babies." She pointed to a sign informing the public that the animals sleeping at the mud wall were adult pygmy hippos.

"Smarty-pants!" Aaron teased. He stopped by a different sign pointing away from the hippos. "Okay, smarty-pants, what are tapirs?"

Izzy smiled. "They look like big pigs with trunks. See?" She pointed. Two tapirs lumbered along bushes in a grassy area twenty feet from the iron fence. One of them stood on its hind legs and mounted the other. It was embarrassingly obvious that this tapir was male. His long penis swung back and forth in clear view, hunting for an opening. It looked for all the world like a separate creature, swinging up to the female's body and poking around, then swaying back down, only to resume its search a moment later.

Izzy pressed against the fence. "What are they doing?"

Rachel touched Aaron's elbow. "Maybe we should…"

But Aaron just shrugged. "It's the way they make baby tapirs," he told Izzy.

"Oh!"

A small crowd began to gather. "Oh, my God," someone said. "They're fucking!" Two teenage boys snickered. Rachel tapped her sister's shoulder. "Let's go, Iz."

Izzy wrapped her arms more tightly around the iron fence. "I want to see."

"It's just sex, Rach," Aaron said in a low voice.

"Yeah," Izzy echoed. "It's just sex."

The crowd grew. The penis finally found its target and penetrated the female. The male pressed against her. Two boys, about 12 or 13 years old, hooted, and a voice with a British accent said, "Good Lord, they're doing the dirty!" Several times, amidst nervous laughter from the crowd, the female's thick body drooped under the weight of the male, and his penis slipped out. He attempted to get a better grip on her back, and his hoofs slipped and fumbled. Finally, he managed to reenter her and stay. And then, as suddenly as it had begun, it was over. The female pulled away, and the two animals trotted companionably toward a muddy pool.

"Let's go see the polar bear," Rachel said. Her face burned. Aaron reached for her hand, but she pulled ahead and hurried over to a drink kiosk.

"I wonder how birds do it," Izzy said when she and Aaron caught up with Rachel. Rachel handed a paper cup of lemonade to her sister. "And porcupines!" Izzy exclaimed. "All those needles. How do porcupines?"

Rachel led them out of the warm sun to a bench in the shade. Izzy set her cup down and scrolled through her phone. "Oh." She read from the screen. "When the female is ready to mate, she curves her tail over her back so that her quills don't impale the male and lays the rest of them flat against her body." She sucked lemonade through her straw. "What's impale?"

Aaron answered. "It means pierce through. Like running a sword through someone."

Izzy's eyes widened. "That's good that she doesn't let that happen."

"That's very good," Aaron agreed.

Izzy looked up at him. "Those boys were stupid," she said.

Aaron nodded. "Sex makes a lot of people nervous. Boys that age… they get embarrassed, and then they act stupid."

Rachel capped her water bottle. "Well, it was embarrassing."

"The animals weren't embarrassed," Aaron said.

Izzy appeared to consider that. "Dogs pee and poop in front of people."

"Exactly," Aaron answered. "Their bodies just do what bodies naturally do. People get embarrassed because society says that those things aren't 'nice.' Churches tell people—"

"Aaron," Rachel interrupted. Aaron bit his lip, and they all went quiet.

Then Izzy said, "That man said 'do the dirty.'" She scratched at a bug bite on her knee. "Someone said the F-word."

Aaron tilted his head toward her. "That's what I'm saying. The F-word. Supposed to be a bad word, right? 'Do the dirty.' Like there's something ugly, something shameful. But sex is just the way that God created to make life go on. To make the human race go on. What's dirty about that?"

Izzy frowned so deeply that her dark eyebrows almost met. "Yeah," she said. "What's dirty about that?"

Driving back later, Aaron spotted a rarity, a parking space only a half block from Rachel's apartment. Watching him put money in the meter, Rachel felt a tingly excitement that came from knowing they'd be alone all night. Mandy had gone home for the weekend.

It was stuffy in the apartment, and Rachel opened her bedroom window a couple of inches to let the cool lake breeze in. She folded up the quilt and set it out of sight on the floor. She and Aaron lay face-to-face on the sheet, barefoot but otherwise clothed. She traced the curve of his forehead, the tip of his ear. He mirrored her movements until they lost themselves in slow, deep kisses, their bodies pressed together. Rachel took Aaron's hand and slipped it under her t-shirt. After a flurry of movement where she wasn't sure what she did and what he did, her bra loosened, and her small breasts gleamed white in the moonlight. His mouth on her, she moaned with the pain-pleasure she felt. Her body lifted from the sheets. Aaron's hand drifted downward, and he…

He cupped his hand over her crotch, triggering two reactions simultaneously: an intense jolt of pleasure that took her breath away, and the shocking realization that she had felt this exact thrill as a child.

I liked it.

She catapulted herself off the bed and slammed her

back against the wall. The sickening thought repeated itself in her mind while she pressed her clenched fists against the sides of her head. *I liked it.* She slammed her fists downward then, and struck her genitals with all her might. *I liked it.* She beat herself in a series of sharp, hard raps. *I liked it. I liked it.*

"Rachel!" Aaron gripped her wrists and held them fast. She made an animal sound and tried to tear from his grasp. "Rachel—"

She hissed, "Let go of me."

But he held tight until her strength seeped out and her arms went limp. Aaron released her wrists, very slowly, until his fingertips were barely touching her. He moved to embrace her. She shrunk back. "I'm sorry," he said. "I shouldn't have… I just…" He reached for her again, but she flinched and pressed against the wall.

Aaron backed away. "Please, Rachel," he said. "Come and sit. I'll stay here at the foot of the bed."

Rachel's gaze swung from him to the folding chair. "Sit there."

He lifted an afghan and a pile of her clothes from the chair and set them down. Then he sat, his eyes wide as he followed her movements: her stepping across the floor, settling herself onto the bed, pulling the sheet and blanket over her. Leaning against the headboard, hugging her knees to her chest. Periodically, a shudder ran through her.

"I should have asked first," Aaron said. He spoke in a

quiet, reasonable tone, but his voice didn't match the look on his face. Even in the dim room, she saw that he looked troubled, and something else.

Wary.

For a long time, they sat in silence. Finally, Aaron stood and took a step toward her.

Rachel gripped the bedding and cringed.

Aaron froze. "Do you want me to leave? Do you want me to stay?"

Rachel blinked. "Yes."

"You want me to stay?"

She shivered violently and pulled the blanket all the way up to her chin. "I want you to leave, and I want you to stay." Aaron picked up the afghan and added it to the bedding already on top of her. Tucking it in, he spotted the quilt on the other side of the bed. "You want the quilt too?"

"No." She shook her head. "No." She shuddered.

"I'm going to make you some hot tea," Aaron stammered. The moment he left the room, Rachel opened the drawer of her bedside table and found her Valium. She swallowed a pill, then buried herself back under the covers, clutching the top of the afghan with freezing hands. She could not stop shaking.

When Aaron returned with a steaming mug, she slipped one hand out from under the covers to take it from him and sipped the hot liquid. Aaron set his own cup onto the bedside table and dragged the folding chair closer to her. "I didn't mean to upset you."

"I know."

He leaned forward, intent on explaining. "I should have asked first. But I thought…" He rubbed his chin. "It's just another part of you, Rach," he said. "Like your elbow." She gave him a look. "Okay, not exactly like your elbow," he conceded. A long time passed. "I need you to say something."

She began trembling again. Thank goodness her mug was only half-full now, or the tea would have spilled onto the afghan, and then she would have needed to take it off, and she wanted the weight of it: the weight of the afghan and the blanket and the sheet between herself and Aaron.

"Never mind, Rach; you don't have to talk." A focused look came over Aaron's face. "How about if I read to you? And you could just drift off. Would you like that?"

Rachel's head swam from the Valium, and her eyelids drooped. A bedtime story. "What would you read?" she asked.

Aaron extracted his phone from his pocket and swiped the screen. "How about…Harry Potter?"

She almost smiled. "You have Harry Potter on your phone?"

He looked a bit chagrined. "He was my hero when I was a kid. You know? A smart boy who defeats the bad guys, not because he's so strong, but because he can figure them out." Aaron shrugged. "What do you think? Would you like me to read that?" At her nod, he switched off the small lamp so that the only light came from the moon and his phone. He began. "Mr. and Mrs. Dursley, of Number Four, Privet Drive—"

Rachel finished the sentence. "—Were proud to say that they were perfectly normal, thank you very much!" They exchanged pleased looks. But a moment later, Rachel's smile faltered. The phrase "perfectly normal" hung in the air between them. Aaron didn't appear to notice it. He just dipped his head and went on reading.

Rachel closed her eyes. She let Aaron's voice take her into the Muggles' world, away from the ache where she had struck her body and from the cold that shivered through her. She snuggled under the heavy covers and saw the owls in the skies, the cat reading a map, and infant Harry with the strange scar on his forehead. When Dumbledore tenderly took the babe in his arms, she drifted off. But the phrase *perfectly normal* echoed in her mind and haunted her dreams.

Chapter 29

The next morning, Rachel's body still ached from the blows. In the bathroom, she gently patted herself dry after peeing. She selected her softest jeggings and her most comfy sweatshirt to wear. She avoided crossing her legs. Yet, even as she protected herself, that same flesh filled her with disgust. At the end of her last class, she gathered her papers into her backpack with relief and escaped to the music building.

In the practice room, Rachel flipped on the light and placed her sheet music on one of the stands. She rosined her bow and lifted her cello from its case. But when she spread her knees to set the cello down, a stab of pain shot between her legs. It seemed right that that should happen. A loathing for that space, a loathing for her whole body, churned in her. The need to punish, to hurt someone, grew in her until it became a tension screaming for release, and she almost struck her groin again. But instead, she brought her clenched fist to her mouth and bit down hard, then harder, until a long shudder went through her, and her body relaxed. She stared for some moments at the ring of red marks in her soft flesh. Then she took a deep breath, picked up her bow, and focused on the notes in front of her.

This was a newer piece, so as usual she tackled the toughest parts first, repeating those phrases over and over while hearing her cello teacher's voice in her head. "Again. And again." While not enabling her to lose herself utterly in the work, this kind of repetition usually focused her attention and shut out the rest of the world.

But not today. Today, no matter how often she went over the notes, confused memories disrupted her concentration: Izzy jumping in excitement, waving her cell phone in the air; her father whispering "I'm so proud of you" while handing her roses after a recital; Aaron tucking the afghan around her; her mother insisting, "You're strong; you'll be all right." With each intrusion, she botched another attempt. In frustration, Rachel kicked the stand. It crashed to the floor, the sheet music fluttering across the shining wood.

When her breathing quieted, Rachel stroked the rich wood of her cello, ran her hand along its graceful curve, and stood it firmly upright again. She brought a simple old Irish song to her mind, a tune her grandma had loved, and that she could have played in her sleep. *Oh, the days of the Kerry dancing.* She took a breath and lifted her bow and played, trying to picture young Irish lads and lassies dancing in a field on a summer's night. Trying to be in that field with them. Instead, the memory of Aaron holding tight to her wrists intruded.

She began again.

Oh, the days…

And again.

It didn't work. Rachel played the music, but all the crushing events of this whole, terrible year persisted. *Breathe into it*, she thought over and over, hoping to lose herself in the tune while her fingers automatically found the right string, her bow arm naturally curved at just the right angle. Instead, she remained acutely aware of the pressure of the strings against her calloused fingertips, the tension in her shoulders, the ache between her legs. After what seemed a hundred repetitions, she flung her head backwards and forward again, as if that movement could release her. Instead, it merely loosened her ponytail and caused long tendrils of damp hair to paste themselves against her sweaty face. Her bow arm dropped to her side, and she breathed heavily in the silent room.

She caressed the curve of her cello. It had been an Aladdin's lamp with magical powers to transport her. Now it was merely a wooden instrument, mute and clumsily balanced on its spike. Another legacy of what her father had done.

She drew her bow again across the strings, intentionally

creating a shrill din. She scraped the bow again and again, each stroke more frenzied than the last, creating a harsh cacophony. Rachel's lips tightened with each screech; the skin on her cheekbones grew taut. Her father! At the height of this feverish agitation, while she was *sawing* away with her bow, a horrible image sprang to Rachel's mind: her father's prick, severed.

Rachel gripped the neck of her cello, dropped her bow and covered her face with her hand. Her head swam. Exhale. Stop. Hold your breath. Inhale. Slow. Exhale. Stop. Finally, the dizziness passed, and she felt able to rise. She placed her instrument gently back in its case. But she moved like an old woman, as if she, like the image in the reversible figure, had been changed from a young woman into a crone.

She stood in the center of Practice Room 8 and glanced around her refuge. How beautiful the sheen of the polished floor, how dear the familiar cluster of music stands, the folding chairs along the wall. How delicate the faint purple streaks visible through the window as dusk descended outside. The peace and beauty of it. Lost to her now. All lost.

Chapter 30

Ever since the Mexican Grill fiasco, Colleen had sent a steady stream of text messages to Rachel, and had not received a word in response. In contrast, Derek had been attentive since the moment Rachel slammed that red door in Colleen's face. That night, he had laid a gentle hand on her shoulder and turned her away from the door, all the while calming Izzy with reassurances that everything would be all right. During that brief walk back to their car, she had had a partner again.

His caretaking had continued steadfastly through these past weeks. "Are you warm enough?" he asked, bringing her coffee this chilly September morning. "It's kind of cold in here." He frowned at the thermostat and adjusted it. A moment later, a whoosh of air flowed through the vent nearest Colleen's chair. Derek gave her a puzzled look. "Did you know it was set at 65 degrees?"

Colleen shrugged. "I forgot to turn it back up this morning." At his raised eyebrow, she explained, "We're under blankets at night, and I'm trying to get our heating bill down."

"You don't have to freeze," Derek said. Then he did something that he had often done in the early years of their marriage, something she'd forgotten. He pointed one index finger toward her. *You.* Then the other toward himself. *Me.* He entwined the two fingers. *Together.* In the next moment, he flushed as if he had committed a faux pas and dropped his hands to his side. But that *You, me, together* moment warmed Colleen as much as the heat that turned the room toasty.

After church, Derek and Izzy kneaded small mounds of red and yellow and gray clay at the kitchen table. "I'm going to make an elephant first," Izzy told her father. "What are you making?" Derek grinned. "Spitballs." He flipped a tiny clay ball at his daughter. She immediately tossed back a red wad that stuck to his yellow shirt. "Hey!" Derek said.

"You're going to make a mess," Colleen warned from the island. But neither Derek nor Izzy so much as raised their eyes to her. Furiously, they continued rolling clay balls to create arsenals.

"I'm not going to be the one to clean up," Colleen scolded. Her husband and daughter exchanged impish grins. "I mean it, you two!" She smiled despite herself.

But when she switched off the light over the island, the gap between the work area of the kitchen and the table where Derek and Izzy sat dimmed and lengthened. Colleen dithered at the side of the stove, refolding the kitchen towel. She felt, suddenly, like a child left out of a party.

Just then, Izzy glanced up. "Mom! Make something with us."

It was faintly ridiculous, Colleen knew, that the invitation filled her with such gratitude. Or that her heart lifted so much when Colleen plopped next to her daughter, and Izzy exclaimed, "All right!" Izzy peered at the thin slices of red, yellow, and blue clay strips Colleen was cutting. "What are you making?"

"A pheasant. I'm going to make a bright, beautiful pheasant." Colleen molded brown clay into the body of a bird and hummed a tune. She pressed the colorful strips together to form a fan and used a spatula to lift the tail carefully. But the center of the pheasant's tail collapsed every time she tried to attach it to its plump body. Seeing that, Derek got a box of toothpicks and together they reinforced the feathers. By that time, Izzy had created a menagerie of clay figures.

Colleen glanced at the clock. "Don't forget you have to practice," she told her daughter.

"I know." Izzy tilted her head toward her father. "Will you listen?"

"Hmm," Derek said, feigning uncertainty. "What's on the program?"

Izzy laughed. "You wouldn't recognize the names. Please, Dad? You can read the paper while you listen."

And what will I do? Colleen thought. *Hover elsewhere in the house while keeping one ear cocked for the music? Try to read? Clean the bathroom?* She recalled the mildew on the shower curtain that she'd noticed this morning. *Shop for a shower curtain?* That's what she'd probably have done in the old days.

Through the patio doors, the burning bush and the gold of the maple tree beckoned to her. Colleen glanced at her husband and daughter, their heads bent over some sort of wall they were building. Izzy gave her a sidelong look. "We're almost done, Mom. Then I'll practice."

Suddenly it seemed to Colleen that all her caution, all her insistence on being no further than a stone's throw from Izzy during these Sunday visits, was nothing but pure stubbornness. A vindictive impulse to punish Derek for the pain he'd put her through. And, weirdly, a way of punishing God as well. A refusal to harbor even the tiniest smidgen of trust in either of them.

A lawnmower whirred outside. Colleen could see Jackie's husband moving back and forth beyond the fence, a baseball cap on his frizzy hair. She'd always liked Tyrone. His easy gait, his joking with the girls. An ugly thought came into her mind. Who knew, really, what Tyrone was like? Who knew about anyone? She glanced at Derek, his head bent over the blue clay wall he was fashioning. He didn't appear different from Tyrone. In many ways, he *wasn't* different from Tyrone. She thought about the conversation they'd had. "I'm not garbage," Derek had said. "I'm a person."

For a moment, while she watched Tyrone, confusion flooded her mind. Because if *anyone* might be a pedophile, she seemed to have only two choices. One was to live in fear that everyone she encountered might be a predator. Who could live like that? The alternative was to accept that Derek was as human as the rest of the world.

She looked up at the kitchen clock, ticking away. Did she really think something terrible would happen if she left the house for an hour?

No. She knew the answer was no.

"I'm going out for a while," she said, scraping her chair back.

Derek's head jerked up.

Colleen frowned at a fleck of clay on her finger and went to wash her hands at the sink. "I want to get a new shower curtain, and maybe some towels for the hall bathroom."

"Pink ones?" Izzy's dark eyes gleamed.

"Maybe."

Derek asked, "So…you're leaving now?"

Colleen forced a smile. "You two will be all right on your own, won't you?"

Izzy rolled her eyes. "Duh!"

Colleen wiped her palms on a paper towel. "I won't be long." She glanced at the mounds of clay on the table, then shifted her gaze to her husband. "I'm trusting you two to behave."

Izzy flattened a green ball of clay with a toy rolling pin. "We'll clean everything up, Mom. I promise."

Derek said, "We'll be fine."

"Okay, then," Colleen nodded. "Okay, then."

Driving down the road, she felt an exhilarating sense of freedom. Such a normal thing to do, to speed away with a wave and a "be back soon!" Head for a parking lot crowded with Sunday shoppers. Stroll down the department store aisles and vacillate between buying only the fluffy pink towels that Izzy wanted or adding the sedate cream ones that were on sale as well. Ultimately, she tossed both sets into her cart. She sifted through dozens of the shower curtains that lined almost the entire wall of the bath section, fanning out those with promising colors. She compared a whimsical one dotted with pink and blue wildflowers with a textured green curtain edged in gold and finally tossed both into her cart.

The long lines at the checkout counters snaked into curves at their tail ends. Colleen joined the line that seemed to be moving fastest, but progress was still excruciatingly slow. Tapping impatiently on the cart handle, Colleen stared at the shower curtains. The towels.

She had to get home. Her head whipped around while

she perused a dozen long lines. Spotting a short line, she barged over to it. In a moment, she realized why it was so short. The checker listened patiently to a customer flipping through what looked like dozens of coupons. After a minute, the woman in front of Colleen made a disgusted sound and left to join a different line. Colleen moved her own cart up and craned her neck. Two of the carts ahead of her held only a handful of items, but the third was crammed. The customer said, "I thought your store was supposed to match the lowest price anyone else was offering."

Colleen rolled her eyes and checked the time on her phone. What was she doing here? Just then the line moved, and she hurried forward. *A few more minutes won't make any difference*, she told herself, *whatever is happening at home. And nothing is happening at home.*

Bang! The cart behind her smacked into her. She whipped around to see a tall man with thinning hair studying his phone, oblivious. "Watch what you're doing!" Colleen shouted. The woman in front of her turned and stared. The man she'd shouted at scanned the space around him, as if searching for the source of the commotion. "I'm talking to *you*," Colleen exclaimed. "You just banged into me."

"Sorry," he muttered, not sounding at all sorry and giving her a look like she was loopy.

"How would you like it if I crashed into you?"

He raised narrowed eyes from his phone. "What's your problem, lady?"

"My problem? I'm not the problem. You're the problem. Why don't you pay attention to what you're doing instead of your darn phone? What are you? A brain surgeon? That's why you have to be glued to your phone?"

"Jesus," the man exclaimed.

Someone sidled next to Colleen, but she was too focused on the jerk to notice who had approached.

Silently, the idiot mouthed *bitch* to her.

Colleen tightened her grip on her cart and drew her whole five-foot, two-inch body straight up and slammed her cart into his.

A large brown hand clamped down on Colleen's cart, and a deep voice said, "Ma'am." Colleen turned her gaze to the heavyset security guard in a navy shirt who loomed at her elbow. *Someone in charge! Good!* Colleen said, "I have a situation at home." She maneuvered her cart as if to pass the customer in front of her. "I have to get out of here."

The guard blocked her, gripping her cart. "Ma'am, if you can't wait your turn like everyone else, I'll have to take your cart out of this line."

"I have to *go*." In a moment of what she later thought of as temporary insanity, Colleen engaged in a tug-of-war over her cart with the security guard. Then his hand clenched her elbow. Marching her past gaping shoppers and through the store doors, he deposited her on the sidewalk like unwanted merchandise.

"Don't come back in," he warned.

But she was already racing, running to her car as fast as her legs could carry her.

She backed out of her parking spot, barely checking for anyone behind her. Seeing the line of cars at the exit of the mall, she barreled ahead to make the left turn. But the light turned yellow and the car ahead of her came to a standstill. Colleen had to slam on her brakes. She swerved out of the left-turn lane and made a right onto the crowded boulevard instead. At the next intersection, she made an illegal U-turn and sped on.

The siren of an emergency vehicle grew louder behind her. Like the other drivers, she slowed, then pulled to the side to let it pass.

But it didn't pass. It pulled in right behind Colleen, its blue light flashing, and a middle-aged police officer ambled toward her car. Squinting in the sun, he made a roll-down-your-window gesture and leaned in. "What's your hurry?"

Chapter 31

Crushing the citation in her fist, Colleen parked her car in the garage and got out. She tripped on one of the two cement stairs that led into the house, and forced herself to slow down. Still, she rushed through the kitchen to the family room.

Derek sat on the recliner, but not in his usual, laid-back, feet propped up manner. Instead, the recliner was upright, and Derek perched stiffly on the edge of the cushion, hands flat on his bent knees. Izzy squatted cross-legged in the corner of the couch, her phone pressed to her ear. She glanced up and spotted Colleen. "Did you get pink towels?"

Colleen blinked. "I didn't get anything. I couldn't find a shower curtain I liked and… I forgot about the towels."

Izzy rolled her eyes and spoke into the phone. "Mom forgot to buy what she went out for." After a long pause, "Oh. Okay. Bye." Izzy frowned. "I thought Rachel wanted to talk to you. She said, 'Let's talk until Mom gets home.' But then she had to go."

Looking at Colleen pointedly, Derek said, "Izzy's been talking to Rachel for half an hour." Izzy restarted the *Sherlock Gnomes* movie and raised the volume. Colleen approached her husband. Quietly, he continued, "Apparently, Rachel thought we had a 911 situation here. Like Izzy needed to stay on the line for as long as she was alone with me." He looked at Colleen, misery in his eyes. "I don't know what to do, Col."

Briefly, she covered his hand with hers, but then drew back. "Rachel needs time. You have to give her more time."

Derek pushed himself up from the recliner and went over to his daughter. "Daddy's got to go, sweetheart."

"Aren't you staying for dinner?"

"No, pumpkin, I've got to leave early today."

"Aren't you going to watch the rest of *Sherlock Gnomes* with me?" Izzy pleaded. But he kissed her on the top of her head and was out the door a minute later.

Izzy hunched in the corner of the couch and began to cry.

Colleen stumbled over to her daughter. "What's the matter, Iz?"

"Daddy's mad at me."

"What makes you think that?"

Izzy's bottom lip trembled, and she crossed her arms in that way she had when she didn't want to talk. Colleen studied her face, scanned her purple t-shirt and the black jeggings she wore, dotted with multicolored stars. Looking for what? She hardly knew.

"I wanted to talk to Rachel," Izzy cried. "I thought Daddy would be here longer. I thought we had a lot of time. Now he's mad because I talked to Rachel for so long." Her face scrunched up. "I wanted to watch *Sherlock Gnomes* with Daddy and now he's gone."

Colleen expelled a breath of relief and drew her daughter into her arms. "Daddy's not mad at you. He just had to go." She rubbed Izzy's back. "I'll watch the movie with you."

Izzy sniffled and nestled against her mother. "'Okay."

While the movie hummed in the background, Colleen's mind filled with images of the indifferent police officer writing out the ticket, the idiot customer who'd banged into her, the guard who had dismissed her so ignominiously from the store. Humiliation burned her cheeks. Worse than all these, she realized, was finding Izzy on the phone with Rachel. A sickening feeling churned in her stomach. She slid off the couch.

Locking the bathroom door, she phoned Rachel. Rachel picked up immediately, but before Colleen could get a word out, her daughter said, "So you never leave Izzy alone with him, huh?" and hung up. When Colleen tried again, the call went to voicemail.

Izzy's attention stayed glued to the film. Colleen tried her best to watch it too, to block the disgust in Rachel's voice. And mostly, mostly, to stop wondering about Izzy. But that she couldn't manage. Periodically, she snuck a glance at her daughter and sought reassurance in Izzy's smooth, unlined face, her wide dark eyes. She wished Izzy would let out one of her belly laughs. That would be a sign, wouldn't it, that Izzy was okay? That nothing had happened?

Why, oh *why*, had she cared about shopping for a lousy shower curtain? *Please, God,* she prayed, over and over while the film rolled on. *I'll never leave her alone again.*

Chapter 32

Rachel dragged her way home from work, shivering despite her fleece sweatshirt. She should have worn a jacket. These late September evenings could turn cold after the sun went down, especially so near the lake. She should call Aaron to pick her up. He was already at the apartment with their old gang, Mandy and Gregorio and Kaitlin. It had seemed the perfect back-to-classes gathering, friends providing a buffer between herself and Aaron, whom she hadn't seen since the night she'd struck herself. But if she phoned, he'd be there so quickly, and she'd be alone with him. Walking home would give herself time to prepare.

A car door slammed and she jolted, then relaxed when she spotted a laughing couple under the streetlight. Turning the corner, she found herself walking more briskly down the stretch of pavement that ran along the edge of park, her fingers tightening around her key. A black expanse of trees and shifting shadows loomed at her side. For a moment, she had the unsettling sense that someone was following her. Her heart thumped in the dark.

On the next block, the feeling of something or someone behind her grew stronger, and she stopped abruptly and whipped around. Nothing there—only wind whistling through the trees. With one last backwards glance down the empty sidewalk, Rachel strode forward, trying to look purposeful. But a few moments later, as if mocking her bravado, faint footsteps sounded across the street. They weren't parallel to her, but some distance behind. She quickened her pace. The footfalls across the road picked up as well. She slowed. She wanted to hold back until the man (of course she assumed it was a man) outpaced her, so that she could spot him and monitor his movements. But his footsteps slackened as well. She came to a dead stop and pulled her phone out. The key she still gripped in her fist now seemed like such a puny defense! She cast a worried glance toward the street opposite her. It appeared deserted, but a man might easily hide behind the thick-trunked trees there. She swiveled her head slowly to take in her surroundings, not really expecting to see him anywhere but across the road.

But there he was, on her left but far away, deep in the park itself. When had he crossed over? Or was this a different person?

Were there two men, working together?

She searched for the emergency alarm on her phone, all

the while darting glances toward the man. The icon was nowhere to be found. Then she remembered that alarm had been on her old phone, the one she'd given Izzy. Surely this one must have a similar app, but where was it? The man's shadowy figure slunk further ahead, still far off. Tracking his movements and seeing the distance between them increase, Rachel relaxed her grip on her phone.

But then he stopped. The moon came out from behind the clouds, and she could see him clearly. Tall. Dark pants, light-colored shirt, baseball cap pulled down. He stared at her from the darkness. How fast could she run? If she dashed into the building across the street and pressed all the bells, would anyone answer? Or would she find herself trapped in the hallway? In a panic, she punched the call icon next to Aaron's name.

A flame flared in the distance. The man had lit a cigarette. When Aaron picked up, Rachel heard the sounds of the party in the background. She spilled out her fears and her location. "I'm on my way," Aaron told her. "Talk loud. Let him know you're talking to someone who's coming." Through the phone, she heard the sound of Aaron's shoes pounding down the stairwell in her building.

She walked briskly and called out loudly, pretending she had a bad connection. "Yeah, I'm by the park, heading toward you. Can you see me yet? That's great, oh, yeah, I think I see you."

Aaron huffed, "I'm going to stop talking so I can run faster, but I'm coming."

The burning ember at the end of the man's cigarette drifted in the darkness. Was it moving forward in tandem with her? Or was it angling toward her, coming closer? Rushing down the sidewalk, she pretended to talk into her phone. Her voice came out high-pitched and unnatural. "Oh, Gregorio is with you? That's great! I wasn't sure if he was coming." Suddenly, the ember of the cigarette veered plainly in her direction, almost streaking toward her. She jogged faster and pictured Aaron running the way he ran on the lake path, racing toward her like a gazelle. She sped up, though she hated the thought of out-distancing the man, of losing sight of that burning cigarette and being unable to track where he was. "Oh yeah, I see you now," she called out, thinking her words sounded so phony, the stalker would surely jeer at them. And then she cried out in a different voice, bursting with relief, "I see you! I do," because there was Aaron, bounding toward her down the block through the pools of light from the streetlamps.

The next minute, panting hard, he threw one arm over her shoulder and glanced around. "Is he still here?" She pointed into the dark, but the red ember had disappeared. The moon had also disappeared behind clouds, and she couldn't make out anything in the darkness. Surely the man lingered in those shadows. Rachel shuddered and leaned her head against Aaron's sweat-soaked t-shirt. Only then did she become aware of the pain, triggered by her running, that pulsed between her legs.

"Why didn't you text me?" Aaron rasped. "Why didn't you call me to pick you up?"

She had no answer, so she merely pressed her face against his chest. His breathing ragged, he said, "Promise me. Promise you won't walk alone after dark." Aaron held her trembling body in his arms. "I got you," he told her. "I got you."

"You need a drink," Gregorio proclaimed the minute Rachel and Aaron crossed the threshold into the bright apartment. "I've got white wine and Stella's, courtesy of my great-uncle."

Rachel gave him a hug. "Wine would be perfect. It's great to see you."

Kaitlin sprang up to greet her. "You okay?"

"I'm fine. Just a run of the mill 'I got scared in the dark' story." Rachel fell onto the overstuffed sofa and sipped the wine Gregorio handed her. Aaron sat thigh-to-thigh with her while Kaitlin and Gregorio squeezed onto the couch beside them. Mandy brought Rachel a plate of latkes with sour cream and applesauce. "Courtesy of Aaron's mom," she said. Gregorio regaled them with a story about his elderly uncle. "He wanted to set an alarm for seven in the morning in order to get to a barbershop that opened at nine. I told him, Uncle Pete, it's only fifteen minutes away. 'People wait on the sidewalk,' he says. 'There might be long line. It's a very popular barbershop.'" A wave of gratitude for their chatter, for their laughter, swept through Rachel. Even their arguments pleased her. They debated who would be on whose team if they played trivia, whether to watch a familiar horror movie they could make fun of or a new one that might actually scare them. Aaron nixed the idea of a new movie and cast a solicitous glance toward Rachel. "You don't want to have nightmares."

Rachel objected. "I'm not going to have nightmares because a man in the dark lit a cigarette. I got a little nervous, that's all. It turned out to be nothing."

"But you do have nightmares," Mandy remarked from the armchair. She gave Rachel a tipsy, apologetic nod. "Sometimes I hear you."

The comment left Rachel feeling exposed. Aaron laid a hand over hers, but she shook it off and stood up. "You guys figure out what we're doing. Whatever you decide is good. I just want to have fun." Gregorio burst into a rendition of "Girls Just Wanna Have Fun" that followed her down the hallway.

In the bathroom, Rachel opened the medicine cabinet. The aspirin container that held Mandy's cache of Valium from her dead grandmother stood next to a box of band-aids. Rachel knew that she had to be careful, since she was drinking tonight, but she downed one pill and then slipped a palmful into her pocket, just to feel safe. Just for the security of it.

Her friends had already started an old horror movie when she came back to the living room. She sunk next to Aaron on the couch and picked up her wine glass. The evening wore on, the warmth of Aaron pressed against her. The laughter each time Gregorio did a parody of a frightened character on-screen settled at the forefront of her mind. Her fear receded. In fact, laughing with her friends and holding her glass out for refills, all the distressing events in Rachel's life drifted further and further away. The man in the park, the violent sawing of her bow across the cello strings, the soreness between her legs. Each shrunk, sip by sip, until they became tiny specks that vanished.

Chapter 33

When Colleen's repeated calls to Rachel went unanswered, apathy returned, and she embraced it like a gift. She wasn't fully *there* anymore, yet no one seemed aware of the change. Derek appeared oblivious to her detachment when he greeted her on Sundays. Her friends, with whom she still walked these cool October mornings, didn't seem to notice. Not even Pat, whom Colleen longed to pull aside so she could spill out her despair about Rachel. But each time, she quashed the impulse. Pat's sympathy would shatter the numbness that she needed so badly.

Then, today, Pat had noticed. The women had been discussing possible Halloween costumes, and Colleen had suggested that Letitia's children trick-or-treat together dressed as bacon and eggs. "Derek and Izzy did that one year," she said, and suddenly her voice had hitched. Pat gave her a concerned look and later invited her to visit after lunch. "You'd be doing me a favor," she'd said. "We could use your van to bring those bookshelves I told you about to Katie, and then we could go for coffee and talk."

Colleen's GPS guided her past a huge shopping center that went on for blocks. She turned left at the next corner as directed, past a strip mall with a dry cleaner, a sandwich shop, and a convenience store. The area struck Colleen as dreary, but perhaps that was because the sky had turned slate. On the opposite side of the street, she spotted the small yellow frame house that Pat had described, the short driveway in front of the garage barely more than an apron. When Colleen pulled in, the van's back end hung over the sidewalk. She let herself through the gate of the cyclone fence, noticing the peeling paint on the house and recalling Pat's comment that her husband was too sick to keep the property up. The contrast between Pat's house and Colleen's own home was stark, and Colleen admired Pat's brave attempt to brighten the cement stairs leading to the back door. Because it must have been Pat who set out the bright yellow and orange mums on the stoop. A light rain began to fall, and Colleen hurried up.

The door swung open before she reached the top step. With her foot, Pat pushed a stack of boxes across the faded green linoleum and made room for Colleen to pass by. "Just put your jacket on the back of a chair," Pat directed. "I'm almost done here." On the table lay a butter dish, a utensil holder, and a sugar bowl and creamer, all decorated with hand-painted blue, violet, and orange pansies. Pat rolled the butter dish in newspaper and placed it in a box.

"I need to get this stuff to Katie for eBay, so I thought we could take it along with the shelves."

Colleen sat across from her friend and rolled the creamer in paper. "I need to talk to you about something."

Pat tilted her head. "You want to wait until we're done here?"

But Colleen couldn't hold it in. "I messed up," she said. "I surprised Rachel with a visit from me and Izzy and her dad, and it didn't go well. Then a couple weeks ago, I let Derek stay alone with Iz. Just for an hour or so." She rubbed her eyes. "Rachel found out. She won't speak to me."

Pat shot her a sympathetic glance but kept working, wrapping a set of small avocado-green bowls that she stacked into a column. "I'm sorry. I just have a little more to do." She lined one side of a cardboard box with kitchen towels, then tucked the bowls against those. While they worked, Colleen told Pat how Rachel had refused to let her and Derek into her apartment, how she'd insisted that she would never forgive her father.

When Pat reached over to pick up the salt shaker, Colleen said, "What happened to your hand?"

"My arthritis." Pat plunged a red, swollen hand into a bowl of water that had bits of ice floating in it. "My own fault." She waved toward the packed boxes. "Besides all this packing, I made homemade soup and spaghetti sauce, and my food processor went on the blink. I had to chop everything myself." She took her dripping hand out of the water and patted it with a towel.

A banging sound made Colleen turn toward the long hallway behind her. A stooped old man with a cane thumped toward them. He must be Pat's husband, Joe. He was on oxygen, the tubing dragging along the floor behind him. Somewhere out of sight, a machine hissed. He needed a shave, and tufts of his battleship-gray hair stuck out in odd places. Just as he reached the counter that separated the rest of the kitchen from where they worked, Pat upended a bag of sewing supplies onto the table.

"What the hell is all this?" Joe said.

Pat ignored him and separated buttons from spools of thread and packets of needles. The silence, broken only by Joe's labored breathing, grew uncomfortable. Colleen turned to him and stuck out her hand. "Hi. I'm Colleen." Too late, she realized that both of Joe's hands were occupied. One gripped his cane, and the other steadied him against the counter. Joe narrowed his eyes at her, and Colleen withdrew her hand. He peered over the counter and squinted at the objects on the table. "Where do you get this crap from?"

"Garage sale," Pat answered. She slipped the loose buttons into an old pill container. "Same place you used to get all your crap."

Joe sneered. "No one's going to buy this stuff." With one swoop, Pat swept the remaining detritus off the table and into a brown bag. "This is good enough, Colleen. Let's go." But before Colleen could move, thunder crashed. The light above the table flickered, and in the distance, the oxygen machine went silent. Joe froze. But the next moment, the kitchen light burned steadily again, and the hum of the machine started up once more. Joe rasped, "Did you order those refills?"

Pat carried a box toward the back door. "I'm calling today."

Her husband puffed. "I asked you yesterday."

Her back to Joe, Pat stared out the window, then turned to Colleen. "Let's get this stuff in the car before it storms. There's a bag in the fridge marked 'Katie.' Would you get that?" Colleen had to pass by Joe to get to the refrigerator. She kept her eyes averted and focused instead on the chipped enamel stove, the door that hung askew on one of the painted cabinets, the old refrigerator with its rounded top. On the bottom shelf, she found a bag labeled in black magic marker: "For Katie. Don't touch!"

"Bring that here, would you, Colleen?" Pat crouched by the open back door, pushing boxes onto the cement stoop outside. Now she used her good hand to grip the side of the door and pull herself up. She took the bag of food from Colleen. "Maybe you could get that last shopping bag from under the table? It's heavy."

When Colleen squatted to pull the bag out, Joe's voice barked above her, "You think you can do whatever you want now, don't you?" Colleen startled. He wasn't talking to her. Of course he wasn't. He glared at his wife, his face flushed and his chin jutting out. Pat didn't spare him so much as a glance, just pushed the last box across the threshold with her foot. Joe smacked his cane on the floor with a bang that made Colleen jump. He muttered an invective. Colleen shrunk back in shock. Had he said *cunt*?

Joe's venomous eyes stayed locked on them the whole time that they maneuvered the bookshelves out the back door. Colleen stumbled in her haste to escape. Tugging on the door handle, she heard the ominous tap, tap, tap of Joe's cane receding down the hallway. She slammed the door shut as fast as she could.

All the way to Katie's apartment, Colleen waited for Pat to say something, but other than giving directions, Pat stayed silent. Arriving at Katie's complex, they passed through a wrought-iron gate, black and shiny, then drove by red-brick townhouses with rustic roofs. Crimson and gold leaves speckled the green grass. After they went by a gazebo and a pond, Pat directed Colleen to a row of parking spaces.

Colleen opened the back of the van, staring at the shelves and the boxes and bags. "We should get Katie to help us carry this stuff." She glanced at the gray sky and felt a drop on her cheek.

But Pat reached for a bag. "Katie will help us at the elevator."

Colleen looked pointedly at her friend's swollen hand. "You shouldn't be carrying anything. Katie and I can get all this."

Pat tucked a cardboard box under her arm. "Katie's agoraphobic. She'll help us at the elevator." Pat didn't ring Katie's bell until they'd stacked the boxes in the small hallway and dragged the shelves to the covered stoop. Through the intercom, she called to her daughter, "We could use a hand down here."

When the elevator doors wheezed open, a tall, thin woman in black sweatpants and a pea-soup-colored jersey top offered Colleen a quick "Hi" before lifting a stack of boxes. Colleen grabbed the loops of three shopping bags and searched for something to say while the elevator ascended. She settled on, "This is a nice complex."

Katie's face broke into a smile that transformed her plain features. "Isn't it? I love it here."

Inside the apartment, Colleen caught a glimpse of stainless-steel appliances, smoky gray cabinets, and white quartz countertops in the kitchen. Katie had chosen gray tones for the living room as well. It held a charcoal couch and chair and glass-topped side-tables with gleaming chrome legs. The dinette area, where Colleen brought the eBay items, had a similar décor. It was too stark for Colleen's taste, but she appreciated the overall effect. What job did Katie have, she wondered, that allowed her to work from home and keep a place so much nicer than her mother's?

She thought of her own Tudor-style home, with its expansive yard and deck and stone walkways. Would she be able to stay there if she and Derek got divorced? Colleen told herself that Derek would always pay the bills. But what if he didn't? What if child support wasn't enough? It hit Colleen that she couldn't keep drifting the way she'd been doing. She needed to think about work. And wouldn't working from home be perfect?

"I do data entry," Katie answered Colleen's question, when the two of them retrieved the bookshelves from the stoop outside. What exactly did "data entry" mean? Exiting the elevator, they lugged the shelves toward Pat, who held the apartment door open for them. But before Colleen could ask Katie for more information, Pat gave her daughter a narrow look and said, "You have a new television."

"I got a great deal," Katie replied, brushing by her mother. Inside, Katie picked up her pace, and Colleen had to hurry to keep from dropping her end of the shelves. They headed for the dining room, Katie chattering, "Jimmy mounted the television for me and connected everything. Jimmy's my brother."

"Oh, right, one of the twins," Colleen began.

But behind them, Pat interrupted, "What was the matter with your old TV?"

"Nothing, Mom. Jimmy moved it into the bedroom." Katie and Colleen maneuvered the shelves to an empty space under the window.

"Katie," Pat scolded.

"You know I sleep better with a television on." The whiny tone coming from this grown woman jarred Colleen. For an instant, she had a disconcerting image of Izzy as an adult, grousing in the same way.

Pat didn't seem to notice. Her face set, she said, "I put the soup and spaghetti sauce I made on the table. You need to find room for them in your fridge." She twisted around. "We should get going," she told Colleen in an irritated voice, as if Colleen had been the one delaying them. Her back rigid, fists at her side, Pat strode to the door, while Colleen scurried behind her and mumbled "bye" to Katie.

As soon as the apartment door shut, Pat spit out, "I can't believe Katie bought that television. We have talked so many times about how she needs to manage her money."

Colleen blinked. "Well. It is her money."

"I'm sure she charged it," Pat fumed, stabbing the button to call the elevator. "She promised not to charge anything else until her cards were paid off."

The elevator came, the doors opening with a wheeze. Colleen shrugged. "A lot of people never pay off their charge cards. It's a different world from the one you grew up in, Pat." She stifled a sigh. She didn't want to spend the afternoon talking about Katie's money problems.

At the car, Pat stopped and faced Colleen. "I think she's stopped taking her medication." All the starch went out of

Pat's stiff bearing, and tears welled in her eyes. "This is how she gets when she's off her meds. Buying stuff."

It started drizzling, and the two women darted into the car just in time to escape a downpour. On this on-again, off-again rainy day, only a small drizzle remained by the time they arrived at the coffee shop. After they'd gotten mugs of tea, Pat led Colleen away from the jumble of tables near the front to a section far back. A line of tables just big enough for two ran along the walls of this narrow hallway. Expansive windows along the wall saved the area from dreariness. It probably looked cheerful when the sun shone. But now, errant drops splattered the glass and only grayness filtered into the space. Watching Pat slump down at the table nearest the washrooms, Colleen saw her friend with new eyes. The brave supporter of Colleen's hopes had disappeared, leaving a husk of a woman who looked as defeated and bitter as Colleen herself felt. Disappointment rose in her. "I didn't know Katie had so many problems," she said. "And Joe? I thought you and Joe were happy."

"Happy?" Pat raised her eyebrows. "Last Tuesday I sat in the basement for two hours, waiting for him to cool down after we had a fight. He can't come after me anymore; he can't manage the stairs. So he waited in the kitchen. Banging that cane on the floor." A bitter laugh escaped her lips. "Happy? The day he dies—that's when I'll be happy."

Colleen crossed her arms tight around her chest. "You

made me think you had a good marriage," she accused. "'As good as most' you said."

"Well, that was true. For a long time. Besides…" Pat stared out the window, where the wind whipped a scrawny tree that grew from a stingy square of dirt in the concrete. "You wanted to believe that your marriage had a chance. Who was I to take that away from you?"

Colleen huffed. "But you have taken it away." She slapped the table, a resounding blow. "Why? Why bring me to your house now? To Katie?"

"I don't know," Pat muttered.

How haggard her friend looked! But Colleen was too aggrieved to let pity displace her annoyance. "From the very beginning, you've thought I should leave Derek."

"No," Pat protested. "I just wanted you to see what can happen. I thought that if you saw what Joe is like now, what my life is like…"

"But you chose that!" Colleen exclaimed. "I'm sorry, but you did. I know you would have struggled financially, but was money really worth living with a man who calls you…" She mouthed the C-word.

"You think I stayed because of money?"

"Well, didn't you?" Colleen glared. "Isn't that what you said once? 'Why should I lose out?'"

"It's not about money," Pat shot back. "It's about *fairness*. Why should my life be harder than his? I'm not the one who did anything. Why should me and the kids have gone without? Been the ones to suffer?" She took a hard swallow of her tea. "And I'm still the one who suffers. I'm not sure he ever thinks about what happened anymore. He's not the one who sits up all night with Katie when she's depressed. It's not him who Ellen tells, 'I'll never let the grandkids stay overnight at your house.' I'm the one they talk to. For him, it's done. But it will never—" Pat choked on the words. "It will never be over for me." She snorted. "Money. If it was about money, I wouldn't be paying half of Katie's rent."

"You pay half of Katie's rent?"

Pat brushed the question away. "I do what I can to help my girls. Katie just happens to need more help than Ellen."

"But you pretended that your girls were okay," Colleen said, her voice rising again. "That you had a pretty good marriage." A pony-tailed young mother passing their table with a toddler glanced at Colleen. Colleen waited until the woman disappeared into the washroom, then lowered her voice. "How could you lie? How could you be so phony?"

Pat's pale eyebrows shot up. "Me phony? You want to have everything you've always had. The house, the stay-at-home mom life, the music lessons—but without Derek. Except when you go to church, and then you put him on display like a store manikin."

After a moment of stunned silence, Colleen shoved her chair back. Pat's hand flew to her mouth. "I didn't mean that," she pleaded.

Colleen pulled her windbreaker on and grabbed her bag.

Pat half-stood. "Colleen—"

But Colleen stormed out of the shop, where sheets of rain just beyond the canopy blurred her van in the distance. She huddled under the inadequate protection of the small awning, feeling friendless and alone. Impulsively, she texted Geeta. She'd been texting Geeta for more than two months, chirpy little messages separated by at least a week. Now she tapped: *Hi, Geeta. Rainy weather here. Made me think of you and the monsoons in India you used to tell me about. Izzy told me that Ritu qualified for the district competitions. Congratulations to her! Hope you are all well. Hope to hear from you. Love.*

She stared at the curtain of rain inches from her nose. If she left now, how would Pat get home? How many eBay items would Pat have to sell to pay for a taxi or Uber? And if Colleen walked away today, who would she have to talk to tomorrow? Next week? She turned back into the cafe.

After a stop at the counter, Colleen shuffled to Pat's table with a blueberry scone for each of them. Avoiding her friend's eyes, she set a scone at each of their places and busied herself with wiping a ring from under her mug.

A long moment passed. "I was mostly telling the truth about my marriage," Pat said. "It wasn't that bad. I just bumped along, for years. I'd think 'after the kids are older,' 'after the twins graduate,' 'after I find a full-time job.' But then there was Katie with all her troubles. It was easier to stay, work part-time at the bakery, live separate lives. I'd visit my friends while Joe went to the off-track betting to play the horses. But now." Pat stared out the window. The rain had lessened, but the wind still blew the branches of the thin tree every which way. "Joe's emphysema's gotten so bad. It's made him mean. And he never goes out any more, except to the doctor. I stay out of the house as much as I can. When I'm home, I keep to my bedroom and listen for his footsteps and daydream about the day I'll be free."

Dread chilled Colleen. "Why not move out?" she asked. "Stay married, if that's better for you financially, but go live somewhere else?"

Pat drained her mug. "I ought to be able to do that. The good thing about Joe being such a tightwad is that he's saved a lot. Invested. But he won't touch that. The only money I control is my own Social Security, and I have to give most of that to Katie for her rent."

"Katie's as old as I am," Colleen snapped. She spent the next fifteen minutes trying to convince Pat that Katie needed to stand on her own two feet, and that Pat had a right to her own money and her own life, away from her husband. Pat responded to each point with a robotic, "Uh huh."

Colleen stopped herself from adding another suggestion. Instead, she considered her friend and then said, softly, "Giving Katie money can't make up for what happened."

Pat's head jerked up. She twisted her gold chain in her fingers. "What else can I do?"

A young woman in stylish suede boots, black jeggings, and a leather jacket strode past their table to the washroom. She was beautiful, with deep amber eyes, bronze skin, and jet-black hair. Colleen glimpsed a sparkling engagement ring on her hand. She pictured her in a bridal dress. So young! So many dreams. Colleen thought of Ellen asking her father to accompany her on her wedding day. Surely, there was hope for Rachel. Surely Rachel was more like Ellen, and nothing like agoraphobic Katie. "I told Rachel about Ellen forgiving her dad," Colleen confided. "I pretended it was something I'd read about in an advice column." She gave her friend a rueful smile. "That didn't go over well either."

Pat broke a piece off her blueberry scone. "I wouldn't say that Ellen *forgave* him," she said.

Colleen struggled to keep the accusatory tone from returning to her voice. "You told me that he walked her down the aisle on her wedding day."

"Yeah. Because Ellen refused to let what her father did affect her. She wanted to have what every other girl had. That's why she insisted on all the usual traditions." Pat grimaced. "Including the father-daughter dance at the reception."

Colleen's heart sank. Ellen had not reconciled with her father. Katie cowered in her apartment and depended on her mother for financial support. Pat hid from her husband in the basement. And Colleen's own daughter slammed her door in her family's face. Misery swept through her. "I'm not doing so well," she quavered.

She reached for her beads, but her pocket was empty. She ran her fingers through her hair. She hadn't had a cut in months, and her locks were long enough that now she could wind them around her finger. "Sometimes, just before I fall asleep, I have this fantasy. I imagine going to a lawyer. A woman. I imagine what I would say, how the lawyer would respond. I work out the whole conversation before I fall asleep. The next morning, when I wake up and I'm still groggy, my heart pounds, and I don't know why. Then the fantasy comes back to me. And I have to repeat, *you didn't do it*. You didn't go see a lawyer. You imagined it. But you didn't do it." The room blurred through her tears and, at the same time, darkened. The sky outside had blackened, and thunder crashed again. "I don't know what to do. I can't..." Colleen felt like a hundred tiny gnats jumped just below the skin of her arms and legs. She couldn't keep still. She twisted her hair, fiddled with her earrings. That terrible sense of being adrift threatened to swallow her. "I'm lost." The words came out in a harsh whisper. Colleen flapped her hands in her lap, then stretched them across the table as if seeking some purchase. In the next instant, Pat enfolded them in her own. Colleen shut her eyes. *It's been months since anyone held my hand.* Little by little, the skittering sensation faded, and her breathing eased. When she finally managed a deep, full breath, she opened her eyes.

The room materialized around her bit by bit. She became aware of the rain beating against the windows, the murmur of customers. An elderly man in a purple sweater scanned a newspaper. Two women exchanged information, tapping away on their laptops. A mother and daughter set shopping bags on the floor. Pat's hands still held Colleen's, but loosely. "Sometimes I feel so adrift," Colleen said.

"I know," Pat answered. She gave Colleen's hands a gentle squeeze.

"I can't do this alone," Colleen choked. "Whatever 'this' turns out to be."

"I know," Pat repeated.

Chapter 34

The white paper bag in the microwave swelled with hot air, and the first kernel popped. Rachel had just poured out her frustration to Mandy, expecting sympathy. But Mandy now stood with her arms folded across her chest. "How can you be so sure that your mother won't leave Izzy alone with him again?"

"I just know. She won't." More kernels popped, creating a cacophony of bursts. Rachel filled two glasses with ice from an old plastic tray.

"You should talk to Monica about it," Mandy said.

But how could Rachel talk to Monica about her mother leaving Izzy alone when she'd kept Izzy's very existence a secret for months now? And what might Monica, a mandated reporter, have to do if she knew that Rachel had a sister who spent time with their father? "My mom wants me to talk to a priest," Rachel said.

Mandy snorted. "What's a priest going to do? Move your father to a different family?" After a final, feeble *pop!*

the microwave went silent, and Mandy drew out the bulging bag. The smell of popcorn filled the room. "You could report him."

Rachel snapped the tabs on two cans of soda. "Don't start, okay?" She added rum to her glass of Coke. Seeing Mandy's mouth compress into a thin line of disapproval, she snapped, "What's with you tonight?"

Mandy turned away and searched the cabinet, shifting aside a box of tea bags and a jar of honey. "Have you seen the popcorn salt? I got that special salt."

That was it? That was all the support her friend was going to offer? Without answering, Rachel padded down the hall in stockinged feet to the bathroom. She flipped open the medicine cabinet door, then blinked. An empty space gaped where the cache of Mandy's grandmother's pills had stood. Rachel scanned the narrow shelves. Nothing. She hurried back to the kitchen, where Mandy was tearing the corner of the popcorn bag open. A puff of steam escaped. "What happened to the pills? They're not in the medicine cabinet."

Mandy dumped the popcorn into a big blue bowl. "I put them in my room. They're almost all gone anyway."

Jokingly, Rachel asked, "You rationing me?" Mandy didn't answer. "I thought we were sharing those pills." Rachel followed her friend into the living room.

Mandy put the bowl of popcorn onto the coffee table and pressed the remote. An Australian comic strolled across a stage while the audience applauded wildly. Rachel raised her voice above the din. "Mandy, I've been having a hard time lately. I just need a few."

"You put rum in your Coke."

"So?"

"It's a bad idea," Mandy said, "to mix alcohol with Valium. I told you that."

Rachel fumed. "I'm not *mixing* anything. I just want a few Valium for later. In case I get panicky."

Mandy stared straight ahead at the television.

"What business is it of yours anyway?" Rachel paused intentionally and waited until Mandy's mouth was full of popcorn. Then she added, "I don't lecture you about what you put in your mouth."

It took Mandy a few seconds to swallow. But then she muted the television and shot back, "I'm not the one finishing off all the wine." She made a visible effort to calm herself before she added, "I'm worried about you." Mandy raised a hand and counted off on her fingers. "You've been sleeping late. Skipping class. Missing cello practice. Tonight's the first time you've come out of your room in a week. And the Valium was disappearing faster than the wine." Mandy's chest heaved. "I'm trying to help you, Rachel."

"If you really want to help me, you'll tell me where you put those fucking pills."

Mandy raised her chin. "I think you're getting addicted."

The blood pounded in Rachel's head. "I put a half-inch of rum in one Coke, and you think I'm addicted. Christ, Mandy, half the campus is drunk every weekend." She shook her head in disgust. "You're worried about me? Worry about yourself. I've seen the crap under your bed, the candy wrappers and potato-chip bags and donut boxes. You think I don't notice how you take out the trash in the morning when the bag wasn't even half-full the night before? All I'm asking for is a few pills." She stared hard at Mandy, who turned her gaze back to the television.

Rachel stomped down the hallway. In Mandy's bedroom, she threw open one dresser drawer after another, sliding her hands under the clothes there, tossing bras and underpants and socks onto the bed. Rachel had just pulled open a drawer in the night table, revealing a flash of bright colors from candy bar wrappers, when Mandy burst into the room. She shoved Rachel aside and slammed the drawer shut. "Get out of my stuff! Get out of my room."

Rachel stood elbow to elbow with Mandy, breathing hard. Then she banged past Mandy and raced to the front hall, where she upended her friend's backpack. Notebooks and papers slid to the floor. She unzipped every pouch, tossing aside pens and tissue packets and tampons, but found no Valium.

She fingered the single pill that remained in her pocket.

In the kitchen, she searched the spice cabinet. Ran a spoon through the sugar bowl and dumped the oatmeal into a plastic container. She shoved ice cream cartons aside and peered in the freezer.

The kitchen was a disaster by the time Rachel slumped on a chair and Mandy crept up to the doorway. Mandy reached behind her neck as if to pull her braid forward, the way she used to when nervousness made her fiddle with it. But Mandy had gotten her hair cut in a different style a couple of weeks ago, and the thick braid was no longer there. She fidgeted with her collar instead.

Rachel took in the mess around her. "I'm sorry," she said. "I don't know what got into me. I'll clean up the kitchen."

Mandy went into the hallway and began gathering up the belongings from her backpack that were strewn on the floor. Rachel followed her, crouching to help. She slipped two pens into one side pocket, a packet of tissues and a roll of mints into another. Mandy put her wallet into a larger pouch and arranged her notebooks in the middle section of the bag.

When the floor had been cleared, Mandy hung the backpack on its hook.

Rachel licked her lips. "So. We good now?"

Mandy's stare went right through Rachel. "I want you to move out," she said.

Chapter 35

Rachel shifted uncomfortably in her corduroy chair. As usual, Monica waited silently for her to begin. *Talk about whatever's on your mind.* That was Monica's stock reply whenever Rachel wondered aloud what to say. What was on her mind was Mandy's demand that Rachel move out. The fact they hadn't exchanged a word since then, that they each moved like shadows in the apartment, slipping back into their rooms whenever the other emerged. How could she tell Monica about their argument? She'd have to admit to using Valium, or lie about what had triggered their fight.

Nor could she talk about the other issue that was on her mind: her stupid mother, who'd left Izzy alone with *him.* She retrieved the small footstool from the corner of the room, slipped off her shoes, and rested her feet on the floral needlepoint that covered it. *If Monica thinks Izzy is in danger, she'll report him.* What would her mother tell Izzy if her father went to prison? That her dad was traveling for a really long time now? Rachel had to fight the hysterical giggle that rose in her throat.

Her gaze wandered down the navy skirt that fell nearly to her ankles. Her tights were a bit long for her short legs and puckered at the tips of her toes. Suddenly she hated her short legs. She hated every inch of her stupid, small, childish body. A wave of dizziness went through her, and she had to make a conscious effort to slow her breathing. Monica sat still, waiting. Finally, Rachel asked, "Do you think that a person can choose to be asexual?"

Monica's forehead wrinkled. "Do you think that you might be asexual?"

"No. No. I just wondered if someone who's not asexual could become asexual. Like these relaxation exercises I've been practicing? Are there exercises that could stop you from…" Her face flushed. "Feeling turned on?"

"You wish you could stop yourself from feeling sexually aroused?"

In the aquarium, the lavender angelfish floated languidly by, waving its delicate tail. "It would be a more peaceful existence," Rachel said. "I wouldn't feel frustrated, or ashamed, or disgusted."

Monica steepled her fingers under her chin. "I don't think you can make yourself genuinely asexual any more than gay or trans or bisexual people can make themselves something different than who they are. Your body, with its sexual needs and desires, is part of the package, Rachel. It goes with you wherever you are."

Rachel sighed.

"So, the question is how to be at peace with your body and your feelings, including sexual feelings. How to accept these as a normal part of being human. A normal part of being you."

Easy for you to say, Rachel thought. For the first time, Monica's words triggered disdain in her. This woman had no idea. Finally, Rachel answered, "The disgust I feel is not normal." She made the declaration as if she *wanted* Monica to concur, perhaps to proclaim Rachel was a lost cause.

Monica said, "Maybe we need to explore where that disgust comes from."

"You know where it comes from."

After a long pause, Monica said, "We understand some things about where it comes from. But clearly there's a lot we don't understand yet—"

"More talk." Rachel looked away. And then she knew why she hoped Monica would simply agree that it was all hopeless. "What good has all this talking done?" she demanded. She glanced down at her fingers digging into the arms of the chair. "So now I realize when I'm angry. Big deal. 'Bring it in here,' you told me. 'When you remember things, bring them in here.' I thought—" Rachel choked up. "I thought talking about stuff in here was supposed to make it go away, not make it worse." Her voice rose. "I don't want to talk anymore. I don't want to remember anymore." She grew lightheaded from the fast breaths that she couldn't seem to slow down. "So, no thank you. I've had enough talking. What I want is what I asked you for my first day here. Something to help me sleep. Something so I don't feel like my heart's jumping out of my chest." She gave Monica a challenging look. "Like Valium. Will you give me a prescription for Valium?"

Monica tilted her head. "Rachel. What's happened?"

Of course, she should tell Monica, should have told her three weeks ago when it happened. And it wasn't so terrible, the bare fact of it. The admission that Aaron's touch down there had disgusted her, made her strike herself. What she couldn't stand was the thought of confessing *I liked it*. Rachel blurted, "Aaron touched me down there, and it disgusted me. Totally."

"So, we're back to the disgust," Monica pointed out, but gently.

"That's why I'm asking you for a prescription. A friend of mine…I got some Valium from a friend, and that's the only thing that's gotten me through this."

"Ah," Monica said, and rested her cheek against her palm. "But you haven't gotten through it, have you? It's still with you. Tormenting you so much that you wish you were asexual. Upsetting you so much that you're ready to explode when I suggest that we talk more about it."

"You told me that sometimes people need medication

when it all gets to be too much." Rachel pointed a stubborn chin toward her therapist. "Well, it's gotten to be too much."

"This friend's Valium," Monica asked, "How much have you been taking? And how long have you been taking it?"

The lies came easily. Less than three weeks, she said. Just since Aaron had touched her that way. And only a single pill, perhaps twice a week, to help her sleep. Even so, Monica launched into a big talk about how addictive Valium could become, how she rarely prescribed it for more than a month, how it could be dangerous, even fatal, when combined with alcohol. At the end, when Rachel made no response, Monica sat silently for a bit before speaking. "Okay. Here's what I think we should do. I'll give you a prescription to help you through this difficult time. But I don't want to add dependence on Valium to your problems. So, we'll go slow and monitor how you're doing very closely. And you must promise me that you'll stop taking pills from this friend."

"That's not a problem," Rachel assured her. "We're not even in touch anymore." Monica waited. "I promise," Rachel said. "I'll only take what you prescribe."

Monica scrawled something, then handed her a slip of paper.

Glancing down, Rachel exclaimed, "Ten? You're only giving me ten pills?"

"For now," Monica said. "This is a really hard time for you right now, Rachel. I understand how much you might wish to numb all these feelings. But you don't have to face this alone. I'll help you work through it in here. You can set up an extra appointment for this week and next week. Okay?"

Rachel nodded. But in her pocket, her fist crushed the paper Monica had given her.

Chapter 36

Ten pills, it turned out, could last quite a long time. If she broke them in half on the little line. If she limited herself to only taking a dose on the nights she just couldn't fall asleep at all. Or when a nightmare woke her at 2:00 a.m. And just one other time, when panic seized her at the thought of lying to her cello teacher, telling him she had to skip her lesson because she had the flu. In this way, a week passed, and Rachel still had one pill left. Tomorrow, she would ask Monica for another prescription.

She'd go to the session, she thought, leaning against her headboard and turning the pages of her Earth Studies textbook. That didn't mean that she had to talk about shame and disgust and these horrible feelings she had about her body. Monica couldn't *force* her to. There must be other ways to rein in the repulsion that she now felt every time she showered, every time she caught a glimpse of herself in a mirror, every time she opened her legs and steadied her cello in that space. She'd been plagued with these feelings all her life, this sense that sex was dirty, shameful, and now, when she'd worked so hard to *deal* with everything, it was worse than ever. How unfair! The time she'd been able to feel pleasure with Aaron had been so brief! He'd come into her life, and like a magician, made the shame disappear with sleights of hand. Replacing embarrassing words with playful language. Philosophizing about the gift of masturbation. Conducting a teasing, fruitless search for shame. And then, like a wizard, he'd transformed shame into passion with just the suggestion that it might be so.

Couldn't he do that again? She'd seen Aaron, but avoided being alone with him since *that night* because she couldn't predict how she'd react. And he'd seemed equally uncertain. Watchful. Giving her a peck on the cheek, a hug when he left her. What she dreaded, more than anything else, was lying next to him and feeling not pleasure, but revulsion.

But what if? What if he could perform that magic once more? What if being with him could turn shame back into pleasure again?

She heard the Late Night show on the television in the living room, and slipped into the bathroom, where she washed her hair and soaped her body under the shower without looking at it. She used the hair dryer and even applied a little light makeup. Then she dressed in her laciest underthings and a clean gray hoodie and soft black jeans. In her room, she fingered the last Valium in her pocket, bit it in half, and washed that down with a swallow of red wine from the bottle on the floor. Her hand on the doorknob of her room, she hesitated. She popped the other half of the pill in her mouth, returned to the wine bottle, and drank deeply before heading out into the night.

The drowsy feeling of the Valium kicking in came to her halfway to campus, and she sighed and inhaled the smell of the fall leaves that crunched under her shoes. Memories floated through her mind. Aaron's stammering invitation to their first date. The laughter they'd shared tumbling down the sand dunes. The evening on the beach when they'd sat around a fire pit, and one of Aaron's old high school friends had strummed a guitar, and they'd all sung.

None of these memories were sexual, yet Rachel felt faint ripples of pleasure recalling them, pleasure untouched by fear or disgust. She smiled in the dark. How great was that? Apparently even just the memory of being with Aaron could restore her. Why had she avoided being alone with him? Clearly, she should have done the opposite, brought him to her bedroom. Her steps quickened, and a few minutes later she stood on the stoop of his dorm building. She texted, "I'm outside."

Minutes passed. What if he wasn't in? Her heart skipped a beat. But then her phone dinged. *Be right down.* She stuffed her hands in her jacket pocket and paced the sidewalk in front of the dorm. The moment Aaron emerged, Rachel sprang into his arms. He embraced her, but quickly stepped back. "What are you doing here? It's almost midnight. Are you okay?"

"I'm fine," she smiled. "I'm great." And she was. She wanted to feel his hands, she needed to feel his hands on her. Ignoring the chill air, she unzipped her jacket and lifted her sweatshirt so that his palms pressed against her skin when he held her again.

"Rachel," he whispered, his breath warm in her ear, "what's going on?"

She silenced him with a long kiss. Then she asked, her voice hoarse with desire, "Can we go up to your room?"

Aaron blinked. "Joel's there. My roommate?"

A pause. "Can you get rid of him?" Aaron's brow furrowed. He opened his mouth, but she stopped his words with a finger to his lips. Then she kissed him, urgently, and suddenly his hands clutched her bottom, pressing her tight against him. She broke their kiss just long enough to repeat, "Can you get rid of him?"

The light in Aaron's room hurt Rachel's eyes, so she flipped the switch off. Now the only light came from a reading lamp near his bed. Rachel stared at Aaron's face in that dim light and let her jacket drop to the floor. She undid the button on his jeans and tugged at the zipper. He stayed her hand. "Rachel, we should talk about this."

She pulled her gray hoodie off, undid her bra, and grinned at him. "Talking is not what I need." She stepped out of her shoes and slipped her black jeans down. Aaron sat on the edge of the bed and untied his running shoes, giving her an uncertain glance while slipping them off. "Aaron," she assured him, "It's all good."

He took his knit shirt off, picked his wallet up from the bedside table, and drew out a packet of condoms. "Do we need this?" She nodded—eager, encouraging.

As he lowered his jeans, his white briefs tented. He sat on the edge of the bed and rolled a condom on. After that he lay back, waiting. She stretched out, facing him, and pressed her mouth to his, pressed her breasts against his chest. Skin. The sensation of her own smooth skin against his wiry hair, the heat of his body. She could lose herself in that warmth. She knew she could. For a long time, the two of them embraced and broke away and reconnected, kissing and nuzzling. She ran her hand down Aaron's face, his scratchy cheek, then lowered her mouth to his chest. His groan sent waves of desire through her.

She raised her breast to him, and the feeling of his mouth zinged right through her. Dropping her hand, she touched herself and felt wetness. See? She was all right; she was fine! Aaron drew back a moment, smiled at her, and tenderly touched her cheek, then gently traced her lips

traced her lips

gazed at her, smiling, running that finger from one corner of her mouth to the other

sealing

her

lips

She twisted her face away. Quickly she lowered his head to her breast and stroked herself, the familiar, compulsive repetitions that had always worked in the past, harder and harder. She might as well have been scrubbing a pot. Anguished, she reached out and felt for Aaron, who moaned at her touch. When she opened her legs, he whispered, "Are you sure, Rachel? Are you sure?"

"Hush." She raised her body and guided him and the next moment, he was thrusting and making soft moaning sounds, while she…

Oh dear God.

She felt the shame prickle her forehead, dribble over her tightly shut eyelids and down her face, down her neck, *oh no please,* a putrid drip down her spread legs to her buttocks, her thighs, her calves, the foul slime squishing between her toes. To keep herself from crying out, in her mind, she sang that old Irish tune, as loudly as she could. *Oh, the days of the Kerry dancing.* Her Grandma Riordan had hummed that tune. She could see her grandma now, humming and stirring a big pot of Irish stew on the stove. *Oh, the ring of the piper's tune.* Rachel's mother sometimes sang those words when she polished the Irish figurines in the curio case. *Oh, for one of those hours of gladness.* Izzy had danced a jig to it one year, wearing a puffy-sleeved blouse with a green vest and a leprechaun cap. *Gone, alas, like our youth, too soon.*

A gasp pulled Rachel out of the song—a gasp that was her own intake of breath when Aaron lifted his weight from her.

"Oh, God, Rachel." He rolled off her, but snuggled against her side, his skin hot and slick with sweat. "Oh, my God, Rachel." He nuzzled the nook between her neck and her shoulder. Apparently, he couldn't sense the scum that had oozed over her body and now dried into flakes, like crumbling, dead autumn leaves.

They lay there a long time.

So. She'd done it.

Her first time.

Aaron's breathing slowed, and his head sunk heavily on her shoulder. He shivered. Rachel pulled the blanket over him. His arm moved as if reaching for her, but she tucked a pillow against his chest, and in his sleepiness, he clasped that instead.

Rachel inched toward the edge of the mattress, lowered herself onto the thin rug, and felt for her clothes. Crouched on the hard floor of that dim room, she dressed herself as though her body was a manikin's. She pulled her panties up with wooden fingers, attached her bra. Lifted her hips from the floor and raised her jeans. She pulled the hoodie over her head, then realized she had it on backwards and had to reverse it.

On the bed, Aaron slept like a child, one arm flung above his head.

She got on her knees, put on her jacket, heaved herself to a standing position and, finally, crept out of the room.

Outside, Rachel breathed in the cool night air sharply. Wandering across campus, she made a discovery. When you're hollow inside—when it's not that you want to die, just that you feel indifferent about whether or not you go on living—then you're not afraid anymore. Meandering toward the lake path, she didn't scan her surroundings. She didn't search for the location of the nearest call box. She didn't even startle when another student, a boy, rounded the corner of a building. Instead, she passed him by as if it was midafternoon instead of nearly two in the morning.

Minutes later, she spotted an entwined couple on a bench, and, curiously, felt no pang of envy. Passion glued that couple in a tight embrace. But she felt no sadness about losing that passion herself. Losing it, it seemed to her, forever. She felt, in a fundamental way, damaged. And that damage excised her capacity to feel anything.

What a relief.

Approaching the lake path now, she caught sight of the moon's rays shimmering on the waves. Moments later, that same moonlight guided her while she picked her way down the craggy edges of the boulders. The crashing sound of the water below grew louder as she descended. Sitting on a cold, flat rock, she let her legs dangle. In novels, characters who thought about drowning themselves imagined a soft, painless death in which the waters embraced them. Hah. Rachel knew what it felt like to have panic sizzling through her like electricity while she panted into a brown paper bag. She knew what suffocation felt like, just as she knew that this freezing water wouldn't envelop her like the warmth of a mother's arms.

Pills, now. Pills were a different story. You could swallow a bottle of pills while snug in your bed and slip unawares into death, not even struggling for a last breath. Of course, pills weren't as certain. You might vomit them up. You might find yourself in an emergency room getting your stomach pumped. You might end up brain-damaged.

For a long time, Rachel gazed at the Chicago skyline in the distance, the chilliness of the rock spreading from her thighs through her whole body, until she shivered. She wrapped her arms around herself for warmth and yawned. Then she stood to make her way back home, letting the numb, nothing-really-matters feeling expand in her, filling her with its strange comfort.

Chapter 37

Colleen dozed on the couch in the midafternoon, then woke from the dream with a start, her heart racing. In the dream, she'd told a divorce attorney, a thin, hawk-faced woman, all about Derek, and the woman had cackled and exclaimed, "Now we've got him!" Colleen staggered to the kitchen and steeped a chamomile tea bag. Sitting at the table, she wrapped her hands around the blue mug. Why, she wondered, was the thought of divorce so terrifying? She'd been independent, alone for days on end, from the very beginning of her marriage. She had spunk. She'd rodded out drains, cleaned flooded basements, waited on hold to argue with cable companies, and dealt with everyone from electricians to landscapers. She stared at her small hands. But instead of seeing their competence, she remembered how they'd looked in the coffee shop with Pat, scrabbling across the table, desperate to find something to hang on to. She clasped them together tightly, then tried rubbing one palm against the other, but ended up wringing her hands frantically.

She stopped herself. There was no comfort in this touch. *Sometimes I feel so untethered*, she'd cried to Pat. Derek's hands had been ever ready when she was distressed. He reached out to her even now, when she repelled all physical contact. He'd held his hand out to her after Rachel slammed that door in her face, and she'd rebuffed him. Nevertheless, while he quieted Izzy on the way to the car, Colleen had felt his concerned glances. He'd understood. More than anyone else in the world, he understood, and he cared. It was for her sake that he'd chosen her "songs of peace" playlist for the drive home. How terribly upset he too must have been at Rachel's words that night. Yet he hadn't sought Colleen's comfort, just offered his own. If only she could turn back time, have just one hour with Derek in the before-time. Press her cheek against his shirt, cuddle with him on the couch, melt into his embrace…

Colleen slammed her mug down on the table. *It's too late. You've lost your husband, and if you don't do something, you're going to lose your daughter too.* But what could she do? Rachel hadn't responded to a single text or voice message. Maybe she should drive to her apartment. Just show up at her door and beg her, through the intercom if need be.

Colleen paced the room. That would be a replay of the surprise visit to the restaurant. But what if she could make

Rachel understand? Make her see that Colleen had only wanted to make things better. She heard Rachel's angry words again. *You're always centering you, Mom.* Colleen let out an impatient sound. "Centering." Why did young people have to use these new expressions, as if the old words weren't good enough? Clearly what her daughter meant was *It's not all about you, Mom.*

Colleen began emptying the dishwasher. *I don't think it's all about me.* Hadn't that terrible phone call from Rachel left her heartbroken? She stacked dinner plates in the cabinet. Hadn't she practically killed herself on the highway speeding to the airport to get to Izzy? She dried a few spots on the glassware. All she'd ever thought about was her children. Her family. All she'd done was for them.

The Irish Kitchen Prayer stared at her from the wall while she put the coffee mugs away. She didn't think it was all about her. It had never been all about her. But didn't she count for something, too? Hadn't she suffered? She held a blue mug in each hand, the cabinet door open, the shelf waiting. Wasn't she still suffering, and not just because of Derek, but because of Rachel?

Rachel's voice whispered: *Centering you.*

Colleen smashed the mugs against each other. One merely cracked, but the other split into pieces, splinters flying. She slumped against the edge of the counter, sucking at the blood that welled from her knuckle.

All over again, she longed for the old Derek. If he were

here, if it was the before-time, he'd sweep up the shards, he'd bandage the cut on her knuckle, he'd get her to smile. She circled the island. He'd help her calm down, and then he'd help her understand Rachel, figure out what to do.

But she knew what to do. She came to a startled stop. Perhaps she'd known what to do for a long time and shrunk from it. She surveyed the blue shards scattered on the kitchen counter. "Save the pieces," her mother used to call out when something had broken. An old expression, meaningless. As if you could glue a shattered mug back together. Or a shattered marriage. But. Save the pieces…

Her phone sat on the island. She stared at its blank face, searching for the right words. Finally, she hit the microphone icon and spoke her text message aloud. "I'm so sorry, Rach. That's all I want to say. That I'm sorry. I know I haven't been there for you. But I…" She caught herself. "'Why' doesn't matter. I just want to say that you're right. I don't really understand what you're going through. But I want to. So. I'm here, if you ever want to talk."

Chapter 38

Rachel counted out her drawer while her boss, Mitzi, watched. It was hard to believe that Mitzi's scrutiny used to annoy Rachel. What did it matter if Mitzi trusted her or not? The numbness she'd felt since the terrible night with Aaron still protected her. It helped that she hadn't seen him, that she hadn't read a single text message he'd sent and that she'd muted her phone. She wondered if, like Novocain from the dentist, the dullness would eventually wear off. Perhaps it was permanent. She'd numbed her way through her session with Monica and left with another prescription for ten Valium. She'd numbed her way through her cello lesson and two classes. Easiest of all, she stayed as unfeeling as straw through her work shifts. She closed out her drawer now.

"You still want those extra hours?" Mitzi asked.

"Yeah. Whatever you have." Rachel picked up her backpack and jacket in the back room and pasted on her automatic smile. "Bye."

Her head lowered, gaze on the sidewalk, she nearly rammed into Aaron when he stepped in front of her. "Oh!"

Aaron's body blocked her, but his arms hung at his side. "Yeah," he echoed. "*Oh.*"

"Aaron." She couldn't think what to say.

"You come to me, to my dorm room, and then you just disappear? You *ghost* me? Not a single answer to my texts, my phone calls. I call Mandy, and Mandy says she can't help. You're not talking to her, either." He blew out a puff of air. "I deserve better, Rachel."

His words were like small barbs. Dangerous to keep listening, dangerous to let his words pierce her armor. "I can't talk, Aaron. I need time."

She swerved round him, but he grasped her shoulders, his hands pressing down on the straps of her backpack. "Time for what?"

She shook her head, silent.

His hands held her fast. "Why won't you talk to me? What is it you can't tell me?"

It was good that the edge of her straps could cut so deep into her shoulders without her feeling any pain. "Please let me go."

"Not until you tell me what's going on."

There was no way she could explain. What could she say? *I'm disabled? I'm too damaged?* That nothing-really-matters feeling ballooned in her, and she realized that it gave her a quiet strength. "Aaron," she told him. "I shouldn't have avoided you. I should have had the courage to tell you this directly." She squared her shoulders. "I want to break up."

He blinked. Then his face crumbled. Not all at once, but plane by plane until the collapse reached his mouth, and his chin trembled like a child's. He whispered. "I don't understand."

She steeled herself. "It's not your fault." His hands went limp, and she slipped from his grasp. All the way down the street, she felt his stare pressing against the small of her back.

At the apartment, for the first time since their argument, Mandy didn't turn ostentatiously away when Rachel reached the living room. Instead, she looked straight at her. "Did Aaron find you?"

Rachel let her backpack slip to the floor. "We broke up."

"What?"

She corrected herself. "I broke up with him."

Mandy stared a long moment. Then she leaned forward, her hands on her knees and her eyes blazing. "Did he do something to you?"

"No." Rachel opened her mouth, closed it again. She fingered her sore shoulder where the straps had pressed. "Nothing like that."

Mandy shifted on the couch. "You want to talk?"

"What's the point of talking?" Rachel asked. She gave Mandy a small smile to take away the sting of her words. "No one understands."

In her room, Rachel's old poster accosted her. *Dance like nobody's watching. Love like you've never been hurt.* Carefully, she peeled the tape away and rolled the poster up. Mandy's footsteps shuffled down the hall and paused outside her closed door.

"Rach?"

She didn't answer.

"Rach, are you okay?"

"Yeah. I just can't talk right now."

Silence. Mandy said, "You don't have to move out. You know that, right?"

Rachel stared at the closed door. That would help; that would give her more time. "Okay," she answered. "Thanks."

The footsteps receded.

More time for what, exactly? To figure out her next steps. Finish out the school year? Drop out now? Quit cello? Her phone dinged. A text from Aaron. She deleted it without reading it. But someone else must have left a text message too, because the icon remained.

That message was from her mother, apologizing for her surprise visit to the restaurant. *I don't really understand, but I want to.* Rachel slumped on her bed. The important thing was to stop her mother from pursuing her, keep her from intruding. She reread her mother's text. Mom wanted to understand what she was going through? Fine. She'd tell her. While she still had her numbness to armor her, she'd tell both of them. And then, just like she'd broken up with Aaron, she'd break up with her parents.

Chapter 39

Colleen knelt on the family room floor and flipped through a stack of CDs, while in the recliner Derek tossed an old tennis ball from hand to hand.

"Izzy's spending the night at Aaliyah's?" he asked.

"Yeah," Colleen answered, scanning the selections on a Mendelsohn CD. "Mood is important, don't you think?" she said. "I don't want anything too heavy, but I don't want anything too light, either. I don't want Rachel to think we're not taking her seriously."

The smacking sound of the tennis ball hitting Derek's palm stopped. "What exactly did she say?"

Colleen slid a Mendelsohn disc into the player. "Just that she wants to talk, but she wants to talk to both of us." She lowered the volume of the music and snuck a peek at Derek. "Maybe she wants to make things better." Derek didn't respond, just resumed tossing the ball. She put the remote controls into the holder on the table and straightened the afghan on the back of the couch. She moved the newspaper from the glass top of the end table to the shelf below and evened the edges of the magazines there. Izzy had left her jewelry-making kit on the floor, and Colleen crouched to slide it on the shelf. But just then, the doorbell chimed, and she startled, dropping the box. Beads scattered helter-skelter.

"I'll go," Derek said. But by the time he'd gotten to his feet, Rachel had let herself in, and she stood in the doorway of the family room, her shoulders hunched under her backpack. She shed the backpack and shrugged out of her jacket, dumping both on the armchair. The hood of her gray sweatshirt was pulled so far forward Colleen could barely see her face.

Derek leapt toward his daughter. "Good to see you, hon." He held out a gift bag decorated with glossy black musical notes. "Got you a little something."

Rachel accepted her father's offering, but she didn't smile or greet him, just peered into the bag and withdrew a Yo-Yo Ma CD.

Derek shifted from one foot to the other. "I heard Yo-Yo Ma in this interview on the radio, talking about Bach's cello suites." To Colleen's surprise, he withdrew a paper from his pants pocket and read aloud. "'I found a certain truth with the cello, and this is it—there's something about this music that actually makes things whole.'" He snuck a glance at Rachel, and Colleen did the same. Such a pitiful attempt to connect with his daughter! Rachel's expression became, if anything, more blank than before.

Derek plowed on. "'Tragedy, comedy, joy, sorrow… I make the listener's ear work to fill in the gaps. That's the secret of why people feel helped by this music when they're in need.'"

Rachel stared at the CD in her hand, silent.

Colleen said, "What a beautiful thought! Yo-Yo Ma is so great. You know, I heard him give a talk years ago. Before a concert at Orchestra Hall."

Rachel raised incredulous eyes to her mother. Disconcerted, Colleen rushed on. "You want some coffee, hon? I just made a fresh pot. Or tea?"

Rachel dismissed her offer with a wave of her water bottle. She brushed by her father and sat at the tip of the couch. While Derek shuffled back to the recliner, Colleen perched on the edge of the cushion at the opposite end of the couch. The beads from Izzy's jewelry-making kit lay scattered there, and she scooped up those nearest her and dropped them into the box.

"Mom," Rachel said, "Would you just leave that stuff?"

Colleen let a handful of red crystals slide and straightened up to face her daughter.

"So," Derek said, false heartiness in his voice. "What's this all about?"

Rachel stood, as if restless, and moved close to her father's recliner. "I have some things I need to say to you." Her words sounded rehearsed to Colleen. "I need you both to just listen, without interrupting." Her daughter's chin lifted. "Is that something you're willing to do?"

Oh, my poor, brittle child! Colleen thought. If only she could take Rachel in her arms. But she imagined her daughter's recoil, her look of disgust. How could she risk that rejection?

Staring across the room at Colleen, Rachel said, "You want to understand what I've been going through? Good. Because it's clear that you don't have a clue." In a mocking parody of Colleen's voice, Rachel said, "'Maybe it wasn't as bad as you think.'"

"I was trying to reassure you," Colleen cried. "When I said that, I was trying to console you. To help you."

Derek reached out and touched Rachel's arm. "We both want to help you."

Rachel jerked away from her father and slammed the CD down on his hand. "You think listening to this will fix me? You think music can cure post-traumatic stress?"

Derek rubbed his hand. "Post-traumatic stress? Rach. That's what happens to soldiers in war. Tsunami survivors. School shootings. I'm not saying that what happened to you wasn't bad, but let's not—"

"Exaggerate?" Rachel put in. Crossing the room, she flung a look of disdain at Colleen. "Make a mountain out of a molehill?" She tugged open the zipper on her backpack and pulled out a sheaf of papers. She flipped through them and returned to stand directly in front of

Derek. "This is a paper I wrote last spring," she told him. Her voice turned wooden. "'Studies indicate that the effects of abuse can persist for decades. As adults, some young girls who are victims of sexual abuse have levels of cortisol as high as Vietnam vets. They are in a chronic state of stress and *never feel safe.*'"

Colleen's heart stopped.

Rachel continued, apparently reading a list from the paper, and each word struck Colleen like a blow. "'Depression. Suicidal tendencies. Anxiety. Phobias. Panic attacks. Addictions. Relationship issues. Sexual adjustment disorders. Cutting.'" Rachel let the paper fall onto her father's lap. "Those are the 'not that bad' problems of abused girls." Rachel turned on her heel and took a place on the couch at the opposite end from her mother.

Colleen sat shell-shocked. Rachel wasn't saying that she had *all* of those problems, was she? She'd always been a bit anxious. But addiction? Cutting? Relationship problems? She had a boyfriend, didn't she?

Derek stretched his hand toward his daughter. "Oh, Rach," he said. The papers she had flung to his lap slid forward. Derek grabbed them and crushed them in his fists, crumpling them into balls and blasting them down to the floor. "I wish to God you'd never remembered."

For just a second, Colleen let herself imagine what a visit from Rachel would have been like if she hadn't remembered. In this family room, Rachel might have been discussing the challenges of her latest cello piece, or laughing at a funny story her father had told, or playing Monopoly with Izzy.

Rachel jolted Colleen out of this fantasy. "The problem is not that I remembered. The problem is what you did."

Derek said hastily, "I understand that."

Rachel's voice broke. "You damaged me."

Damaged. The word insinuated itself like a stiletto, slow and unbearably hurtful, between the two ribs just below Colleen's breast. It hurt to breathe. Colleen heard Rachel say, "The damage would be here whether or not I ever remembered."

Rachel looked alien as she sat there, her arms crossed over her chest, and her hands rubbing up and down the long sleeves of her gray sweatshirt. Colleen watched, remembering how Rachel had scratched her arm so hard that she'd drawn blood. The hands moved faster. Colleen shifted closer to her daughter and grabbed her hands, stopped their frenetic journey up and down her arms. "You're not damaged," she insisted. "Look at you. You're young and beautiful and talented and funny and smart. Right now, you're upset. But you're strong. You're all right. You're going to be all right."

Rachel tore her hands from Colleen's grip and slapped them over her ears. And then she howled. A horrible, primitive, unending outcry. Colleen couldn't bear it. She slammed her palm over Rachel's gaping red mouth to stop it. Rachel twisted her head to free her mouth and, when Colleen wouldn't loosen her hold, bit down hard. Colleen tore her hand from her daughter's teeth.

"You have to stop pretending!" Rachel shrieked. "You have to stop."

Colleen cradled her sore, throbbing hand against her heart.

Rachel flung her hands up in a helpless gesture. "I'm not all right. I've never been all right." Tears streaked her face. "You think I was all right when I woke screaming from nightmares? Did you think I was all right when you put paper bags in my lunch box in case I needed to breathe into something? You think I'm all right now? When I stay in bed half the time? When I can't sleep without pills?"

The stiletto drove further into Colleen's heart. She swiveled her head wildly, as if there must be some solution, some help in the room. But there was only Derek. Colleen turned back to her daughter and pleaded, "But the pills? They're helping, aren't they?"

Rachel turned wooden again. "Yeah, Mom. They help. But I almost hate to tell you that, because you'll bounce right back to 'Rachel's all right. We don't have to worry about Rachel.' You'll go right back to la-la land, where if we just all act happy, everything will be fine. Everything is not fine. I don't care about anything anymore. Not anything, understand? I broke up with Aaron, and I don't care. I'm falling behind in my classes, and I don't care. I haven't picked up my cello for two weeks, and I don't care."

The stiletto in Colleen's heart twisted. She could barely breathe through the anguish. She understood, now, that she had never really taken in Rachel's pain. She'd shrunk from opening herself to it from the very first moments of that terrible phone call.

"Who's Aaron?" Derek said. "I didn't know you had a boyfriend."

"Why would you need to know? To give me some fatherly advice?" Rachel turned back to her mother. "I don't think I'll ever be able to have what you had with Dad. Be with someone who knows me inside and out and still loves me. How can I ever have that?"

"I wish I never had had it!" Colleen cried out. "It would have been better to never have had that than to have this happen." She cast a pleading look at her daughter. The smallest gesture from Rachel would do—a softening of the hard line of her mouth, a brief touch on the hand that Colleen extended to her now. But Rachel drew further into her corner and scratched at her long sleeves with hands bent into claws, an ugly, desperate motion. From the corner of her eye, Colleen noticed Derek rising from the recliner. Rachel's hands continued their frantic journey up and down her sleeves. Derek moved so close to Colleen that she felt his pant leg brush against her knee. Rachel raised her eyes to her father. In an acid voice, she said, "Go ahead, Dad. Now is when you calm me down. When you tell me everything will be all right."

Derek squatted on the floor so that he was eye-to-eye with his daughter. He packed an amazing amount of compassion in the single word he spoke. "Rachel."

Rachel inclined toward her dad. The movement was so miniscule that Colleen would have missed it entirely, had Derek's whole countenance not been suffused with tenderness in response.

"Still?" Colleen cried out. "He's still the one you want? To comfort you?"

Rachel retreated from her father. "No! I don't. I don't want him." Derek rocked back on his heels. In a choked voice, Rachel said, "I want who he was before."

Colleen took a moment before she answered. "Me too. I want who he was before, too."

Derek rose clumsily to his feet and folded his arms across his chest. In a tight voice, he said, "I'm right here, you know. And I am still who I was 'before.' There's only one me." He drew himself up. "I knew I might hear some hard things if I came here today, Rach, but I hoped I could make you understand how bad I feel, how much I care about both of you." He walked toward the recliner, picking the Yo-Yo Ma CD up from the floor on his way. "I know this isn't enough," he told Rachel. Turning to Colleen, he added, "Or fixing the toilet, or cutting the grass. But I hoped…"

He shambled to the recliner. "I would do anything to fix this, Rach."

"You can't be the one to fix this," Rachel cried out. "Can't you see that?" She lifted her feet to the couch and hugged her knees to her chest, her Doc Martens heavy against the fabric.

Just in time, Colleen stopped the automatic admonishment to take her shoes off. There was something strange about the way Rachel stared at her feet.

"Remember how you used to tease me, Mom? Tell me how weird I was. I wouldn't get a pedicure because I didn't want anyone seeing my ugly feet." She gave Colleen a sad look. "'All girls like pedicures,' you said."

Confused, Colleen answered, "I just wanted to have some mother-daughter fun together. What does that have to do with—"

"I never understood either," Rachel broke in. "Until things started coming back to me. But that's how he began. Taking off my shoes and socks and tickling my foot and pretending I was little. Playing *This Little Piggy* until he got to the last one." She stifled a sob. "'Wee wee wee,' and he ran his fingers up my leg to… to…"

Revulsion rose like vomit in Colleen's throat. She stared at Derek where he sat, still as a statue in the upright recliner, his white-knuckled hands gripping his knees.

"Do you see now," Rachel asked her mother, "why I can't meet you at Water World and act like we're one big, happy family?"

Colleen's face burned. "I do," she answered.

How could she not have seen that months ago? Somehow, she'd managed to hold the reality of what Derek had done at arm's length, just as she'd kept her distance from Rachel's pain. She'd placed her own pain center stage. "Rachel," she asked, fully focused on her daughter, "what do you want to do about this?"

Rachel looked as if she couldn't make sense of the question.

Colleen said, "I've read some things about this. There's no statute of limitations in Illinois for child sex abuse."

The Mendelsohn symphony drew to a close. Silence buzzed in the air louder than the music had been. Derek pushed forward on the recliner and flattened his feet on the floor, his hands still gripping his knees. His voice was hoarse when he spoke. "You know what I've been saying to myself this whole time you two have been talking? That prayer. 'Let me not so much seek to be understood as to understand.' I am trying so hard to understand both of you, but I'm wishing that you would try to understand me, too. Just a little." He swallowed visibly. "Understand that you are both the world to me. Understand that I'm better than the worst thing I've ever done."

His face darkened with shame.

Colleen's heart hardened, tight and small as a peach pit. "You poor thing," she said.

Across from her, Rachel's eyes widened.

"You poor thing," Colleen repeated. "You want our pity?"

"I want a little compassion," Derek blurted. "I wanted just the smallest bit of hope that someday I could make this right, or—I don't know. Suffer enough to satisfy the two of you?" He shook his head dejectedly. "Col, how many times did I give you second chances? Didn't I try to understand? Every time your temper got the best of you?"

Colleen gaped at her husband. "You think what you did and me losing my temper are equivalent?"

"No. I'm just saying that I always knew you didn't *want* to get angry like that; you didn't mean to lose it." His tone of voice sounded exactly like it always had when he'd calm her after an outburst. Understanding. Reassuring. He tilted his head, "I knew you regretted it later. That's all I'm saying. I understood you, because I know what that feels like."

"It's not the same!" Colleen exclaimed. "It's not the same at all."

"I'm not saying it's the same!" Derek yelled back.

Colleen had to catch her breath before she could speak. But finally, she was able to say, more calmly, "The things you're saying now to try to make me feel bad for you? They turn my stomach." She looked directly at her husband. "I'm filing for divorce."

After a moment, Derek stood, his shoes smacking the floor. "This is impossible." His chest heaved. "There's no way I can make you understand, because you don't want to understand. You're judge, jury, and executioner all in one. My all-purpose wife." He clomped toward the archway, then came to a halt and turned again toward Colleen. "Is this fair? Do you think you're being fair to me? Because I don't. I've done everything in my power, these past months. And back then, too. I did everything in my power." He paused a long moment. Then he let out a weird chuckle. "What an idiot I've been! 'Everything in my power.' I don't have any power, do I? You two have all the power. 'No statute of limitations,'" he muttered, stumbling out of the room.

Colleen and Rachel froze in place, their heads cocked. But instead of the slam of the front door, they heard only a soft click.

Rachel's face had gone white.

"You don't have to do anything unless you want to," Colleen assured her. "But I'll help you if you want to." She waited. When no response came, she added, "No matter what you decide, I'm going to do something. I'm going to file for divorce."

Colleen searched her daughter's face. "I didn't understand before," Colleen told her. "I didn't realize."

"I know you didn't," Rachel said. "How could you?"

Colleen reached for her daughter. "If only you'd told me."

Rachel pulled away.

"I didn't mean that as a criticism," Colleen rushed on. "I meant for your sake. I wish you had told me back then, for your sake." She wiped her tears with her sleeve. "Why didn't you tell me?"

Rachel's eyes widened. When she spoke, her voice was small. "I knew you'd be mad."

"Oh, sweetheart, no! Not at you." In some confusion, Colleen added, "Never at you. How could you think that?"

"Because then you'd find out everything." Rachel rubbed one eye with the heel of her palm, the way she used to as a small child. "Maybe you don't even know this. But me and Daddy made fun of you." Her face flushed. "I didn't really understand the other stuff, but I knew it was wrong to make fun of you. I knew that." Colleen sat speechless. Rachel didn't appear to notice her shock, and she went on, earnestly. "It would have hurt your feelings if you'd known we made fun of you. I knew Dad was right about that."

So that was how he'd done it. So simple. Such duplicity. Colleen smothered her rage. She would not repeat her past mistakes; she would not make her anger the center of attention. Instead, she took her daughter in her arms as she hadn't done in years. "I'm so sorry," she said. Rachel burst into tears. "I'm so, so sorry," Colleen repeated. Rachel convulsed against Colleen's chest, driving that razor-sharp stiletto deeper with each sob.

When Rachel left nearly an hour later, she appeared exhausted, but calm. Colleen watched her make her way until she'd disappeared around the curve of the cul-de-sac. She gathered up the crumpled pages of Rachel's term paper and smoothed them. Izzy was spending the night with Aaliyah, but who knew how early she might show up in the morning? Colleen brought the papers upstairs. Sitting on her bed, she noticed a paragraph highlighted in yellow. "It is this sense of betrayal, shame, and shared guilt that damages victims so terribly. For that reason, the greatest psychological damage occurs when the abuser is a father or father figure."

Colleen howled her daughter's name into her pillow. *Oh, Rachel! Rachel!* She rocked back and forth. *Dear Lord, I can't bear anymore.* She prayed, over and over. *Please. Take this away. Please.* She repeated those words, but that sharp needle of pain remained lodged in her breast. *Then give me the strength to bear this,* she finally prayed. After a long while, her breathing slowed, and a longing crept over her to feel close to her daughter. She stumbled down the hall to Rachel's bedroom.

When she'd still hoped that Rachel would live at home during the summer, Colleen had restored her bedroom to what it had been before the move to Arizona. She'd tacked up Rachel's musical posters, Beethoven and Mozart and Yo-Yo Ma alongside cartoons of Lucy, enamored of Schroeder as he played the piano, and portraits of jazz artists from Coltrane to Charles Lloyd. She'd arranged Rachel's costume jewelry in the small, decorative boxes of Asian design that her daughter favored, and unpacked her old American Girl mini-dolls to display along the top of her shelves. She sat on Rachel's bed now and fingered Annie, her daughter's beloved ragdoll, that lay on her pillow. Because of a split in the thin fabric at her neck, the doll's little face, framed with red yarn-hair, lolled to the side. "Poor Annie," Colleen said aloud. "I never did mend you, did I?" She smoothed the doll's gingham dress. The hem was torn, and the loose edge drifted down Annie's stuffed leg.

Colleen fetched her sewing box. "I'll have you fixed up in no time," she told the doll. She threaded a needle—a very small, thin needle almost as keen-edged on its threaded end as at the point. On her first stitch, the end of the needle pierced her finger. She sucked on the well of blood and wrapped a tissue around the spot. Continuing to repair the doll's neck, she slipped the needle through more carefully to avoid hurting herself. But when she lifted the dress to fix the hem, she saw that one of the legs had a large tear. Thick stuffing oozed out. "I should have seen that," she told the doll. "I should have done something about that a long time ago." She finished stitching the drooping hem, then studied the damaged leg. The area required a patch, and the stitches would have to go through the bulky stuffing as well. The needle didn't slide easily; with each push, it hurt the pad of Colleen's already sore finger.

She knew she should use a thimble, but she didn't want to. She pulled the thread through, telling the doll, "I didn't know." The end of the needle pierced her finger, and she winced. "I didn't know," she repeated, "but I should have known. I should have paid more attention." She searched the ragdoll's face, but Annie's cross-stitched eyes remained blank. Colleen's finger throbbed, and her gaze wandered to the thimble in her sewing box. "What if?" she asked Annie. "What if I hadn't lost my temper?" The little doll looked white-faced back at her, and in her visage, Colleen saw the pale face of eight-year-old Rachel backing away from her mother's rage. Backing away and running to this very bedroom, while Derek moved down the shadowy hallway to comfort his daughter. Colleen thrust the needle through the bulky material, puncturing her finger so badly that she cried out. But though her swollen finger throbbed with each stitch, she steadfastly mended the floppy leg until it was attached securely to beloved Annie's little stuffed body.

Chapter 40

Mandy must have been listening for Rachel's footsteps on the stairs, because she flung the door open the second that Rachel hit the landing and gave her a searching look. "How'd it go?"

"Different than I expected." Rachel blinked. "But good." She hung her jacket on the hook and flopped down on the couch, but then jumped up immediately. "It's weird. I'm exhausted, but I can't sit still."

Mandy rubbed the back of her neck.

"My mom's going to file for divorce," Rachel said. She laughed, a laugh that surprised her so much it made her laugh again. "How crazy is that? My mom's getting a divorce and I'm happy? C'mon." She grabbed Mandy's hand. "Let's make some cookies."

While they prepared the cookie batter, Rachel told Mandy the story of her meeting with her parents. "I hit my father with a Yo-Yo Ma CD," she said, pounding butter to soften it. "And I yelled at my mother that she had to stop pretending." She scrounged through a shelf to find the shortening. "And she did. It was like she finally heard me, and she got it, and said she was going to divorce my father. And I don't know exactly how, but all my anger at her just went poof."

"So, you stopped protecting your mom," Mandy mused, cutting open the bag of chocolate chips, "and she survived."

"Yeah," Rachel reflected. "No more walking on egg shells." A thought struck her. "I don't have to be the mother anymore." It seemed such a momentous realization that she spun around, expecting Mandy to look astonished as well.

But Mandy merely muttered, "About time," and folded the chips into the batter. Then the two of them spooned little mounds of cookie dough onto the sheet. They cleaned up, the smell of baking cookies filling the kitchen. Mandy gave Rachel a sidelong look. "Have you talked to Aaron?"

The timer on the old stove dinged, and Rachel put a mitt on and drew the cookie sheet out. "Not yet." She lifted the cookies with a spatula and slid them onto a large plate, her mind flashing with images of Aaron's dorm room, of the moonlight on the lake that night. "I'm not sure what to do about Aaron."

Mandy gave her a curious look. But Rachel just opened the fridge and said, "I need to figure some stuff out. You want milk?"

They shared warm cookies with melted chips and cold glasses of milk while Mandy told Rachel about the half-hearted search for a new roommate she'd made after their fight. "Rebecca said she was interested, but she couldn't move in until next semester."

"Oh, Mandy. *Rebecca*?"

Mandy chuckled. "I know, right?" In the midst of their laughter, a deep contentment filled Rachel, and she knew that she'd sleep that night without medication. She'd shut her eyes, remember the feeling of her mom's arms around her, and sleep like a baby.

Chapter 41

The rest of the week after that terrible meeting, Colleen woke each morning thinking *Rachel*. While she made her bed and brushed her teeth, images of her daughter invaded her thoughts: Rachel standing stiff and hidden in the shadows of her dark, hooded clothes; Rachel clawing at her arms; Rachel's eyes tightening to hold back her tears; Rachel's body shuddering in Colleen's arms. Colleen gave Izzy moments of attention, but the second that she waved Izzy off to school with her lunch box, Rachel once again claimed Colleen's thoughts. During the day, she spoke long, rambling text messages to Rachel into the microphone on her phone, but deleted them each time and instead typed brief words meant to encourage. Often, she sent a single question: *Where are you now?* or *What are you doing?* "I just want to be able to picture you," she explained, when Rachel complained of her intrusiveness. It was as if, by following her daughter's footsteps to class, or imagining her in the practice room or studying in the laundromat while her clothes tumbled in a dryer, Colleen could hold Rachel in her mind and so keep her safe.

She barely gave Derek a thought. When he did occur to her, she focused on the fact of his absence. On the relief she felt from the certainty that she wouldn't smell coffee percolating when she descended the stairs on Sunday morning. With that assurance in her mind late Saturday night, she drifted off to sleep, feeling something akin to peace.

But then the phone rang in the middle of the night, and a disembodied voice said, "Mrs. Moretti? Your husband's been in an accident."

He died. That was her first thought. Then: *God never gives you more than you can handle.* Had God decided that Derek alive was more than she could handle?

But Derek hadn't died. Cuts and bruises, an especially nasty head laceration—but only his leg had suffered serious damage. Colleen waited at the hospital to hear from the orthopedic surgeon who was working to repair a break in his tibia that required pins to hold it together. Colleen and Izzy sat in the family waiting area, an immense space in which a dozen couches and chairs were arranged in clusters, like little living rooms plunked down into a cavern. A deserted cavern, except for a group huddled at the far end of the room. That family sat in silence, eyeing the swinging doors each time they creaked open. Once a nurse came, and once someone in scrubs, and once a priest. Each time, the family stiffened, looked toward the door when it opened, and stood when the person came in their direction. The muted sounds of their distress echoed across the space. A small cry, a low moan, a sympathetic murmur from the professional.

Colleen had been assured that Derek's injuries were not life-threatening. Still, as she waited, scenes from various television series played across her mind. Bad things happened in surgery. Unanticipated reactions to the anesthesia. Unexplained drops in blood pressure. A doctor pressing paddles against the patient's chest and yelling "Clear!"

If Derek died, would *that* be more than she could handle? Or would it be a relief? Colleen glanced at Izzy, who tapped on her cell phone with her thumbs. "Izzy, what are you doing?" But before Izzy answered, those wide doors swung open again, and Derek's surgeon strode across the room. Colleen stood up. The surgeon smiled as he took the last steps toward her. "Everything went well. Your husband is doing fine." He went on, matter-of-fact, upbeat. Of course, Derek would need rehabilitation; it would take a while, but the surgeon hoped for a complete recovery. The nurse would let Colleen know when she could see her husband.

Izzy blurted, "But what about his brain?" The surgeon gave her a puzzled look. "Didn't you operate on his brain?"

The doctor leaned toward Izzy. "No. Why did you

think I operated on his brain?"

Izzy turned a trembling mouth toward her mother. "I heard you on the phone. You said, 'a head injury.' I heard you. And then you said he needed an operation."

"Oh, Izzy! You misunderstood. Daddy cut his head when he fell. That's all. Nothing that made him need brain surgery. The operation was on his leg." The surgeon nodded in confirmation. But long after he'd disappeared, Izzy's forehead remained creased. "Iz, I told you Daddy was going to be fine."

"That's what people always tell kids." Izzy flung herself against Colleen. "I thought he was going to die." Colleen wrapped her arms around Izzy's bony frame. "He's okay?" Izzy hiccupped. "Daddy's going to be okay?"

"He's going to be fine. He'll be in a cast. Probably he'll need crutches, he won't be able to drive for a while, stuff like that. But he'll be fine."

A slow smile spread over Izzy's face. "He won't be able to drive? So, he'll be home. He'll be home all the time, not just Sundays?"

"Well," Colleen stammered, "He has to go to rehab, and…"

But Izzy wasn't listening. She twirled in a circle, chanting, "Daddy's okay, hurray hurray, my daddy's okay!" Colleen grabbed her daughter's arm and put her finger to her lips, nodding toward the other family. Izzy eyes widened. She whispered, "Sorry!" and sat down. But she kept grinning and humming. From time to time, she leapt up and bounced in little circles around the couch where Colleen sat.

Just then the doors creaked open again, and a man in a dark suit came through. The waiting family gathered round him, and he led them down the hallway into a little room. A really small room, from what Colleen glimpsed before the door shut. It seemed too cramped to accommodate all those family members. Abruptly, a thin keening came from inside that room, and Izzy jerked. The wailing swelled. Izzy sprang to Colleen's side. "Mommy!"

"It's okay," Colleen said. "It's… someone died, I guess. The people are sad because someone died."

Izzy clutched at her mother's arm. "Not Daddy, right?"

"No, of course not Daddy."

Izzy blew out a long breath. Colleen pressed her own face into her hands. *Not Daddy.*

Parting the curtains around Derek's bed, the nurse said, "Mr. Moretti, do you see who's here? Do you know who this is?" Colleen scrutinized her husband in the muted fluorescent light. He had an IV in one arm, and a gauze bandage on his forehead. Encased in a cast, his right leg propped up on a pillow, Derek looked pinned to the bed.

His eyes fluttered open. "Colleen."

"Yes," said the nurse. "It's your wife, Colleen." The nurse placed her hands on Izzy's shoulders and moved her closer to the bed. "And who's this?"

One side of Derek's mouth rose in a crooked smile. "Izzy."

Izzy laid her small hand on the sheet. "Hi, Daddy. Does it hurt a lot?"

Derek mumbled, "A little." The nurse pressed something plastic against his palm. "You'll need this when the anesthesia wears off. Remember what I told you? Just press the red button at the top."

After the nurse left, Derek asked, "Is Rachel coming?"

Colleen blinked. "I haven't called Rachel."

"I did," Izzy announced. "I texted her." She scrolled down her phone, frowning. "She didn't answer yet."

Rachel won't come, Colleen thought. Aloud, she said, "Bea is on her way. She's going to take Izzy home with her."

"They won't let me stay," Izzy grumbled to her father. "You have to be older. Why?"

Derek started to answer, but then he winced.

"Maybe you need to use that painkiller," Colleen said.

Izzy leaned over the side of the bed. "Can I push the button?" But Derek shook his head, and just then the door opened, and Bea burst in. "My goodness!" she kept repeating. "When you think what might have happened! It could have been so much worse." She chattered about some friend who couldn't mount her stairs or drive her car for more than a month after breaking her leg.

"A month!" Izzy exclaimed, casting shining eyes on her father. "You'll be home for a month."

"Your dad could sleep in the family room," Bea observed, solving the problem of the stairs in their house. "Doesn't that couch open into a bed?"

Colleen nodded mutely in response, and at the same time, Izzy's mouth stretched in a huge yawn. "Give your dad a kiss goodbye," Colleen told her.

Finally alone with Derek, Colleen stood over her husband. "What happened?"

Derek's eyes were barely open. "I fell. I slipped and fell in front of a car."

"But where were you going? What were you doing downtown in the middle of the night?"

"Oh, Col," Derek said, his mouth turned down. "Nowhere. I had too much to drink."

"And the weather was terrible." Colleen went on as if he hadn't spoken. "Freezing rain. Where were you going?"

A pause. "It doesn't matter."

Colleen pressed. "You must have been going *somewhere*."

Derek shut his eyes briefly. When he opened them, he didn't look at her. He gazed off to the side. "Remember that song you like? 'I got peace like a river in my soul'? The lights reflecting on the river were so peaceful."

She took a moment with that. "Are you saying the bridge was where you were headed? That was your destination?"

Derek shifted his glance and looked directly at her. "Where else was there for me to go, Col?" he said, his voice rough. "Where else?"

Colleen wanted to shake him. At the same time, she wanted to flee the room and shut her ears to whatever he might say next. But she was done with fleeing. "Derek, are you saying you went to the bridge to… you were thinking about jumping off that bridge?" Derek looked away. "You know God can forgive any sin except suicide. You realize that, don't you?" Colleen said.

He tsked. "I was already in hell." His body stiffened, and he winced again.

"You should use that painkiller." Colleen reached for the dispenser, but Derek snatched it away and pressed it to his chest.

"It won't fix anything," she told him bitterly. "You suffering won't fix anything." Her voice rose a pitch. "Killing yourself wouldn't have fixed anything either. What do you think that would have done to Izzy? To Rachel?" She took a breath. "To me?"

Derek stared at the wall chart, where the names of the night-shift nurse and the doctor were printed in thick magic marker. "I checked the life insurance," he said. "It would still cover me. And we have mortgage insurance. The house would be paid for. You'd be okay."

He grimaced in pain again. Colleen's teeth clenched. "I'm not going to sit here and watch you be a martyr. Use that medication, or I'm leaving."

He raised bleary eyes to her. "I feel so terrible, Col."

But Colleen merely crossed her arms over her chest and waited until his thumb rose and pressed the red button on the top of the dispenser. "You want to do something," she said, "go to confession. Start with that. Make things right between you and God."

After a long while, Derek said, "Would you come? Would you come with me? Just, you know, wait in the pew while I go in." His hand crept toward her across the sheet, like a plea.

"I don't think you'll be getting to church for a while," she said. "But Father Ambrose would come to you at the hospital. Or the rehab center."

Derek drew his hand back. "I'll wait," he said, "until I can go to church. Go into a confessional."

Colleen nodded. She could understand Derek's need for darkness, for anonymity—the priest's profile hazy behind the grill, his eyes not upon you. "Okay," she said. Derek turned his palm upward in another appeal, but she didn't touch it. After a while, his eyelids stopped fluttering, and Colleen watched his chest rise and fall. The plastic medication dispenser fell from his grasp and lay at an angle against his side.

Resting her head in her hands, Colleen recalled Bea's words: *When you think what might have happened.* She didn't want to think about what might have happened.

She didn't want to picture any of it. Not Derek on that bridge, or the look on his face a few days ago when she'd said the word *divorce*. Not Rachel's ragged sobs at the end of that terrible meeting, or Izzy's anguish an hour ago in the waiting room: *I thought he was going to die.* But those images haunted her, and shutting her eyes only made them more vivid.

Derek's gold wedding ring caught the light. Colleen thought, as she had so many times before, *How could he?* How could Derek sit at the kitchen table and drink his coffee from a mug touting him as "World's Best Dad"? How could he return time and again to their home, to sweep Colleen up in his arms and take her to their bed? How could he have gone to church Sunday after Sunday, sung the hymns lustily by her side? "How could you tell me you loved me," she moaned softly, "and then do this to me?" Colleen dropped her face into her hands. She cried the way she had cried days before for Rachel, but this time she cried for herself. She cried until the wads of tissue she grabbed from the box on Derek's table were soaked, and her throat felt so dry that she couldn't swallow. She blew her nose and sipped the tepid water in the Styrofoam cup.

He was a big man, but on the bed, he appeared shrunken. She stared at his bandaged forehead, at the purple bruise that ran down the same forearm that held his IV drip, at his leg in its heavy cast. Something moved in her heart. What did she feel for this man? Not love. Pity, maybe. But not exactly. The word finally came to her. Compassion. She felt compassion for this flawed, broken man. She moved one of the extra bed pillows to the foot of the bed, rested her cheek on it, and closed her swollen eyes.

She had nearly dozed off when the curtain rings scraped against the rod, and Rachel slipped in. She scanned her father's cast, then stared at the small gauze bandage on his forehead. "I thought Dad had brain surgery," she said in a low voice.

Colleen whispered. "Izzy got it wrong." She felt too weary to explain.

Rachel settled onto the folding chair near her mother. "So it's just his leg?"

Colleen angled to face her. "It's a bad break. He'll need to be off it for a long time, and he'll need a lot of rehab. But, yes, the main damage is to his leg."

Rachel's gaze wandered back to her father, her face nearly as pale as his. "I thought he was dying."

"I should have called you myself," Colleen murmured. "I'm sorry."

Rachel licked her lips. "So what happened? Izzy said a car accident?"

Colleen hesitated. How much should she say? And how should she say it? "Your dad fell in a street downtown. It was dark and icy, and the driver couldn't stop in time."

Rachel's forehead creased. "He wasn't driving? He was crossing the street?"

"Not exactly crossing. He…" Colleen gulped. "Listen, Rachel, this wasn't your fault." At Rachel's startled expression, she hurried on. "I'm only telling you this because you said you want honesty." She took a deep breath. "Your dad fell when he was climbing the bars on the Michigan Avenue bridge, the one that goes over the Chicago River downtown." Her heart pounded like a drum as she waited for understanding to dawn on Rachel's face, but all she saw was more confusion. "Rachel, he'd been drinking and he was depressed."

"Depressed," Rachel echoed. Her mouth opened a little and her breathing became audible. "Well, goddamn!"

Colleen nodded slowly in agreement. She scooted her chair so close to Rachel that their knees touched. "Not your fault," she repeated.

From the bed, Derek whimpered, and the two of them stood and peered down at him. Rachel said, "Dad told you this?"

Colleen nodded.

"And you believe him? You think he really meant it?"

Colleen cast a startled glance at her daughter. "Of course."

"How do you know, Mom?"

In some confusion, Colleen answered, "Why would he lie about something like that?"

Rachel stood stiffly next to Colleen, her arms tight around her chest. "He got your attention, didn't he?"

Derek shuddered in his sleep, and a low moan escaped him. Colleen thought, *He meant it. He had to have meant it. That's the only possibility I can live with.* Derek grimaced, and Colleen reached for the gizmo that delivered pain medication and pressed the red button. "There's no way to know how serious he was, half-drunk on that bridge," she told Rachel. "I doubt he knows himself." She looked at her broken husband. "I know he was hurting. Desperate." She looked back up at her daughter. "Don't you think a person has to feel desperate to even think of doing that?"

Rachel's face crumpled, and she lurched a little toward Colleen. Then she slumped against her mother the way she used to as a small child when she was distressed—her arms hanging helplessly at her side, her mouth trembling, and her eyes awash with tears. "We could have been standing over a casket," she choked.

Colleen wrapped her daughter in her arms, the two of them pale green in the glow of the monitor that flashed Derek's blood pressure and oxygen levels. She meant to hold her, to let Rachel cry out all her tears in her mother's embrace. But before Colleen knew it, sobs tore through her own body as well. The pain of them took her breath away, and she tightened her hold on Rachel just as Rachel clung more fiercely to her.

Chapter 42

Rachel's gym shoes squeaked as she crossed the tile floor of the hospital foyer to Aaron. In the dimmed lights, he looked like a smudge in the circle of chairs in the distance. The smudge rose and moved toward her, gradually taking on his compact shape. As soon as he was within hearing distance, Rachel said, "My father is fine." Her words echoed a little. "He didn't have brain surgery. Izzy got that wrong. He's got a broken leg. That's all."

Aaron eyed her. "So… that's good, isn't it?"

"Oh, sure," Rachel said in a dull voice. "It's great. Everything is just great."

Outside, they saw their breath in the frigid November air. Aaron strode alongside Rachel through the near-empty parking lot. In the car, he ran the motor and turned the heat to high. "Rachel—I don't understand what's going on."

A bitter laugh escaped her. "Who does? Who understands what's going on?" She stared straight ahead.

"My father tried to kill himself."

"*What?*"

"He fell into traffic when he slipped on a bridge. He was going to throw himself over that bridge because of me."

Aaron angled his body toward her. "Why would you think that?"

Winding her arms tightly around herself, Rachel said, "Just drive."

Aaron heaved a sigh. "You can't not talk to me, Rachel."

Rachel retreated deeper into the hood of her jacket and stabbed a button on the dashboard. Late-night jazz filled the car.

Aaron snapped the radio off. "You called me in the middle of the night. And I'm glad you did, okay? I was happy! You needed me. But then you make me wait downstairs while you see your dad, and now you're all… I don't know what you are. Because you won't tell me."

"I'll tell you," Rachel cried. "But drive, okay?" After a pause, he turned his piercing gaze away from her and shifted gears.

She waited until they were on Lake Shore Drive. "When I was eight years old," she began. Aaron gave her a sidelong glance. "Don't look at me." She pulled her sunglasses out of her bag and put them on. The moonlit night darkened even more. "When I was eight years old…" She squeezed the words out, one by one. "My. Father. Abused. Me." The heater didn't work that well in Aaron's old car, and the cold air seemed to cut her breath short. She inhaled sharply. "He would come into my bed, and—I don't know. I don't know if he pulled down my pants or had me do that or just slid his hand… I don't know. What I remember, clearly, is the feel. His cool, thick finger touching my skin." Her head spun. After the dizziness passed, she said, "The other thing I remember for sure is him pulling my hand under the covers and showing me how to touch him."

Long moments passed. Rachel's shaky breaths were the only sound. Aaron's gaze was fixed on the road, his mouth a tight line. "Say something," she whispered.

"I can't drive and talk to you about this at the same time." With shocking speed, he swerved across two empty expressway lanes and onto the exit. He drove down a few side streets until he came to an empty stretch and parked, leaving the engine running, the thin heat on.

Rachel snuck a glance at him. Did that turned-down corner of his mouth signify disgust? That little muscle by his eye jumped. He probably wished he hadn't pushed her to confide in him. Or wished he'd never gotten involved with her in the first place. *Say something*, she wanted to scream.

But he didn't say a word. He just opened his arms to her. It wasn't easy to hug with the console and the gear box between them, but she managed to press her face into his jacket while his arm wrapped around her shoulder. He stroked her sleeve, a gentle touch over the area she'd so often clawed. She snuggled into him as best as she could in this cramped, awkward space.

Finally, Aaron spoke. "I could kill your father."

A small bubble of hysteria rose in her. "He almost took care of that himself, didn't he?" The wind whistled outside.

"Oh, Rachel," Aaron said.

The car seemed a bit brighter, and she realized that her sunglasses had fallen off. She extracted herself from Aaron's arms and fumbled around the car seat until she retrieved them. "Tell your story," she said, sliding the glasses back on. "That's what everyone says. You have to tell your story." She clutched at her arms. "I *hate* this story. Too many girls can tell this story, or others, much worse." She added, her tone now challenging him. "Really. When I think of how much worse it could have been, I feel like I should be able to seal it off and live my life. But the next second, I could kill my father myself..." She made a helpless, open-palmed gesture. "I don't know what to do with that. I don't know where to go with what happened to me. There must be some other place, somewhere between 'no big deal' and hating him. But I don't know how to get there." Her voice turned hoarse. "I don't know how to get there."

Aaron took his gloves off, and when she felt his warm hand cover hers, she clutched his thumb as if it were a lifeline. He stammered. "I think, maybe, Rachel… I'm sorry. I thought I could help you; I really did. And I'm here, okay? As your friend." He cleared his throat. "And as your boyfriend. But… maybe you need to talk to someone. A professional." His hand tightened a little on hers, and she almost told him then, about Monica and the sessions she'd been having since June. But something held her back, some intimation that she needed to keep that part of her life separate from Aaron. She answered, "I'll talk to someone, Aaron. I promise. I will." His hand relaxed over hers. "Good," he said. "Good." A cold shiver ran through Rachel, and for the first time she understood how much she'd hoped that Aaron could save her.

Make her normal.

Make her whole.

Chapter 43

Rachel fingered the slip of paper in her jacket pocket as she headed toward her father's room in the Rehab Center. She didn't really need the paper to remind her of the questions she wanted to ask, but she thumbed it. As if that could give her the courage to ask: *Did you really mean to kill yourself? Why? Did you go to that bridge because of what I said? Where will you go when you get out of here?* And the scariest one: *Will you try again?*

The door to Room 214 was ajar. Rachel peered through the opening at a slender Filipino woman in a green uniform who stood at the foot of the bed. "Mr. Moretti," the aide cajoled, raising a crutch in one of her hands.

A jutting wall blocked her father from Rachel's view, but she could imagine his frustrated look from the tone of his voice. "If you'd just give me the walker, I could *hop* to the bathroom myself! And it would be faster."

Rachel backed into the hallway. The aide murmured, "We'll get you all set here in just a second. I'll help you swing your leg. That's right."

She heard scuffling sounds and a gasped "Oh, Christ!" and then the bang of her father's crutches hitting the floor while he made his way to the bathroom. Slow bangs, interspersed with muttered curses. There was a moment of quiet, and then the aide said, "Good job. Here we are." Rachel snuck a peek into the room. Through the wide-open bathroom door, she glimpsed her father stepping toward the toilet, the aide close behind him, gripping a wide green band around his waist. "You remember how to turn yourself?" the aide asked, and at the same time she clasped his waistband and began to lower his tracksuit. Rachel twisted away from the sight and bolted down the hall.

She paused by the open doors of the PT room, where an elderly woman held on to the bars on either side of her and took a step forward. One physical therapist followed her with a wheelchair, while another held onto a band that encircled the old woman's waist. "You're doing great," he told her. "Let's try for two more steps today. Just two more." Catching the grimace on the patient's face when the woman forced herself forward, Rachel wondered if her father walked that painful path during his sessions. She distracted herself from that thought by scrutinizing other patients: a gray-haired man who bounced a big ball; a middle-aged woman on a treadmill that went so slowly it barely seemed to move at all, a frowning young man who lay on a mat, raising a small weight. Rachel kept watching until she felt certain that her father must be finished in the bathroom.

When she rounded the wall that obscured his bed, he was leaning forward, craning to see who had come in. "Oh! Rachel."

She stayed silent, suddenly at a loss for words.

"Could you…I dropped my phone." He gestured to the side of his bed. "Someone tried to call. Was that you? Did you just try to call me a few minutes ago?"

Rachel crouched to reach under the side bar of the bed. "That wasn't me." She handed him his cell phone, and he set it next to a lunch tray, where an unfinished lump of chicken salad congealed and a white plastic spoon stuck out of the pasty yellow pudding. "Are you done with that?" she asked.

He shot her a grateful look. "Yeah. Could you put it over there?" He nodded toward a shelf across the room that ran almost the length of the wall. "Have a toffee," he added, indicating a small gift bag next to the tray.

Rachel picked up the tray and carried it to the shelf. From behind her, her father said, "So. Busy time for you, I guess. Your term will be over soon."

Returning to his bed, she angled the chair so that she could see his face.

He coughed. "Exams coming, all that."

Rachel fingered the paper in her pocket. "I'm not doing

small talk." He gave a little start. She went on. "There's stuff I want to ask you. About what happened." She met his eyes. "Why did you go to that bridge?"

Her father blinked. "Didn't your mother tell you?"

"Kind of. But. What were you thinking, exactly?"

"I wasn't thinking," he countered with a sigh. "I'd had too much to drink."

"Was it because Mom said she wanted a divorce?"

A long moment passed. "Partly, I guess."

It felt chilly in the room. She kept her jacket on and wrapped her arms around her chest. "It was because of the stuff I said, wasn't it?"

He shook his head, an adamant no. "It's not on you, Rach. You could only say that stuff because of what I did." His face filled with misery. "What I did to you. To Mom. To our family." He rubbed a reddened eye. "I couldn't see any other way out, Rach."

It took Rachel a second to find her voice, but when she did, it came out clear and cold as ice. "Why would you get to do that?" she said. "What gives you the right to leave while the rest of us live with the mess you made?" She wished there was a way to shove her father's face into that mess, make him smell its stink, make him *eat* it, make him sick on it the way that it sickened her. "I hate you," she said. Her heart went all jittery in her chest. "If you kill yourself, I'll hate you even more. If you kill yourself, that'll just be another mess I have to live with." She gulped air.

The blood drained from her face, and her throat closed up.

With one swift motion, her father dumped the toffee candies out of the gift bag and pressed it into her hands. She dipped her mouth to its opening and breathed as slowly as she could. For some moments, the room seemed to darken, and she lowered her head almost to her knees. From the corner of her eye, she glimpsed a wheelchair across the room. The wide green strap that her father had needed around his waist to get to the bathroom hung over the back of it. The sight of it, the memory of him clumping into that bathroom, the image of him in pain, triggered another wave of dizziness. She breathed into the bag for what seemed like forever, but when she recovered and lifted her face, she saw from the clock that only a few minutes had passed. She gave her father a bitter look. "You don't get to leave," she told him. "You have to promise me that. I shouldn't have to wake up in the middle of the night wondering if you've jumped off a bridge."

He ran his fingers through his hair, exposing an ugly black thread at the edge of his bandage, near his shaved hairline. "That won't happen, Rach."

"Don't think it's because I care about you." Because she didn't, she didn't care about him, she would never again care about him! Shutting her eyes, she transported herself to her practice room. In her mind, she played a dissonant piece on her cello, hearing every discordant note, down to the last jarring chord.

When she finished and opened her eyes, her father was staring down at the crumpled sheet on his bed. His white calf, with its wiry hairs, was exposed, and he flicked the sheet in an attempt to cover it. Suddenly the room reeked of indignities. The sidebars that enclosed the bed, the plastic urinal that hung within his reach, the gadget to call the nurse's station pinned to the mattress, and on that shelf, the leftover lunch that congealed on his tray.

"None of this is your doing," her father said gently. "None of it ever was." He propped his elbows against his pillow and leaned toward Rachel. "None of it is your fault."

His tenderness threatened to melt the cold numbness that gave her strength. She stood abruptly, turned her back on him, and left the room.

Chapter 44

"Don't look at me that way," Colleen told Pat. "I haven't decided for sure to let Derek come home. But Rachel's okay with it. 'Whatever you want, Mom.' That's what she said."

The two women curled up on the couch in Colleen's family room, one at each end, a patch of sunlight on the cushion between them. Pat shook her head. "But why would you do that?"

Colleen sighed. "He can barely get around. He can't manage stairs at all. He can't drive."

"Those are his problems."

Colleen lifted her chin. "What do I tell Izzy? How do I explain to her why her dad's not coming home to recuperate?"

"Try saying, 'Your father and I are getting a divorce.'" Pat took in the distraught look on Colleen's face. "I understand that's hard to do."

Colleen kept her eyes downcast at the couch cushion.

"Who am I, after I get a divorce? I used to think that was a totally stupid question. I'd see these magazine articles. Who are you? And I'd think, how can anyone not know who they are? I knew. I was a singer, a music student, my parents' daughter, my brother's sister. Then I was Derek's wife, a homemaker, a mother, a really creative mother who encouraged her daughters in music and writing and drama. I was a volunteer. At school, I started the fourth-grade drama program, I arranged to get the music for the youth orchestra. Now who I am? Rachel's not living at home, and when I get divorced, I won't be a wife anymore. Once Izzy's out of school, I won't be anything."

"You'll always be a mother," Pat said. She gave Colleen a rueful smile. "We never get to stop being mothers."

"A mother who failed her daughter." A heavy silence fell between the two women. Colleen sighed deeply. "And the other thing is, I don't want to have to tell Izzy just before the holidays. All the kid's favorite Christmas memories? The way the whole family decorates the tree, and bakes cookies together, and helps me set up the stable. Izzy puts baby Jesus in the manger, and then I play the piano and we all sing, even Derek. The dinners with our family, my brother Shawn and Bea and Amber. We play games, we laugh—I don't want to take that away from Izzy. If I tell her now, it's like I'm not just ruining this Christmas, I'm ruining her memories of all the great Christmases we've had in the past, and we'll never have another one." Colleen blew her nose and took a fresh tissue and dried her cheeks. Pat leveled a thoughtful look at her. "What?" Colleen demanded.

"If you let Derek come home, you're going to start pretending again."

"I'm not pretending. It's not the same as before. I've made a decision; I know what I'm going to do. It's just a delay. Just for a while."

Pat pursed her lips. "A while can go on and on." Colleen opened her mouth, but Pat held a hand up. "Let me finish. You're still at the beginning, Colleen. A lot of terrible stuff has already happened, but still, you're just at the beginning. You can't imagine how it goes on forever. You walk out of a movie because suddenly you realize the scene is going to be about incest. You make up stuff when people ask what you're doing to celebrate your wedding anniversary. Your grandkids—" Pat's voice caught. "Your grandkids aren't allowed to stay overnight with you." Pat swallowed. "The years slip by. You think you have forever. But you don't. No one has forever." Pat's eyes welled with tears. "I had a mammogram." She gulped water from her glass. "Then an ultrasound. Now they want me to have a biopsy."

"Oh!" Colleen leaned into Pat and hugged her. "A lot of times it turns out to be nothing."

"I know. I'm trying not to worry. But it hit me hard, Colleen. The idea that he could outlive me. After all this time, just when I can see the light at the end of the tunnel, he could outlive me?" She shook her head. "It's unbelievable. Joe had a scan for his emphysema. It showed something on his lung, and they want him to have a lung biopsy. You watch. His will turn out to be scar tissue and mine will be cancer." Her face got a determined look on it. "If I make it through this, I'm going to change things."

"Why wait?" Colleen urged. "Change things now. You could get away from him now, if you just put yourself first. Stop giving your money to Katie, stop putting her before yourself."

"If you let Derek come home, you're doing the same thing," Pat said. "Putting Izzy before yourself."

Colleen brushed the remark off with a wave of her hand. "You could move in with Katie. You're paying half her rent anyway."

Pat's face closed up. "That would be worse."

"Worse than living with Joe?"

Pat stroked her locket. "Living away from Katie," she said, "I still worry about her. And get mad about some of the stuff she does, like buying that television. But I don't *see* her do those things. I don't have to come home and see boxes of stuff she can't afford piled in the hallway. I can sit with her when she's really down, even stay overnight if I'm getting really worried. But I don't have to witness her going downhill, day to day. I don't have to wake up every morning and see the door to her room shut and wonder if she's still breathing in there." She raised her eyes to Colleen. "I can't live with Katie. Maybe I should, but I just can't."

Colleen took a long time to answer. "Of course, you can't," she said. "And I…I can't just let Derek go off somewhere after rehab, alone. I don't think he'll do anything, but…it's like he fell into a pit, and now he's struggling to climb out. He's climbing out, and he's not that far from the top, but he can't quite make it. He needs a hand to pull him over the top, and then he needs to rest a while. Then he'll be all right— he'll be able to start off again on his own. But not yet. See? He needs that last boost." She shook her head. "You don't see someone you've loved for twenty years barely holding onto the edge of a pit, and just walk away. You just don't do that. No matter what they've done."

"I'd walk away," Pat said. "In a heartbeat." She raised her eyes to Colleen. "I wish Joe had felt guilty enough to take his own life."

"Oh, Pat, you don't mean that!"

An odd look crossed Pat's face. "You meant it, didn't you?" she said. "When you got that phone call from the hospital, and you thought maybe Derek had died?"

Colleen drew back on the couch. "It's not the same," she said. "For a second, I thought that things might be easier if he had died. That's not the same as wishing that he had." Colleen glanced at the empty seat cushion between her and her friend. Earlier, buttery sunlight had warmed that space, but now it sat in shadow, a chill gap between them.

After Pat left, Colleen slumped in the corner of the couch. The problem with having only one friend who understood was that when they didn't understand, you had no one. *You don't just walk away*, Colleen asserted angrily in her mind. Momentarily, she wished her mother was there. But of course, she could never have talked to her mother about any of this. She wished Geeta was sitting with her now, even though she couldn't have confided in Geeta either. But Geeta's calming presence, her bare brown feet tucked under her, her smile—Colleen would settle for just that much. She checked her text messages. Geeta had failed to respond to a single text over the past months, and the time between Colleen's messages to her had grown longer. But she texted now, briefly telling Geeta about Derek's accident.

Less than a minute passed before she heard the ping! of a message alert. She almost didn't want to look. If it wasn't Geeta…

But it was. *So sorry to hear about Derek. When is a good time to talk?*

Colleen's eyes stung with tears. She couldn't tell Geeta everything, but she could tell her about the divorce, she could tell her about Derek at the bridge. She tapped at her phone. *Would now work for you?*

Chapter 45

"You've done so many really hard things these past two weeks," Monica told Rachel. "Talking to your parents, to Aaron, dealing with your father's suicide attempt, visiting him in rehab. I hope you feel good about how you've handled all that. Proud of yourself."

"I am proud of myself," Rachel said. "And in a lot of ways, I feel better. I'm sleeping better. I'm definitely calmer. But after I saw my father in rehab, I don't know. I felt really good at first, but later I felt ashamed of myself. It's like shame is a virus I always carry, just biding its time to infect me. Lying in wait." Her heart thumped, and she took a moment to breathe deeply. "So, I think I'm ready to try that thing you talked about."

Monica nodded. "And you brought something today that gives you comfort?"

Rachel lifted her old rag doll from her wide cloth bag. "This is Annie."

Monica smiled. "Good," she said. "An old friend."

Rachel tightened her grasp on her doll. "So, now what?"

"Now we invite Rachel in. Eight-year-old Rachel, who understands so much about this shame business. We invite her in, and you talk to her."

Rachel gulped. "If I talk to her, it might make it real."

Monica pulled her chair close. "It's already real, Rachel. It's always been real."

"But what if I yell at her? What if I blame her, say, 'Look what a mess I am! Look what you did to me!'" Rachel clutched Annie to her heart.

"We need a way that you can see that child without being afraid of what might happen. A way to have her here, but put some distance between her and you. So that you feel safe, and she feels safe, too. Sometimes it helps people to imagine a thick pane of plexiglass between themselves and the person they need to talk to. Do you think you might want to try that?'"

Rachel focused on the aquarium, on her cadre of fish slipping in and out of the fronds. "No," she said slowly. "I'll look at her through the aquarium." She raised her eyes to Monica. "The aquarium is a safe place." A nervous laugh escaped her. "It sounds stupid, but shame can't get where the guppies are."

"Good," Monica said. "That's good. So, hold onto Annie and look through the glass of the aquarium while I take you through a relaxation exercise."

Rachel had done this before. But this time, even though

her eyes stayed wide open, trained on the aquarium, on the little fish who darted around carefree, safe and sheltered, Monica's voice grew fuzzier and more distant than it ever had. A heaviness came over Rachel's body and grounded her firmly in the chair.

"She's there," Rachel whispered. For young Rachel's face was forming, a little wavy and indistinct through the waters, but clearly there, on the other side of the aquarium. The child stared at Rachel, watchful. "She's afraid of me," Rachel said, astonished that this could be so.

Monica's voice came from afar. "What do you want to say to her?"

"She's shrinking back." Rachel whispered to the girl, "Don't be afraid. I'm not going to hurt you." Rachel stroked Annie's hair, but kept her eyes on the child. "Oh, you poor, poor thing." Rachel began to cry. "So scared. Sweetheart, no one's mad at you. No one is going to yell at you, or throw things." The girl had been crouching, but now she stood a bit straighter. Rachel said, "I wish you could come to me, sweetheart. I would rock you in my arms. Rock you in my arms, and never let anyone hurt you again." The child's bottom lip trembled. "You didn't do anything wrong," Rachel told her. "You never did anything wrong. You are good." Now the child's face, like Rachel's, was wet with tears. "You are good," Rachel repeated. She rocked her rag doll, a constant stream of murmurs coming from her lips. "You are good you never did anything wrong you are good." Then she stopped rocking, and instead pressed her face against Annie, while her body was racked with sobs.

After a long, long time, Rachel raised her wet face to the aquarium. The child was gone. The guppies flashed scarlet and gold and indigo in the water. She looked down at little Annie in her hands, then turned to Monica. "I never did anything wrong, did I?"

Monica took her hand. "You never did anything wrong."

Chapter 46

"Happy birthday!" Rachel called down the stairway while Gregorio made his way up to the apartment. He took in her floral print leggings and pale lavender top. "Look at you! What happened? Did you lose your job at the funeral home?" At the top of the stairs, she gave his arm a playful punch and led him into the living room, where Aaron and Mandy were already in the throes of a Scrabble game.

Gregorio feigned dismay. "You started without me?"

"What nerds we are," Rachel laughed. "A Scrabble tournament to celebrate your birthday."

"Plus Greek food," Aaron reminded her.

Kaitlin arrived a few minutes later, waving a bottle of ouzo. They were excited to be together; none of them shared a class this year. While they played Scrabble, the conversation meandered from how their classes were going to the latest scandal in D.C. to funny YouTube clips that they passed their phones around to share. Rachel basked in the camaraderie of her old gang. Then Gregorio startled her by asking, "How's your dad?"

Before Rachel could think of how to respond, Aaron said, "I told Gregorio about your father's accident." Rachel mumbled a few words about rehab going well, and Gregorio expressed the wish that her father would be out by Thanksgiving. "Hospitals and rehabs are such dismal places to have to spend a holiday," he said. To Rachel's relief, he turned then to Kaitlin. "Are you going home for Thanksgiving?" and the conversation drifted.

Dinner arrived when Mandy and Gregorio were in the final game of the tournament, Mandy ahead by 17 points. "Who ever heard of 'ki'?" Gregorio complained, moving the game to make room for stuffed grape leaves, gyros, hummus, and spinach-cheese pie.

"Gotta keep up," Mandy said.

"You're pocketing your letters?" Gregorio exclaimed.

"Just a precaution," Mandy answered breezily. "I told you I was competitive."

By the time the food was consumed and only an inch of ouzo remained in the bottle, Mandy had captured the Scrabble title. "So, who's coming with me to the movie?" Kaitlin asked. They were showing a newly released comedy in her dorm. Aaron shot a questioning glance at Rachel, but she shook her head. Within a few minutes, the apartment cleared and they stood amidst the clutter of half-empty glasses and the remnants of their meals on paper plates. Neither made a move to tidy anything.

Instead, Aaron came up to her, and she moved silently into his arms.

The first time they'd made out after Rachel had told Aaron about the abuse, his every gesture had seemed tentative, as if he awaited some kind of permission from her. He'd kept his shirt on even after she'd removed her own top. And after she'd pulled him down to the bed and nuzzled his shoulder, he'd unexpectedly pulled back and ran his hand across her forehead, like a mother checking to see if her child had a fever. "I'm not a porcelain doll," she'd told him. They'd reinstated their nothing-below-the-waist rule, and he'd relaxed.

But tonight, Aaron seemed tense again. For a moment, she felt his hardness against her thigh, but then he immediately edged away from her. She leaned over to kiss him, but he pulled back, leaving a foot of space between them. In the moonlight that came through her bedroom window, he lay flat on his back, cupping his hands behind his head. He stretched out, perfectly still, yet it seemed to her that he vibrated with need. In a way, hadn't he been vibrating with need ever since the night she went to his dorm? Her gaze wandered to the poster she'd recently taped back up on her wall. *Love like you've never been hurt.* She touched his shoulder. "Aaron. I'm not, um… ready to have sex, but I could, you know, do something for you. Is there something I could do for you?"

He gave her an uncertain glance. "Well.

Maybe…maybe you could give me a hand job?"

She startled.

"Never mind." Abruptly, he sat straight up. His face turned beet red. "I can't believe I said that."

She pulled herself up next to him, leaning her back against the headboard, but pressing against him as well, shoulder to shoulder. "No, that's okay. I mean, I asked you." She scanned the length of his blue jeans, her glance momentarily arrested by the bulge under his zipper. *Why shouldn't I do that for him?* she thought. Hadn't Aaron tried to answer her needs—her confusing, ambivalent, changeable needs—all these past months? Her need to draw him near, her need to pull away. Her need to feel his hands on her, her need to still them. *I could do this for him,* she thought. *It doesn't have to be a big deal.*

She patted the sheet and gave him a weak smile. "Come on. Let me do something for you. Take your jeans off." When he'd undressed, she said, "Get under the sheet," and laid next to him, but on top of the covers. She kissed him and stroked his bare chest. After a while, she sat up, her back to him, and slid her hand under the sheet.

He was hard, but his skin felt velvet-soft. Automatically her hand pumped, slowly. Up and down. A sour substance rose to the back of her throat, but she focused on the wall poster. *Dance like nobody's watching.* Her hand slipped a little and she rearranged herself. Up and down. *Sing like nobody's listening.* He said her name. "Rachel." When she didn't turn, he pleaded, "Rachel, look at me."

She looked. *This is Aaron.*

"Could you… a little faster…" Bile rose in the back of her throat, but she kept her gaze on him—on his half-closed eyes, the sheen on his brow. A moan escaped him, and he tightened his hand around hers—

Love like you've never been hurt

and he quickened her movements,

Don't throw up

then slowed them.

Love like you've never been…

He moaned one last time and breathed heavily for some moments before withdrawing her hand from him.

His semen dripped onto her wrist. *Don't throw up.* She wiped it on the sheet as best she could. Aaron lifted his head, an apprehensive look on his face. He appeared so vulnerable at that moment, his look touched off such an immense tenderness in her, that she mustered her most reassuring smile.

"Can you hand me some tissues?" Aaron asked.

She grabbed the whole box, set it on the bed next to him, and offered another smile. "I'll be right back."

When she returned from the bathroom, Aaron had pulled back the quilt and wiped the sheet with a wad of tissues. He didn't meet her eyes. "You want to change the sheets?" They pulled off the sheets and, in silence, remade the bed with fresh ones. Aaron sat on the edge of the bed and gave her a helpless shrug. "This was a mistake, wasn't it?"

Rachel swallowed.

"I'm sorry," Aaron cried.

Rachel shifted closer and wrapped him in her arms. "No, it's all right. Really. I'm okay. Not great, but okay. I wanted to do something for you. But I'm still figuring things out." She looked at Aaron's troubled face. "I've got a long road to travel," Rachel said, repeating her therapist's words. She touched his cheek. "But there's no one I'd rather do that with than you, Aaron. No one."

Chapter 47

Except for a brief text promising to let Colleen know when she had her biopsy, Colleen had heard nothing from Pat. Each time she took out her phone to call her friend, she hesitated. She had to decide within the next few days whether or not to let Derek come home after rehab, and she didn't want Pat to influence her. But today a text message from Pat had come when Colleen was scrubbing the tiles in the downstairs bath. *Can you come? Joe in ICU.*

Leading Colleen through the intensive care unit, Pat talked nonstop. "I took him for that lung biopsy yesterday. They told him it was risky. I tried to talk to him about a second opinion, but he never listens to me. Anyway, something went wrong when they took the tissue samples. His lung filled up with blood, and his pressure dropped to nothing. I didn't know anything about this. I was in the cafeteria. But when I got back to the waiting area, they come up to me and the next thing I know, they take me into this little room and shut the door and tell me he's in a coma, and they're transferring him to the ICU." Pat turned into a room and moved to a green vinyl chair in the far corner, the furthest possible distance from where Joe lay, a ventilator breathing for him.

"Where are your kids?" Colleen looked around, as if these adult children might be lurking somewhere unseen.

"Ellen came yesterday afternoon. Jimmy and Johnny will be here later. I didn't call Katie. Katie won't come." Pat spoke matter-of-factly, but Colleen flinched.

Joe moved restlessly on the bed. Though his eyes were shut, his mouth grimaced around the white tube that protruded from it.

"Sit," Pat said, motioning to a nearby chair. She half-whispered. "You'll never believe what I did." She glanced at her husband on the bed. "I should have left him, Colleen. I know that now. But at the time, whenever I thought about it, I always ended up at the same place. Why should he get to win?"

"But Pat, he is winning. That's why I said get away, get money for yourself."

"Exactly!" Pat's cheeks pinked up in excitement. "Yesterday I get home from the hospital and see a statement from Joe's retirement account in the mail. My name's on that account, too, but he doesn't like me to open those. I did anyway. Then I phoned." Pat bounced a little on her chair. "I just wanted to find out exactly what you have to do to take money out, you know? I just wanted to ask a general question about that. But this lady says, 'I have to ask you some questions first.' She asks for my social security number and those questions about my mother's maiden name, that kind of stuff? Then she asks for the password. I thought, that's that. But I was sitting right by the big open file drawer, and I see the folder called 'Invest.' And there it was. The password scrawled inside the cover. So, I give it to her, and she says how much did you want to withdraw? I started to say, oh, I don't want to take any out, I just wanted to know how to do that, but then—I couldn't believe I did this, Colleen—instead I said $20,000." Pat nearly sprang out of her chair in her excitement. "The next thing I know," she raced on, "she's asking, do I want them to take tax out? And I don't know what to say, but she makes it sound like that would be a good idea, and says that if she makes the amount $22,000, then they can take some tax out and I'll still get $20,000. And I say, okay, let's do that. All casual, like I do this every day!"

"Twenty thousand dollars," Colleen repeated.

"Yeah." Pat grinned. "They're sending a check to the house."

"Oh my God." Colleen felt a little giddy herself, but scared, too. She glanced over to the bed. Joe's eyes were closed, but he moved restlessly from time to time. Colleen mouthed: *Can he hear us?* When Pat stood, Colleen followed suit, and they both watched Joe struggle against the restraints that pinned his hands down. "Why did they do that?" Colleen whispered.

"He tries to pull the tube out." Pat spoke in a normal tone of voice. "The nurse said they do that. It's uncomfortable, to have something down your throat." Joe grimaced and twisted his body. "The nurse said he's been getting more alert." Pat made a face. "I'm supposed to talk to him, say his name."

She shuffled closer to the bed and bent over her husband. "Joe? Joe? Can you hear me?" It startled them both when Joe's eyes flew open. Colleen stumbled backwards. *It's foolish to be afraid*, she told herself. *Joe can't even speak, with that tube down his throat.* But her heart thumped. Had he heard Pat talking about the money? There were stories about people in deep comas who later claimed they'd heard conversations in the room the whole time.

Pat raised her voice. "Joe, you're in the hospital. You're going to be okay." He jerked at the restraints. "You have to stay tied down." His hands stilled and his eyes narrowed. "They'll untie you, but first they have to be sure you won't pull the tube out." Joe twisted his head toward the restraints and widened his eyes at her. When Pat told him, "We have to wait for the nurse to untie you," he tried to force his shoulders off the bed, but was only able to raise them a couple of inches. "You need the tube to breathe, Joe. You're on a machine that helps you breathe. That's why I don't want to untie you." Joe shot a venomous look at his wife. "Fine, you old goat," Pat exclaimed. "Let the nurse explain it to you."

"You want me to find a nurse?" Colleen asked. Joe's gaze darted toward Colleen then, and he nodded vehemently.

"I'll get someone," Pat sighed. She reached for the gizmo with the call button that was pinned to the bed near Joe's hand. Joe clamped down on Pat's hand like a vise, so hard that his knuckles turned white, and she cried out. For a second, Colleen was too stunned to move. But then, with Pat struggling to pull Joe's hand off her own, Colleen lurched forward to help. She pried his index finger loose. In reaction, he wound it so tightly around Colleen's own finger she thought it might break. With her other hand, she scratched him as hard as she could, and he jerked his hand away, freeing Pat. She backed away from the bed, cradling her hand next to her body. "You son of a bitch!"

Just at that moment, a nurse stepped into the room. She only paused a second at Pat's words, then walked briskly toward the bed, not meeting anyone's eyes. Adjusting something on the monitor, she said, "Patients don't always know what they're doing when they come out of a coma. The loss of consciousness, the drugs. They can be very confused." The nurse tipped her head to read the hospital bracelet on Joe's wrist. "Mr. Callahan, do you know where you are?"

Colleen never heard Joe's response because, with her undamaged hand, Pat dragged her out of the room and down the hall. "I want to get some ice in the cafeteria," she said.

Suddenly furious, Colleen exclaimed, "He knows how much that hurts!"

They joined the people milling around various kiosks. Pat begged a baggie from the server at the sushi station and filled it with crushed ice, while Colleen got a tall paper cup of iced tea. At the table, Pat wrapped the ice-filled baggie in her scarf and pressed that gingerly against her arthritic hand. Colleen stabbed her straw through the plastic top of her drink. "You sure you don't want anything?"

Pat shook her head. "He's back," she sighed. "Worse than ever." She looked the picture of dejection. But after a moment, her frown faded, and she grinned. "But I'm getting $20,000. I still can't believe I did that."

Colleen rolled the edge of a napkin between her thumb and forefinger, and spotted a red scratch Joe must have made on her hand. "Won't the check be made out to Joe?"

"Probably, but I won't have to actually cash it, will I? I can just deposit it into our joint account. Then I'll transfer it to…" She gave Colleen a sly look. "I have another account he doesn't know about."

Colleen got goosebumps. "But eventually he'll find out."

Pat stared at her ice-packed hand. "I don't care anymore. I really don't."

A thought struck Colleen. "What happened with your biopsy?"

Pat shifted the bag of ice. "That's next week. Then it'll take another week or so before I get the results." She forced a smile. "I'm not going to worry about that. I'm going home to enjoy being in my own house, *alone*, and wait for that check to come."

"You could move out," Colleen said. "Right now. You could stay with one of your kids until you find a place of your own." She looked expectantly at her friend.

"Maybe," Pat said. "I haven't gotten the money yet." She looked around, searching the table, the empty chair next to her. "Shit. I left my purse in his room."

Colleen offered to retrieve it while Pat waited outside the wide ICU doors. If I were Pat, Colleen thought, I'd be out of there. I wouldn't spend another second in that house. So why, she asked herself, are you still thinking of letting Derek come home? Why did you spend every Sunday with him for months? Derek's not anything like Joe, she told the accusing voice in her head. But aren't you just like Pat? the voice countered. Aren't you also concerned about money, about changing your lifestyle?

Colleen shoved the door to Joe's room open as though she could push those thoughts away with the motion. Joe appeared to be asleep on the bed. He no longer had the tube down his throat. She stared at him. His face was slack now, but she pictured him the way he'd looked when he fought against the restraints, his eyes narrowed and his face contorted with hatred. The contrast with how Derek had looked in his hospital bed could not have been starker: Derek, bruised and repentant and broken, his eyes begging Colleen for compassion.

Joe made a noise, and Colleen's heart turned over. She tiptoed across the room, lifted Pat's paisley bag from the chair, and skittered out. Halfway down the hall, she noticed the same nurse who had been in Joe's room earlier. The nurse stood in the doorway of a patient's room, pulling latex gloves on her hands. Colleen didn't know why she felt she had to say something, but she whispered, "Um. We're leaving now… Joe's sons should be here pretty soon."

The nurse cocked her head toward the sleeping patient. "You can talk out loud. He's in a coma." She gave Colleen an appraising look. "Come in for a second."

The nurse straightened the bed covers around the man, talking all the while. "When stuff like this happens, it's very stressful. Family members don't always know what they're saying, any more than the patients know what they're doing. I'm always amazed that more people don't lose it. And when you've been married a long time, and your husband has been sick a long time…" The nurse uncovered the man's bare feet, inspected them, and then adjusted them so that his heels no longer pressed against the pillow beneath his ankles. "One thing I've learned is that it makes things easier when you can keep the real person in mind." She gestured toward the bulletin board in the room, jam-packed with photos. Colleen recognized the man in the bed in a large photo with a baby who wore a yellow "I love Grandpa" bib. In another, the same man stood on a dock by a sailboat, his arm flung casually over another man's shoulders. "His brother," the nurse said. For the first time, she looked directly at Colleen. "We tell the family of coma patients to bring pictures. They do it to remind us that there's more to this person than the body we attend to. But I think sometimes the family needs the reminder even more than we do. There's so much more to every person than their condition." The nurse peeled off her gloves and dropped them in a container by the door, squirted antiseptic from the dispenser and rubbed it into her hands. "You have a good day now."

On the surface, the nurse's tone had sounded neutral. But hadn't there been a judgmental edge to it? Suddenly angry, Colleen thought: *She knows nothing about Pat. About Joe.* Colleen hurried the last few feet to the wide ICU doors, and exhaled in relief when they sealed behind her. Returning Pat's purse to her friend, she hugged her goodbye, then made her way through the halls to the north parking lot exit.

An aide pushed a man in a wheelchair toward her. Encased in a cast, the patient's leg extended straight out, his heel resting on the edge of the foot support. That would be Derek when he had to leave rehab next week. To go where? She couldn't decide.

She'd told Rachel that she'd support her if she wanted to file charges against her father, and she'd told Derek that maybe he could come home until his leg healed. She'd told Izzy her dad would be home with them for Thanksgiving. Her head ached. What was she doing? What was she supposed to do? She felt as if hands tugged at her, pulling her in every direction. She leaned against the wall, shut her eyes, and wrapped her arms around herself. But cries assaulted her ears: Derek's pleas, Rachel's accusations, Izzy's "but not Daddy, Daddy didn't die, did he?" They ricocheted in her head, clamoring, until she shouted, "Shut up!" and her eyes flew open. The corridor was empty except for two women a few feet down the hall who jerked to a stop, then gave her a wide berth when they passed. Colleen floundered, her hand trembling so much that she could barely latch onto her rosary once she'd found it in her bag. *You have to help me,* she whispered. That's when she noticed a stained-glass window set in a door a little further down the hall. Its brilliant orange and turquoise hues were reflected in a patch of color on the floor, as if the light projected from the heavens themselves. The window drew Colleen toward it like a beacon.

Inside, she saw the source of that light. One wall of the chapel was all glass. Through it, Colleen saw a small garden, where sunlight brightened golden mums. She slipped into a honey-colored pew, stared at the dust motes in the sunbeam, gripped her beads, and waited. Surely that beacon of light promised peace.

Instead, the cries of all the people who needed her rose again. Snatches of Rachel's confrontation with her parents came back to her mind in ugly whispers. *This little piggy* triggered a wave of nausea. Disgust for her husband prickled her skin again. How could she possibly live with Derek, even for a few weeks while he recovered? She should listen to Pat's advice. She should listen to that undercurrent in Rachel's voice when her daughter had muttered *Do what you want, Mom*. But what did she want?

I want more time, she thought. *More time before I have to witness Izzy's heartbreak when I tell her that we're getting divorced. More time before I have to face the questions from family and friends. More time before my life changes forever.*

But her life had already changed forever. She raised her eyes to the cross, and fingered her beads and admitted: *What I really want is for all this ugliness to go away. For Rachel to be healed like Jesus healed the sick with just a touch. For Derek to be a husband who had no dark underside. For a miracle.* She wept into the wad of tissues in her hands.

She, who rolled her eyes at stories of statues that shed real tears, who knew that God was no bearded old man in the heavens, but a source of life, a source of grace—she longed for an old-fashioned, out-of-this-world miracle. It hit her then that on some level, she'd hoped that the charade she and Derek had enacted these past months might one day magically become true. That if they behaved as though they were a real family, as if they had a real marriage, if she acted as if she might one day forgive him, then God might make that happen. How foolish!

She wanted a miracle, but the most she could hope for was more time to come to grips with it all. To come to some sense of peace with her decision, some readiness to divorce. Time for Derek to accept that, too. Because he hadn't been utterly wrong-headed, had he, months ago when he'd wished they could somehow get through this together?

If he came home to recoup, that would give them a month, six weeks until the New Year. No longer pretending. Both of them knowing this was a stopgap measure. But at the same time, learning what was possible. Discovering how they might salvage remnants of their friendship from their tattered marriage. Learning, she realized suddenly, if it was possible for her to forgive him. Not as a way to sustain their marriage or to get her old life back, but as a way to heal and move on to a new life.

She prayed the rosary. The sun lowered in the sky, and the little chapel grew dim. There was a tiered display of votive candles to the left of the altar. So many of the candles had been lit for the sick, for the dying. Their flames shone brightly in the darkness, flickering. Like—

Like that summer night on a camping trip years ago, when she had stood with Rachel and Izzy and Derek, all of them enchanted by the towering evergreens where thousands of fireflies flickered. They had lit up the branches like strings of tiny Christmas lights. Thousands! Blinking on and off. Derek had beamed. "It's magical, isn't it?" Then he had wrapped his arms around all three of them and said, "I love having a family."

The peaceful shadows of the chapel settled lightly on Colleen's shoulders like a velvet throw. God had brought this memory to her mind—this reminder of Derek, the loving father. To even consider letting Derek come home, she needed some way to keep that image foremost in her thoughts. The nurse's words came back to her. "Don't look at patients only through the lens of their illness." *Don't look at Derek only through the lens of what he did.* But how to manage that?

In the next moment, an idea flashed through her mind, and it seemed to her that God had sent it.

Chapter 48

"Don't twist around," Colleen said, brushing through the last tangles at the back of Izzy's head. The doorbell chimed. "And put away your dolls before you come downstairs."

"Maybe that's Amber, or Rachel." Izzy scooped up the dolls, plucked them down in a jumble on the shelf, and sped past Colleen into the hallway.

Colleen followed, but then hesitated at the open door to Rachel's room. On the wall next to the closet, she'd taped photos in the shape of a heart. Most were snapshots, but in the center of the heart, she'd placed an 8"x10" shot of Rachel and her father at her eighth-grade graduation. In it, Rachel wore a white dress with a scarlet sash and cradled a dozen white-and-red roses in her arms. Derek looked handsome in a blue suit. Flushed and happy, Rachel tilted her face up to her father.

Colleen dithered, then carefully peeled the photo off the wall. There were several marks around the spots where the tape had been. The marks weren't quite aligned, because of the many times during the past week when she'd removed that photo and then replaced it. At the doorway, she sighed and looked again at her daughter in that picture. Surely there was love in Rachel's eyes. Colleen reversed course and taped the picture back up.

Later, in the kitchen, while the smell of roasting turkey wafted through the room, Colleen and Rachel peeled potatoes and Bea minced garlic for the green beans. Izzy traipsed in carrying an armful of games, Amber in tow.

"Not in here," Colleen called out. "We're cooking."

The girls did an about-face and headed for the family room, but moments later Izzy called out. "Mom. There's no room in here."

With an impatient "Tsk!" Colleen set her peeler on the counter. Bea followed her down the hall.

"See?" Izzy said, pointing at the mess that surrounded Derek and Shawn, who were intent on the football game.

It was true that the room was more crowded now that Colleen had changed it to accommodate Derek. Stacks of his clothing cluttered the card table she'd moved in here. His laptop and papers from work, including a thick training manual, were strewn over the end tables.

"I could move some of this stuff," Bea said, picking up Derek's laptop. But then she looked up at the wall above the fireplace. "Oh! That's new."

"It's a clock," Izzy told her aunt. "Isn't it cool? Instead

of numbers, it has pictures of our family. I helped Mom pick them out." Etched in gold letters in the center of the large glass clock over the fireplace were the words *Time Spent with Family is Worth Every Second.*

"Nice," Bea said.

Colleen scanned the untidy room. She hadn't had enough time to organize things for Thanksgiving, that was the trouble. She let out a sigh and turned to Izzy. "Just go play in the living room."

Izzy's mouth fell open. "Really?"

Colleen adopted a devil-may-care tone. "Why not?"

"Whoa!" Shawn exclaimed. "Did someone cast a spell on my sister?" He turned to his daughter. "Careful, Amber, I don't think a kid's ever been allowed in that room."

"That's not true—" Colleen objected.

"And you didn't even make us take our shoes off when we came in!" he recalled.

"I only ask you to do that when it's wet outside," Colleen began to argue, but then she stopped herself. "I've decided that's the small stuff."

Shawn raised his eyebrows in mock surprise. "Now I know you've been abducted by aliens or something." He cast a grin at Derek, inviting him to join the teasing. But the sight of Derek, with his heavy cast propped on the ottoman, wiped the smile from Shawn's face. He gave Colleen a serious look. "Right. Don't sweat the small stuff."

Perhaps the glass of wine she'd been sipping had gone to Colleen's head, because she found herself giddy at the thought that her brother assumed Derek's accident was the big event that had changed her. She felt a reckless impulse to blurt, *Oh, it's not about the car hitting him. That wasn't a big deal. It was more him wanting to throw himself over a bridge. And me planning to get a divorce. And what he did to…* Colleen's hand flew to her mouth, and a deep red flush spread over her face. She fled back to the kitchen, Bea at her heels. There, Rachel washed the potatoes in a colander and then began chopping them. Colleen started to peel a sweet potato. But Bea stayed still, giving her a considered look. "Good for you," she said.

Good for me?

"Sometimes it takes a near-tragedy, doesn't it?" Bea added. "To put things in proportion."

"Right," Colleen said. A moment later, she wiped her hands on her apron and escaped to the formal dining room. This was another room they only used for holidays and special occasions. The glasses set on Grandma Riordan's antique white tablecloth sparkled, and the silverware gleamed. While Colleen scrounged through the hutch drawer looking for matches, Rachel came in and set the salt and pepper shakers down. Then she stopped and took in the display Colleen had created in this room: a shadow box on the wall made up of carved letters that spelled out LOVE. She had inserted family snapshots in the nooks between them. Rachel turned to her with narrowed eyes. "What is all this?"

Colleen struck a match and lit one of the cream candles in the crystal holders. "Just something to remind me. Like you said once, about those reversible figures? How you can look at it from different perspectives. These photos help me keep the perspective I want in mind."

She struck another match, trying to think of a better way to explain.

"This is your new house of cards, Mom."

Colleen leaned over to light the second candle. "What was good is as real as what was bad," she murmured. But she didn't know if Rachel heard her, because when she looked up, her daughter had disappeared.

Shawn helped Derek get settled at the head of the table, his encased leg elevated on an extra chair. When they held hands for the blessing, Colleen bowed her head, but peeked at Rachel from the corner of her eye. Derek said, "I'll keep this short and sweet. We're grateful for this food, and I'm more grateful than words can say to be here." Unexpectedly, he choked up. In the silence that followed, Colleen saw Bea nod as if she understood the roots of his emotion. Derek recovered and went on. "I'm more grateful than I can say to be here this Thanksgiving and to have all my family here with me."

Rachel's eyes were shut tight. Was she blinking back tears? Remembering that night at the hospital? Colleen whispered a prayer to God to help her daughter. She wasn't asking for a miracle. She was sure of that. It was more a prayer that God would help Rachel find a way to forgive her father, for Rachel's own sake. Because wouldn't it help Rachel heal, if she could do that?

Later, while Izzy played the violin for them, Colleen's gaze wandered around the circle. Bea leaned forward a little on the hard chair she preferred. Amber curled up on the big armchair. Shawn, restless as usual, glanced at his phone through much of the piece, while Rachel sat with her eyes shut, her head cocked toward the sound. And from the couch, his leg extended onto the ottoman, Derek gazed at Izzy with the doting look he always had when his daughters played. Unexpectedly, he glanced in Colleen's direction and smiled.

Without thinking, she smiled back. She felt a kind of fondness. But was it genuine, or an artifact of the setting? A resurfacing of her ingrained response to Derek's pride in his daughters? A startling thought flashed through her mind. What if the fondness was real? What if love *could* come back?

The family burst into applause. "Play one more," Derek requested. "Play 'Danny Boy.'"

Izzy made a face. "That's so easy." But she foraged through the books that were stacked on the shelves and set the music on her stand. Derek looked over at Colleen and tipped his head, his raised eyebrow asking: Would she sing? Colleen nodded.

When she came to the lyrics, "Oh Danny boy, I love you so," she felt an ache. An ache of love for Derek? Or an ache of wishing it might be possible to feel love again? When the piece ended, she whispered a prayer. *Please, Lord. Help me. Send me a sign. A Christmas rose. A shooting star.*

Instead, God sent an ice storm.

Chapter 49

The ice storm gathered fury during the dark, predawn hours that Friday, while Colleen slept. She woke to the sound of wind lashing against the bedroom window, and stared out at a world of diamond-studded trees. Even before she'd had her coffee, she bundled up and went out to throw salt on the stairs and the driveway. By midmorning, a brilliant sun brought people out, despite the bitter cold, to photograph the glistening trees. Now, in the late afternoon, the sun had faded. There were flutters of snow, and the wind had turned brutal again.

Colleen smashed a shovel against the two front stairs to break up the gray slush that had frozen there. The sound of a motor made her turn, and her mouth dropped open at the sight of Pat's car. The car shimmied, then slid until the front tire skidded onto the grass. Throwing handfuls of salt from her bucket, Colleen walked gingerly toward the car. "What are you doing here?" she said, when Pat lowered her window.

A thick gray scarf hid much of Pat's face, and her gray knit cap covered her ears. "I needed to see you." The scarf slipped a bit, revealing a purple bruise on Pat's cheek.

"What happened to your face?"

"I fell," Pat mumbled. She threw her car door open, forcing Colleen to step back. "I have to pee," Pat said.

Colleen laid a hand on her friend's arm. "Walk behind me." Pat's boots crunched on the trail of salt Colleen threw down as they made their way to the door. They stopped at the bench in the hallway to get out of their boots, but waited until they were in the kitchen to shed their damp jackets. They stood shoulder to shoulder at the double sink, where Colleen wrung out her mittens and Pat drank a glass of water thirstily. In the bright light, her bruise shone a deep purple. "What happened?" Colleen demanded.

"I slipped on the ice when I was salting our walk."

Colleen tried to picture it. How would you hit your *face*? Wouldn't you break your fall with your hands? "Joe hit you, didn't he?" she said. "You drove here in this terrible weather because you were afraid to stay with Joe."

"No," Pat insisted, shaking her head. "I fell, and then I just had to come tell you the good news." Colleen gave her a skeptical look. "Really," Pat said. "Remember my biopsy? The doctor's office called today. I'm fine. I don't have cancer."

Colleen dropped her sodden mittens in the sink and embraced her friend. "That's great! That's great news!" She held her at arm's length and added, with a meaningful look, "so now you have a second chance."

Pat blotted the tears from her eyes. "You're the only one who can really understand." With a last glance at that bruise, Colleen went to the refrigerator and took out a bottle of Chardonnay. "To celebrate," she said.

But Pat shook her head. "I don't really drink. And I have to drive home." Colleen put the bottle back, opened the freezer door, and waved a box of Dove chocolates in the air. "Perfect!" Pat said.

They talked while they waited for the chocolates to thaw. There was no reason, Colleen argued, for Pat to delay making a new life for herself. With a pointed look at her friend's bruise, she urged her to get away from Joe, now. Today.

"Stay here tonight," she said. "You can sleep in Rachel's room. Izzy's not even here. She's having a sleepover with Aaliyah." A thought occurred to her. "I know you don't want to see Derek. But you wouldn't have to. He's in the family room, not upstairs."

"It's not that," Pat said. She gazed out the patio doors, where the light from the kitchen illuminated a row of thick icicles hanging from the gutter. "I think I should get home."

The wind howled outside, and a chill went through Colleen. "If you go back there, I'm going to be scared for you all night long."

Derek must have turned the TV on in the family room, because suddenly a commercial blared. Colleen stood to shout that he should tune it down when a forecaster said, "We expect some warming by Saturday and temperatures back to normal on Sunday, but for now, stay off the roads."

"Another reason you should sleep here tonight," Colleen said, helping herself to a chocolate. The anchor's voice continued. "And keep those flashlights handy. There have been numerous reports of power outages, and Com Ed expects more."

"Power outages," Colleen repeated.

At the same time, Pat answered, "Okay, I'll stay here."

Colleen hesitated. "Good. But what about… do you want to call home? Make sure everything's okay?"

"We have the backups," Pat said. "He's okay."

Colleen said, "Maybe you should let Joe know that you're staying here tonight."

Pat nodded. "Yeah. It might seem strange if I never thought to call him."

It seemed an odd statement to make, and an unsettled feeling crept over Colleen. Pat searched her pocket, pulled out her cell phone and stared at the black screen. "I forgot," she said. "I turned it off in the library."

"You went to the library?"

"I had a book to return, and then I stayed there a while to warm up. They have all those signs about silencing your phones, and I don't know how to do that, so I just turned mine off." She held the power button down. Moments later, the phone emitted a string of insistent beeps. Pat's fingers trembled as she tapped some numbers. She pressed the phone to her ear and her face took on a waxy quality. She looked up at Colleen. "That was Ellen. My daughter, Ellen?" As if Colleen wouldn't know who Ellen was. Pat's voice sounded calm, but her whole body began to tremble.

"Joe is dead."

Chapter 50

While they watched the movie, Rachel reclined on the couch, her legs stretched across Aaron's lap. He drew circles on her gray leggings, sending little tingles up her spine. The characters on the screen raced through a rainstorm and ended up in the guy's apartment. Of course, they would now have to get out of their soaked clothes, and the inevitable sex scene would follow.

It seemed like the perfect opportunity to make her suggestion. Here they were, cocooned in an ice storm that glazed thin white webs on the storm windows. But each time she opened her mouth, the butterflies in Rachel's stomach took her breath away, and she remained silent. The couple on the screen locked gazes.

Rachel couldn't figure out what to call the thing she wanted to propose. "A kind of game to improve your sex life" was open to way too many interpretations. In the movie, desire had predictably overwhelmed the couple. Why, oh why, Rachel wondered, did film passion so often lead to sex on the kitchen countertop, or the guy smashing the woman up against a wall? The least comfortable arrangements she could imagine, and ones that appeared to require Olympic-level athletic skills and strength.

She noticed that Aaron's hand had stilled, coming to rest on her knee while he peered at the movie. She sat up. Aaron apparently took that as an invitation to sidle closer to her, his eyes still focused on the television while the couple reached the finale of their sex scene.

If she didn't say something soon, Aaron would kiss her and then… Good. A completely different scene came on the television—people answering phones in an office. Rachel took the plunge. "There's this thing that I heard about…it's supposed to improve your sex life."

"Oh?"

"It's kind of like massage," she told him. "But you're more like—just touching the other person. Like this." She grabbed his hand and drew her thumb across his palm, then stroked his fingers, one by one. Aaron smiled and tried to reciprocate. "No, you take turns. Like if it's my turn to… pleasure you… then you stay completely passive. Until it's your turn to give me pleasure."

Aaron's brow furrowed. "Okay," he said, uncertainty drawing out the "O."

"And you're both naked when you do this."

"Oh!"

The couple on the television were back, rolling on the

living room rug. Rachel turned the TV off. "But you don't touch sexual parts," she added.

"So, the idea is…?"

"You basically avoid being sexual while you touch all the other parts of the person in a sensual way." She gave him an uncertain look. "Does that sound too weird to you?"

"So, it's a kind of foreplay?"

"Not exactly. It doesn't necessarily lead to sex. I guess in the beginning, it shouldn't. For tonight, I'd like us to agree that we won't make out or kiss or anything, even afterwards. Because the whole idea is to experience the sensations of touching or being touched, without worrying about what happens sexually." Now he looked really confused. "Aaron, it avoids my triggers."

"Oh."

"You want to try it?"

"Sure," he said. But his tone was hesitant.

"Let's try it," Rachel urged, and unbuttoned her blouse.

His eyebrows shot up. "Here? In the living room?"

"Mandy's gone home," she answered. She slipped out of her blouse, glad for the old radiator that hissed and clanged while sending sheets of heat into the room. She wanted to be here, in this room that held no reminders of her child-self, no multicolored quilt that she needed to set aside before she could lie on the bed with Aaron. And no memories from the night she'd struck herself. "Come on, take your clothes off," she urged.

Aaron grinned. "Just to be clear," he asked, "we're both getting barefoot all over?"

"Stark naked," she laughed. With the heat coming up, the room quickly grew overly warm, and she undressed without so much as a shiver. When their clothes lay heaped on the floor, they perched at opposite ends of the couch. Rachel kept her gaze on Aaron's face, a protection against accidentally drifting too low and seeing him, for the first time, in the bright light of day. He seemed to be doing the same, his look trained on her forehead.

Rachel said, "I'll start. I'll touch you first. You just lie back; I'm the one giving you pleasure."

He squinted. "But not sexual pleasure?"

"It might feel sexual. Or become sexual. You let yourself feel whatever you feel. It's just that we don't... you stay passive, and I don't touch you anywhere directly sexual." She waited until he slid down on the couch cushions. Taking his hand in hers, she once again traced slow circles on his palm and ran her forefinger up and down the sides of his fingers, across the soft skin of his wrist. While making her way up his arm, she focused on the texture of his skin—the softness of his inner arm, the roughness of his elbow, the hardness of his bicep. An image of her father's soft upper arms flashed in her thoughts, and she rubbed Aaron's muscle as if to imprint this difference in her mind. Something similar happened when she ran her hand lightly down his chest. Aaron was much less hairy than her father, and his hair was paler, walnut brown. She trailed her fingers down the hairs that formed a ridge in the center of his chest, and he sighed with pleasure. She took his face into her hands, and pressed her palms against his smooth-shaven cheeks and looked into those beautiful dark eyes speckled with gold.

"Rachel," he said, reaching for her.

But she put a finger on his lips to hush him, and lifted his hand off her bare hip. Then she tugged playfully all around his curly head of hair, explored his ears (how soft the lobes, how surprisingly flexible the outer ridge) and stroked his eyebrows. She went straight from his head to his feet. His heels were much rougher than hers, and she wondered if it was running that affected him that way. The hairs on his toes, like the hairs on the back of his fingers, were sparse, another contrast with her father. It seemed to Rachel that with every touch she claimed Aaron as Aaron, solidified him as someone utterly separate from her father.

Aaron's knees were rough, but the skin on his thighs was soft and covered with a light down. When she moved her hand up and down his leg, her thumb grazed his inner thigh, and he gasped. She ran her palm over his taut stomach, and his penis sprang up from its nest of curly hair. *This is Aaron*, Rachel reminded herself. Circling his belly button with her thumb, she snuck a sidelong glance, and noticed the soft little cap atop his rigid penis, the bluish veins running down its side. She had the surprising thought that she could clasp him now, give him pleasure with her hand—even, maybe, take him in her mouth— and it would be all right. It would be, simply, a way of loving him.

But she didn't do either of those things. She stayed with their agreement to avoid sexual contact. Instead, she asked him to turn over, an action that itself reverberated with vulnerability. Then she explored every inch of his compact body. She kneaded his neck and shoulders, then ran the heel of her hand down the broad muscles of his back, over his tight butt, and across his toned runner's calves, until she had reached his bare feet again. She wriggled each of his toes, and though—just for a second—the words *this little piggy* sprang to her mind, she replaced them with Aaron's reassuring words. *No shame here.*

"Wow," Aaron said when she'd finished, and they both sat up, facing one another.

"Yeah," Rachel smiled. "Wow."

"So, you ready to…"

Her heart drummed with anticipation. "Give me a minute."

Aaron let out a long sigh. "Wow," he repeated. Then he looked at her steadily. Under his scrutiny, just the *thought* of sliding her barefoot-all-over body down the couch flooded Rachel with waves of pleasure.

"Remember," she admonished him, "no sexual stuff. And don't start until I say."

He made a cross-my-heart gesture over his bare chest and rested his hands on his knees, patient as a Buddha.

Chapter 51

Colleen put her car in low gear and inched out of the garage down the dark driveway. The car swiveled, but the antilock brakes kicked in and it steadied again. Pat repeated, "You don't have to drive me home. I can drive my own car."

"Of course I'm going to drive you home," Colleen said. She looked at her friend out of the corner of her eye. "Are you sure you don't want to call Ellen back? Tell her you're on your way?"

Pat shook her head. "We'll be there soon enough."

But on the icy roads, it took Colleen nearly twice the time to get there. Ellen met them at the back door, wearing a down jacket and carrying a flashlight trained on the floor. A candle flickered on the kitchen table. "Where were you?" she asked her mother.

"At Colleen's house. This is my friend, Colleen." Pat turned a bit, to bring Colleen forward, and then asked abruptly, "Who's that?" A dark form hovered in the corner of the kitchen.

Ellen replied, "That's Maura. She's been wonderful. She's with the police."

"The police?"

"I called 911. They sent the police and the paramedics. There was nothing they could do, Mom." Ellen's voice broke. "Maura insisted on staying with me until I could reach you. Until someone could come." Pointed downward, her flashlight made a pool of light on the faded green linoleum. "I thought I was fine. But Maura had me wait in the bedroom when they came to take Dad. And then… I could hear them." Ellen choked up. "Zipping the bag. That was a terrible sound, Mom." She burst into tears.

"I'm sorry," Pat said. "I'm sorry you had to be the one to deal with that."

"I tried to call you. I called here first when I heard about the power outages, and then I remembered that when you lose electricity, your phones don't work. So then I tried your cell, but it went right to voicemail. I tried the twins, but they're both probably still out on snowplows. I got scared. And I forgot all about wellness checks. I should have called the police to do a wellness check." Ellen wiped her face with a tissue. "Maura said it probably wouldn't have mattered, it was probably too late already, but… Anyway, then I drove here."

Pat pulled off her gloves and loosened her scarf. Ellen squinted at her mother, then pointed the flashlight directly at her. "What happened to your face?" The shadow that was Officer Maura stepped out from the corner.

"I fell on the ice," Pat said.

Ellen went back to her story. "I could see that the house was all dark when I drove up. There were no lights, no candles, no flashlights. It was freezing in here."

"Yeah," Pat said. "The furnace stops working when we lose electricity. I never understood why; it's gas heat." Her voice drifted off.

Ellen tugged at her mother's sleeve. "I shouted for Dad when I came in. I ran down the hall. Mom, I *tripped* on him. He was in the hallway, and I tripped right over him."

Pat put her arm across her daughter's shoulder, and they leaned into one other. "I'm so sorry," she repeated.

"Why didn't he use his portable tanks?" Ellen went on. "He was *right there*, right outside the TV room!" Pat answered something, but Colleen couldn't hear it, because suddenly the kitchen light blazed on, and the TV down the hall blared one of those horrendous commercials with the speaker yelling a mile a minute that you have to *act now*. Officer Maura came forward. She wore a black leather jacket that didn't look very warm. Colleen heard a whoosh as the furnace started up again. In the next second, cool air blew through the vent near her feet. The officer said, "Maybe we can take a look at that now. At those oxygen tanks?" Her eyes on Pat.

At the end of the hallway, Joe's bedroom door yawned

open. Pat gestured vaguely toward the bed. "There's one in there," she said. Then she pointed into the TV room across the hall, where some game show contestants yahooed and jumped up and down. Maura picked up the remote and turned the television off. In the quiet, Colleen heard the wheeze of the oxygen machine. Four portable canisters stood neatly in the corner, next to the flat-screen television. Pat said to the police officer, "Those are all full. They just delivered them."

The surge of relief that came over Colleen at Pat's words shocked her. Yet when Maura asked, "How can you tell how much oxygen is in these things?" Colleen found herself tensing up again. Pat appeared unruffled. The officer wanted to see what you had to do to actually release the oxygen. Colleen glanced at Ellen, who seemed absorbed in her mother's explanation. Pat twisted a lever, and a hiss of air rushed out of the canister.

Shivering in her wet shoes, Colleen wondered how long it would take for the house to feel warm again. She shifted nearer to the wall vent, where hot air now blew out. Her shoe landed on a glossy magazine and slipped a little. There were a bunch of magazines and junk mail on the floor, half of them under the end table. Colleen knelt down and gathered them, turning her face to the warm air. That's when she noticed the envelope that fluttered, its edge caught under the leg of the table.

Maura asked Pat, "What time did you say it was when

you left the house?" Still crouched on the floor, the stack of magazines in her hand, Colleen freed the envelope. Pat said something to Maura about spending time in the library just as Colleen slipped the envelope between the magazines. Maura said, "So the first you knew that anything was wrong was when you listened to your daughter's messages?"

"Yeah," Pat answered.

"What time was that, then?"

Colleen glanced at the three of them in the corner. Pat stood there, her profile to Colleen, while Maura reviewed the information she'd written on her pad. The electricity was on when Pat left the house, right? And she always kept her car in the garage? Pat began telling the officer about the crime in the neighborhood, the people two apartment buildings down who everyone suspected dealt drugs, but the police couldn't seem to do anything about it. That was why she always kept her car in the garage, locked. Colleen thought, *The electricity had to still be on when Pat left the house. It had to be on, or she wouldn't have been able to get the car out of the garage.*

Back in the kitchen, Maura sat on a chair and pulled on her heavy boots. "How are you getting your car back from your friend's house?" It seemed an odd question for her to pose, and no one said anything for a moment.

Then Ellen looked at Colleen. "It can stay there a day or two, can't it? It's not in the way?"

"Leave it as long as you need to," Colleen assured her.

When the officer zipped up her jacket, Ellen flinched. *It was terrible when they zipped up the bag, Mom.* Maura said, "Well, anyway, the electricity's on again, so you won't have any trouble getting the car back into your garage." She glanced at Pat. "I guess there's some way of opening that door even when you've lost electricity. Isn't there?" She sounded genuinely curious.

"I don't know," Pat mumbled. Then suddenly, "Oh, yeah, there is a way. I have to ask Joe how to do that, I should learn how to do that—" She halted abruptly, looking dazed.

Ellen put her hand on her mother's shoulder, and Pat raised her eyes to her daughter. "Dad's really dead?"

Maura stood up. "The medical examiner will have to get confirmation from your husband's doctor that he had end-stage COPD, but it doesn't look like that will be a problem." Her hand rested on the doorknob. "I'm sorry I had to bother you with all these details, but this way we can close things up." She turned to Ellen. "We may never know for sure what happened. Maybe your dad fell, maybe he was in the bathroom when the power went out, and he just got too short of breath to make it to the tanks. Who knows?"

Maura turned to Pat then, appearing to consider that discolored, swollen cheek a long moment before she spoke. "I'm sorry for your loss." And then she slipped out, frigid air flowing into the kitchen even though the door only opened for a second or two.

"Pack some things," Ellen told her mother. "You can come home with me."

"I'd rather be in my own house."

Ellen sighed. "Mom."

"I'm all right," Pat said. She searched her daughter's face. "You know I'm all right. The only thing I feel is relief."

Ellen's face hardened. "Right. Well. Me, too, Mom. For your sake." Her eyes filled with tears. "But he was my dad."

Something tightened in Colleen's chest.

Pat looked down at the floor, and a stubborn look crossed her face. "I'd rather be in my own house," she repeated.

Ellen's shoulders slumped. "Okay. Then I'll stay here with you."

"Isn't Scott out of town?"

"The kids will be okay for one night."

Pat tsked. "This storm isn't over yet. What if *your* electricity goes out? And they're home alone? No. You should go home."

"I can stay with your mother," Colleen offered.

"I don't need anyone to stay," Pat objected. But this protest sounded weaker.

"I'll stay," Colleen told Ellen.

Ellen went down the hallway and returned with a pillow, sheets, and an electric blanket in her arms. "I'll make up the couch for you."

Colleen shook her head and took the linens herself. "Go home, before the storm gets any worse. I'm fine here."

While Pat got ready for bed, Colleen made tea and toast for her, then set it on her bedside table. After a single bite, Pat leaned against her headboard. "I can't really eat." Her eyelids drooped heavily.

"Get some sleep," Colleen said, and shut the bedroom door. Back in the TV room, she spread the sheets on the couch. At first, she didn't see a place to plug the electric blanket in. Then she spotted an outlet in the corner behind the same end table where she'd found the envelope. She had to pull the table out and lean over to reach the outlet. Pat would be embarrassed by the dust that had accumulated in that corner. Colleen extracted three silver paperclips, a crumpled ball of paper, and a candy wrapper. She carried those to the recycle bin. A sudden, long-ago memory of standing by the bin in Arizona with a letter in her hand froze her in mid-motion. She dropped the candy wrapper, but she smoothed out the crushed wad of paper on the counter. The crumpled letter confirmed the withdrawal of $22,000 from Joe's investment account.

Chapter 52

The next morning, the weather forecast on Colleen's phone predicted a clear day, but one that would still be frigid. She stared at the phone in her hand. Unbidden, Pat's statement that she'd turned off her phone in the library because she didn't know how to silence it came back to her. Hadn't she seen Pat silence her phone on more than one occasion? She pushed the thought away. But her hand shook, and she fumbled the edges of the sheet as she folded the bed linens. Before going to the kitchen, she folded the letter from Invest and tucked it into her pocket.

Colleen found Pat pouring water from a large measuring cup into the coffee maker, her bruise now a sickly greenish yellow. "How does your face feel?"

Pat made a so-so sign. "It hurts a little to talk. It hurts more to smile." She gave Colleen a half-smile with the undamaged side of her face. "You know," Pat said, "how you hear about people, after someone dies? How they wake up, and for a second they forget that the person died, but they feel this heaviness? And then they remember?"

Colleen blinked. "Is that what happened to you this morning?"

Pat gave her that crooked smile again. "Kind of, except the opposite. When I woke, I felt this *lightness*, and then I remembered. And I felt…oh, Colleen, I felt so happy!" She took two mugs and two small plates out of the cabinet, and a package of cinnamon rolls from the bread box.

Colleen glanced anxiously around the room, as if someone hidden there might have overheard Pat's comment. Aloud, she said, "I got really nervous when that police woman asked you about the oxygen tanks. I thought, what if you forgot to call for refills?"

Pat retrieved milk and butter from the refrigerator, her back to Colleen. "I didn't forget," she answered absently. Then, turning sharply, "What are you saying?"

Colleen opened a drawer where she thought spoons might be, shut it again. "Just. I was afraid the tanks might be empty."

"You thought Joe died because we didn't have backups?"

"No, not really."

"You thought we didn't have backups because I *intentionally* didn't order them?"

Colleen opened a different drawer, and pulled out two spoons and a butter knife. "It just made me nervous, that's all. I don't know. The police being here, you coming to my house in that storm, that bruise." She laughed anxiously. "Anyway, the tanks were full." The coffeemaker hissed, and a thin brown stream of liquid dripped into the pot below. "But I wondered," Colleen pressed on, "did you really have to pee?"

"What?"

"When you came to my house. You said you needed to pee. But you didn't head straight to the washroom. You stood by the sink, drinking a glass of water. Who does that?"

Pat's hand flew to her mouth. "Oh, don't Colleen, please. Don't make me laugh. It hurts to laugh."

Colleen felt cross. And stubborn. "No, I mean it. When you have to pee really bad, you don't drink water *first*."

"Oh, my God, Colleen. So, you thought, what? That the electricity went out, then I did what? Oh, I know, I moved the oxygen tanks down to the basement where Joe couldn't get to them. Then I drove to the library and to your house, so I'd have an alibi. No, wait, first I had to wait for Joe to die, then come back to my house, bring the oxygen tanks back to the TV room, and *then* go to your house."

Colleen pointed her chin at her friend. "You wouldn't have had to move the tanks at all. You could have just kept Joe from getting to them. That's maybe when he hit you. And then you could just wait until it was all over. And then leave."

Pat faced her. "Do you really think I could stay in this house and sit calmly by while my husband died, and then come and spend an afternoon with you eating chocolates?"

Put that way, it sounded ludicrous. "Of course not," Colleen answered. "But I don't think you fell on any ice, either." From where she stood, she could see out the large kitchen window, across the yard to the garage. "The electricity must still have been on when you left, or you wouldn't have been able to get your car out of the garage."

Wide-eyed, Pat exclaimed, "You really did suspect me."

"I'm sorry," Colleen blurted. "But I keep thinking about it. Why didn't Joe get to his tanks? What really happened? Don't you wonder about that?"

Pat poured coffee into their mugs. "I think Joe came to the kitchen for something. A cup of coffee, a bag of chips. Who knows? I think the electricity went out while he was in here, and he panicked. Maybe he was already out of breath from the walk to the kitchen. Any exertion wipes him out these days." Pat handed the box of rolls to Colleen, and the two of them sidled over to the table. "The electricity goes out, and the machine shuts down, and he realizes he has to get to the back-up tanks. He's scared, he's breathing hard. Maybe he gets dizzy. Loses his balance and falls. Whatever. He's short on oxygen. He passes out. That's what I think happened." Pat took a roll from the box and sliced it into quarters. "I'm not going to pretend that I wish I had been here to help him, Colleen. I'm glad

I left the house. And I'm not sorry that the electricity went out. But," and here Pat's voice became firm, and she looked straight into Colleen's eyes, "I never hid any oxygen tanks. I never stopped Joe from getting to his backups. I was not *in* the house when we lost electricity." She took a bite of the cinnamon roll and licked flakes of white frosting from her upper lip.

The tightness that had taken up occupancy in Colleen's chest loosened, and she inhaled deeply. After she let the breath out, she asked, "But he did hit you, didn't he?" Pat nodded. Colleen pursed her lips, then burst out, "I'm glad he's dead. I'm *glad*."

"I'm glad too," Pat answered, licking a finger. "The way I'm different from you is that I don't feel guilty about being glad."

Someone rapped hard on the back door, and Colleen startled. Before either woman could move, the lock turned, and a middle-aged man in a Blackhawks jacket stepped into the kitchen. "Jimmy!" Pat's whole face softened. She stood up, half-turning to Colleen. "This is one of my twins."

Jimmy stared at his mother. "What happened to your face?"

"Nothing. I fell on the ice yesterday."

"Oh, Ma! I told you, I'll shovel." He leaned toward his mother and gave her a hug. She barely came to the middle of his chest. He stepped back. "So," he said, "Dad's gone."

"He's gone," Pat echoed. The two exchanged a look that Colleen couldn't decipher. "This is Colleen," Pat said. "My best friend. She stayed with me last night."

Jimmy's quick nod was friendly enough, but it seemed perfunctory, and suddenly Colleen felt like a fifth wheel. "I'm going to get going," she said.

Jimmy blocked her way. "Let me salt the stairs first."

Colleen put her jacket on while they watched Jimmy through the window. "You don't want Jimmy to know that Joe hit you," Colleen observed. "Even now."

Pat shrugged. "It's complicated."

"Joe must have been in a rage when he found out about the money. Oh!" Colleen reached under her jacket and felt for the letter in her jean's pocket, but before she had a chance to extract it, Pat said, "Joe never found out about that money. I got lucky, I guess. He died before that happened."

Time stopped. Colleen recalled how the police on TV shows try to catch suspects in a lie—often a lie about something trivial, but one the interrogator leverages later. She pulled the folded letter from her pocket and thrust it toward Pat, who gave her a confused look. But in the next moment, understanding dawned on Pat's face.

"Why did you lie?" Colleen demanded. Pat took the paper from her and stared at it. "I know you didn't stand by and watch Joe die," Colleen said. "But why lie? Why say that he never found out about the money? Why not tell me the truth about him hitting you?"

A scraping sound outside drew their attention to the window. They saw Jimmy smashing ice on the stairs. "Remember how you felt," Pat said, "when you thought Derek might have died in that accident? How you wished, just for a second, that he *had* died?" When Colleen didn't answer, Pat pressed on. "If Derek had texted you saying he was on his way to that bridge, what would you have done? Texted him back? Phoned him? Gotten in your car to try to stop him?" Colleen opened her mouth to answer, but Pat forestalled her. "I don't mean now, when you're thinking about it. But then. Right at that moment. Say you were nearby and you had to act right then to keep Derek from jumping. Would you have?"

Colleen's throat closed up, but she forced a swallow and answered. "Of course I would."

Jimmy was just outside the thick window now, tossing salt on the landing.

Pat said, "And what if you knew that if you reached Derek in time, he might shove *you* over the bridge instead of throwing himself? What would you do then, Colleen?"

A long moment passed. In a low voice, Colleen said, "What did you do, Pat?"

Pat shook her head. "I didn't do anything. What I did is that I didn't do anything." Pat gripped the edge of the table. "I was so happy that morning," she said, "because of the phone call about my biopsy. I forgot to watch for the mail. I forgot how anger can give a person a surge of adrenaline. I couldn't believe how fast Joe came after me down that hall. I stopped to grab my coat and my purse and keys, because I wouldn't have put it past him to lock me out in the cold. I had just made it to the back door when he smashed me with that damn cane. But I got out, I got out of the house. I backed the car onto the apron and closed the garage door with the remote. The windshield iced up, and I squirted fluid on it, and that just made it worse. So, I turned the heat on and waited for the heat to clear the windshield. After a while, I looked in my rearview mirror and noticed the dry cleaners'."

Colleen recalled the strip mall across the street from Pat's house, the brightly colored lights shaped like clothes hangers at the top of the store windows. "Those lights are always on," Pat said. "But they weren't on then. It hit me that they'd just lost electricity, and maybe we had, too. But maybe not. It's patchy in my neighborhood. Sometimes we lose power, and they still have it next door. I couldn't see any light in our kitchen, but then Joe might have turned that off. I thought about going to check on him. I did. But I could imagine him standing right here, where we are now. Peering through the window, watching my car idling in the driveway."

Involuntarily, Colleen's glance went to that short strip of cement where Jimmy now stood, tossing more salt.

"And then watching me make my way back to the

house," Pat said. She took a shaky breath, and looked directly at Colleen. "I thought: If he's all right, do you need to go in there?" She pressed her lips together and shook her head in a silent 'no.' "Then I thought: If he's not all right, do you *want* to go in there?" She shook her head again, slowly. *No.*

Chapter 53

Three days later, Colleen slipped into the crowded room at the funeral home. She hadn't expected so many people. But of course, Pat had four grown children who would be accompanied by their spouses and children and visited by their friends. Colleen was glad for the throng of people. She hadn't seen Pat since that moment in the kitchen when Pat had admitted driving away from that house.

She spotted her friend in the front row, talking to a young teenager seated at her side, undoubtedly one of the grandchildren. Her twin sons stood nearby, somber in their crisp white shirts and dark suits. Pat waved her fingers at Colleen and gave her what she no doubt meant to be a conspiratorial smile. It made Colleen queasy, and she turned away and approached the open casket.

Joe looked neat and clean-shaven in his white shirt and blue suit, rosary beads wound around his fingers. Those same fingers that Colleen had pried off when he'd crushed Pat's hand in the hospital. Those same hands that had swung that cane. The same hands that had violated his daughters. *How can I blame Pat for anything?* Colleen thought.

And yet. Pat had stayed in that loveless marriage. At least for a time, while she tried to make her marriage work, she must have allowed those hands to touch her. She must have had sex with her husband. What had that been like? Colleen wondered. It had to have been at least okay, hadn't it? Otherwise, how could Pat have borne it? She glanced at her friend, who was grinning at something Jimmy whispered in her ear. The gap between her and Pat widened. *There's no grief here*, Colleen thought. *The saddest thing about this wake is that there's no real grief here.*

Colleen made the sign of the cross and trained her eyes on Joe again, forcing herself to pray for his soul. A white silk pillow, stitched with roses and the words "Beloved Grandpa," lay near his head. A bouquet of pink and lavender flowers lay at the foot of the casket, a wide blue satin ribbon with the words "Rest in Peace, Dad" stretched across it. How phony this whole display seemed! Someone sidled up to Colleen. At her elbow, Pat snorted. "All this was Ellen's idea. She even made me get something." Pat indicated a small spray of white roses. "What do you think?" she whispered, a sly smile on her lips. The gold inscription read "Gone, but Never Forgotten." Pat embraced Colleen in a close hug and whispered, "I knew you'd understand."

But Colleen took a step back. "I don't," she said. "I don't understand." She turned on her heel.

Letting herself into the kitchen later, Colleen cocked her head and listened for Derek. Sometimes he cold-called potential clients, relentlessly upbeat as he thanked them for their time and promised to email information. But no sound came from the family room today, and she found him crouched, not over his laptop, but over a legal pad. He hadn't dressed; he still wore his white V-neck undershirt and drawstring pajama bottoms. But glancing at him, Colleen suddenly pictured him in a shirt and tie and blue suit, laid out in a funeral home like Joe.

He looked up. "How's Pat doing?"

Colleen blinked. "Okay. As good as can be expected, I guess."

"Must be hard," Derek said. "All those years together."

Colleen hesitated before answering. "He was sick a long time." She perched on the edge of the armchair and stared at her feet, unable to shake the picture of Derek in that coffin. "It could have been you."

Derek gave a little start. "Oh, Col." He reached for his crutches, but she hurried over to sit next to him on the couch. When she leaned into him, he put his arm over her shoulders. Her voice now a little angry, she repeated, "It could have been you."

"I was a coward," Derek admitted. "I thought I was

being courageous, but it was a coward's way out. I know that, Col."

Colleen pressed her cheek against the tangle of coarse hairs that sprouted at the V of his t-shirt. Her big old teddy bear. They stayed like that for a long time, each afraid to break the fragile connection. Then Izzy burst in from school waving a paper that had a gold star, and they settled back to hear her read the story she'd written.

As the days went by, they got into a routine. Colleen brought Derek breakfast, and they watched the morning news together. Then she busied herself with Christmas shopping and decorating the house, including the huge tree that Shawn brought over, strapped to the roof of his car. It had grown too cold to walk the prairie path, and she reopened her old gym membership. She scanned job openings on her laptop until the twenty-year gap since her two years of college seemed like a hopeless barrier to anything other than retail work. When the sale of their Arizona home came through and eased their financial pressure, she switched to reading online college course descriptions. She imagined going back to school for a degree in music education, and talked on the phone with Geeta about the fine line between excitement and fear.

One night, she phoned Rachel. "How are you doing, hon?" Rachel responded with a detailed account of looming exams and term papers due. But then Colleen said, "I mean, really, how are *you* doing?"

A long pause. "Not too bad. I'm sleeping better. I'm working on stuff in therapy." A small chuckle. "I'm not so angry all the time."

"Oh, good. That's good."

"Yeah. And things are good between Aaron and me."

In the background, Izzy's voice rang out. "I'll be right down, Dad."

Colleen said, "I've been meaning to ask you—"

"Is Dad still on crutches?" Rachel interrupted.

"Yes, but he might get the cast off next week, then he'll be in a boot and starting to put weight on the leg. He can hardly wait. You know your father—he needs to be active. He does everything he can around here, paying bills, dealing with our lawyer in Arizona about the closing, helping Izzy with her homework, but he's getting a little stir crazy."

"He'll be able to get upstairs then? When he has the boot?" Rachel asked.

After a long pause, Colleen answered. "Yeah. He could probably scoot up the stairs on his butt now. But to walk, he still needs his crutches. When the bone heals enough and his muscles get stronger, he can get by with one of those three-pronged canes." She paused. "You don't have anything to worry about," she told Rachel. She wished her daughter would *say* something, but there was only silence on the other end of the call. Colleen took a deep breath. "He went to confession, Rach." A tsking sound, so faint that Colleen wasn't entirely sure she'd heard it, came across the line. Then nothing but a hush. She blurted, "By the New Year, he should be able to be on his own. I mean, go back to his friend's townhome." She rushed on. "Anyway, I was thinking about how well Thanksgiving went, and I wondered about Christmas. I figured Aaron probably has nothing going on. Being Jewish. Maybe you'd like to invite him for dinner at Aunt Bea's?"

The silence went on forever. "Mom," Rachel finally said, "Aaron doesn't want to meet my father. Aaron wouldn't want to shake his hand."

Colleen's cheeks flamed. After ending the call, she sat on the edge of her bed for a long time, praying the rosary until she felt calm enough to return downstairs. There, she spent more than an hour meticulously dusting all the photo displays.

Most evenings, Izzy and Derek played games or worked on Izzy's homework. Tonight, while she scrubbed a pan in the kitchen sink, Colleen heard Izzy's burst of laughter from the family room. Setting the pan in the drainer, she realized, *I haven't thought of it once today.* She tilted her head. Or yesterday. Possibly not the day before, either.

In her bedroom, she drew out her journal and flipped past her notes to the chart at the back. Each night, she'd tallied how often she'd obsessed on what Derek had done; how often she'd needed to go to a family photo to keep good Derek at the front of her mind; how often she'd watched him anxiously when Izzy was nearby. She didn't need to count the marks to see the improvements over the past three weeks, the blank spaces that showed another day had passed without her once thinking about *it*.

She glanced at their wedding photo on the dresser. Their old photo was now encased in a new silver frame that had the inscription: *With God, all things are possible. Matthew 19:26.* Rereading the phrase, she felt soothed, like a child when their mom assures them that there's nothing to fear, that everything will be all right.

Several nights later, after Izzy had gone to bed, Colleen scrolled down the movie list on the television screen. "How about *Ghost*?"

Derek hoisted himself into a standing position, using the arm of the couch on one side and his newly-acquired three-pronged cane on the other. "*Ghost* is good." He took a painstaking step toward her in his boot. She rose to meet him. "No," he said. "Stay there." He steadied himself with his cane and slowly crossed the two feet of space between them. "Pretty good, huh?" Derek held out his hand to her. "You want to sit by me on the couch?"

She settled close to her husband to watch the old movie. When the song "Unchained Melody" came on, and Demi Moore danced with Patrick Swayze, Derek handed Colleen a box of tissues. "It's the music," she sniffed. But it wasn't exactly the music, or the doomed yearning of the two lovers. It was that the music triggered Colleen's own yearning. *I hunger for your touch*, the Righteous Brothers sang. Derek rested his hand on her thigh for a moment, and a shockingly intense wave of desire rippled through her. *God speed your love to me.* Could that happen? Could God speed love to her after this long, lonely time?

Chapter 54

Rachel strode into her therapist's office and plopped down on the soft corduroy chair. She had to make a conscious effort to keep her fingers from digging into her arms. "I'm afraid my mom might be changing her mind about getting a divorce," she told Monica. "She slips in these little remarks about how nice my father is being to her. 'He went to confession,' she tells me. Like that's some huge accomplishment."

"Have you talked to your mother about how you feel?" Monica asked.

Rachel shook her head.

"Why not?"

"Let me ask you something first. You remember that thing I had to sign when I first saw you? About confidentiality. Does that mean… what if, just as an example, what if I got worried that my father might do something to my cousin? She's eleven. If I told you I was worried about that, what would happen? Would you have to report him? I mean, just on the basis of my fear that he might?"

Monica rested her chin on steepled fingers. "Are you afraid that your dad might abuse your cousin?"

"No. Not at all. I'm just trying to understand when you have to keep something confidential and when you don't."

"Well, if you thought that your father might be a danger to your cousin, or anyone else, I'd ask you what your fears were based on. We'd explore the evidence. We'd explore what you might want to do to keep your cousin safe." Monica's gray eyes gazed steadily at Rachel. "Like talking to your mother about it, talking to your cousin's parents. Or reporting that your father molested you. What I would be compelled to do would partly depend on what triggered your fears about him, and on what you decided to do."

The blood drained out of Rachel's face. It was one thing to know, as an abstraction, that she could report her father if she wanted to. It was another to hear that option listed so matter-of-factly, as though it were a menu item.

"For example," Monica went on, "you might urge your father to see an attorney to explore his options, including the possibility of reporting himself. That would up the chances that the courts might accept his participation in a therapy group, along with his being on the sex offenders' registry, rather than making him face formal charges."

Rachel's heart thudded. *Thank God*, she thought, *thank*

God I've never mentioned Izzy in here. "I don't think my father's a danger to anyone," she said. "It's just that I get all tense when I think my mom might not divorce him." Rachel watched the golden guppy with the orange fringe veer away from the glass wall. "Sometimes," she told Monica, "I think I'm doing so good. And other times…" She shrugged.

"It's a long road back from trauma," Monica said. "And you've come a long, long way. But you're still excavating feelings that you weren't even aware of before." Monica folded her hands in her lap. "Learning how to deal with them takes time."

"I still have nightmares sometimes," Rachel said.

Monica nodded acknowledgement.

"But not nearly as often," Rachel added. "And things are better with Aaron." She grinned. "I *love* sensate focus." The yellow guppy hung motionless behind a frond. "I want to go beyond that. I even went on the pill, two weeks ago. But what if it's like before? The only time we had sex, and all that shame came back?" She considered what she'd just said. "But I don't really think that will happen. I don't know what I'm afraid of, exactly."

"Maybe you're afraid you'll shut down?"

Rachel gave that some thought. "I don't think so. I get really aroused when we're making out, and when it gets too intense, I make us stop, but it's not like before. I don't stop because I'm all numb. Just the opposite."

"When it gets 'too intense,' you stop. Because?"

Rachel's face colored. "I feel like if he touched me, or I touched myself, I'd have an orgasm." Her mouth curved the tiniest bit. "Aaron calls it a starburst."

Monica smiled, then steepled her fingers under her chin. "So, is it having intercourse that scares you, or is it having a 'starburst' with Aaron?"

Rachel tossed that topic back and forth a bit. She didn't want to return to the question of her father. But then she found herself telling Monica about her mother wanting to invite Aaron to Christmas dinner. "That was another thing that made me think, what's happening? Is she going back to la-la land? That makes me feel so—"

She almost said "angry." But at the last second, she filled in, "hopeless and helpless."

"Are you helpless?" Monica said.

Automatically, Rachel gave what she thought was the expected answer. "I guess not," she muttered. She thought a bit longer. "I feel helpless when I think I have no choices because I have to protect my mother." A quiet strength surged through her, making her sit up straighter. "But I'm not helpless, am I? If my mother goes back on her promise to file for divorce," she told Monica, "there are things I can do."

Chapter 55

Three days before Christmas, Colleen went to the salon. She'd neglected her hair for so many months that it had grown long enough to try a different style, and when the stylist finished, she found herself looking in the mirror at layers of russet waves framing her face. The stylist had chosen a windblown look. Colleen's long bangs were parted in the middle and fell in wispy strands to the sides of her face. Later, she and Izzy did their nails, brushing sparkly pink polish on Izzy's, mauve on Colleen's. Izzy blew on her fingers and waved her hands in the air after Colleen finished her last pinkie. "Let's go show Daddy!"

Colleen trailed Izzy to the family room. Derek exclaimed, "Look at you, Iz!" Izzy shook her head, and the colorful beads that Aaliyah had woven into her jumble of black curls bounced. "Beautiful!" Derek said. He caught a glimpse of Colleen. "My two beautiful girls."

That little hitch.

Every time there's a hitch, Colleen reminded herself,

that's a chance to get back on track. She wandered over to the glass clock with her carefully arranged family snapshots. *It's like that reverse figure of the old woman versus the young one,* she reminded herself. *Which image do you want to see?* She focused on Derek's tender expression in the wedding photo.

Izzy tugged at her hand. "Mommy, I want to show you something."

Upstairs, patches of felt, wooden beads, buttons, and coin wrappers carpeted Izzy's bedroom floor. "I need help making finger puppets," she said.

Colleen spotted a tube of glue lying on some folded newspaper. "You better do this at the kitchen table."

"But I want to surprise Daddy!" Izzy gave her mother a grave look. "I'm being super careful."

Colleen worked with Izzy long enough to complete one finger puppet, a replica of Derek, complete with a miniature cane made from toothpicks. "I got it now," Izzy said. "You can go." Colleen left, but not before she'd glimpsed the red yarn surely destined for another finger puppet representing her. Her glance flew back to her daughter's face, scrunched in concentration over the father puppet. Izzy was all right. If they stayed a family, if they were somehow able to be a family again, Izzy would snuggle into that reality as though nothing had ever changed.

Instead of returning downstairs, Colleen went into her bedroom. She picked up their wedding photo from the dresser and clasped it in both hands. She sat on the bed where she'd slept alone for months now and recalled the particular moment she'd fallen in love with her husband. It wasn't triggered by anything earth-shaking. They hadn't even been in a romantic setting. But for her nineteenth birthday, Derek had paid for time at a recording studio so she could make a CD of her own. She'd stood behind the glass waiting for the first chords from her musician friends. Derek had caught her eye and given her that crooked smile and the tiniest nod of encouragement. A "You can do this" nod. Something had swelled up inside of her, a joy that burst through when she opened her mouth to sing.

She picked up her cell phone and scrolled through her music files. *Why not have the music ready,* she thought, just in case God did decide to send love to her again? She thought of Pat's loveless marriage, and reminded herself how different Derek was from Joe. How different she was from Pat. She chose "Unchained Melody" as the first song on the new playlist.

That night, Colleen made Derek's favorite dinner, pot roast with rich gravy and tender, falling-off-the-bone meat, along with mashed potatoes, carrots, and green beans. Derek poured red wine for himself and Colleen. After dinner, the three of them stayed in the kitchen and played a very competitive game of Sorry, then Chinese checkers. Finally, Izzy went to bed. Colleen wiped the counters, washed the pan she'd left soaking in the sink, and started the dishwasher. When she went to check on Izzy, she saw a band of light under her daughter's door. "Izzy!"

"Don't come in! It's a surprise."

Colleen spoke through the closed door. "It's time to go to bed."

"I'm almost done."

"You can finish those puppets in the morning. I mean it. Turn the light off. Now." She heard vague grumbling sounds. But the light went off.

Downstairs, Derek sat on the couch, his laptop resting on his thighs and his foot in the boot propped up on the ottoman. "Want to get that wine bottle?" he said. Colleen carried their wine and the half-filled bottle to the family room and set them on the end table nearest Derek.

While she poured, Derek tapped keys on his computer. "Are you working?" Colleen asked.

"No." He smiled. He set the laptop on the coffee table, tapped another key, then gripped his cane and heaved himself up. The strains of Bryan Adams singing "Everything I Do" filled the room. Derek leaned on his cane with one hand and opened his arm to her.

She thought of how they used to dance on the bare floor of the living room in his fraternity house, Derek spinning her across that room until they collapsed, breathless, on the overstuffed couch. "I don't think dancing with your cane is going to work," Colleen said. But she smiled.

"You can be my crutch." She came close, and he steadied himself by resting his hand in the crook of her arm. They didn't dance, not really. But they leaned in and swayed to the music. Each time Bryan Adams sang, "Don't tell me it's not worth fighting for," Derek gave her arm a little squeeze. When the song ended, he sunk back down on the couch and drew Colleen to him. She rested her head against his chest and listened to his heart beat. Derek said, "Remember the first time we danced? At that karaoke place? You had just been up at the mic, and I thought you sang better than the original artist."

She remembered. "You wanted my phone number. But you were drunk."

Derek grinned. "Only a little. You said you wouldn't give it to me when I was drinking. Meanie."

"I gave it to you the next day."

They took turns remembering.

"Remember," Derek laughed, "when we missed the show because we didn't know there were two entrances, and we waited for each other for an hour at opposite ends of the building?"

"Remember how you changed the station on your car radio so I wouldn't know how much you liked country music?" she said. Derek put on an *aw shucks* look.

"Remember our first Fourth of July," he said, "when we

left the dock where they were shooting fireworks, and we went back to our cabin to make love and—"

"—the grand finale came right at our own," she finished. They chuckled at first, but the chuckles grew until they were laughing as hard as they'd done then, so many years ago.

When they'd quieted, Derek said, "Remember the first time you got really mad at me, and you picked up that alabaster statue from Italy and hurled it across the room? And then you started crying. You kept saying, 'I didn't know it was breakable.'"

"I was afraid you'd leave, because it was your mother's." Colleen's voice fell to a whisper. "And you said, 'Don't worry. My love's not breakable. You can smash all the statues you want, but you can't break my love.'"

Derek moved his booted foot off the ottoman. "Sit," he said. "I'll give you a massage." He kneaded her shoulders while she sat. She thought: *Remember when you used to give me a back rub, and after a while I would turn over and say "Now do my front…"*

As if he knew her thoughts, Derek embraced her from behind, crossing his arms over her chest. "Colleen," he said, his voice husky. She felt the warmth of his body pressed against her back and his breath on her ear. "Can you get upstairs on your own?" she asked.

"Absolutely. With my cane and the bannister? I just need a little time."

"Wait until I call you, okay?" Over her shoulder, she gave him a smile so self-conscious it was almost shy. "I have a surprise for you."

Chapter 56

"I have a surprise for you," Rachel told Aaron, sliding the last of the Scrabble letters back into the box. A minute later, she dragged a kitchen chair into the living room and set it opposite him. "Stay here. I'll be right back."

When she returned with her cello, she'd changed into her white silk blouse and the long black skirt she wore for recitals. She arranged herself on the chair three feet in front of Aaron, close enough that she could see the golden flecks in his eyes. She rosined her bow. Tuning the cello, she tightened a peg or two. Finally, she widened her knees and centered the cello on its stand, the filmy folds of her skirt drifting down her thighs. With a smile at Aaron, Rachel lifted her bow.

The room faded. The music played itself through her bow arm, through her fingers, which flitted up and down the fingerboard. When the notes spoke of regret, it was her own anguish that pressed her calloused fingertips against the strings. During a passage communicating longing, her emptiness merged with the great hollow in the center of her cello, and the two of them mourned together. And when the feather-light, upswept notes of hope slipped in, she followed them like signposts out of despair until joy shone in her like the gleam of her cello. When she drew the bow across the strings for the last phrase, her arm relaxed and her contentment mirrored the peace of the music.

Inhaling slowly, she became aware of her body again. How her bow arm drifted to her side. How the silk of her blouse caressed her neck. How sensual it felt to have her knees spread on either side of the cello. Last came her awareness of Aaron in front of her, solid and sturdy and present, and part of what she'd just experienced.

Chapter 57

Soaping her breasts in the hot shower, Colleen let herself feel the ache for her husband's touch. She dried herself with a fluffy towel and donned an emerald gown before she turned off the bedroom light and lit the candle on the dresser. Moments after the flame flickered, the room filled with the smell of vanilla. Colleen called down the stairwell. "Derek, you can come up now."

When she was young and shy about sex, Derek would sometimes ask her: "Would you unbutton your top? Would you do that for me?" And later, "Would you undress, stand over there, just let me look at you?" And her face would flame with excitement. She heard Derek's halting ascent up the stairs now, and she moved near the bathroom again, standing in such a way that the doorway framed her, the light from the bathroom illuminated her. When the bedroom door creaked open, she clicked on the playlist, and "Unchained Melody" began.

Derek gave her a long, appreciative look, a broad smile

spreading across his face. He leaned on his cane, stepping fully into the room, and clicked the door shut behind him. The Righteous Brothers sang *I hunger for your touch,* and Colleen tugged the edge of the little cream ribbon at the throat of her gown. Derek's gaze stayed steady on her. Soon, she thought, undoing the first tiny button. Soon she would feel his fingertips, his hands on her. The song went on. *I need your love.* She smiled at her husband. He moved his cane up a bit so that he bent forward when he leaned on it, inclining toward her eagerly. Desire rippled through her as she undid the last button. *God speed your love to me.* Her breath caught at the words of the song, and watching Derek closely, she used both hands to loosen the sash and slowly opened her gown.

A shadow of disappointment flashed across Derek's face. It came and went so fast that Colleen wasn't sure of what she'd seen. She gripped the edges of her gown. "What?"

"Nothing," Derek said quickly, giving her a sheepish grin.

Colleen pulled the gown closed.

"Col, no, you're beautiful! You look beautiful. I just…When you said you had a surprise, I thought…You used to shave for me. That's all."

It had been years since Colleen had thought of that long-abandoned predilection of Derek's. But grasping his meaning now, she recoiled violently.

Chapter 58

With the strains of the cello piece still echoing in her mind and vibrating through her body, Rachel lay naked with Aaron under the sheet, the small lamp providing just enough light for them to see one another. They kissed with that tentative, exploratory approach they'd taken in the very beginning. Rachel took his hand and touched her lips with his finger. He caressed her the way he'd done so many times recently, but this time when her desire heightened, she didn't stop him. She laid one of his hands on her breast and brought the other down between her legs. She shut her eyes and luxuriated in the sensation of his hands on her.

Aaron.

From time to time, she opened her eyes and glimpsed the curve of his shoulder, or the ridge of his collarbone, or his eyes looking straight at her. Her attention fluctuated back and forth from Aaron to the exquisite feelings that mounted in her.

Until the very last moments, when she cried out and lost herself utterly in the starburst that exploded in her.

Chapter 59

Colleen's shoulder struck the door frame as she recoiled from her husband. Derek gripped his cane and took a step toward her. "Oh, honey…"

She raised her palm. "Don't."

He stared at her for a long time. Then he collapsed slowly, bone by bone, onto the edge of the bed, and Colleen recalled Rachel's words. *A house of cards.* Derek's cane clattered to the floor. "Colleen. Sweetheart." She bent and picked the cane up, staring at the three prongs on the end of it as if she couldn't figure out their purpose.

"Can't we try a do-over?" Derek appealed. "I'll go back downstairs, come up again?" She turned away, and her glance landed on their wedding photo. *With God, all things are possible.*

She'd been wrong. She'd acted as if somehow, whenever she shifted her perspective to Derek the good father, she eradicated the Derek who lusted after young girls. She'd failed to recognize an essential truth about reverse figures.

Both were always there, regardless of which you perceived at any given moment. No matter how often she managed to keep her focus on the loving husband and the good father, Derek the pedophile persisted as well.

Derek stared at her strangely and inched clumsily away from her, toward the door. Colleen wondered why he didn't use his cane. Then she realized that she still held it, though she couldn't remember how it had gotten into her hands. Hardly knowing what she did, she gripped the cane and raised it to her shoulder like a baseball bat. Derek scooted to the far corner of the bed, grabbed onto the back of a chair there, and pulled himself up. Colleen stumbled toward him. Derek moved away and pushed the bedroom door open. He gripped the doorframe to steady himself, then took a step backwards into the hall.

Where he bumped into something.

"Daddy! See what I made?" Izzy wagged the finger puppets on her hand, the tiny replicas of their family. She wriggled her fingers. "I made them all by myself. Almost." Seeking confirmation of that fact, she glanced at her mother, then blinked at the raised cane in Colleen's hands. "What's going on?"

Derek said, "Nothing, sweetheart. Nothing's going on."

Izzy stepped uncertainly into the room, looking back and forth from her mother to her father. Colleen tipped Derek's cane toward him. meaning for him to take it, but

Derek drew back and cringed.

Izzy began to weep.

"Oh, don't cry, sweetheart," Derek said. "Everything's all right. Why are you crying, honey?"

"I don't know!" Izzy sobbed. "I don't know why I'm crying." Her father leaned down to embrace her, but Colleen sprang to life and snatched Izzy into her own arms.

Chapter 60

Alone in her dark bedroom, Colleen laid back on the pile of pillows stacked against her headboard and stared at the silver tray atop her dresser. It was crowded with bottles of cologne and lotion and lipstick tubes. For want of a better place, she had put the laughing Buddha near that tray, alongside a simple statue of a young Virgin Mary holding her infant. In the shadows from the nightlight, the shapes looked like a throng of friendly gods. *Maybe I'm going a little crazy*, Colleen thought. Because in the dim room, the items on her dresser did seem like little gods. Gods who were talking with one another, having a pow-wow with Mother Mary and the laughing Buddha. A friendly discussion about what she should do.

Pray, she thought. *That's what I should do.* But instead, she found herself thinking that if she had a troupe of gods, she'd say: Okay, which one of you is responsible for all this pain? Where were you all when Derek climbed into that bed with Rachel? Who put that urge in him in the first place? Which of you came up with *that* map of the world?

Colleen would bet money that one or two of the gods glanced toward her. Others angled a bit toward the wedding photo, cocking their heads as if wondering why it still stood there. Why did it? She got out of bed, and the little gods dissolved back into bottles of cologne and perfume, lipsticks and lotions. She slipped the wedding photo into a drawer. Climbing back into bed, Colleen stared again at the top of her dresser. Nothing had changed, except there was now emptiness where the wedding photo had stood. The little gods returned, tilting their heads toward her expectantly.

All this time, she'd believed that if she could forgive Derek, then she might be able to stay with him. But now she saw that if she stayed with him, she would never be able to forgive him. Year by year, she would become more like Pat. If he was unhappy, she would think he deserved to suffer. If he was happy, she would be even more resentful. And buried under whatever veneer of acceptance she felt able to extend to him, there would always be that well of disgust.

She had to leave him.

It seemed to her that the little god-figures on the dresser nodded. *Yes, you see, it's simple.* The Buddha grinned, and Mother Mary cast a sympathetic glance her way, and at that moment, it did seem simple. Simple and clear and a profound relief.

Chapter 61

"I appreciate you coming," Colleen said, watching Rachel unwind the blue woolen scarf at her neck.

"No problem." Rachel gave her a quizzical look. "But I thought you wanted to wait until after Christmas."

Colleen bit her lip. "I just can't have him here anymore."

Rachel's head whipped around, her scarf halfway off her neck. "Did he do something to Izzy?"

"No. No, nothing like that. I just—"

The doorbell chimed. Derek's shadowy figure darkened the glass panel in the side of the door. "He doesn't have a key anymore," Colleen told Rachel, and went to let him in.

Derek did a double-take when he spotted his daughter. "Oh! I didn't know you were going to be here."

"To support Mom," Rachel responded.

He kept his gaze on Rachel a moment longer, then hefted a briefcase. "I need some papers I left in the family room." Barely touching the floor with his cane, he moved gamely toward the room on his boot. Rachel took a few steps in the same direction, then stayed planted at the archway of the room. "What happened to the clock?"

Colleen made a dismissive gesture.

Rachel turned away from the family room, walked to the formal living room, and peered in.

"I took them all down," Colleen said.

"Good," Rachel answered just as her father emerged with his briefcase.

In the kitchen, Colleen didn't offer the usual coffee and tea, cookies or scones, and the three of them sat at the bare table. Colleen opened with, "We need to talk about how to tell Izzy."

"Col," Derek responded. "Do we really have to do this, five days before Christmas?"

"I can't have you here," Colleen answered. "I just can't."

"I don't have to be here. We could pretend that I went to visit my sister, and then just wait until after Christmas—"

But Colleen shook her head and went on as if he hadn't spoken. "We also need to talk about what we want to do. Illinois has no-fault divorce, so if you don't contest anything—"

"I'm not going to contest anything," Derek said.

"If you don't contest anything," Colleen repeated, "I

don't have to say anything about the grounds for divorce."

Derek took a moment with that. But then he merely repeated, "I'm not going to contest anything."

Colleen's elbows rested on the table, and she leaned her chin on her palms. "When we talk to Izzy, the important thing is that we assure her that the divorce isn't her fault. Because kids think it's their fault somehow, even when they *know* it's not."

"The other important thing," Derek said, "is that she knows we both still love her, and that I'm still her dad. She'll still see me."

"The *important thing*," Rachel interrupted, directing her remarks to Colleen, "is to be sure that Izzy is safe if she's going to see him."

"Of course," Colleen answered.

Derek's hands had been folded in front of him on the table, but now they tightened into fists. He visibly got hold of himself before he spoke. "You know," he said, "there's this thing human resources talks about when they train you to do screening calls. The idea is if you really like something about a job applicant, or you're really impressed by one thing they did, it's like they wear a halo that makes most everything about them look better. The halo effect. You have to be careful not to let that cloud your judgment."

Colleen stared at her husband. *What in heaven's name was he talking about?*

He went on. "But there's the opposite. The shadow effect. A guy loses a big client, and ten years later everyone still thinks of him as "Max-who-lost-the-Fortune-500-account." He addressed Colleen. "That's me, isn't it? Shadow-man? I'll always be 'the-husband-who-destroyed-our-family,' the 'father-who-hurt-our-daughter.' I'll always be the shadow."

Colleen stiffened.

"All I'm asking," Derek appealed, "is that we don't hurt Izzy any more than we have to. She's going to be devastated. So, I'm just saying. Let her know we both still love her. Let her know she's not losing me."

A heavy silence hung over that barren kitchen table. Colleen took as deep a breath as she could manage. "I was thinking, what if you asked for a transfer? You always say Tony has trouble getting people in Des Moines. Then I wouldn't have to worry about you being with Izzy, but you and Izzy could Skype."

A vein in Derek's forehead bulged. "Jesus Christ, Col! How can I convince you that Izzy is safe with me?" He flipped open his laptop with an angry jerk. "See this website? I've practically memorized the advice they give to help people…not cross the line." He tilted the screen toward Colleen, but she turned her face away.

"You want me to accept responsibility?" Derek exclaimed, "I've accepted it! This is all on me, all right? The divorce. Izzy being torn apart when we tell her.

Rachel's—Rachel's problems. I'm just begging you not to take away the only thing I have left."

Colleen pondered a moment, then addressed Rachel. "Maybe he could see Izzy, and I would just make sure that I was there."

Derek turned toward her, his expression hopeful but wary. "So, it will be pretty much the same as it is now?"

But Colleen shook her head. "That would be confusing to Izzy. I'd have to be more like… a monitor."

"What does that *mean*?" Derek roared. "You come to the movie, but sit in the aisle behind us? Watch us play a game in the family room from twenty feet away?"

"If Rachel reported you," Colleen said, "it would be much worse."

Derek's mouth dropped open. He turned to his daughter. "Is that what you're planning?"

Rachel's face was frozen.

"Because if that's what you're planning," Derek said, his mouth a tight line, "I'd just as soon have it happen now. Get it over with. Go ahead. Report me." He read from the screen on his laptop, nearly spitting out the words. "Holding yourself accountable for the harm that has been done may mean facing legal consequences, including possible probation, imprisonment, financial penalties or fines, and public registration." He slammed the laptop closed. "Public registration means big restrictions on where I can live. Where I can go." He looked at Colleen. "No attending any school plays that Izzy is in. And how long would Tony keep me if a client came across my name on the sex offenders' registry?" He pressed his forehead against the palm of his hand. "Just do it, Rach," he said. "If you're going to do it, just fucking do it. I don't want to live with that sword over my head."

"I never said I wanted to report you," Rachel answered. "I don't want you to lose your job or go to prison."

"No one wants that," Colleen said sharply. "Who would that help?"

"Except." Rachel rubbed her eye. "What about other children? What if he married again and had more kids?"

"Oh, my God." Derek threw his hands into the air.

"He can't have children," Colleen assured Rachel. "We took care of that after Izzy was born. And I don't think he'd touch another girl. I really don't."

Rachel nodded, then leaned toward her mother. "If they were Skyping, you wouldn't have to watch over them. Izzy wouldn't entertain fantasies that you two were still together." She turned to her father and a cloud of pity came over her face. "It wouldn't be forever."

Colleen nodded and told Derek, "Just until Izzy's older."

But now Rachel's brow furrowed again. "How old?" she asked her mother. She turned to her father. "How old was I when you lost interest in me?"

Derek reddened. "Nothing happened after I started

traveling. I told you. That's *why* I traveled so much. So, you were, I don't know. Eight and a half?"

"I didn't ask when you stopped *abusing* me," Rachel said. "I asked when you lost interest." Her voice slowed. "I mean, it must have still been a problem for you, or you wouldn't have had to keep traveling. Right?"

Thirteen, Colleen thought. Because Rachel had been in eighth grade when Derek had suddenly managed to work almost entirely from the Chicago office. An unexpected memory flashed through her mind: Derek complaining, his disgust thinly disguised. Did they have to have all this "female stuff" out in the open in the bathroom? He'd meant the box of sanitary pads that Rachel had failed to put back in the closet. He'd meant the used pad that Rachel hadn't completely wrapped up before putting it in the wastebasket. Aloud, Colleen said to Rachel, "Izzy will be all right after she gets her period."

Derek's gaze stayed glued to the kitchen table top. "Fine," he said. "I'll talk to Tony. Go to Iowa. You know, my commissions there will never match what I can make here."

Colleen noticed the silver tips in his receding hair line, the lines of fatigue on his face. "We'll figure out the money," she said. "I don't need this big house for just me and Izzy. There are ways I can cut back." *Does Izzy really need violin lessons?* she wondered, and the question stopped her breath for a moment. How much could she deprive

Izzy and Rachel? "And sooner or later, I'll be working," she added.

Rachel offered, "I can get more student loans."

Colleen shook her head. "You shouldn't have to sacrifice. You, of all people, shouldn't have to sacrifice."

"Mom." Rachel addressed Colleen, but her glance took in both of her parents. "We all have to sacrifice. Even Izzy."

Even Izzy, Colleen thought, and she braced herself to call Izzy at Aaliyah's and tell her to come home now.

Chapter 62

Pat hovered at the door, a shiny red tin decorated with elves stuck under her arm. "I won't stay," she told Colleen. "I just wanted to drop off some cookies." She held the tin out like a peace offering.

"Come in for a minute," Colleen invited. When she opened the door wider, Pat peered down the hallway. "Derek's not here," Colleen assured her.

In the kitchen, Colleen glanced surreptitiously at her friend while she arranged Pat's cookies—trees and bells and stars dotted with red and green sprinkles—on a plate. Had Pat's cheekbones always been so sunken? The skin at her throat so wrinkled? When the teapot on the stove whistled, Pat said, "I didn't know if you would want to see me again."

Colleen poured water over their tea bags. "I didn't know either." She tipped a teaspoon of sugar into her mug and looked up. "I tell myself that what you did was self-defense. Joe attacked you. You didn't attack him. All you did was walk away." She took a shaky breath. "I tell myself that, and I believe that. And still every cell in my body cries *it was wrong*. That there should have been another way. I don't know. Call 911? Get a neighbor to go back in the house with you?"

Pat set her mug gently on the counter and turned to leave. But Colleen stayed her with a touch on her arm. "Then, Pat, then I have to admit that I might have done the same thing. That I would want to do the same thing." The two women regarded one another. After a moment, Colleen handed the plate of cookies to Pat while she picked up their mugs of tea, and Pat followed her to the kitchen table. Plopping down on her chair, Colleen said, "I kicked Derek out."

"Oh!"

"I decided not to wait until after Christmas. I'm filing for divorce." Pat stayed silent. Colleen bit the top off a bell cookie sprinkled with red dots. "You can say it. I know you're glad."

Pat smiled, seemingly despite herself, and then the hesitant smile turned into a wide grin. "So, it worked? Me making you meet Joe. Showing you what Derek could become."

Colleen didn't answer. The ticks of the kitchen clock echoed through a long silence, and Pat's smile faded. Finally, Colleen said, "It was more that you showed me what *I* might become."

Pat flushed. "I came here today because I didn't want

to lose you as a friend. But I think maybe I've already lost you." She fiddled with the locket at her throat. "You'll never look at me the same way again."

Colleen flipped her palms upward in a *who knows?* gesture. "Maybe not. But we're all we've got, Pat. My messed-up self and your messed-up self. And you and I—we know a lot about what's messed us up. What we've been through. That's worth a lot, isn't it? That's worth keeping a friendship. Isn't it?"

For a second, Pat's whole face wavered, as if it was underwater. Then she shut her eyes tight. Colleen was catapulted back in time to the coffee shop, where she'd been the one to squeeze her eyes shut. When she'd felt so lost that she'd reached out blindly, and Pat's hands had been there. She could do that for Pat now. She could at least do that. Colleen took her friend's hands in her own. Pat's eyes, glistening with tears, shot open, and she gave Colleen a grateful squeeze. They sat there a few more moments, the friendly tick of the clock a backdrop to a kind of quiet contentment. Colleen had the surprising thought that it was this contentment she had craved all her life. This quiet closeness was the elusive goal of all her meticulously planned romantic interludes with her husband, all her carefully orchestrated family outings. What was this feeling she had so hungered for, she wondered? In the next moment, the word came to her. *Intimacy*, Colleen thought. *This is intimacy.*

Chapter 63

Colleen waved as Rachel poked her head around the doorway of the living room. "I'm just finishing Skyping with Geeta," she told her daughter. "Showing her our tree." She turned her laptop so that the camera faced the towering tree and caught Rachel placing two Christmas presents under it. Geeta said, "Your Christmas always reminds me of Diwali, our festival of lights celebration." She paused. "And maybe I shouldn't say 'Merry Christmas,' because this is such a hard time for you, but I'm thinking of you, Colleen. I'm sending my love." Colleen blew her friend a kiss, then waited until Geeta signed off to close her laptop.

By the tree, Rachel cupped one of the musical instrument ornaments in her hand. "I remember the year you got these, Mom."

Colleen blinked. "Oh. That was your dad. He found those one Christmas in that music store."

Rachel let go of the silver harp, and it swung on the

branch a bit. "How's Izzy doing?"

Colleen steeled herself against the memory of Izzy's desperate plea when they'd told her about the divorce ("It's a joke, right? You're making a bad joke?"). "Not as bad as I feared," she said. "But maybe that's because the reality hasn't completely hit her. We'll see when your father doesn't come with us to Mass tonight. When he misses Christmas dinner tomorrow at Aunt Bea's."

Colleen watched the play of emotions on Rachel's face. Sadness? Worry? Resignation? They resolved into a determined look that reminded Colleen of herself, and Rachel said, "I could come back home until my classes start in January. Spend more time with Iz." Colleen had a glimpse, then, of how her relationship with Rachel might evolve into a kind of partnership in which they looked out for Izzy and somehow, through that, came to terms with all the ways that Colleen had failed to look out for Rachel. "That's a really nice offer," she said. "But you have work, and Aaron. You're still seeing Aaron, right?"

Rachel nodded.

"So, you'll want to spend time with him too. You can see Izzy without moving back here. You can visit. Izzy will be all right."

Rachel hesitated. "If you're sure," she said. "Because I also promised Mandy that the two of us could do some stuff together. She's coming back a few days before classes start."

"That'll be good for both of you," Colleen said.

Rachel shifted from one foot to the other. "And Izzy could join us, me and Aaron and Mandy, for some things."

"Sure," Colleen said. "It's all good." But a little wave of loneliness swept through her.

Rachel went to the foot of the stairs. "Hey, Iz! If you want a good seat, we need to get going."

At church, Colleen had Rachel enter the pew first, so that she could sit between her daughters. They had come up to the balcony for a better view of the fourth-graders who always began the Children's Mass with a reenactment of the nativity story. Colleen laid their jackets on the pew to save spaces for Shawn, Bea, and Amber. When they arrived, seconds before the drama started, Amber scooted in first to be by Izzy. Izzy craned her neck to get a better look at the boy at the microphone, who intoned: "The Roman emperor told all the people that they had to go to their hometowns to be counted." Mary and Joseph walked down the aisle, a very plain-looking little girl beside a tubby boy. Perhaps the parish intended to make a point with those choices. Colleen hoped so. She wondered who had volunteered their baby to be Jesus this year, then spotted a woman hovering in the shadows of the makeshift stable, her brown face barely visible under the folds of a blue mantilla. An infant squirmed in her arms. Halfway down a side aisle, Joseph knocked at the door of a confessional. "Please, sir. We need a room for the night."

"No room at this inn!" a gruff voice called from inside.

Colleen glanced around. Shawn tapped on his phone, but put it away when he noticed her frown. Bea leaned forward, intent on the little play below, but then she turned to Colleen and smiled. Izzy whispered something that made Amber giggle. On Colleen's other side, Rachel looked pensive, but untroubled. *This is my family*, Colleen thought. After the shepherds found the baby Jesus and the three Kings brought their gifts, Father Conklin began Mass, and Colleen lost herself in the familiar patterns of the liturgy. In his sermon, Father Conklin said, "A sign in the skies. That's what we'd all like. A new star in the heavens that no one has ever seen before, to lead us to the love and joy and peace that is Christmas."

Colleen had misread so many signs this past year. In her desperation, she'd believed that those articles on resisting temptation showed that Derek had never yielded. Rather than proving that it might be possible to sustain her own marriage, Pat's life had turned out to be a cautionary tale. And she had believed that if she tried hard enough, she could protect Izzy, forgive Derek, love Rachel back into the family. But she couldn't. Rachel's terrible word came into her mind. *Damaged.* They were all too damaged. That's why she needed someone whose infinite capacity for love and forgiveness was undamaged. That's why she needed God. God wouldn't change reality for her, or undo the past, any more than Colleen could do that for Rachel. But like Colleen herself, God was stubborn. God would be there for her, just as she would be there for her daughters, no matter how long it took her to embrace Him again.

Wouldn't it be nice, Colleen sighed when the Mass drew to a close, to have some little sign, some small reassurance from God? *There I go again*, she thought. But it would be such a gift if God made something happen tonight, something that would bring her and Izzy and Rachel together, something that would lift their spirits and give them hope.

A slip of a girl stepped up to the microphone near the stable to sing the final hymn. She looked especially diminutive from their seats in the balcony. The woman with the infant came forward as well and stood nearly at the elbow of the young singer. With her lacy blue mantilla and sleeping baby in her arms, she was the image of the Virgin Mary.

In keeping with the Children's Mass tradition of featuring the church's youth, the teen vocalist couldn't have been more than 14 or 15 years old. Even from this far away, Colleen saw how nervous the girl was, clutching the microphone one moment and fiddling with strands of her long, dark hair the next. Colleen had watched a lot of *Got Talent* performers. Some of them, like this girl, looked like nonentities, and then stunned the audience with extraordinary performances. Colleen had a heady sense of anticipation as the organist played the first few chords of the *Ave Maria*. The Ave Maria! Hail Mary. Wasn't that a sign? That prayer had been Colleen's mainstay, and music was the shared passion that bound her and her daughters together. She reached out and clasped their hands. The next moment, the mouse of a girl opened her mouth. Colleen held her breath and waited for the strong, pure tones of a practiced soprano to come out of this nondescript teenager and stun the congregation.

Gripping the microphone, the teen emitted a thin, reedy treble. After just a few words, she went flat. Izzy and Rachel exchanged alarmed glances. The soloist quavered through the next words, as if searching for the right note to get her back in tune. "She's terrible!" Rachel whispered. A snicker escaped Izzy. Just then, the vocalist hit the high note on "Maria." It came out shrilly, and the baby Jesus wailed. Izzy giggled, and Rachel followed suit. Try as she might, Colleen could not contain herself. All the tension she'd been under these past months burst out. She let go of her daughters' hands and pressed her scarf to her mouth to stifle her laughter. Something sharp jabbed her in the back. When she whipped around, a vexed woman hissed, "Shh!" Colleen faced forward again, trying to get a grip, but then Izzy mimicked the disapproving woman, drawing her dark eyebrows together, and sternly telling her mother, "Hush!" Izzy and Rachel collapsed in contagious laughter. The harder Colleen tried to stop, the more her body shook. She snuck a glance backwards and glimpsed the woman's face, florid and angry. "Sorry," Colleen muttered, "we've all been under a lot of stress lately." But that understatement struck her as hilarious, and she doubled over, barely muffling her guffaws. As if this gave her daughters permission, Rachel laughed out loud until she snorted, and Izzy almost howled. The three of them collapsed in the pew. They laughed until tears ran down their faces, they laughed even harder when Izzy squeaked, "I think I wet my pants!" They laughed, barely able to breathe, while far below the hapless singer plowed through her terrible rendition of that exquisite hymn, and Shawn and Bea and Amber stared in open-mouthed astonishment.

A note from the author:

Please consider writing a review for *Once You Know*.

Ratings and reviews are important to all authors, but especially to newly-published folks like myself. Besides informing potential readers, reviews open other doorways. For example, for a novel to even be considered as a Book Bub selection, it needs to have at least twenty reviews posted.

I learn from and appreciate all reviews posted by my readers.

If you'd like a personal response from me, you can contact me through my website, www.madeleinevanhecke.com

Thanks!

Acknowledgements

I am very grateful to all the friends and family over the years who have supported my writing and given me valuable feedback, including Priscilla Grundy, Molly Klowden, Soon Har Lewis, Shirley Lundin, Mary Corazza Parks, Orick Peterson, Claudia Rufo, Judith Warren, David Wulatin, and Kalyn Wulatin. A special thanks to my long-time writing partner, Ranjini Iyer, for her insight and friendship. Finally, this book would not be in your hands today without the guidance of Alida Winternheimer, developmental editor/writing coach extraordinaire. Quite simply, Alida taught me how to write a novel.

Many thanks to all.

Once You Know
Book Club Discussion Guide

1. Colleen's reactions when she first becomes suspicious that her husband may be having an affair show that she has a great capacity for denial. In what ways does her denial help her cope? How does it make her situation worse? How do you personally feel about denial as a coping mechanism?

2. Colleen's daughter Rachel judges her harshly for carrying on a pretense that the family is intact when Rachel's father has actually moved out of the house. Colleen does this for her daughter Izzy's sake and is torn because she cannot fulfill both Izzy's needs and Rachel's desires. Do you agree with Rachel's criticism of her mother, or do you have more sympathy for Colleen's decision? What options do we have when we're caught in the middle of people we love?

3. Colleen's friendship with her older friend Pat plays a major role in the story. How did learning about Pat's

situation initially impact Colleen? Pat made a momentous decision during the ice storm. How did you react to her decision?

4. The idea of family secrets is central to the plot of this book. Is it sometimes better not to know the truth? Not to disclose the truth? How do you decide?

5. Throughout the story, the question of what forgiveness is and whether it is always possible to forgive is raised. Rachel argues that some things are unforgiveable; Colleen says we should forgive for our own sakes so that anger doesn't eat away at us; the priest in Arizona tells Colleen that forgiveness is a choice, not a feeling; and in his sermon, the priest back home argues that forgiveness is an act of compassion. How do you define forgiveness? Do you believe that some things are unforgivable, or that sometimes it's better to withhold forgiveness? How do you decide when to forgive?

6. At one point, Colleen's husband Derek expresses the idea that everyone is more than—and better than—the worst thing they have ever done. Colleen makes some valiant attempts to see Derek as more than the hurt he's caused. How possible do you think it is to keep both good and bad aspects of someone we love in mind? How possible is it to focus on the good, and, in so doing, control the emotions we feel towards them?

7. Throughout the novel, Derek longs for understanding
   and compassion from his wife and daughter. To what
   extent did you feel able to extend compassion to him?
   Is there anything he might have said or done that
   would have increased your empathy? When we do feel
   empathy towards people whose actions we abhor, what
   triggers it?

8. The recent events of the *Me Too* movement form the
   backdrop to this novel. Along with the class on gender
   and violence, the movement influences Rachel and
   Aaron. How does their heightened awareness of these
   contemporary issues impact their relationship, for
   better or for worse? What are some challenges young
   adults today face related to sexuality and sexual
   intimacy?

About the Author...

Bio

On the outside... I'm a nonfiction author (*Blind Spots*, Prometheus Press, 2007 and *The Brain Advantage*, Prometheus Press, 2011), a former college professor (North Central College, Naperville, IL) where I taught courses in psychology, creativity, and critical thinking, a lecturer (Common Ground, Deerfield, IL), and a game inventor (*Wicked Words*).

Behind the scenes... I've been a closet fiction writer, now able to use my retirement years to study the craft of novel writing more intensively.

In my personal life, I'm a widow who still wears her wedding ring and her husband's old flannel shirts on cold winter mornings. Greg Risberg, the love of my life who made me laugh nearly every day, died in 2014. My daughter Kalyn, son David, and granddaughter Claudia are my great joys in life.

FAQ's

1. Um. Not to be rude, but aren't you kind of old to be publishing a debut novel?

I am. And I can't even blame procrastination. I was the kind of student who had term papers finished a week before they were due. But it takes courage to put yourself out into the world. I think it's taken me all these years to be brave enough to do that.

2. So, why now? What made it possible?

One reason is that I found an absolutely wonderful developmental editor/writing coach, Alida Winternheimer who, quite simply, taught me how to write a novel. Like a symphony, a novel is incredibly complex. It has so many moving parts and blends different character voices. Though books on writing and week-long writers' workshops have been helpful to me over the years, I needed something more intensive to even begin to master that intricate artistry. Alida's astute guidance gave me that.

3. What made you want to write this particular book, *Once You Know*?

Women have confided in me. So often the hurt that caused them the most pain was the hurt of being betrayed by someone they loved and trusted. What to do may appear obvious to those on the outside of that situation. But it feels much more entangled and problematic to the person within the relationship. That's what I tried to capture in *Once You Know* in the hopes that this story might help women in similar situations make the best possible decisions for themselves.

Contact the author through
www.madeleinevanhecke.com